Diamond Curse

Diamond Curse
by Burt Hurlock

Amazon Edition

In 1989 a Silicon Valley venture capital firm funded a technology called Continuous Flow Cell Free (CFCF) protein synthesis. CFCF was developed by the Soviet Union's Institute for Protein Research (IPR) to unleash industrial scale protein production to supply the burgeoning genetic engineering field.

In-Q-Tel is an investment vehicle launched by the CIA in 1999. Its mission is to identify and invest in companies developing cutting-edge technologies that serve United States national security interests. *Wikipedia*

In October 2003 *The Guardian* reported that the Nama Tribe of Richtersveld, South Africa had prevailed in a court battle to regain lands and mineral rights in their homeland worth billions of pounds.

In July 2004 *The Washington Post* reported that DeBeers SA, which controlled an estimated 60 per cent of the world market for rough, uncut diamonds pled guilty to price fixing in Federal Court and agreed to pay $10 million to settle the 10 year old indictment.

In March 2014 Liberia confirmed two cases of Ebola. By early 2015 the outbreak had spread to Guinea, Ivory Coast, Mali, Monrovia, Nigeria, Senegal, Sierra Leone and the United States. The Center for Disease Control was forecasting up to 1.4 million cases before the epidemic could be contained.

By August 2015 the World Health Organization announced a highly effective vaccine against Ebola. 11,100 people had already died including 507 doctors and nurses. 26,900 had been infected.

Chapter 1

Harry Achermann awoke to two measured knocks on the door. "Good morning, sir. It's time," he heard Dirk LeBeau growl making a futile effort to whisper. Dirk's baritone voice rumbled from deep inside his colossal frame, reverberating like thunder through the cold, still farmhouse. His imposing physique served him well as Club Manager at the Donner's Forge Rod and Gun Club. Throughout the fall hunting season he served a rarified community of understated and powerful men, by whose sway in business and political circles the establishment lived, but whose tangled webs barely factored in lives like his. To a man they were no match for his brutish countenance, and at Donner's Forge Dirk LeBeau had the last word.

Low in the darkness over the old farmhouse a dense patchwork of jagged clouds funneled eagerly into the cramped valley, blotting out the remnants of starlight in the waning blackness before dawn. Like stage hands vanishing in the wings, the creatures of the night stilled and retreated to their lairs, the crisp leading edge of a spring cold front enveloping the diminutive building, and tossing the surrounding treetops with careless malevolence.

The club was a special place, tucked into the foothills of Dutchess County about an hour north of Manhattan. It was unknown but to a close circle of avid, well-heeled hunters – men who retreated to plantations in Georgia to shoot quail, and to Scotland and Argentina to shoot grouse and dove. Its acres of ponds and wetlands, and rolling fields and wooded foothills served a rich menu of game – pheasant and duck, partridge and turkey, woodcock, deer, beaver and fox, and even the occasional bear. The guides and club staff counted their tenure in decades, and members and employees mingled easily in a civilized, unassuming manner, like veterans at a regimental reunion. The members arrived well-dressed, in imposing, low-slung foreign cars only to clamber aboard mud-caked, terrain-conquering made-in-Detroit pick-up trucks with enough ground clearance to straddle a vintage sports car. Members spoke softly, possessed impeccable manners, and shared with the guides a reverence for etiquette, especially field etiquette. Dirk LeBeau promoted that reverence with missionary zeal, calling every member by his surname even though he was better known to some than their spouses. Harry heard him amble down the hall, pausing on each threshold to issue the identical knock and barely stifled wake-up call, the old pine flooring wincing and whining under the burden of his great frame like a barque under sail.

He checked his watch, a bristling chunk of Swiss engineering with the sticker price of an automobile. It was four a.m. May 1st, 2004, the opening day of spring turkey season in New York State. The cool morning air, hostage to a turbulent Canadian low-pressure system, was washing like a flash flood into the Hudson Valley, and wafting through the open window. Harry closed his eyes, luxuriating in the warm layers of wool camp blankets, and summoned the pleasing image of a youthful woman on the kitchen staff he had encountered some months before. He wondered if he would see her again today. The rapturous whirring and peeping of countless amorous amphibians rose, like a call to prayer, from the woods and wetlands around the farmhouse.

In the unfolding hours across the state tens of hundreds of turkeys, both toms and yearlings, or jakes, would strut and gobble to their deaths, drawn to camouflaged gunmen by skillful calls and astonishingly realistic decoys. On this particular dawn the farmhouse accommodations were at capacity with a dozen members, a rare event, even by opening day standards. The gathered crowd knew the trophy birds that survived opening day became leery and elusive, like cats in a kennel. The turkey's reputation for shrewdness was well-earned and these were busy men, unaccustomed to disappointment, and unrepentant for hunting the birds in the early spring when their guards were still down. Most of the hunters would be rewarded for their effort by sunrise, and then scatter, like sated wolves, dispersing to weekend social engagements.

The age of the club members spanned three generations, from spry octogenarians whose humility reflected the deprivations of their Great Depression-era parents, to baby boom arrivistes who had dedicated their short lives to self-actualizing by consumption. There was a healthy contingent in between, representing the silent fifties, whose silence was not beyond despairing of the immodesty displayed by younger members. Harry knew he epitomized that immodesty, and that his wealth was the subject of endless speculation. To the retired set he was young and brash and transparent. To the rest he was plainly nouveau, but his beguiling, irreverent charm would guard the club from stodginess and keep things fresh. All of this made him happy.

He let his eyes adjust to the shadows in the unfamiliar circumstances. A beam of light from the hall caught the brass hook of the garment bag hanging from his door. In the corner, draped over a cane rocker, lay a full suit of camouflage: silent breathable waterproof overalls, a coat, a baseball cap and face netting – enough to make any man invisible. Certainly enough to fool grazing deer, which passed close enough to count ticks the size of grapes, or to remain undetected at close enough range to blast the head off a turkey. Between the rocker and the garment bag were three pairs of shoes, aligned in neat array: a pair of black wingtips he had worn in Manhattan the day before, a pair of unscuffed leather boat shoes to wear inside the club house, and a new pair of hand-sewn hunting boots.

As he lay there, the features of the room came into focus: plain white stucco walls, substantial wooden door and window casings with heavy brass fixtures, and a simple shaded light bulb suspended by its electrical cord from the ceiling over the dresser. A heavy iron radiator rose like a headstone from the wide pine floor boards beneath a window, and above the radiator dangled the worn macramé loop of the shade pull. All the shades were precisely half drawn. The original elements of the utilitarian farmhouse had been well preserved to retain the authenticity of an unadorned hunting lodge.

It was a moment of calm in which to reflect on the unlikely path by which he secured his coveted membership at Donner's Forge. The superior grin on his face masked a pitiable condition, like the beguiling cover of a dreadful book. He scoffed at the ersatz rustic charm of the room, which he thought bore more resemblance to a theme restaurant than to the grim realities of the rural life into which he was born.

His accomplishments had come against long odds. Conceived unexpectedly to an unhappy emigrant couple in a decrepit coal-mining town in West Virginia, Harry had dedicated his life to erasing the tracks back to his origins. He could still recall each muddy, rut-pocked road leading to another in a web of hillside switchbacks like Dante's circles of hell. Recessed in the shadows of clearing after clearing were brooding, ramshackle cabins with corrugated tin roofs. Rows of decomposing trailer homes cowered along the untamed fringes of the primordial forest, and festooned across front yards and side lots lay disorganized heaps of firewood, rusted-out cars, appliances, and heavy machinery of uncertain origin. There were, in places, signs of faded luxury - a rotted, lime-green, canopied glider swing, purchased at K-Mart sometime in the late sixties, judging from the color.

Harry had been the only issue of a distant father. He possessed a healthy appetite for attention, compounded by loneliness, exacerbated by paternal indifference, like a green shoot reaching for the light in a dark closet. His most prized possession from adolescence had been an incomplete deck of cards he found in the parking lot of the Moon Valley Saloon, a small tavern set inside a double-wide trailer home with a turquoise plastic awning, emblazoned with a tortured strand of Christmas lights that flashed year around. Dog-eared and sticky, the cards smelled vaguely of beer, and launched Harry on a journey of amazing self-discovery.

Because it lacked half a dozen high-point cards, the deck was useless for games, so Harry used the cards to master sleight of hand. Like a top-hatted stage magician he awed his schoolmates with trickery, pulling cards from thin air and tossing them back into the sky from whence they never returned. He became practiced at selecting willing and gullible assistants, and at distracting them with flattery to work his cunning legerdemain, a ruse to which he would return time and again over his business career. Indeed, Harry's zeal for deception and his natural, unstudied instinct for showmanship made him a born grifter.

Before they knew better, the boys inhabiting the clusters of trailer homes around the mines gathered to test their mettle in betting games with contrived rules and names… two and torture, three-card killer, and one-down dead man. The fabricated games were spontaneous inventions incorporating what little the boys knew of blackjack and poker, and playing them, Harry discovered his penchant for numbers. Like a psychic discovering his powers, he became aware of a gift for anticipating outcomes – a gift that any trained mathematician would have pegged for the knack some people possess to estimate probabilities.

His proficiency with cards and his confidence in using them to his advantage burgeoned. Even when his numerical intuition failed him, his dexterity did not, and when he was not counting cards, he cheated. Most card counters played comfortably knowing the odds. Harry liked the odds even better when they were stacked. To his contemporaries in Appalachia he was a genius and a fabulous entertainer, but no one to be invited to games for money.

For Harry, life in West Virginia had run its course by his twelfth birthday, a day that came and went with all the others. Even astride the highest local peak, there was nothing to see but endless forest, blighted by mountains decapitated in the search for anthracite. He never questioned the unsentimental urge to leave, not from the moment it struck him on the evening of his twelfth birthday, even though he took two more years to act on it.

On a warm spring day in eighth grade Harry was called home from school to his father's bedside. Detached and distant, like awkward extras in a black and white movie, Harry and his mother watched his father die. Emphysema from years of coal mining and two packs a day ended the short, hard life of a father Harry barely knew. Not twelve hours later Harry was on his way, all his worldly possessions - some overalls, t-shirts, a pair of sneakers, buck knife, and an incomplete deck of cards - packed in a canvas bag slung across his back. No one he would encounter in the next forty years would have any notion of his origins, nor that he left a mother and an unburied father behind in Appalachia.

He rolled his feet on the floor. First light would come in little more than an hour. The sounds and smells of hunters stirring drifted down the hall. Iron beds creaked and the floor buckled as men paced about, following their morning routines. They stood around semi-clad in towels and long johns, gathering bleary-eyed around a bank of common sinks where they took turns brushing their teeth and shaving. It was not until they were dressed and filing down the narrow crooked staircase into the sitting room on the ground floor that Harry appeared on the landing looking and feeling like a rookie, his crisp, clean gear contrasting awkwardly with the faded attire and well-worn, oiled leather boots of the other men.

He was the last to appear in the room downstairs which was crammed with every kind of stuffed indigenous game. The fauna was mounted in minimalist dioramas, the way they would look in the woods and fields. Against the dark paneled walls and the fieldstone fireplace, and beneath the rough-hewn crossbeams, on tables, on walls, over door jams, and in recessed panels were massive trout, leaping bass, a crouching beaver, the majestic heads of two eight point bucks, two careening otters, a coyote making off with a partridge, a skulking fox, several pheasant in flight, a variety of duck standing on a muddy shoreline, an omniscient wide-eyed owl, and a tom turkey in full strut that in life would have weighed not less than thirty pounds.

God's a comedian, he snickered to himself, taking in the scene - a room full of hunters and their guides milling about beneath the vengeful glass eyes of the mounted game. What they would say if taxidermy could give voice. He supposed LeBeau and his guides were the nearest relation to frontiersmen this century had to offer, and he pictured their pick-up trucks idling outside, old and weather-beaten, accessorized with kennels and gun racks, with dusty dashboards cluttered with ball caps, flashlights, dry pens and old cigarette boxes. Their short gruff phrases felt certain and clear, and strangely familiar and comforting. He was sure they were unused to turning out well-groomed at any hour, let alone four a.m. Most had not shaved in days, and some for considerably longer. They wore threadbare camouflage, and when they smiled their teeth betrayed a life of cigarettes, black coffee, and chewing tobacco. Not one possessed a treadmill, that was sure, but they were powerful, rough-hewn men, well able in Harry's estimation to bear their weight in gear and game over long distances in double-time.

He supposed the lives of their clients were of passing and generally inaccurate conjecture. It was obvious the members were out of place anywhere but the club grounds in the vicinity of High Rock Township, like overdressed tourists from a faraway place where benevolent regimes dispense fortunes, no questions asked.

He knew that a few members, or "Guns" in club parlance, had long-standing allegiances to particular guides, with whom they had tromped the acreage of Donner's Forge for decades; but to describe these loyalties as friendships, as some Guns did, would be exaggerating. The Guns were excellent marksmen but amateur outdoorsmen, which accounted for the allegiances; and the guides were well-paid and generously tipped, and enjoyed wonderful hunting when the Guns withdrew to their leafy suburban redoubts. Like loyal footmen, Harry marveled, the guides knew their clients' limitations, and understood they came to Donner's Forge as much to hunt as to keep the company of men in similar stations.

The guides of Donner's Forge were renowned, or so he had been told, even among guides at lesser clubs. Stalking and dog-handling and bird calling were the reserve currency of the guide community. They all cackled and purred, and putted and yelped, but it was precise imitations of the turkey's wild courtships that separated the great guides from the good. The bird marked for death would ride the dawn on a rapturous roller coaster of high and low emotions, before he was felled like a grand old redwood by a single twelve-gauge blast to his bare, wrinkled head.

As he surveyed the room Harry recognized the LeBeau boys, whom he met the prior evening. All the guides were men's men. They had the look of hard work and an air of accountability earned in hard-scrabble blue-collar homes; but the LeBeau boys had ambitions, too. He recognized the look, a restless individuality that bridled at life in the service of wealth and privilege. The LeBeaus were celebrities, or they were at Donner's Forge, judging from the conversation the night before. Ron, the elder, had worked as a guide since high school. He was clearly in demand and the Guns liked him, partly for his superb dog-handling, but also because he knew things about the members and talked more than he should. During the week he attended the police academy, intent on becoming a federal marshal, or so he was known to say. His younger brother, Rick, was highly regarded, too, admired as much as sought. He was the match of his brother and father as an outdoorsman, and he had joined the army on his eighteenth birthday. He completed ranger school and sniper school before deploying during the first Gulf War where he supported Special Warfare units inside Iraq before the invasion proper. Rick was uncharacteristically small and inconspicuous for his family, and he was thought to have seen enough action to demur from the inquiries of curiosity seekers. He had come home to High Rock to settle down, and he worked part-time as a guide when the Guns outnumbered the regular staff.

Without warning Dirk LeBeau brought the room to order.

"There's coffee and Danish in the dining room," he announced, his voice swelling to a measured bellow, "which will still be there after I read the guide assignments," he added, arresting the crowd's subtle migration.

"Mr. Sunstrom, you're with Roscoe; Mr. Whitaker has Ron; and Mr. Fletcher, you're with Stu. Mr. Fletcher's guest is with Tommy." LeBeau was referring to Mr. Fletcher's forty-year-old son who was well-acquainted with Guns and guides alike having accompanied his father to the club for a dozen years; but he was not a member, and in LeBeau's conception of the universe only members drew the honor of being called, like raffle winners, by name.

"Mr. Achermann, you're with Rick; Mr. Cargill you're with Huey."

Harry was surprised and pleased to draw Rick LeBeau. Perhaps they were paired because neither was a regular. He saw Rick approach him from across the room, extending a sinewy powerful hand, and his brilliant blue eyes locking on Harry's like a diamondback cocked to strike.

"Good morning, sir," he said, his upstate New York accent riding hard on the "r"s and vowels. "You take your time. Get some breakfast and I'll be ready to go when you say so." There was something vexing about him, like contained spite, though he spoke respectfully. On closer inspection Rick contrasted starkly to the other guides. He was close shaven for a start, with a clear, taught complexion and clean, pressed camouflage, and his shirt was neatly tucked at the waist. Apparently the habit of being squared away had grown on him in the army. His build was naturally strong and rangy, and he fixed his gaze with purposeful determination, his unrelenting eyes not prone to wander.

"Thank you, Rick. Don't mind if I do. Can I get you something?"

"No thanks, sir. I already ate. I'll meet you by the front door."

Harry entered the dining room where he found himself at the end of a loosely organized coffee line forming around a long oak table better suited to banquets than coffee and Danish. A dozen men stood in compact circles of three and four, some speaking in hushed conspiratorial tones while others were bursting with familiar, jocular laughter. Sarcasm and good fellowship were exchanged in equal portion between unseemly mouthfuls of Danish, like football recruits at a training table. The atmosphere was collegial, friendly, even warm for a conclave of highly competitive men.

He stood at the back of the line recognizing some familiar faces from the club New Year's Eve party, his first club event as a new member. One of them was the girl on the kitchen staff, who was approaching him with a Danish on a small plate and a fresh cup of coffee. He was happy and a little surprised that she seemed glad to see him, and he thanked her for seeing to his breakfast before the food ran out.

The stilted mannerisms and high diction of the gathering pleased him. They were reassuring qualities of distinguished company, and but for the camouflage and Danish, he could be at a Fifth Avenue cocktail party. He had received warm welcomes from a number of the Guns, and was tasting the belonging he craved when a voice rose above the others, friendly but firm.

"So Jack, have you found your thief? Do you have your man?" It was Truman Ballantyn, a thirty-year veteran of the club born to a large enough trust fund that neither he nor generations of his issue need work. Even so, he finished law school, built a thriving litigation practice that he graciously gifted to his partners, and became district attorney to Philadelphia. He was eventually elected lieutenant governor of Pennsylvania before joining the Department of Justice, where he served for eight years under President Ronald Reagan before retiring. Ballantyn was a man with an over-inflated sense of justice because he could afford it. He was addressing Jack Whitaker, deputy director of the CIA, who was seated quietly in a back corner sipping coffee.

Like Ballantyn, Whitaker had joined the club long before becoming a visible public figure. While the Secret Service detail that followed him about had once been a curiosity, it was little more than an inconvenience now. Whitaker was a better shot than his bodyguards anyway, and nobody resented the distraction they created more than he, or so he said. The detail of large, anxious men charged with his safety was trained to dislike everything about sitting in dark woods filled with gunmen, and they compounded the difficulty of attracting a trophy gobbler for Ron LeBeau, Whitaker's long-time guide.

Whitaker and Ballantyn shared an uncommon fellowship, found in a duck blind and bound in the nation's service. They were like eighteenth century whalers who shipped together on a youthful lark, unaware they would count their absence in years and ply the seven seas in weather fair and foul. They relished public jousting, which escalated to awkward poignancy so often that familiar spectators made for the exits as soon as they locked horns.

This particular question, delivered without warning, hushed the room, like an indecent noise in church. Twenty-four hours earlier the *Washington Post* had published a story about a discreet and desperate manhunt led by the CIA for a market-maker in biological agents. The story alleged that a government insider with access to secure Department of Defense labs had pilfered and sold an especially virulent virus. The article continued, like a breathless romance novel, to speculate in obvious ways about likely buyers and doomsday scenarios. It concluded by alerting the fair reader to prepare for the escalation of the terrorist threat level to maximum alert by Homeland Security. The Department of Defense was afforded one quote: the virus was developed "explicitly for the purpose of testing antidotes to possible terrorist attacks."

Whitaker was caught off guard, as Ballantyn intended. The atmosphere of collegiality dissipated, the vacuum filled by a palpable uneasiness, like the first cool stirring of a sea breeze.

Even if nobody in the room read the *Washington Post*, and everybody except the guides did, there was no way to have missed the story. It had been screamed by paraffin-perfect dyed blond news bunnies, and shouted by boyish and believable news anchors across scores of cable news shows since the Friday edition posted to the web. A few of the guides, for whom television had become too stupid to be borne, stood by impassively, making little sense of the question, if they heard it at all; but to a man, they understood the gauntlet had been thrown. Harry tensed as a Secret Service agent materialized at the door.

Career members of the intelligence community like Whitaker infrequently lowered their guard, but Whitaker counted Donner's Forge among the places he could. This was a loaded and indelicate question, even by Ballantyn's standards, so the repartee was slow to form. The eyes of the room were upon him, the coffee in his hand hanging unwaveringly on his lips. He held it there, his hand steady as a marksman, his back ramrod straight, like a column of justice. Harry felt himself perspire, beads of moisture pushing through his skin beneath his eyes. He stepped back without thinking, the blades of his shoulders meeting the chest of the Secret Service agent standing behind him. He heard the old oak farm chair beneath Whitaker creak as the man appeared to swell with righteous indignation, his eyes becoming cruel and narrow, like meurtriers in a medieval castle. A few Guns unaccustomed to the show shifted uncomfortably as the old hands waited excitedly for the counteroffensive.

"Thief?" Whitaker replied with dripping sarcasm. "What thief?" he posed contemptuously, with a fiendish, provocative smile. The room erupted with laughter.

But his smile dissolved as quickly as it appeared, and the gawkers held their breath like witnesses to a blundered knife-throwing trick. Whitaker's expressionless eyes took a slow turn of the room, his merciless stare finding each member, guide, and secret service agent, a second having materialized at the door. His message was clear: theft or no theft, news leaks be damned, a line had been crossed. The nation had been betrayed and he would hunt the thief down. His eyes found Harry last, at the far end of the table, and stayed on him longer, before he bowed his head and smiled conceitedly.

"We have our man," he quipped, and drank from his cup.

Ten minutes after the Danish ran out Harry sat in the passenger seat of a John Deere Gator, a souped-up, high-clearance, all-terrain golf cart with two seats in the front, a flat bed, and a roll bar. The two-stroke engine clattered so loudly through the pitch black that Harry could not imagine wildlife of any description staying within a hundred miles of where they were careening across the countryside. Why the flood lights mounted across the roll bar were off was anyone's guess. He couldn't see five feet ahead in the darkness at the bottom of the valley even though the cold front had passed, the cloud cover was dissipating, and a thin line of magenta set the ridgelines to the east in black relief against the clearing sky. Only one of the two headlights mounted on the front fender worked, and it was pointed at the ground, like a vintage jeep rigged for blackout. The Gator was built for rough terrain, and it was proving itself up to the task. Harry held tight to the heavy metal bars of the roll cage. He guessed his chances of surviving a roll-over were low, and the likelihood of ejection high, and neither held much appeal. He was in Rick's hands.

The guide must be certain of his route, Harry assured himself, because the downcast headlight would fail utterly to give sufficient warning of an obstacle if they had to brace for impact. The uneven earth was whizzing beneath the front grill like the evening edition on a high speed press. Rick bounced and rolled with the terrain, like an apathetic subway rider. Harry was not so relaxed, and the rocking was making him feel ill. The Gator plowed across a shallow stream and lurched to a halt where the base of several large tree trunks suddenly appeared in the headlight. Rick cut the engine and the headlight flickered out.

Harry could tell they had reached the base of a foothill bordering the valley. He was looking into an abyss of darkness even though the sky overhead glowed with black light, like a television switched off in the dark. Rick was out of the Gator and rummaging in the flatbed as Harry waited for his eyes to adjust. The guide reappeared in a camouflage utility vest with a snap-on game bag, and a seat cushion with a camouflage slip cover that rode snugly against his lower back. Apparently it deployed like a mud flap over his posterior to cushion him during long waits on the hard forest floor. Harry didn't feel like moving. He wasn't feeling well.

Rick pulled a soft, wide-brimmed camouflage hat low over his head. He looked like a South American guerilla fighter. He stood before Harry in a wide relaxed stance, swiveling his head through one hundred and eighty degrees, his ears scanning the retreating night like counter-posed radar dishes.

"Yeah, this is a bit of a hike," he finally said in a coarse whisper. "Pretty steep the first half mile or so… you need help with your gun?" he offered.

This kind of patronizing might be right for the regular membership, but Harry knew something about walking mountains. He wondered if his agility on a rocky slope would raise or lower him in Rick's esteem. His ascendancy through the moneyed ranks was in no small part in denial of his origins, and in the presence of another Gun he might have graciously accepted Rick's assistance. But in the company of a lad with roots not so foreign to his own, Harry shed his affectations.

"No, I'll be all right. You lead the way."

"Sure? It'll be loaded," Rick observed with concern.

"Yes, I'm sure," he replied confidently, taking to his feet. He really didn't feel well at all, and steadied himself on the roll bar.

"You'll be needing this," whispered Rick, holding a single twelve-gauge shell vertically like an hour glass between his thumb and forefinger.

"Is that a special load?" Harry inquired.

"Yes, sir. Same fire power but fewer, larger balls than a field load."

"Only one?" Harry asked.

"Only one. You won't get a second shot." Rick said. Harry took the shell and fumbled for the breach in the darkness. The gun was not his – it belonged to the club – a semi-automatic Remington with a five shell magazine. Not many members possessed their own turkey guns, which were painted in flat earth tones, or wrapped in camouflage-patterned athletic tape. They would look out of place, a bit too *country*, next to the oiled walnut stocks and hand-engraved alloy chambers of the English Purdies, Belgian Brownings, and German Merckles.

"Here, let me help you with that," Rick whispered. He stepped forward, placing his hand over Harry's, and guided the shell into the breach. The spring-loaded magazine hatch beneath the barrel surrendered easily to the shell, which snapped with mechanical procession, like the turn of a dead bolt lock, into the chamber.

"There you go," Rick said, checking the button beside the trigger guard. "Safety's on. Leave it there until you're ready to shoot."

"Thank you," Harry heard himself say.

"Here we go," said Rick, starting into the abyss. Harry followed close, gun perched on his hip, barrel pointing skyward. The soft dirt path soon gave way to granite, with patches of spongy moss and lichen filling the depressions like mousse served in ramekins, and then the trail turned abruptly uphill into a steep treacherous incline. Harry's confidence wavered as Rick waded into the mountain without breaking stride. He managed to keep pace the first hundred vertical feet, but then he started wheezing. The sound was surprising, unfamiliar, like the deathbed rattle of his dying father, who had escaped his thoughts for forty years. He became annoyed as the endurance of his youth failed him, and he began to feel sapped like a generous blood donor.

At least he could see better in the coming light. The magenta from the east was overtaking them, the deep blues and purples from overhead reaching down the mountain, breathing life into the rugged terrain, which loomed into focus. Harry labored to put one foot in front of the other, pouring concentration into every step, until he lost his footing on a small fissure of loose rock waiting to give way beneath the dry leaves. As he fell he jammed his knee into a branch lying across the incline, and a small stream of stones tumbled free, tracing the path he would have taken but for the lucky presence of the limb. He caught his balance, regained his footing, and joined Rick where he was standing still, in suspended animation, on a small plateau overlooking the gulch below.

"What is it?" asked Harry between gasps.

"Thought you might want to catch 'urr breath," Rick replied sounding amused.

"No, I'm all right," he said, his false bravado ringing hollow as he lay down the gun, braced his arms on his knees, and sucked on the morning air like an asthmatic. It was not until he was upright again that he noticed Rick channeling the forest. He was turning his head again in smooth mechanical orbits as if tuning his senses to a celestial signal, his eyes bisecting quadrants, fixating on a series of vanishing points like a dancer spotting turns. Without the noise of their feet tearing through the dry leaves the woods were silent and heavy, like a blizzard dawn.

He felt himself mesmerized by the intensity of Rick's concentration, and his perceptible intimacy with his surroundings. The woods were speaking to him transcendentally, in metaphysical riddles. Harry shifted, detritus beneath his feet crunching under his unblemished boots. Rick flared his hand, *be still*, but too late. The beating of enormous wings drummed the air in a prehistoric eruption from the treetops overhead as a giant roosting turkey spooked and took flight, cackling and yelping, over the canopy.

"What was that?" Harry asked in amazement.

"I hope it was a hen," Rick whispered with a smile. "... you good to go?"

"Yes. Sure," Harry answered. Rick leaned in close to his ear and spoke in a barely audible whisper, his breath feeling cool on Harry's perspiring neck.

"They've been roostin' right over that ridge past few mornings. They ain't come down yet, so we've got time to set up." Rick's feet were still planted where they first landed on the plateau, even as he dipped one shoulder like a running back, and swung an army issue gunny sack from where it was riding on his back to where he could reach it on his hip. It contained a good many mysteries judging from the sound of his rummaging. He eventually found the object of his search, lifted it to his mouth, cupped his hands to his face, and blew. A deafening, territorial crow-call lifted into the dawn. It was summarily assailed, even before the echoes subsided, by a primitive emotional sound the likes of which Harry had never heard.

"What the hell was that?"

"Shock gobbles," Rick whispered. "Territorial warning. Good news is they're still in the trees," Rick continued, sounding confident in their prospects. "They sure hate crows, though, don' they?" he said chuckling to himself before pushing on. Harry followed, tromping another hundred yards to where the woods opened on to an abandoned logging road cut into the side of the mountain. The road was overgrown with shrubs and weeds, but no trees had taken root. Even Harry could see it offered an unobstructed field of fire.

He looked on as Rick crept up on the first substantial tree bordering the road. He paced around its base, studying vantage points the way golfers study lies. After some deliberation he stepped back looking satisfied.

"You're goin' to sit right dere," he whispered. He had removed the glove from the hand he was using to point at the base of the tree and it glowed in the dim light like a phosphorescent prosthetic.

"Lean your back against de base of dat tree and get comfortable in your shooting position, like this," Rick said, deploying his seat cushion. He nestled his skinny frame between two large roots that embraced him like the arms of a starfish, perched his left forearm on his cocked left knee, and lowered his cheek to the stock of an imaginary gun.

"This is how you should be before we ever see a bird. Them Toms is real sensitive to movement, so keep still when they come into range. Should come right up that ol' road, there," he said pointing straight ahead, making it look easy. "I'll keep calling until he's on to us," Rick said gliding forward on to his feet with his seat cushion trailing like a beavertail. "When it's time to shoot I'll give him a warning call, sort of like a *putt, putt, putting* sound. Up his head will pop an' you shoot. That head won't stay up long," he cautioned, fumbling in his shoulder bag for a slate turkey call, and replacing his glove once he had the instrument of treachery in hand. Harry tried hard to register Rick's instructions. Some combination of the hour and the darkness was making it harder than it should have been.

"I'll be right 'ere behind you. Let's just sit 'ere a while, and let 'em settle back down 'fore I start calling. Good luck," he whispered auspiciously, and disappeared from sight on the opposite side of the tree.

Harry squatted and tipped back against the tree. He didn't fit between the roots as easily as Rick, but he was not uncomfortable. Time would tell. He cocked his left knee, the way Rick had demonstrated, and lay the back of his left hand on it. He placed the pump action fore stock of the semi-automatic Remington into his open palm, felt with his right hand for the trigger guard, and pulled the camouflage face netting up from around his neck over his nose and beneath his eyes. His hearing became acute, the silence of the forest accentuated by the first stirrings of its diurnal residents, and he set to rehearsing his firing sequence - lowering his head to the barrel, releasing the safety, and taking aim - slowly and softly, like a dirge. The foraging around him intensified with the improving light. Squirrels and chipmunks and God knows what else were rifling the loose, dry leaves in frenzied delight. Song birds launched into illustrious, full throated cries, and a light breeze excited the treetops.

Harry had been waiting, as instructed, for the birds roosting in the vicinity to "settle down," when he became aware of something familiar, something from his youth, in Rick's bearing. Perhaps he saw in Rick the man he would have become had he remained in the woods of West Virginia. There was in Rick something of a noble savage: simple, tough and sentient. A man so much at ease with himself, so attuned to his surroundings, that he personified wisdom, or the presence of it, with his reserved invulnerability. It was a grand, abstract quality, like holding the secret to happiness. What Harry admired but was loathe to admit was that they both came from nowhere, and Rick remained uncompromised. There was an absent minded freedom to Rick's guilelessness of which no man of Harry's

vices was capable; and for a moment Harry had the faintest
recognition of self-betrayal.

It was a noble thought swept away by a chorus of gobbles that
rolled up the road like a wave to the shore. Behind the tree, Rick
issued a short sequence of clucks, standard protocol for a hen
catching a gobbler's eye. The clucks were met with silence. A few
more gentle clucks drifted up from behind the tree followed by a
soft, slow-rolling noise like a purr. That got the attention of
something because Harry heard a scraping sound like dragging
heavy furniture. There was movement down the road, on the level
ground where the overgrowth fell away. His heart was pounding and
his stomach roiled.

The sun had advanced on the eastern foothills, and the light was
good, and once Harry knew where to look he could see an enormous
gobbler in full strut, the bottom of his wings skirting his legs and
breast like sheaths of armor, plying the undergrowth like plow
shares. Rick had spotted him too, and the coy hen in his fingertips
started prattling in measured, intermittent *purrs* and *clucks*, textbook
flock-talk, in guide parlance. It was putting the gobbler at ease,
Harry could tell, and bringing him closer, and his eyes began to
water. He hadn't blinked in dog years.

The tom advanced two steps at a time, tucking his head, fanning
his tail, and blurting half-hearted gobbles. Rick seemed to know it
was an unexceptional performance, undeserving of praise, and he
frustrated the gobbler with silence. This fueled the bird's aggression,
as with all unnoticed men, and achieved the desired effect. The tom
hastened his approach, chugging through the undergrowth like a
tractor in high corn, and Rick rewarded his advance with a gentle
patter of clucks. The impassioned creature homed in on the sound,
altering course like a helmsman on a mark, and progressed with
fresh vigor directly for Harry. As the gobbler closed, induced by
fatal passion, Harry lowered his cheek to the stock, touched his right
index finger to the trigger guard and depressed the safety with his
thumb. The safety released with a loud *click* and the tom froze right
over the tip of Harry's barrel, just out of range, vaguely aware of
something irregular.

Now was the time for *cutting*, a series of sharp clucks that
reliably inflame arousal, a siren song for distracted gobblers,
especially when they're already *henned up*. Rick served a banquet of

cuts, and the tom flared his commanding wings, tucked his grisly head, spread his heroic tail, and erupted in a vainglorious gobble. The game was all but played and the tom advanced in full strut, closing, closing, only to halt again and strike an unrepentant exhibitionist pose. A few more yards and the bird would be in range. When he finally entered the kill zone Harry was ready, but the bird's wretched head remained tucked, shielded in the recess of its inflated, iridescent chest, the prelude to a dazzling finale.

The tom stopped, girded his loins for another gobble, and let fly. And then a shot crashed through the dawn. The first thing Harry felt was outrage, for he never pulled the trigger, and the bird was gone, melting into the forest like a sprite. Then he felt the blow, a punishing wallop with a sickening sound, the sound of a high velocity round tearing through flesh; and then panic as his shoulders went numb, and he felt the warmth of his own blood spilling from his throat down his chest. He clutched his neck to staunch the bleeding and found the hole where his Adams apple had been, the gaping wound ejecting thick spurts of blood against his fastened collar. Then overwhelming dizziness to which he capitulated, falling helplessly in the direction the bullet had driven him. Rick had hissed "not yet!" before he realized the shot came from elsewhere, and now he was skirting the tree trunk on his belly, coming to Harry's aid. Harry tried to speak and heard himself gurgle, a gravelly sound reminiscent of his voice, muted by his own blood. He felt Rick roll him to his back and pull his hands from his throat. With nothing to obstruct the hemorrhaging he saw his own blood pulsing in jets, arcing through the morning air like sprits from a fountain. He saw Rick's face, steely and sure and comforting, until Rick left. He must have been crouching, staying low in the shadow of the tree, fearing a second shot. He could hear Rick's breath, and the stirring of detritus, and pictured his guide triangulating on the shooter. When his face reappeared Harry pleaded through his eyes, beseeching Rick for help as only the speechless can; and he saw Rick's hesitation and watched with sinking horror as the guide made a cool calculation of his chances for survival. For God's sake, why wouldn't he help? At least put pressure on the wound. But Rick continued to study him, even as he spilled blood, even as he clutched the wound to stem the bleeding himself, and his peripheral vision began to fade, and he began to lose the battle for consciousness.

And then pressure on his neck as Rick pressed his left thumb into the first intact section of the carotid artery he could find, and reached into the gaping wound with his right index finger to open the remnants of the trachea. Rick must have cleared torn flesh blocking the airway for Harry felt a clean deep gulp of cool mountain air fill his lungs. To what he owed Rick's change of heart he did not know, but he was, for the first time in his life, grateful.

Harry knew he was bleeding to death. It would soon be over if Rick removed the pressure from his neck. He could hear Rick rifling his gunny sack with his free hand until he fumbled a whistle awkwardly into his mouth. Rick's first attempt was hopeless. He was going to die on this mountainside because his useless guide couldn't blow a whistle; but eventually Rick developed conviction, and Harry could feel him blowing himself breathless with the full force of his sinewy frame.

Harry began to feel light, the weight of his body falling away, until he saw himself from a distance, spread across the forest floor, his guide struggling to save him. He could only hope the whistle at dawn on the opening day of turkey season would bring every guide in hearing distance to his aid. He could see Rick putting pressure on his carotid artery with one hand while he used the other to keep the trachea unobstructed, the whistle clenched in his teeth, sending up the alarm in a continuous chorus of shrill blasts. He looked every bit the veteran Harry heard he was, combat so fresh in his memory he was pressed hard to the forest floor, in the shadow of the tree he had put between himself and the position from which the shot was fired. He was prone, reaching over his head and working on Harry's throat by touch while he blew with the force of a steam whistle. Between Rick's blasts and the raspy sound of his own breathing, Harry heard the ignition of pick-up trucks and the abrasion of all-terrain tires tearing across gravel down in the valley near the farmhouse. Help was on the way.

As they lay head to head, Harry on his back and Rick on his belly, there was reason to hope. He felt his gurgling gasps subside, and his breathing come more easily, and to see the world through his own eyes again, glimpsing the sky through the canopy overhead.

"Hold on, Mr. Achermann," he heard Rick say. "Stay with me. The boys are almost here." But the regularity of his breathing did not last and he felt himself starting to pant, shallow and erratic like a tethered water dog. He saw Rick's face materialize above him.

"He's in shock," Rick mumbled. He felt his blood pooling anew in the opening of his trachea. Rick rolled him on his side to drain it, but the numbness was spreading, the blood running around his ear, and there was nowhere to look but Rick's eyes as the guide held him on his side. He was too spent to panic and too confused to feel anything more than a cold vacating sensation like wet paint bleeding in the rain. The sun had cleared the eastern foothills, and hovered over the brim of Rick's camouflage hat, shimmering like a halo. Harry's last view of this life was the image of Rick's bloody face, and in the guide's eyes he saw hatred.

Chapter 2

Charlotte Stockton marched through the drizzle of another grey London morning. She despised the city's sidewalks in the rain. Leaping between lily pads of protruding flagstone like a school girl playing hopscotch slowed her progress and distracted her from her work. She was presently obsessed with recent developments in a court case she had covered for the *Washington Post* for just three of the ten years it had wound its way through the U.S. legal system. In recent days she had detected a subtle but unmistakable change in the tone of a DeBeers executive she proudly hounded like a paparazzi. The flutter of activity reported to her by a stringer on site in the Columbus, Ohio Federal Courtroom hearing the case compounded her suspicions.

She passed the Lamborghini dealership on the way to the South Kensington tube for the twenty minute ride into the city. Approaching the end of her fifth year as an expatriate, the glamour of being posted to London was losing its luster. She remembered feeling promising and intelligent when she arrived, a single twenty-something in ascendance. Now she was thirty-something, with numerous and important by-lines to her credit, but still single and vaguely discouraged. She renounced a long-running romance when she left for London, rejecting as eligible a proposal of marriage as any girl could want from a boy back in Washington she thought she loved. It seemed to her then that he or someone like him would always be there and love her just as well. She had been wrong on both counts, she knew that now, and consoled herself with the thought that you couldn't have everything, and she had gotten what she wanted. She tucked her head and raised her spirits, assuring herself there were no expectations and no regrets in her sporadically brilliant and repeatedly doomed dalliances with city bankers. Each one reinforced her impression of the last. They were interchangeable automatons in the polyglot financial diaspora ceaselessly swirling between European capitals, surging like a tide about the baffles of a rotting pier. The aspiring writer in her hung on the deconstructed forms of gleaming Lamborghinis reflecting on the dirty rainwater. Nature had a way of undoing objects of desire, she observed, dismissing the insight like a fortune cookie proverb, and departing the sidewalk in the direction of the tube station.

The infamous DeBeers diamond cartel came under federal indictment in 1994, when Charlotte was still in journalism school, for price-fixing in the worldwide market for industrial diamonds, rough stones, and cutting and polishing. General Electric had been named a co-conspirator, but was acquitted early in the proceedings. The pending case meant that no senior executive of DeBeers was free to enter the United States, the world's largest market for precious and industrial diamonds, without risking arrest. Nobody she interviewed who knew a thing about diamonds questioned the veracity of the allegations.

"There's something going on with the DeBeers case," she chortled as she tossed her rain-soaked satchel on the return of her Formica cubicle. She pulled the hood from over her head and felt curlicue swirls of her unruly blond hair stick to her damp cheeks in clumps, like the waves on the head of Venus de Milo, she flattered herself. She hung her coat on a grey plastic hook that was glued to the fabric cubicle divider, and moved down the hall to the office kitchenette, shaking out her mane, desperate for a coffee.

"Really?" Elliot Schiller shouted back. He was sitting as usual with his back to the door of his office, his feet on the credenza running the length of his window. She could see the *Washington Post* London Bureau chief from the kitchenette. He had the *Financial Times* European Edition open to the business pages which meant he had already scanned the electronic editions of the *New York Times* and the *Wall Street Journal* which were just now going to press back home. He would be getting around to the *China Daily* and eventually to some good but tiresome articles in *Barron's*, assuming no distracting office dramas. Along the way he'd steal guilty glances at a handful of publishing industry trade rags, the way traders peek at pornography, but she did it too. She, like Schiller, was a creature of the industry, and there was no industry more self-conscious than the media. Even so, Charlotte admired him for keeping his bearings, for staying grounded in a world increasingly defined by hyperbole and half-truths, insinuation and exaggeration.

It was no accident that his back was turned to a bank of video monitors hung from the ceiling outside the glass wall of his office, where pointless pontificators on CNN, MSNBC and Bloomberg carried on in muted pantomime. She envied his front row seat on the world, to which he seemed indifferent, and his aloofness drove her to distraction, especially during the early conquest years of her career. But envy turned by degrees to respect – respect for the timing of his obliviousness, and for his understanding of current events and their significance in the broad sweep of history.

The rain streaking down the outside of his office windows presently obscured his view of St. Paul's Cathedral, but on a clear day the exalted dome reflected light like bone china in the sun, the purity of its whiteness against a cloudless cerulean sky a constant symbol, he frequently observed, of the soaring devotional aspirations of a kingdom in decline. By the window he had hung a celebrated photograph - the unyielding dome amidst flames and smoke as London burned again after another of countless Nazi bombings. The cathedral was never hit, he liked to remind visitors. It was a stalwart testament of that time to the empire's destiny, and a reminder to the present of how far the world had come since the last time the peoples of Europe attempted to eradicate each other.

Coco, as she preferred to be called, emerged from the kitchenette under a head of steam, covering the short distance to her cubicle like the light brigade. She and Elliot were the early risers, and found themselves together often before the British staff landed at their desks. These were awkward moments in the early years, for she was taken with his charm and sophistication, and enjoyed flirting with him. He was never opposed, but it was a parlor game, as she quickly learned. His marriage of twenty-five years and the children born to it sustained the man. It was easy to understand why. Elliot's wife, Liza, embodied every virtue of a devoted wife and mother. Her youthful beauty left the false impression that Elliot fell willing prey to a trophy hunter, and that she was his second time around, at least. In fact, Liza and Elliot had been high school sweethearts, and their affection for one another was nauseating. People admired their charmed romance the way circus-goers wait for the trapeze act to fall.

Coco was soon the recipient of Liza's legendary kindness, which was dispensed with even hand to all the office staff. She never missed weddings or birthdays, and knew every wretched child by name, and over time she took a special interest in Coco. Liza nursed a deeply felt empathy for Coco and for the whole generation of women who came to adulthood with untenable expectations for families and careers. The attention while comforting was irritating. Surely, Coco thought, Liza regretted being kept, for sacrificing the chance to be her own woman. That explained her interest in Coco's innumerable paramours, and she vetted Coco's suitors the way jewelers grade stones. Or perhaps she was revisiting choices, which made Coco squirm, to think her suitors made Eliza grateful for the choices she made. But there was no denying her good intentions and Coco came to feel a part of the extended Schiller family. She knew Elliot and Liza would do anything for her, and it was in some part their compassion that kept her running in place, a single American girl in London, passing through her prime.

Coco had walked the beat long enough to trust in her well-developed divining rod, and it was twitching like a seismograph. Something important was about to happen in the DeBeers case. She pressed the *on* button of her computer, and settled into her cubicle.

"What makes you think there's something going on with DeBeers?" Elliot barked from his office. He looked more like he was swinging from a hammock than managing the largest foreign bureau of an important U.S. newspaper.

"Sam sounded different when he called back yesterday."

Coco was talking about Sam Dunkelsbuhler, great grandson of A. Dunkelsbuhler, a Jewish merchant who agreed in 1893 with Cecil Rhodes and nine other Jewish merchant families to purchase the entirety of De Beers' South African diamond production. This seminal event marked the formation of the first diamond monopoly, and set the stage for more than a hundred years of *managed* pricing and distribution practices.

Coco had stalked many senior figures at DeBeers' London headquarters at Seventeen Charterhouse Street. They came and went like Russian oligarchs in sleek German cars with tinted glass windows and Aryan drivers. Sam had been the striking exception, making himself an easy target for Coco. She was thrilled to discover that he walked to the tube from his home in the Boltons, and from the Chancery Lane stop to DeBeers world headquarters. She expected him to be austere, and as calculating as a mongoose, but she was wrong. He was downright chatty, and self-effacing and earnest, too earnest she presumed to be disingenuous, and she accepted his agenda on its face, which was righting old wrongs, like a repentant school-yard bully at a class reunion. He acknowledged the catalogue of grievances against his company, which were chapters from a bygone era, he said, a storyline he would be glad for her to publish.

Schiller had counseled her to keep her distance, but she dismissed his advice out of hand. A symptom of his aloofness was the trap of old stereotypes including the ones about Sam's company, but times were changing. The era of shadowy global conglomerates churning out ill-gotten gains beneath the noses of an uninformed public was over, and the age of internet-enabled enlightenment was here. Astute leaders like Sam knew it and were wise if not shrewd to come clean. Sam was no rube. He was disarmingly media-savvy, but he had been friendly and forthcoming from their first chance encounter, which she had staged on the steps of Number Seventeen.

He would have *no comment*, of that she was sure, so she planned on the encounter being brief. Like so many leaders of high station in Europe, the executive suite at DeBeers had developed a constitutional aversion to American reporters, so she went with a single purpose which was simply to establish contact, so he would recognize her when they met again. Her source-building schemes were art, she flatterer herself, choreographed over months in staged chance encounters at chic city restaurants, invitation only receptions, and exclusive business conferences, where the access of her press pass gave her *open sesame* powers. The ingenuity of her plots made her a world class schemer, she used to think, but as the formula became routine she began feeling like a dog trainer. She built rapport and nurtured it into trust, which was obedience by another name, with the right tone of voice. If Sam were like all the others he would lose sight soon enough of the difference between pleasantries and the little story-breaking intimacies that were supposed to be reserved for friends. That was Coco's secret to good sleuthing. That's all there was to it.

She reserved so little time for their first meeting that she planned to meet a suitor at a pub around the corner just minutes after Sam usually bounded from his building. It was a modern, fortress-inspired pile with a stone façade, a portcullis-sized main entrance, and tall narrow windows designed, it appeared, for archers. She came armed with reliable information that he always departed work on the stroke of five o'clock, a small but revealing detail about the man's reverence for structure. On the stroke of five he emerged from the doorway, a twitchy skip like a springbok in his step. To Coco's astonishment and Sam's apparent delight they were sipping skimmed lattés at a self-important patisserie by half past five, with Coco's date waiting around the corner, and glancing at his watch like a stationmaster.

His curiosity surprised her from the moment she introduced herself as a *Washington Post* reporter. He was fascinated by the media's interest in DeBeers. The turnabout was surreal, the way he dominated the questioning, and gave Coco a dose of her own medicine. It was a measured but pointed cross-examination the intent of which, he said, was to decode what he called "the American obsession with fairness."

Was it not the objective of superior corporate strategy, he argued, and quite persuasively she thought, to secure *unfair* advantage? What enterprising business, he wanted to know, would find success without unfair advantages. His family had for generations risked the company's viability to preserve the tidy balance between production and consumption, and he charmed her like a new age prophet with seductive ideas about sustainability, long-term profits and stability by which all the constituents of a benevolently managed monopoly flourished.

"Imagine," he proposed, "a world in which diamond miners in South Africa, cutters in Amsterdam, and retailers in the United States are thrown out of work with every announcement, real or fictitious, of a new find." When she pressed him on the charges in the court case back in Ohio, he said he was precluded by the proceedings from commenting; but he made no pretense of disputing the facts. He was an unapologetic advocate for the practicality of managed economic models over populist notions of free enterprise, and he was unabashedly proud of his heritage. It was Sam's great-grandfather, she learned from him at this meeting, who hired a sixteen-year-old apprentice from Friedberg, Germany, named Ernest Oppenheimer.

"What did he say?" Elliot murmured distractedly.

"It's more like what he didn't say," she shot back from her cubicle.

"I don't have time for the cloak and dagger stuff, Coco," he replied. She could tolerate a good many workplace inequities, especially in Europe, but not superiority and not from a fellow American. She jumped to her feet and marched to his door, coffee still firmly in hand.

"I'm serious. He was really different, as though he were tip-toeing around something he couldn't say."

"Called you back to say nothing at all?"

"That's just what I thought. It was like he wanted to say something but couldn't or wouldn't. Maybe he returned the call to be polite. I don't know. He sounded strange. You ever have a source do that to you? Suddenly change on you?" she said, trying to sound deferential.

"All the time. Probably wants to retract something, scared as hell he said too much." She noticed he wasn't reading his paper at all, but manipulating a miniature Rubik's cube in one hand, moving its segments in bursts with the practiced dexterity of a shell-game impresario. Eventually he flipped the unresolved cube on to his credenza, folded his paper into a tight roll, and wheeled around from his window, the slug of newsprint hitting the circular file at the same time his feet reached the floor. He looked at her strangely, a look she had seen from her parents the time a guy broke her heart, and he leaned towards her on his elbows, his chin on the arch of his clasped hands. It made her uncomfortable.

"Coco," he finally said, "what do you know about these people?"

"What do you mean, *these people*?" she replied irritably, for she already knew his mind. "You mean the people who work at DeBeers? Or do you mean Jews in the diamond trade?" she continued impertinently. On this subject she sided with Sam, who credited anti-Semitism for much of his company's recent legal troubles. Elliot never bought it, being Jewish himself, and familiar with anti-Semitism in its many subtle shades. It made him invulnerable, she often thought, to that variety of presumptive guilt for which WASPs like herself were defenseless.

"Tell me what you know, Coco."

"As you know, Elliot," she began, containing herself, "I think they're much maligned, and maybe a bit unfairly."

"Sam has gotten through to you."

"No. I just don't think Oppenheimer did anything Andrew Carnegie or John D. Rockefeller didn't. That was the time."

"That's right," Elliot conceded, "it was a bad time to be anywhere but the top. That was the point of antitrust legislation, wasn't it? and that was a hundred years ago."

"Not anywhere but America, Elliot. Certainly not in South Africa. More to the point, the monopoly was never the goal. It was a survival strategy, a direct consequence of brutality going back to the Spanish inquisition. There's a kind of poetic justice to it if you ask me," she said, feeling righteous, *poetic* justice being the purest form.

"I see," he acknowledged. "So there were no alternatives to fixing prices, controlling distribution, and driving free-market competitors out with a litany of predatory practices."

"That was the effect, Elliot, after many centuries of persecution, not the cause." This was such well-trodden ground between them that she began to suspect him of an ulterior motive, a trap he would spring when he was ready; but she was so sure of herself on historical grounds that she plowed ahead as she had before: Jews were banned for centuries from most guilds, two of the exceptions being money lending and gem cutting. Coincidentally, gems were good collateral, and became to lending what steam became to industry. Capital formation among Jews was a natural consequence of the professions they were permitted to pursue.

"History drove them to the gem trade, not the other way around," she concluded authoritatively.

He looked especially drawn this morning, his chin weighing like ripe fruit on his clasped fingers, and his expressionless face frozen like a curling match spectator between boredom and intrigue.

"All you're telling me, Coco, is that the conspiracy has lasted a hundred years longer than it should have," he said as he raised his sagging head and reached with both arms behind his neck. Why such uncharacteristic patience, especially at the hour during which he tolerated disruption least. Perhaps he was having a change of heart and now was the time to press her case.

"Chicken or the egg, Elliot," she said with growing confidence. "The cutting talent, knowledge about gem stones, experience valuing collateral, it was all concentrated in the Spanish Jewish community. The dumb Spaniards drove a thriving industry out, and the Jews picked up and moved on. Bad luck for Spain that diamonds and cutting tools travel well. It was probably the first significant instance of capital flight, even before there was a word for it," she noted defiantly. "So the Jewish stone cutters reassembled in Amsterdam, which was transformed almost overnight into the world center for diamond trade. In fact, did you know it was Jewish diamond merchants who financed the Dutch East India Company, which organized its own trade routes to India because that was the primary source of precious gems at the time? I didn't," she concluded admiringly. His unusual reserve made her conscious of her fervor and wonder if Elliot could be right. Was she proselytizing her own boss with the cartel-sanctioned version of world history? Had Sam been that clever? Nonsense, she thought, and carried on undeterred.

"It's persecution that made them fanatics about protecting their market, and perpetual fear of expulsion that burnished their reverence for diamonds, because diamonds were easy to carry and easy to hide, and the surest way to transport wealth discretely. History explains why Jews circled the wagons around the diamond market. They'll do anything to protect it," she concluded, running out of breath.

"Like what?" Elliot asked with a darkening tone, a reliable sign of the opening on which she feared he had been waiting. His eyes had been on her for an uncomfortably long time, but there was distance in his stare, an undefined distraction. She resumed her charge, but nervously this time, a trill in her voice she found hard to contain.

"…like the community moved again from Amsterdam to London when Britain succeeded Holland as the dominant sea power, because protected trade routes were vital to the enterprise. Or when huge finds were made in South Africa, ten Jewish merchant families, all related by marriage, banded together to absorb the supply, contracting to purchase one hundred percent of DeBeers' South African diamond production…" She was sounding defensive and she knew he could hear it, despite her command of history. That look on his face – was it cynicism or pity? She felt strangely at risk and gulped inadvertently for air.

"Elliot, why are you looking at me like that?" she found the courage to ask. "You're not telling me something." He did not deny it.

"Keep going," he said, "what happens next?"

"You know the rest. Sam's great-grandfather hires Ernest Oppenheimer, who goes to South Africa to work in the Dunkelsbuhler buying office there. He travels around, learns mining and sorting, and quickly grasps how a single rogue diamond producer can threaten world diamond prices..."

"Which is exactly how he takes control of DeBeers, isn't it?" Elliot interjected like a prosecutor. "He starts his own mines, independent diamond producers that he trades back to his own employer for ownership interests," he said.

"What's wrong with that?" Coco replied, wondering if she had missed the point.

"It's blackmail, Coco, don't you see? It's the beginning of the cultural underpinnings of the whole enterprise, not a simple merger of business interests as you like to contend. He threatened to flood the market and depress prices unless he got what he wanted from DeBeers. He blackmailed his very own employer, for Chrissake!"

"Not exactly," Coco protested. "What would be the point of actually flooding the market when it would destroy his own business along with theirs? He gave them a vision for stabilizing the market, that's what he did," she replied feeling vindicated.

"You don't say. Let's imagine that conversation with his boss: 'Rest assured I'll never dump these diamonds, but tragedy could befall me and they could find their way to market another way. Satisfy yourself it won't happen by buying me out now with a few shares of DeBeers. Is that what you think happened?" There it was again, his insufferable superiority.

"Of course not, Elliot. It's more like: 'Let's combine our interests so we're not competing,'" she said, holding her ground but sounding less certain.

"Or else..." Elliot added. "That's blackmail, Coco, no matter how you spin it."

Elliot could do this. Give you the rope to hang yourself before checking your research, and using the hard facts to paint a completely different story. Every time he did it he reminded her of over practiced lawyers for whom the trade of conscience for technique sat easily. At least they were alone and he was being civil about it. That wasn't always true.

"By the way," he started back in, "do you know where the name Anglo-American came from and how it ended up controlling DeBeers?" Of course she knew, better than he.

"Well, the war…." she started, but Elliot interrupted.

"Do you think things would have gone differently without the war?"

"Of course I do," she shot back. Getting Elliot to play his cards was always the challenge, and now that he was talking instead of giving her that bemused, patronizing grin, she recovered her train of thought.

"Oppenheimer put these gold mine deals together for some German clients of DeBeers. When World War I broke out Britain moved to expropriate enemy interests abroad, and his German investors faced a total loss. So he formed a new company with a distinctly Allied ring to its name, disguising the nationality of his investors and preserving their economic stakes. Isn't that what he should have done? Isn't that what history taught him to do?"

"Coco, you sound like the damn DeBeers public relations department. I warned you about getting too close." He was warning her, kind-heartedly, which unnerved her further still; until the empathy on his face dispersed like molt on the wind, and he began choosing words more carefully.

"So far, Coco, you're describing a tradition of blackmail and deception. With a torrid affair and a grisly murder we'll have a fabulous second class novel for the beach this summer." He was driving at something. He reserved glib jabs for his most cynical moods, when he succumbed to his darker angels. His cynicism, she often thought, was the transparent self-defense of an essentially optimistic man whose nose had been shoved like a puppy in life's accidents. It was a palatable way of getting at horrible truths, which she was usually inclined to let pass, except the word *beach* reminded her of Oppenheimer lore that was harder to reconcile, lore that had survived the scrutiny of historians.

The new name, Anglo-American, had been more than a ruse to disguise enemy investors. During the war there had been a German colony on the west coast of Africa. On a beach somewhere between the border of present day South Africa and Namibia, German colonists supported by investors back home discovered a staggering deposit of diamonds littering the sand. They were alluvial diamonds, carried for centuries by erosion and runoff from the coastal mountain range and high plains of western South Africa, and dumped like gravel on the coastal floodplain, where they were lifted by the tides and troweled like frosting on the virgin shores.

German soldiers conscripted local railroad workers to gather the diamonds, forcing them to crawl like Greek fraternity pledges in lines across the beach, sifting the sand as they went, and gagged like Chinese cormorants to prevent them from swallowing. The strike had the power to upend the cartel and Oppenheimer recognized the threat. No stranger to political opportunism, he prevailed on the South African prime minister to seize the find with South African troops. The German investors financing the discovery panicked like a stalked herd, and Oppenheimer responded with signature cunning. Through relatives back in Germany he soothed his frantic prey, offering to trade their seized interests at appalling discounts to Anglo-American. With the strike in his control he renamed the company and promptly traded Consolidated Diamond Mines for another large stake in DeBeers and a seat on the board. Subsequent and opportune purchases of stock made him the most powerful shareholder of DeBeers, and the architect of perhaps the only corporate takeover engineered entirely from within the hapless target by a salaried employee. Whether Elliot knew, she could not tell, but the events would strengthen his hand.

Office workers were appearing now in ones and twos, with rain-soaked overcoats and wet umbrellas by the score that were accumulating like kindling in the lacquered umbrella stand by the front door. The staff lacked enthusiasm for arriving at work, and she watched with amusement as Elliot noted the arrival times. He seemed distracted and unwilling, or too discouraged to rejoin the debate.

"Let's take a walk, Coco," he said after an awkward pause. The suggestion was irregular, out of character in her experience, the only one of its kind in five years under his employ. She peered into her gaunt patron's face, replaying the conversation for a faux pas sufficient to earn a reprimand offsite. Was she guilty of an impropriety too egregious to confront in his office? It seemed unlikely given her rising star status, and she was well-liked by her colleagues, even if they found her obsequious.

He picked up his briefcase and headed for the door, the same way he did when he left for the day. There was nothing relaxed or cordial in his demeanor anymore, like he had summoned his courage for something.

"Shall we?" he said. Coco knew better than to dispute him. It was better to stand down and listen. She returned to her cubicle, placed her coffee on her desk, and reached for her raincoat.

"Will we be coming back?" she whispered, to soften the abrupt departure.

"Why don't you bring your things," he replied, and she felt herself panic.

"Okay," she croaked inaudibly. They exited the office hastily, the eerie glow of steam from her hot coffee rising like a genie from a bottle in the light of her computer screen.

Chapter 3

Wayne Guthrie sat at his favorite corner table at the Mad Hatter Tavern, two gritty blocks south of the downtown Poughkeepsie police station. In a few short hours the tavern would be throbbing to live music, jammed wall-to-wall with young adults, descended from the hills encircling the city, or risen from its pervasive decay. Over time Guthrie learned that Poughkeepsie was like so many redoubts of civilization scratching out a living against the granite heights along the Hudson River north of Manhattan. Her post-industrial decline was now decades in the making, the skeleton workforce holding fast to vestigial family businesses still fighting for survival in the city's lengthening shadows. More recently the region's largest employer, a revered high technology company with a downsized three letter name, eliminated more than ten thousand jobs.

The job cuts reduced a once-proud middle class to groveling for work they never imagined wanting, at a fraction of the income they had come to expect. Not everybody could afford to stay, and the housing glut that followed the exodus attracted low-wage office staff from Manhattan, willing to endure the fitful two-hour commute on the Hudson branch of the Metro North train service into Grand Central Station. The middle-aged and elderly, who shared fond memories of Poughkeepsie's brilliant past in the heart of the indomitable American high tech revolution, could feel the city's soul draining away, like coal from the belly of a hopper car.

Guthrie admired the city's young, who set upon the world unburdened by misty longings for the past, leaping like fledgling seabirds from dense colonies on towering heights, soaring into a new day on untested wings. If they were still in Poughkeepsie they subsisted happily on hourly labor in what remained the most beautiful landscape in the East. This was the generation that would soon cram themselves cheek-by-jowl around the stage in the Mad Hatter, undulating rhythmically to the base chords and drum beats of another unintelligible local band. They would drink away their paychecks, dancing and laughing and fighting with careless abandon, entwined in the fraying weave of another American city in decline, curled in the embrace of the Hudson Valley foothills.

He looked forward to being fast asleep, snoring like a hibernating bear, by the second set, tucked into a dark corner of a stone gatehouse he rented on a Dutchess County horse farm that belonged to a plastic surgeon in Manhattan. Until the crowd drove him out, Guthrie would sit quietly at the sun-splashed table by the window overlooking Market Street. This is where he came to mull the evidence, to let his intuition run like a loosed colt on the first day of spring.

He felt out of his depth only thirty-six hours after the crime, a homicide, negligent or premeditated, unlike any he had worked before. The crime scene alone gave him pause. It would thrust him soon enough into the impregnable realm of elites who would buffalo his investigation as only the establishment can. He could only imagine the scramble for cover already taking shape across Fairfield County phone lines a dozen miles south as he gazed absent-mindedly at the front page of the morning's *Poughkeepsie Journal* which blared *Millionaire Banker Killed in Local Hunting Accident*. It wasn't the truth as well he knew, but Poughkeepsie was still a small enough town that the chief of police and editor-in-chief played darts like fraternity brothers on Saturday nights, and did each other favors, no questions asked. The editorial decision to withhold the police department's suspicion of foul play was accomplished in a thirty-second phone call, greetings and all. Guthrie had worked other assignments that made the papers, but they were newsworthy for the madness of the crimes, not the station of the victims, who were formerly unknown and remained so. This would be different, the other way around.

The limelight had found him before, at unimaginable cost, and he had always feared it would find him again. The spotlight foreshadowed tragedy, that was his experience, and he was haunted by the idea that he had earned his misfortune, for indulging his ego, by heeding the call to stardom.

"Pride goeth before the fall," he reminded himself more often than he cared to remember. He even wrote a prayer for moderating guidance, and built structure and discipline in his daily routines to slay the ambition he feared was a curse.

This is how *procedure* came to factor so prominently in his modus operandi. Procedure was a place to keep his animal spirits caged, and he clung to it with superstitious compulsion. Procedure was already in evidence on the table beside the *Poughkeepsie Journal*, in a stack of preemptively labeled, mostly empty files, which would spill with abundance like Christmas stockings before he dared venture a theory for the crime - because *procedure* meant accumulating the facts until they spoke for themselves notwithstanding the temptation to speculate.

Soon he would have every description of evidence available to a modern murder investigation, from crime scene photographs to forensic reports, from three-dimensional maps to radio traffic transcriptions. The empty files were already color-coded with thumbnail-size Post-it notes in all the rainbow colors of a gumball machine, and guarding them from prying eyes, like a sentinel among them, his ever present mug of steaming black coffee.

In the shadows of the tavern he spotted Charlene, a heavyset waitress with more than half her fifty years given to lapping the Mad Hatter. She cruised the premises in predictable orbits, topping off his mug whether he needed it or not. He was grateful for her silence – she had a penchant for gossip - and he could tell by her proximity she was laboring to contain her nosiness.

He leaned back in his chair and squinted in the soft filtered sunlight reaching through the window to his table. Brilliant blue flashes from his loosely pursed eyelids were magnified by the thick oblong lenses of his wire rimmed glasses, and gossamer tendrils of his thinning ginger hair sparkled like tinsel in the sunlight. He was aware but indifferent to his changing appearance, which still bore the signs of his athletic youth, a time during which he went by the unflattering nickname of "bucket head." It was a term of endearment inspired by his prodigious head, which rested like an obelisk on the muscular column of his neck. He had shoulders to rival a bridge span and a chest to rattle a superhero, expanding in all dimensions from the waist like an inverted pyramid. But he was not immune to gravity and relentlessly battled its ravages with a regimen of rigorous workouts at the local high school gym.

He knew his appearance made him intimidating and even unapproachable to some, but it was the only part of his Wichita, Kansas youth he couldn't let go. His memories of making the 1970 starting offensive unit of the Wichita State football team were not the stuff of legend retold by other college football heroes. In that closed chapter of his life he had been a blazing fast two hundred and eighty-five pound pulling guard who tore holes in a defense the way excavators move earth. *The Wichita Eagle* had been writing about him since high school, and he turned down bids to Alabama and the University of Texas to stay near home. Not because he would miss being a local celebrity, that was old news, but because family and football went together, and one was no good without the other. On October 2nd, 1970, one of two planes carrying players, staff and fans to a game in Utah struck the treetops on a hillside near Loveland Pass in Colorado, killing thirty-one of forty passengers.

Among them were most of Guthrie's teammates and best friends, the coaches, the trainers, and his father, a booster who had been by his side from the day he first tottered around the backyard in his father's old football helmet. Guthrie was one of nine survivors to testify before the National Transportation Safety Board that everyone aboard survived the initial impact. And then the fully fueled aircraft caught fire and incinerated thirty-one, eleven of whom including his father survived long enough to reach area hospitals where they lingered for days before succumbing to infections that took hold in their oozing burns like cultures in a Petri dish. From that day forward the image of his dying father felt like cosmic retribution for the blind ambition that put them together on that chartered private airplane.

The investigation that followed exposed numerous FAA regulatory violations, but the National Transportation Safety Board eventually blamed the pilot. The pilot flying the other plane carrying second-stringers and water boys followed *procedure*, taking the prescribed route over the continental divide and the time and distance to reach a safe altitude. The pilot flying Guthrie, his father and his teammates decided on a whim to impress his guests, treating them to a sight-seeing tour and a low altitude pass into a dead end canyon, with walls that rose too fast to climb, and closed too quickly to escape. The canyon had always been there, beckoning like a Venus flytrap to passing aviators tempted to sacrifice procedure along with everyone aboard, for a flight of fancy. There began Guthrie's distrust of the limelight and his yen for obscurity, his contempt for conceit and his devotion to *procedure*. He wondered

sometimes if he became this way to spite himself, because pride
came easily to him, with his powerful physique and his expansive
mind, and pride was the hand maiden to conceit, which was bound to
end in tears.

He was not always soft-spoken and introverted, but being that
way grew on him as he searched in somber desperation for some
way to atone for the guilt of surviving, and for being the reason his
father was on the plane. For a time he tried to fill his father's shoes,
consoling his mother and tending to his sisters when he was not
wandering Wichita in a despondent haze, all that he had lived and
loved about family and football incinerated amid sage brush and
prairie grass on a Colorado hillside. Even today, sitting in the Mad
Hatter, he could see the fuzzy ink ribbon letters of the NTSB report,
a document to which he turned again and again the way doubting
Christians search the Bible. Guthrie believed, or wanted to, that no
accident like the one he survived began with bad intentions. They
were avoidable tragedies born of lapses in judgment for which there
was no explanation but a failure of self-discipline. Anybody could
have been that pilot, diverted from *procedure* by unregulated pride.
He knew it was irrational to comingle the pilot's culpability and his
own guilt, and in the reasoning recesses of his mind he managed the
separation, but he never shook the feeling of accountability, the
irrationality of which he could articulate but not tame. Knowing he
was wrong made the burden no lighter, but subjugating himself to
procedure kept his ego at a distance and his lethal pride at bay. His
fealty to order became a way of life, a self-taught skill, and it
worked. After the media circus around his testimony at the NTSB
inquiry Guthrie faded into a life of unexceptional domestic routines.

The transition to law enforcement came naturally, the appeal of
due process irresistible. The law was there to guard against failures
of self-restraint which made him a natural agent of its enforcement.
It pleased him to count himself among the law's most unbending
stewards and he was unapologetic for his intensity, whatever his
classmates at the Kansas Police Academy said about him. "Guthrie's
grudge," they called his zeal, for that look in his eye on the firing
range. The Academy Commander showed scarcely more
understanding.

"He's a nut all right," Guthrie once heard the Commander say,
"but he's our nut. Just don't be downrange when he opens up." The

story of his survival preceded him to all his Kansas State Police Force assignments, the legend of his indestructibility swelling with his advance, like the bow wave of a ship; and with an eye on due process he never disappointed, swooping in mercilessly where scofflaws tarried, thanking God for the duty to purge menace from society.

He had fathered a daughter, the love child of a short passionate union to his high school sweetheart, who went cold on Kansas and left Wichita for the West with the sparkle of a Forty-Niner in her eye, final destination unknown, and there was nothing left to do but divorce her, by the book. When his daughter followed her fiancé to New York City, Kansas couldn't hold him and he settled at a safe distance, in Dutchess County, where he was too far to pry and close enough to restore order if trouble began.

Poughkeepsie suited him fine, an obscure locale to which no ambitious New York State police detective aspired, and he was pleased but not surprised by the warm welcome from the Poughkeepsie Police Department. He fit like an old work glove on the community's extended hand, and settled into the bucolic, half-speed life of the decent if simple folk of his newfound territory. There was a familiar rhythm to life in the farm country of Dutchess County. It held much in common with life in Kansas, and Guthrie discovered peace if not resolution traveling the pastoral byways between fatal traffic accidents and senseless drug crimes. If he missed anything at all it was the challenge of hard cases, for there was little taxing work in Poughkeepsie's petty crime scene, and even less to invoke the smoldering moral imperative for which he was renowned in the west. Hard cases in Kansas found him for his local celebrity, a condition that failed to follow him to his beat in Dutchess County, and with time he took to wondering of his competence, and if it might be flagging both with age and for want of practice.

He had the sinking feeling that he solved fewer cases in the east, but he had never reviewed his statistics to be sure. The itinerant nature of the eastern criminal element made crimes more random and criminals harder track, he told himself. They washed into town like Hudson River driftwood, cast by night on the shore to wreak their havoc, and drifted away again as mysteriously by dawn.

The case lying on the table before him was, in his experience, without precedent. The conspicuousness of the locale could not be overlooked. The members of Donner's Forge were no more acquainted with violent crime than a sporting read of the town police blotter for a chuckle at the youthful indiscretions of the neighbor's children. The membership personified the idea of *power elite*, a term that was meaningless back in Kansas. A cursory glance at the Donner's Forge membership book was a crash course in white Anglo-Saxon hegemony, each member branded by important sounding titles at august institutions where their impeccable credentials predicted they would land.

Achermann's biography fit right in with the bankers and lawyers, the publishers and politicians, like another well-rounded egg in the carton, at least at first. On closer inspection Guthrie smelled a rat. There was something unharnessed in Achermann's face, an unruly aberration among his fine featured colleagues, a man easy to picture with enemies. And as for the setting, the exclusive community, conspiracy among the power elite was practically a cliché. No doubt the denizens of Donner's Forge schemed like robber barons over pellet-riddled brazed duck to bend elections and monopolize industry. But murder? It felt like a reach, too crass, or insufficiently enterprising for so ambitious a conclave of men.

There was little to suspect about the guides either. No recent hires and no misfits, everyone traceable to within twenty miles of Poughkeepsie and all the way back to the year of their birth, like the predictable flight paths of migratory birds. Not long on education but no rap sheets either, and a few with distinguished service to the nation evidenced by medals, like Rick LeBeau's. Guthrie was taken with the graciousness of the place, and especially how members and staff mirrored each other's manners. They were all of one breed, despite the distance between their origins, like a smooth mountain lake fed by disparate streams that suffered malingerers and malcontents and misanthropes poorly. The pattern of rectitude was itself conspicuous, like a contemporary order of the Templar Knights.

Of course with so much success the members were bound to have enemies because envy and collateral damage were likely always nearby. For instance, "Chainsaw Jack," a member's populist name, was earned orchestrating the firings that brought the region to its economic knees. Were Chainsaw the victim suspects would abound, and that accounting only for the local community. But the question of the hour was who were Achermann's enemies? Why would they follow him here? And how would they have known where to find him? To the last question, which might answer the others, there were only two explanations. Either Achermann and LeBeau were followed, or Rick LeBeau tipped the gunman to where they would be and the gunman was waiting when they arrived.

His hunch was the latter, even if suspecting so failed procedure. Well before opening day the guides scouted their territories, like thieves casing a neighborhood, for the roosts and feeding patterns of their quarry. Opportunities to plan a shooting abounded, although none of the guides raised suspicions, and he had already spoken to them all. They were sincere and forthcoming, concerned and contrite, as predictable as their patterns said they would be; and none thought the shooting an accident. Rifle hunting long after deer season? It was like "turning up to a squash match with a tennis racquet," said an eavesdropping Gun. No experienced hunter would carry a rifle this time of year, unless he were a poacher, and a poacher would be stupid to be lurking near the clubhouse, especially with all the activity that dawn.

The alternative to an inside job was a well-planned hit, a sophisticated assassination by a gun-for-hire. It was possible, even likely, that Achermann had been tagged with a GPS dot, a tiny signal-emitting device the size of a watch battery that an assassin could have used to track his movement on the grounds of Donner's Forge. But the gunman would have had to move quickly once Achermann was stationary, and quietly to remain undetected, and there were no obvious entries from the perimeter of the club grounds from which to approach the murder scene inconspicuously. He could see from a simple road map that the untamed terrain around Donner's Forge formed a thickly wooded mountainous moat that extended for miles, with no passable access roads. Finally, nothing like a GPS dot had been recovered from the body or Achermann's clothing.

He also felt the gun-for-hire assassination theory fell apart on the location. Achermann was so easily accessible in so many other venues better suited to staging a hit that Guthrie counted the location among his top clues. Rick LeBeau was under obvious suspicion for being present, and the only witness to the crime, but it was hard to explain why a more lethal shot had not been administered at point blank range from a weapon that remained unrecovered. Or perhaps there was a struggle and Rick had finished the botched job with his bare hands before help could arrive. Why he would plan a murder that so plainly implicated him was hard to reconcile, never mind that Rick hardly fit the profile of a murderer, and had no motive. In fact, the EMTs had high praise for the measures Rick had taken to save Achermann's life. No, there was another scenario, which though it may elude him now would not forever, for these were the sorts of cases that succumbed to procedure. LeBeau bore further observation, but the answer felt further afield.

Guthrie and his staff had hastily questioned the few club members who remained on the grounds by the time they arrived on the scene. For men he expected to enjoy hearing themselves talk they were mute as mimes, nothing to say whatsoever about events of early yesterday morning, or Achermann himself; in fact not a one owned to an association with Achermann, as if he came and died as an uninvited guest. The guides and Guns he spoke to had corroborated each other's whereabouts, which meant the cover-up for a conspiracy, if one were afoot, was already underway, and piercing the veil would be well-nigh impossible. The alibis were bullet-proof, the relationships enduring, and the loyalties deep enough to keep the secret of a well-orchestrated murder far from the public eye.

This one would be complicated, and attract public attention. The dreaded limelight, he was thinking as the sun dropped below the buildings across Market Street taking his optimism with it. An avant-garde of evening patrons had drifted in on the quitting hour like sea tangle on the tide. The fashion of the hour was denim accessorized by leather work boots and stiletto heels, canvas work vests and spaghetti strap camisoles, with baseball cap and costume jewelry accents. He could smell the grill being pressed into service, seared beef and fries and perfume and aftershave infusing the tavern with combustible possibility.

He was stirring his coffee with considerably more success than his investigative muses when he turned to the sparsely populated files before him. A protégé, Jimmy Doolan, had helped himself to a Donner's Forge membership book from which he had cropped member portraits and biographies. The impetuous young detective had stapled the decoupage to accompanying notes of yesterday's interviews, and the sets were neatly stacked in the file labeled *Interviews,* per procedure. The spine of that file lay in his left hand while he ran the thick calloused thumb of his right across the pages, doing it repeatedly like a dealer loosening cards. When the file eventually fell open it did so to the photograph of Jack Whitaker.

Whitaker had been ushered from the premises by his security detail long before Guthrie arrived, but he had been surprisingly easy to reach on the direct line to his desk at the CIA. He was solicitous beyond all expectation, due to his impregnable position, no doubt, and he was the only exception. The common conclusion from the handful of other interviews was that the Guns were no strangers to questioning and excelled at multiple choice and one-word answers – *yes, no, I can't recall* – which made Whitaker an enigma. He was garrulous, curios, and willing to speculate on motives and suspects, as if he were game to drop what he was doing and throw himself into the investigation.

Guthrie's suspicion of curiosity was no less developed than any detective's. The foremost concern of all perpetrators was always for their own safety, and unnatural curiosity in the progress of an investigation was a widely accepted tell; but the deputy director of the CIA? Whitaker made no disguise of his interest, encouraging Guthrie to share what he could, and assuring him of utmost discretion and unparalleled powers of surveillance if Guthrie could find a use for them. It was peculiar, high-handed, thought Guthrie, unless he was foreshadowing disclosures to come. Guthrie closed the folder and tossed it back on the table, inadvertently cueing Charlene to swooped in and top off his mug. She did so with such enthusiasm that it puckered the cellulite in her cheeks and reduced her eyes to heavy furrowed seams of mascara.

Guthrie ignored her, and focused pessimistically on the folder labeled *Crime Scene.* The area in the immediate vicinity of where Achermann was shot had divulged little except a small fragment of a large caliber, high-powered round recovered from a stump several yards from where the victim fell. The forest floor in a fifty-foot radius of where Achermann bled out had been trampled beyond recognition by the guides, who responded to Rick's whistle like dogs to a dinner bell. Guthrie imagined that the ghastly scene they encountered triggered a sort of hostile territorial panic that sent the guides into the woods in marauding bands, with guns and dogs like a frenzied lynch mob. The secrets the forest might have told were sacrificed to the thirst for vengeance. As Guthrie could have told them the search on foot was fruitless, despite the assembled tracking skills. Everyone, especially the guides, knew it was the work of a competent marksman who could have fired from as far away as a mile, and been long gone by the time a search party picked up his trail; but the futility of the hunt in that moment was irrelevant and failed utterly to discourage hot tempers.

A few of Achermann's personal effects, like his smartphone, had been recovered from the clubhouse on the chance that something in his movements and contacts in the hours before his death would present a meaningful lead, but Guthrie was skeptical. He doubted the scraps of evidence in the possession of the Poughkeepsie police department would yield much. The murder felt too well-planned.

And then there were Achermann's business interests, which would defy comprehension by his skeleton crew of country detectives. The file labeled *Professional Associations* was empty, the job of filling it shortly to be assigned to Jimmy. The paper trail was certain to dwarf the Poughkeepsie phone book, but it was an avenue they had to pursue. Jimmy had coded the file green, to symbolize currency or to honor his Irish heritage, one could never be sure, but with Jimmy there was always a reason. The sums of money at Achermann's disposal defied the imagination – they might as well be counting in light years - and where it came from and to what dubious practices it owed its accumulation could never be known. They would need a forensic accountant just to trace Achermann's trading partners, whose anonymous stockholders would never be found, especially if the perpetrator were among them, and he could easily imagine the murder was for money. Drug dealers in Poughkeepsie killed for much less than Achermann's stakes. Reflecting on those realities sank his optimism further and raised the unappealing prospect of another unsolved case until he reminded himself of a constant on which he could dependably rely: violent crimes were often rooted in uncomplicated impulses from which complicated circumstances might easily distract.

A basic ungoverned urge would explain the murder of Harry Achermann, and he should guard against diversion from the primary search for motive. Under pressure to get Guthrie started, Jimmy had gathered information about Achermann's wife, and the marriage was a powder keg of crossed purposes. On paper they were the quintessential Manhattan power couple. The file labeled *Family* included a photograph of Astrid Taylor Achermann, which Jimmy had located in an article published by her medical school alumni magazine. She was formally attired, in the company of tuxedos, standing by a wall of dark wood paneling. She had the unforced elegance of a fairy tale heiress, who was bound for newsstand scandal and ruin by the limelight. Photographs lie, and this one probably did, but the look in her eye caught him off guard, lightened his heart, and tumbled his belly like new summer love. Her eyes conveyed a pathos Guthrie had seen before in people of relentless optimism like missionaries and social workers in destitute circumstances. A call to her office that morning was met by the cool, contemptuous voice of a woman calling herself Dr. Achermann's assistant, who doubted Dr. Achermann's availability any time soon. It was a discouraging and familiar reception, and one that fueled his suspicion that Dr. Achermann would be well coached by lawyers when he finally reached her.

He turned the page and scanned a disjointed biography of the former Astrid Taylor. Jimmy had started the search for those murderous qualities so easily overlooked in decent society, and wholly absent from her ethereal gaze. She had an impressive list of accomplishments to her credit, even before encountering Harry Achermann. She was as peripatetic as her husband, according to the magazine, which begged the question of their intimacy. An arrangement of convenience? Lives tacitly reordered were always easier than messy divorces. It was a choice people made all the time, restless couples parting ways by degrees, straying like tectonic plates shifting by inches into continents separated by oceans. There was ample opportunity for transgressions on both sides, which in Guthrie's experience meant there were, and lovers scorned many a crime explained; but unrequited love missed the mark here. For reasons he was sure his procedure would find, avenged infidelity was no more likely to explain the crime than alms are to buy salvation.

Not now, but soon he would sense the killer's wake, and until then he was content to wait. He stacked the files like graham crackers into a neat rectangular pile as his eyes wandered the room. The closing crowd and dwindling light meant his departure was overdue, and he swept the files from the table.

Charlene was practicing her sixth sense for disappearing when you needed her so he slid five dollars under his coffee mug even though it was twice the tab. He searched the room hoping to pay his respects, for she would surely make him regret sneaking out on her. Charlene was gone, but something caught his eye - two familiar figures darkening the tavern door. He saw it for the first time only yesterday, the world-weary gate of Rick LeBeau, his center of gravity rocking smoothly from one leg to another like a saddle sore cowboy, and his brother, Ron, following him. He expected them to melt in the burgeoning throng, but they bypassed the crowd and made for a table obscured by a stage that extended into the room like a Paris catwalk.

Guthrie studied them, searching for something overlooked. He felt guilty doing it. Rick had served his country, and honorably. He was beating his own path to the world, outside the shadow of his father, and none of that jibed with attaching himself to a murder that would suck him like Charybdis back into a world he had left before. And yet Guthrie was no stranger to the ironic impulses of the subconscious, to the self-defeating acts that drag us back to our origins with the intractable sureness of gravity. People were bound to their circumstance in psychological dimensions too complicated to unravel; and Guthrie had learned to count on reversion to the mean, on people falling back on their patterns however haunting, the way salmon leave the ocean to die where they were spawned.

Guthrie perched his glasses on his forehead and rubbed his eyes, stretching and cracking his voluminous neck like the victim of an indelicate chiropractor. Let procedure run its course, he told himself. Maybe his instincts about Dr. Achermann would prove wrong, or a disenchanted business partner would surface, or his intuition would serve him better tomorrow. Tonight he was drawing a blank. Replacing his glasses he saw her, a radiant young woman with the unmistakable self-assuredness of striking beauty. She cast a spell through the murky light as she entered the bar with a gaggle of friends. Almost immediately, on the far side of the room, he saw Rick take to his feet only to be jerked by his shirt tails back to his seat by his brother who was speaking to him like a psych ward counselor.

Interchangeable young men were perched about the bar like vultures tasting the air for carrion, and they noticed the girl too. Guthrie could see them in ones and twos, craning their necks indiscreetly to ogle her with hopeless ambition. The girl had long, jet black hair that tumbled in curly dollops across her shoulders and down her back. She wore a form-fitting fire-engine red blouse that accentuated the fullness of her figure, and deepened the darkness in her eyes, which she flashed with animated exuberance in the dissolving light. The stage lights reflected in her full red lips, which looked ripe enough to burst, and her thigh-length overcoat was stylishly flared. Too light for fall and too heavy for spring, Guthrie observed, suspecting its use was disguise. She wore tight black leggings that encouraged the appreciation of her height, and slender black heels with thin black ribbons that climbed her delicate ankles like vines from the underworld. When she shifted her weight from one leg to the other she balanced the opposing foot on its toes and swung her hair to the opposite shoulder, to preserve her symmetry, Guthrie supposed.

He glanced back at the LeBeaus, who were about to be served by an approaching waiter with what looked from a distance like two house cheeseburger platters. They were glaring at the tall pretty girl like puritans at a witch trial. Ron was well into his cheeseburger when Rick rose again, and this time the girl saw him. He marched for the exit scowling as he went, his accusing eyes trained on her like the barrel of a gun. His brother followed in hasty pursuit, still chewing as he passed through the door.

Charlene materialized over Guthrie's shoulder.

"Always been a looker, that one," she offered unceremoniously. "Too pretty for her own good and don't know how to handle it, or maybe she do, if you know what I mean," she volunteered, nudging him salaciously with her chubby elbow before exploding in a burst of coarse, bawdy, belly laughs.

"Awe, Charlene, now that's not a nice way to talk. She looks about my daughter's age," Guthrie observed sympathetically as he watched Charlene plant a pudgy fist on each of her generous hips and pose like the overseer of an abattoir.

"Well, that one right there… Mr. Detective-man, don't get me started. You know better than that," she cautioned, commencing to cackle again, her amusement rising until the raunchy full-blown belly laugh Guthrie had heard before disintegrated like a shipwreck on the foamy spew of her menthol cauterized throat.

Guthrie studied the girl a minute longer. She was cutting her eyes playfully between the stolen glances of admirers.

"I see," said Guthrie, "she's a flirt," and he watched Charlene's pudgy fists turn white as she clenched them with frightening force.

"And you don't like that, do you Charlene," he toyed. "Why don't you like that, Charlene? I bet you were a flirt in your day, weren't you?" Charlene exploded into such a peal of laughter that Guthrie thought she would tear.

"You're naughty, Mr. Detective-man. Now don't you make me spill my coffee all over your pretty files."

Guthrie was proud to make an art of nurturing community relations. He knew questioning the locals made them uneasy, and in a small community like Poughkeepsie, accustomed to long winters and dwindling prospects, it was wiser to go along and get along than to risk making himself unapproachable. Loose talk, especially to the law, could drive the few friends one had into hiding, and asking questions was the surest way to deny himself answers. When he grew curious the locals became suspicious, and he was well aware that impatience could be his own worst enemy, frustrating discovery the way wet fish slip a tight grip. So he depended on gossip, an urge as irrepressible in humans as the howl of a wolf at the moon, and he tuned himself to the moment, registering Charlene's covetous glare. She looked like a house cat guarding a mouse hole.

"All that beauty and not a lick of sense," she finally muttered loud enough to be heard.

"Really?" said Guthrie.

"She's plenty smart, all right, jus' not smart enough to know a good thing… to know a good thing when it's staring her in the face," she continued, glowering. Guthrie recoiled theatrically to encourage her ripening cynicism. Strong feelings took shape on Charlene's face, struggling to find voice before the spirit abandoned her.

"Oh, I s'pose we're all young and stupid sometime, ain't we, Mr. Detective-man? And we grow out of it, don't we," she offered wistfully. "You just hope you don't do something you can't take back," she said as she squeezed another constricted cackle from her calloused throat; but the sad wisdom of her years defied disguise.

"I don't know, Charlene," Guthrie interjected cheerfully, to keep her talking, "did you?" he said, shooting her a provocative gleam through his bespectacled blue eyes.

"Now don't you start," she chortled. "Too long ago for me to remember and none of your business anyway," she said with a wink.

"Yeah, me too," said Guthrie, directing his attention, and with any luck hers, back to the pretty girl at the bar.

"Now that one, there," she began obligingly in a discretely disapproving tone. "She don't want nothin' she can have, and everything she can't. One day she'll wake up with nothin', and she won't look like that no more, neither."

"How's that?" Guthrie asked.

"She's from here, from a good family, hard-working sorts, that raised her nice. But she's greedy and ungrateful, tarting around and flipping that hair, thinkin' of nobody but herself. She's broke some hearts 'round here," she chirped coquettishly in a voice revived from her youth.

"Including Rick LeBeau's?" Guthrie asked as inconspicuously as he knew how.

"Well, I don't know about that," Charlene replied dismissively before turning on her heels, "and I must be about my tables, Mr. Guthrie," she hailed from over her shoulder, rounding the corner and disappearing behind the wait station, above which her pudgy hand briefly reappeared to place the coffee pot back on the hotplate.

Guthrie had broken procedure, crossing the invisible line he attempted so strenuously to observe. He had asked the question the answer to which Charlene would have volunteered, and probably more, had he been more patient. He gathered the neat stack of mostly empty files in his gigantic hands, slid them into his briefcase, and turned to wave a perfunctory good-bye when he caught Charlene staring at him.

"What did you say her name was?" he inquired indiscreetly with nothing left to lose.

"I didn't," Charlene replied like an obstinate child, "but it's Kelley Sutton, if you must know." Guthrie smiled. It was a start.

Chapter 4

One hundred and forty-five degrees south and seven hours west
Astrid Taylor Achermann took shelter from the blistering midday
heat in an open-sided, standard issue World Health Organization
field tent. She was accompanied by two health officials from Cape
Town, a white doctor, Peter Hammond, and a black translator, Sisulu
Botha. She was pleased that her escorts reflected the new political
realities of South Africa, and together they had pitched their tents at
the foot of a mountain range running through Richtersveld National
Park. She was already *in country*, too late to turn back, when she
learned that Richtersfeld was the most remote and least visited of
South Africa's seventeen national parks, tucked in the furthest
reaches of northwest South Africa, bordered by the sea to the west
and Namibia to the north. The travel guide included with her
supplies was vaguely ominous, warning of the park's extreme
climate, and the indispensability of four-wheel drive. *"Especially*
difficult are some steep and rocky mountain roads and some sandy
river crossings... Good maps and a compass are
indispensable...since sign posts have not been erected."
Richtersveld National Park existed to protect the sensitive, high
mountain desert ecosystem within its borders, not the destitute
people Astrid had been sent to observe, and it was home to flora and
fauna found nowhere else on earth. The flora included the
halfmensboom, or half-person tree, whose thick truncated canopy
resembled a human head perched atop a fat, awkward trunk. Much
of the park's desert habitat consisted of ancient alluvial flood plain
on which rivers still flowing from mountains in the east had
deposited thousands of years of sediment. Authorities permitted few
parties entry to the park, and Astrid and her team had checked in at
the ranger station on their way in, as required.

At almost fifty Astrid was still powerless to discourage
advances, even though she still wore her wedding band. Barely five
foot three inches tall, she had a curly thick head of fertile chestnut

hair with faint streaks of grey she was too busy to color. In the field she wore it back in a tight ponytail forcing the curls to erupt in all directions from the back of her head. She knew the many purposes of her gun-metal blue eyes, including the switch from warm-and-friendly to furious in a blink. She was less aware of the bestial beauty of her full, pouting lips and the vigor of her thick, dark eyebrows and her physique retained many of the attributes of her athletic youth. When she strode across the sand the striated muscle in her shoulders and triceps formed hairline shadows, like fish bones, as she swung her arms back and forth. Her intensity as much as her athleticism had landed her in the coxswain's seat of an Ivy League men's eight heavyweight rowing team. She could make eight oarsmen each one more than twice her weight pull in fearful unison. Yet despite her appearance, or maybe because of it, she had been luckless in love, and made a prison of her vows, even though she alone observed them.

"And what brings *you* so far from home, my dear young woman?" Peter Hammond had inquired too familiarly on the long ride out to camp. Astrid Taylor never set out to be a World Health Organization field doctor. She came fourth in a line of five children born to an established New Orleans family headed by an irreverent entrepreneur. Everything Billy Taylor touched turned to gold, from oil wells, to real estate, to speculating in commodities, and she grew up expecting hard work and selflessness to be rewarded. Astrid Devant Taylor, Astrid's mother, supervised the household with hell-fire and brimstone Baptist zeal, and the children were raised *in the church*. Between God and work, the Taylor children marched a narrow path. She admired but disapproved of three of her siblings who rebelled against the family's capitalist underpinnings and made lives for themselves as musicians and artists. They survived comfortably supported by Billy, whose success they tolerated as the price for the financial support they expected. But Astrid, like her oldest brother, had been determined to make her own success, and she had.

With a Magna Cum Laude pre-med undergraduate degree, she matriculated directly from the coxswain's seat to a highly selective northeastern medical school, completing her residency at Massachusetts General Hospital in Boston. With good intentions and modest ambitions, she joined a small family practice in Cambridge where she found joy in her work, and from which she planned to retire, until a renowned faculty member at Harvard Medical School called to have her join his prestigious research staff. She and her new colleagues were in pursuit of an antidote to the recently identified AIDS virus, and she soon caught the attention of the Columbia-Rockefeller Center for AIDS Research, which recruited her to a new program being launched in coordination with the Center for Disease Control in Atlanta. Shortly after moving to New York, she met Harry Achermann, a colorful, charming, self-made commodities speculator, probably like her father as she imagined him in his youth.

They married quickly and spent little of the next decade together, she pursuing research, and he following markets around the world and around the clock. Sometime not so long ago, the exact year eluded her, with a catalog of research breakthroughs to her credit, disillusionment set in. Did the emotional bottom haunt her, or did she willfully revisit it, to keep herself on course? She had been sitting in the luxurious solitude of the sprawling Fifth Avenue apartment she shared with Harry when she was struck by the absurdity of her existence. She felt stupid and indulgent, separated from her crazy, colorful southern roots, caught in an unfulfilled marriage, and bound to the emotional sterility of the lab bench. She vowed on the spot to resume practicing medicine, to care for patients who needed her, and in the company of compassionate caregivers. Without delay, and with the same ferocity that propelled her meteoric rise, she resigned her research position and applied for a posting with *Medecins Sans Frontieres*, the French not-for-profit known for delivering medical care to the most God-forsaken corners of the earth. For the next four years she toiled in desperate conditions in refugee camps and war zones throughout Africa, thriving in places short on love and long on suffering.

But Hammond need know none of that, nor did he need to know her mission was not strictly relief. In the months following the events of September 11, 2001 the World Health Organization issued a call. The WHO wanted physicians with knowledge of communicable diseases and experience working in Africa. It had been strongly encouraged by its largest benefactor, the government of the United States, to monitor ever more frequent Ebola outbreaks in sub-Saharan Africa. A team of WHO researchers working with NASA engineers using satellite imagery and rainfall data had established a link between the onset of rains following unusually dry seasons and outbreaks of Ebola. Astrid had been sent to Richtersveld to evaluate reports of an Ebola outbreak among the Nama tribe, whose range included the park and surrounding regions locally known as Namaqueland. The most perplexing aspect of the outbreak was its virulence, and the anomaly of its appearance in a region with a steady, moderate climate, no rainy season, and a long way from any known cases.

Nothing Astrid learned about the Nama before her arrival surprised her. Like countless uncelebrated African peoples, they had suffered deplorably before wave upon wave of Dutch, German, and British colonialists. Directly descended from the Khoikhoi bushmen to the east, they migrated west to the Atlantic coast after a fierce quarrel with their ancestors. This brought them in contact with 17th century European immigrants, who promptly enslaved them by the hundreds. Many perished in the smallpox epidemics that swept southern Africa in 1713 and 1755. With their fine features and pale skin they were easily distinguishable from other native Africans, but their most arresting quality was their language. They spoke an abstracted version of click language that UNESCO classified as endangered. Miraculously, the language had survived, despite being abandoned by the tribe after the Apartheid regime prohibited its teaching in schools. As if banning the language were not deprivation enough, the regime banished the tribes from their homelands in a needless coup de grâce to ancient traditions.

The Nama inhabiting the park still lived in small clutches of mat houses, dome-shaped shelters built on a lattice work of light, flexible, wooden poles held in place by an overlay of hand-woven sedge mats. The mat houses were ideally suited to the environment and highly adapted to the Nama's nomadic way of life by virtue of the speed and simplicity with which they could be pitched and struck. The aerodynamic dome resisted high desert winds. In dry conditions the sedge contracted, leaving a semi porous membrane that provided excellent ventilation. In rain the sedge expanded, closing the gaps and sealing the shelter. Much to Astrid's consternation the mat-houses encouraged the sort of communal gatherings known for propagating virulent contagion like Ebola. She had come to Richtersveld to gather facts about the outbreak, and to counsel the Nama on treating the disease and slowing its spread.

With only several thousand Nama populating the park, an outbreak of Ebola could have devastating consequences.

She knew the hour must be noon because Peter Hammond rose from where he was reading a novel in a folding camp chair and approached the VHF radio powered by a U.S. Army issue RUPS, or rugged uninterruptible power supply. The WHO medical party had been instructed to check-in daily by radio with the park ranger station. Hammond switched the volume knob to "on" and adjusted back the interference with the squelch knob.

"Richtersveld Park, Richtersveld Park, this is World Health party, over."

"Loud and clear Dr. Hammond," the radio crackled in heavily Afrikaans-tinted English. She thought the reply came conspicuously fast.

"Checking in. All well here, no change among the Nama, I'm afraid. New cases every day. Do you have an update on inbound staff and supplies?" This time Hammond waited. Her already piqued curiosity turned to apprehension.

"Do you copy, Richtersveld?" More delay. They were withholding something, she was sure, and she pictured them bunched around the radio like family at a wake.

"Yes, we copy," the radio finally crackled. "No news on the relief party, but we have a request from Cape Town that you break camp and bring your party out without delay."

"Nonsense," she said to herself, skewering Hammond inadvertently with a look.

"Why?" she barked from the shaded work bench where she was organizing blood samples. Hammond looked skeptical too, and he paused before depressing the push-to-talk button.

"Say again, Richtersveld?"

"Request you break camp and come out, Dr. Hammond."

"No way. They know what's going on here," she said.

"Is there a reason?" Hammond inquired deferentially. She would have taken another tack, but she could tell he was intimidated by the heavy handedness for which the South African authorities were renowned.

"Orders are to come and collect you, Dr. Hammond, if you're unwilling to come on your own," came the response, but it didn't sound like an order.

"Richtersveld," Hammond began with purpose, "situation among the Nama is grave. A dozen already dead, many more sick and dying. Cannot leave before relief. When is relief coming?" More delay. Astrid stood up and marched like a storm trooper to the VHF where she snatched the microphone from Hammond.

"We're not leaving until this situation stabilizes, do you copy?" she barked.

"Stand by," crackled the radio. She and Hammond stared at the radio like castaways when the water runs out.

"What the blazes are they doing?" he asked after several minutes had passed.

"I don't know, but we're not leaving," she assured him. Several more minutes passed before the radio crackled back to life.

"Dr. Achermann, there is a plane en route from Cape Town to collect you. Your team may stay, but with respect, Dr. Achermann, we must insist you return to the park station. We are instructed to come out and collect you if necessary." She knew better than to fight futile battles, but she had to understand.

"Can you please tell me what this is about?" she snarled through the microphone.

"No, I'm afraid I cannot. You are urgently needed back in the States."

"Why? By whom?" she demanded. "What could be more urgent than the present situation? Without the right attention the whole damn Nama tribe will be gone in two months."

She searched Hammond. "What could this possibly be about, Peter?"

"I've no idea. Why don't you ask them?"

"Richtersveld, I'm not leaving." In the long delay that followed rose a growing sense of dread.

"Do you copy?" she demanded.

"Dr. Achermann, I regret very much to inform you that your husband has been killed."

She heard the words, but they failed to register, and the skeptical grimace she reserved for the witless park rangers carried into the look she gave Hammond. The idea was preposterous, like a tabloid headline.

"Say again, Richtersveld?" she heard herself protest half-heartedly, the words closing on her like a fever.

"I regret to inform you your husband has been killed. I'm very sorry Dr. Achermann. We have no details other than arrangements have been made for you to travel to Cape Town."

Her first reaction was to picture Harry dead. She had seen countless dead, knew how death looked, and how it smelled and felt. But Harry's world and the world to which she owed her intimacy with death never intersected. The dissonance between Harry and her many pictures of death was a null set, a non sequitur, and the thought of death brought her back to the plight of the Nama. She sank slowly to her haunches, the mic resting in the open palm of her hand.

"My God," Hammond whispered, "My God, Astrid. I'm so sorry. I'm so very sorry." Was it the remote locale, or the incomprehensibility of the news that explained her indifference? She remained on her heels by the radio as Hammond came to her side and reached for the mic, but she tightened her fist and put it to her mouth.

"How was he killed?"

"Dr. Achermann, we have no details. I regret very much giving you this news." She put the mic down and left the tent leaving Hammond to conclude with the Richtersveld rangers whom he assured Astrid would be ready by sundown.

She didn't care what Hammond thought of her stoicism. He couldn't know there was a part of her that had always been embarrassed by Harry. In her heart she was sure he had earned his fate, whatever it was, and she felt guilty for the sentiment. What she never expected to feel was relief, but the catharsis was irrefutable.

For all his failings, and there were many, her memories of their early years were not gone. When they found each other in all the excitement of New York City, they were young and talented and attractive, each one full of promise, she as a researcher, and he as an arbitrageur. But the romance and promise faded like a shriveled party balloon, succumbing to time and the grinding regimen of careers. Occasionally she comforted herself that they forgot to have children, distracted by the demands of their considerable achievements. It was a convenient self-deception that failed on the facts, as she well knew. She chose to wait, and somewhere between rising risks and declining opportunities, hope for conception withered like berries in the sun. Sometimes she thought that fading intimacy was the price of success, but that too overlooked the truth.

His attentions to younger women became legend, and somewhere in the devolution of their lives self-deceptions became preferable to knowing the full scale of his infidelities. Their romantic encounters grew rare and eventually loveless, until promise flickered out like the lights on a doomed ship.

What survived of the marriage was not without its merits. It preserved their position in certain social circles, and access to the people and institutions that were important to them. Unions of convenience were not so extraordinary, especially as they navigated middle age. In and out of love their paths rarely crossed, though nobody knew it by the appearances they cultivated.

She was gazing into the sinking sun as the ranger pulled into camp, admiring the mountains as they glowed through the sea fog advancing on the plateau. The truck rolled to a stop and a lithe, weather-beaten man in a perspiration-stained safari shirt and shorts climbed out. He failed to notice her as he bounded to the tent where Hammond and Botha could be heard trading gags as they familiarized themselves with the eye protection, gowns, face masks and gloves they would need in her absence. She would have to remind them that the masks and gowns were insufficient for disposing of corpses, which oozed contagion long after death. Body suits and breathing apparatus were among the supplies she expected to arrive with the relief party. The ranger was already inside when Astrid poked her head beneath the canvas where a heavy dew had begun collecting.

"Dr. Achermann?" the ranger inquired solicitously.

"Yes?"

"Very sorry, madam. Very sorry indeed. Norris Sanderling, at your service. My mates call me Sandy," he said optimistically. The Afrikaans polluting Sanderling's English betrayed his breeding.

"Yes. Hello. I'll be right with you."

"Are these your things?" inquired Sanderling, pointing to a large travel worn duffel bag and an aluminum, crush-proof case.

"Yes. But I will carry them, thank you," she said.

"No," said Sanderling, "I insist," and he reached for the aluminum case marked with a large red cross on a circular field of white. There were other decals too. *Warning. Danger. Handle with Care*, pasted helter-skelter like bills of passage on a steam trunk.

"No, Mr. Sanderling," said Astrid, using the tone she reserved for New York cabbies. "I handle that one. You may take the other one if you wish."

"Yes, Dr. Achermann."

In a show of force designed to impress, Sanderling heaved the duffel bag over his shoulder, marched it to the truck, and dumped it unceremoniously into the rear. The farewells to Hammond and Botha were easy. It was the eyes of the chief that hit home. The leader of the Nama and two elders had wandered into camp late that afternoon bearing more sad news. Conditions in the village were deteriorating.

She called for Botha to convey her sympathies and a promise to return. When Botha finally appeared he looked like a surgeon, masked, gloved and gowned. The absence of clicks in the muffled sounds of the dialect he used left her doubting his faithfulness to her sentiments, and her doubt deepened as she stared into the chief's helpless eyes. They were resigned and sweet, like an abandoned shelter animal waiting to be euthanized. It made her angry, to leave when she could make a difference, for the demeaning purpose of cleaning up after Harry, even if it was for the last time. Harry was dead. There was nothing to change about that. She reached out with both arms, her unprotected hands falling gently on the shoulders of the chief.

"I will be back. Do you hear? I will be back." He stared at her despairingly, the promise ringing hollow, like all the others of centuries past. "Well, then," Astrid said with questionable resolve, "see you soon," she said optimistically, knowing it might not be soon enough.

She marched past the back door of the truck Norris Sanderling held ajar for her and climbed into the front passenger seat, the crush proof aluminum case clutched in her arms. "Sure you don't want me to put that in the boot?" Sanderling offered, climbing into the driver's seat.

"This stays with me," she snapped.

"Medical supplies, is it?" he said, turning the ignition. He jammed the truck into gear and steered it through one hundred eighty degrees until the wheels found the tracks he left on his way into the camp.

"No. It's tissue and blood samples."

"Tissue samples?" he said.

"Yes. From the Nama dead."

"Bloody hell," Sanderling exclaimed. "I knew there was a flu or something that had the tribes a bit under the weather, but dead? How many dead?" he asked in disbelief.

"Not sure. At least a dozen. There will be more in a fortnight."

"Is it contagious? Are you sure you want that in here with us?" Sanderling asked, concern for himself foremost on his mind. Astrid smiled.

"Not to worry, *Sandy*," she said having a go, "at least ten percent survive, maybe fifty percent with the more benign strains. Shouldn't be surprised if a man of your stamina pulled through."

Sanderling's shoulders flagged, more with relief than pity for the Nama she supposed. "Rest assured," she added cheerfully, "you would have to come in contact to actually contract it, at least that's the current thinking," she said, squinting like a short-sighted copy editor as she second-guessed herself. "This one might be a bit different, not sure yet, actually."

"Bloody hell," Sanderling repeated, more quietly than before.

"Yes, well that's pretty much how it turns out for the victims. It comes on just, as you say, like the flu, or a bout of malaria or typhoid fever. You know, chills, headache, fever, so one jumps to the usual diagnoses. Then in five days or so the fun begins. First a rash, usually about the torso," she said, her hands finding her hips like a stewardess demonstrating a flotation device, "accompanied by nausea, abdominal pain and chest pain, and then vomiting, diarrhea and hemorrhagic symptoms," she finished matter-of-factly, watching Sanderling wet his lips.

He was forming a question, impeded by the evident queasiness she had quite intentionally induced.

"What does that last bit mean?" he inquired uncomfortably.

"You know, bleeding, from all your mucus membranes. The bleeding intensifies, weight loss accelerates, followed by shock and then multiple organ failure. Then you're dead. That's about it, really," she concluded clinically, to disguise her satisfaction with his vulnerability.

"How do you suppose it started? I mean, how do you suppose they caught it, the Ebola, or whatever it is?"

"That's a mystery," she replied, wondering at his curiosity.

"I mean, they must have caught it from someone, or something, musn't they? These things don't just start spontaneously, do they?" He was more than curious. He was afraid.

"Yes, that's the mystery. The Nama are so isolated, so far from any documented outbreaks. Maybe you can tell us. Do they move around? Leave the park? Visit other tribes?"

"No," Sanderling replied, rather abruptly she thought.

Sanderling's multiplying physical discomfort was hard to overlook. It was always the he-men who had no stomach for clinical shop talk. Doubtless he fainted at the sight of blood. He was having a common and involuntary reaction to graphic subjects known as a vasovagal response that triggers dilation of the circulatory system. He had all the telltale signs - color loss, perspiration, elevated breathing - nothing a change of subject would not cure.

He seemed to know it, too, and focused intently on staying in the tire tracks from his outbound journey. The sand was soft, he had explained, and departing the ruts which were vanishing into the advancing dusk, would be straying from the path of least resistance and slow their progress. The colors sweeping the desert and lapping against the distant mountains gave Astrid a pleasant distraction. They were changing rapidly in the flat beams of retiring sun, from muted sienna browns and burnt umbers to brilliant splotches of reds and oranges where the light caught the ridges and peaks. The distant range looked like pastries in a confectionary, intensifying in a crescendo of brilliance until the sun succumbed to a single high peak, and the lustrous splotches faded as quickly as they had materialized, dissolving in the earth's shadow, bleeding into purples and blues, the colors of cold desert nights.

"Could germs or a virus, or what have you, be carried in?" he finally asked.

"Sure, of course, people can be carriers. They can carry the infection for days, even weeks before showing signs of illness. That's how it spreads."

"No, not like that," he countered. "I meant, could things like second-hand clothing or blankets, things of that nature be contaminated, donations of the sort charities distribute?"

"I doubt it very much. There's nothing like that in the case histories. Bush meat and unsanitary living conditions are more likely pathogens. I suppose it's possible, some form of mutation maybe, but very unlikely. Why do you ask?"

"Well, that does come as relief," he said loosening his collar. "Just a few months back we started delivering relief supplies, from charities and such, as I say. We South Africans have developed quite a conscience in recent years, you know."

"So I've heard."

"It's none of my business, Dr. Achermann, but what's your interest in these matters? Why would you come all the way from the States to a place like this to do this sort of work?" he inquired skeptically as if to say, "who volunteers for these types of outings anyway?"

She was tired of *Sandy*, and felt no obligation to explain herself.

"The answer to that is far too complicated, but it has something to do with helping the helpless," she said, confident the subject of compassion would fail to hold his interest.

"Don't you worry about catching one of these bloody diseases?" Just as she expected, the idea of putting others first never occurred to oafs like *Sandy*.

"We take precautions," she said, communicating her boredom by taking in the landscape.

"What's pressing enough to risk your life for a bunch of bloody tribesmen?" he persisted. His ignorance was infuriating, and his curiosity conspicuous.

"What do you know about Ebola, Mr. Sanderling?" she posed nonchalantly.

"A lot bloody more than I wanted to, ma'am," he said trying to be amusing, but Astrid was not amused. One of the disenchanting aspects of her work was the insufferable stupidity of the officials she encountered. She could predict it by now.

"Well," she muttered to herself, "let's hope you will not learn more." Regrettably, Sanderling was not to be dissuaded.

"What more is there to know?"

"Quite a lot, actually."

"I'm interested, genuinely," Sanderling said sincerely.

"Well, it goes something like this," she started. "We don't know if the virus even existed until thirty years ago. The first confirmed outbreaks were in the seventies in the Sudan, two separately documented events, several years apart. It didn't show up again until the 1990s, and it had moved to Gabon and Cote d'Ivoire, and then to the Democratic Republic of Congo. In 2001 it appeared in the Rift Valley in Saudi Arabia and Yemen, and in Uganda, too. Do you know your geography well enough to see a pattern, Mr. Sanderling?"

"It's spreading, in all directions."

"Yes, it's spreading like an ink blot. Each strain is different. Each one highly contagious. The outbreaks vanish as abruptly as they appear. We don't know how it starts or why it stops, except to say that it runs out of victims. But for a lucky few, it wipes out the small, isolated communities where it surfaces. We have no models for what happens when this family of viruses finds its way into densely populated communities, like Cape Town or Johannesburg, so do you see the concern?"

"Is that next?" Sanderling asked fearfully, running a rough-hewn hand around the back of his neck, and across the stubble bristling from his ruddy checks. He shifted uneasily in the dilapidated naugahyde driver's seat and checked his rearview mirror, in the most desolate desert on the emptiest continent. Something was eating at him, Astrid felt sure.

"Don't know," she said dispassionately, but fatigue was finally catching up with her. She felt parched by the day's heat, despondent about the news of Harry, and restless with a long night ahead. She was thinking his inquisitiveness was finally satisfied only to discover she wasn't that lucky.

"You see, Dr. Achermann, what I don't understand is why anyone in the States would care? So Africa loses a few indigenous peoples. It's been happening for centuries, hasn't it, and it's bound to continue. Bloody Darwinian if you ask me." Another Neanderthal. It was wasted effort, but she could not help herself. Ignorance galled her the way red antagonizes bulls.

"A disease like this, Mr. Sanderling, could have geopolitical ramifications… especially in the wrong hands, if you get my meaning," she started, scolding him like a schoolteacher. She never did tame the urge to set dunces like Sanderling straight, despite her embarrassment at rising to the bait.

"Geopolitical… what?" Sanderling replied doubtfully. "Don't be daft. Who would give a toss about the Nama?"

"Never mind." For once she didn't have the strength and turned away, gazing out the window at a prehistoric landscape fading into the encroaching night. She felt her eyelids closing, her head teetering. It would be hours before they reached the ranger station, and sleep would be a fine alternative to the uninspired company of Sanderling. She made a last, half-hearted attempt to enlighten him.

"You are aware of recent world events, aren't you? I mean, you have read a newspaper, or watched a television, or chatted with someone who has," she said speaking quietly into the darkness. He looked at her searchingly, like a falsely accused child, the lights from the dash reflecting emerald green in the droplets of perspiration bubbling on his forehead and beneath his eyelids. She felt cool in the moist evening air. Why was he perspiring?

"I'm not following you, ma'am," he said contritely.

"You have heard of terrorism, even down here, haven't you?" she said. "Do you know what a disease like this could do in the wrong hands?"

They were lurching through the darkness before the conversation resumed.

"How can you possibly know where you're going out here?" Astrid said, more by observation than inquiry.

"I'm just following my tracks, Dr. Achermann. If the wind doesn't come up the tracks will take us all the way to the station."

"And if the wind blows?" she countered.

"We drive due east until we pick up the Orange River and follow her back to the station."

"I see," she said, fatigue creeping back in.

"Life's pretty simple out here, Dr. Achermann."

"Unless you're a Nama."

"I suppose you're right. History has been unkind to the Nama. I'd never heard of the Nama until I came out here."

"Really?" she replied unsurprised. "And where were you coming from?"

"East Coast. Port Elizabeth. That's where I'm from, originally. Spent twelve years between here and there as a mine foreman."

"That's quite a change. Mine foreman to park ranger?"

"I suppose it is," he said. She expected an explanation but none followed, or at least none that she was awake to hear. When she woke the truck stood still in the darkness, idling in its tracks, and Sanderling was slumped over the steering wheel.

Chapter 5

Coco two-stepped in unsettled pursuit, cutting left and right in
Elliot's wake as he weaved in purposeful silence through determined
commuters crowding the half block between the office and a small
coffee shop tucked down a side street. She was used to the rain,
which was falling again in heavy, blowing sheets. Pedestrians
skittered in undulating waves, like plumes of panicked reef fish
darting for cover beneath awnings and doorways. She was close on
his heels as he blew through the door of Le Café Paris and braced the
door against the storm until she cleared the threshold, landing in the
cramped entryway dripping and diminished like a sopping cat.

The café was almost full, procrastinating patrons reluctant to
relinquish their cozy roosts. Clinking teaspoons and the clattering of
institutional grade porcelain mixed with the animated voices of
managers and secretaries trading age-old gripes about bosses and
colleagues, nattering like dyspeptic starlings. A gentle haze of
cigarette smoke hung in the air. At least the walk had been diverting.
Now she stood beside Elliot with growing discomfort as they were
approached by a young, skeptical-looking hostess wearing a black
beret, a red neckerchief, black pants and a tired white blouse. She
had a heavy cockney accent and showed them to a table in the
middle of the room. For reasons Coco preferred not to imagine Elliot
shook his head and requested the empty booth next to the kitchen at
the back of the café. The hostess accommodated him with huffy
impatience, pitching two greasy laminated menus on the table before
saying something indefinite about returning to take an order. Elliot
sat first, which she found bizarrely out of character, taking the bench
facing out at the café, and leaving her with a view of the kitchen and
a yellowed poster of the Eiffel Tower hanging cockeyed over Elliot's
head. He had slung his briefcase ahead of him into his side of the
booth before sitting down without removing his coat, and she
followed his lead, letting the water pool on the vinyl seat around her.
He was rushed or nervous, and she had never seen him nervous.

"What's wrong, Elliot? This is weird," she ventured, trying to lighten the mood. He looked resolved, like a sphinx.

"Coco," he started, pain taking shape on his face.

"Liza and I… well you know how fond of you we are," he said in a way that sounded as reassuring to himself as it was meant to sound to Coco. "You know we would do anything for you," he continued, only now with empathy like a hospice counselor. "You would come to us for help if you ever needed it, wouldn't you?" The furrows in his brow and the sadness on his face portended something dismal.

"What kind of help, Elliot? What are you talking about?" she said, forcing a smile. "You're scaring me." He wiped the pathos from his face and started again.

"Coco, can you think of any reason someone would want to blackmail you or me or the *Washington Post*? Have you unearthed anything around the DeBeers story that would be a threat, I mean a serious threat, to anybody…like a DeBeers executive?" He was speaking from a dark place, and she sensed his distress. In a curious expression of defensiveness, or megalomania, her immediate reaction was to feel flattered. Had she stumbled unknowingly across something big? Had she asked such sensitive questions that Sam had gone over her head to Elliot to have her muzzled? It was the highest form of praise to an aggressive reporter, like penalty time to a hockey player for punching the opponent's lights out.

"Almost everything I've reported," she said feeling encouraged. "We're reporters, Elliot. What do we report that doesn't threaten someone?" She saw his patience expire. He reached for his briefcase, lifted it into his lap, unlatched the buckles and flopped the worn leather cover on to the table. Reaching in he produced an oversized yellow envelope, the kind radiologists use to file x-rays. He placed the envelope delicately on the table in front of Coco, averting his eyes in an unconvincing display of disinterest.

"What's that?" she blurted with more trepidation than she intended. He had no words for her, no perceptible response, but to prop his elbows on the table and lower his forehead into his palms like a grieving widow.

"Open it," he finally said staring at the table. Coco bent back the duck-billed tabs restraining the flap on the envelope. She compressed the edges to force the mouth open and glimpsed the white border and grainy edges of a black and white photograph. There were several. She looked to Elliot for a clue but he refused to acknowledge her, his eyes boring into the table like magnified sunlight.

She slid the photographs part way from the envelope before losing her breath and jamming them back in. Her first reaction was to gasp, and then snort, a comedic sort of outburst at the indecency, which was dismal to the point of absurdity. She knew right away it was the wrong reaction by how it exacerbated Elliot's distress. He was appalled, distraught, his old-fashioned sensibilities under siege. She guessed he would spare her the obvious moral judgments, but what came next? She waited for what felt like an eternity.

"Are you okay?" she finally asked.

"Not really," he replied, plainly discouraged by her response. "Are you?" He sounded angry. "Look, nobody expects you to lead a life of abstention, but what the hell, Coco! Why is this crap coming through my mail slot, hand delivered? You can see there's no postage, can't you?" Her mind raced ahead. Who took the pictures and how did they come into Elliot's possession? It was indiscrete, to be sure. She did not consider herself promiscuous, but she was not a prude either. She had glanced at one photograph only long enough to recognize herself, and now her gnawing curiosity yearned to look again, to identify the man.

"I apologize, Elliot. I need to take a closer look," she murmured, doing better to sound contrite. She supposed the mores and commonplace intimacies of her generation were unfathomable to men like Elliot. Inured to indiscretion by the pervasiveness of prurient digital imagery, erotica and nudity did not leave her breathless the way they did Elliot.

"Please give me a minute, to figure out who… I mean, when these were taken." Elliot stifled a gasp. She regretted leaving him few but the worst conclusions to draw about her private life.

"Coco, it's not so much *who* or *when,* but *why?*" he replied, drawing a deep breath. "That's what we need to talk about." She felt her expression wilt, not so much because she was intrinsically ashamed but because she knew she had disappointed him.

"Let's sit here for a while," he continued, calming himself. "I have nowhere to go and we're going to need to talk about this."

"Does Liza know about these?" she whined more plaintively than she intended.

"No." Elliot assured her, "and she won't. Nor will anybody, I hope," he added sounding doubtful. "Here's the problem. I don't know where these came from. They were in my mail at home last night, addressed to me - no note, no threats, no demands," he reported apprehensively. "We all know you can't be in our business for long without being threatened, but we usually know what it's about. Whoever delivered those pictures has an overdeveloped sense of suspense, or there's another shoe to drop." He looked uncomfortable as hell.

"I'm so sorry, Elliot. It was a mistake."

"Of course, Coco. We've all made mistakes. But there's a problem here, do you understand?" Her amusement had crested and she began to feel hollow and numb, and perhaps a little afraid, because Elliot was afraid, and he never was.

"Sure," she said.

"The problem," he continued, "is that I don't know what whoever sent these wants, or what they're prepared to do. Obviously, I'm worried about you. Only you can know if there's worse to come," he said. It felt like a jab, the implication being there was a side to Coco he could scarcely imagine, a side he did not want to know.

"If this is connected to anything you're working on," he began, letting the thought hang like a sinking kite... then you can be sure these will come to light to discredit you, and," he paused, "probably me." Elliot's meaning took time to register.

"Is what you're saying you have to fire me," Coco replied. "I mean, to distance yourself, to protect yourself?"

"I didn't say that, but you're compromised until we know what this is about," he replied.

Coco had not achieved her professional status by tactical retreats. The more she contemplated gagging by malicious forces too cowardly to show themselves, the more incensed she became. She felt under siege, like a frontier widow burned from her home.

"So what, Elliot?" she began, knowing he admired her spunk. "So I'm not a virgin. Is that hard news?" His look needed more than spunk.

"Tell me who the guy is," he replied. She turned to the envelope more deliberately this time, and slipped the photographs free, flipping quickly, and swallowing shame, frame by glossy frame. The face of the man in the photographs was obscured in all but one exposure, and she recognized him immediately.

"Him," she said.

"Keep going," Elliot prodded.

"He was a friend of Sam's."

 "How much do you know about him?"

"Probably not as much as I should."

"Do you know where he is now?"

"No. That was the last time I saw him. Pretty sure."

"Do you know," Elliot countered abruptly, before softening his voice to a whisper, "his name?"

Coco became distracted by the skeptical Francophile waitress, who had been in orbit like a nosy relative for some time. She had aborted more than one final approach already, out of respect, Coco guessed, for the scene the waitress presumed was playing out between herself and Elliot. She guessed they looked like other mismatched couples the waitress had witnessed before: Elliot's age, her obvious vulnerability – it must have the dismal look of so many affairs that had unraveled in Le Café Paris before. How sad, thought Coco, that the world still expects young women to fall for old men, whose elderly appetite for sweet after-dinner ports bears no resemblance to wedding champagne. She caught the waitress's eye, conveying in a glance she could use the interruption. The skeptic swept in like a world-weary meter maid, order pad in hand.

"What's your pleasure?" she inquired in her cockney accent as Coco was finishing her thought.

"Harry Achermann," she said to Elliot, "that was his name."

Chapter 6

The Nama chief lay splayed across Astrid's lap vomiting convulsively, the blood coming in sporadic bursts, small gobs of tissue intermingling with greater frequency in the thick viscous fluid that dried almost instantly to Astrid's bare legs in the hot desert sun. She could see a thin ivory crescent of sclera through the sliver of the chief's eye lids, his irises beginning the slow roll to the back of his head. She rocked him like a colic child, furnishing what comfort she could in these his last hours. From the corner of her eye she saw the chief's arm rise from the packed sand, his hand swaying in the air like a hypnotist. He reached for her, seeking comfort she presumed in the loose hold he took of the supple dry skin on her neck, until his fist clenched shut with mechanical brutality around her windpipe.

She reached for his wrist, to wrest the hand free and found it immovable. Even the physiological weakness of the opposed thumb she found impossible to exploit. She let go the hand supporting his head, seizing the chief's wrist with both hands, and wrenching with all her might, even as his fingernails cut and she felt the skin on her neck break. The dying chief appeared to be mustering every last measure of strength for misplaced retribution. She called for Hammond, to no avail, for she barely managed a stifled gurgle. She could feel herself losing the struggle to contain panic when the chief convulsed again, rolling into her torso and landing squarely across her hips, pinning her beneath his cadaverous frame, gravity fortifying his grip and crushing her larynx in the arch of his palm. She flailed like a beetle, her limbs strangely incapacitated, heavy and awkward rather than burning the way she would have expected from oxygen deprivation.

She could see Hammond in the distance, his back turned, sitting at the camp table. Surely he could hear her, the sound of her distress, and was bound to turn and see her struggling. She tried again to scream but with piteous effect, a shapeless empty moan fading with her strength. As consciousness slipped away she heard an earsplitting knell - the toll of the grim reaper she presumed. No, not yet. This was not her time, she vowed, and she jack-knifed at the waist with the remnants of her strength, rising from the sand like a cobra.

She bolted upright in bed, stuck to sweat-soaked sheets, the red message light on the hotel telephone pulsating in staccato sympathy with each jarring burst of sound. Gasping for breath, she tore the sheets free and lurched across the room, guided by the message light to the receiver. "Hello," she croaked into the mouthpiece.

"Hey there," replied the familiar voice.

"Hello?" Astrid said again, triangulating on the American accent.

"It's me, it's Katrine," the chipper voice chirped. Astrid fell back into the institutionally upholstered arm chair by the writing desk, nauseous, disoriented, and relieved. Where she was and how she got there remained foggy, but she recognized the voice and it was comforting, like the humid embrace of New Orleans spring air.

"Hey Astrid, are you okay?" Katrine's husky bright voice inquired, working like an antidote to the grisly vision of the Nama chief. Slowly, the sensation of suffocating dissolved along with the smell of dried blood and the gritty texture of hot sand; and reluctantly, shadows of events over the past thirty-six hours lifted.

"Astrid, say something." She flicked on the light, becoming marginally more sentient, and more aware of the rolling waves of nausea roiling her insides. She had gotten herself out of Richtersveld National Park, and Sanderling to a cot at the ranger station where she expected he would die. He was symptomatic, all his indications identical to those she had observed among the Nama: a sudden, incapacitating hemorrhagic fever from which none of the Nama recovered. He had to have been infected well before pulling into camp to collect her for despite its aggressiveness the strain took time to incubate. She took the precaution of donning a surgical mask as soon as she realized Sanderling was contagious, as much to protect others as herself if she were already infected. The World Health Organization had arranged her flights to the Johannesburg Airport, and from there to New York, connecting through London, scheduled travel time about twenty-two hours.

But Astrid knew what awaited her in New York. She had no patience for the nosy journalists and officious estate lawyers who would circle and hover in nervous delight, like buzzards over a carcass; nor was she feeling sentimental enough to plan funerals and memorial services, or to reply to obsequious condolence letters from the cadre of sycophants with whom her husband surrounded himself. The insufferable indignities would survive the delay her detour required.

In London she skipped her connecting flight to New York and booked a new one to Atlanta, placing a call from Heathrow airport to an old friend from medical school who worked at the Center for Disease Control, alerting her to her imminent arrival.

"Can't talk now," she had said evasively, "about to miss my flight."

Katrine Burkhardt and Astrid had navigated medical school almost effortlessly, and if not effortlessly, then with so much unrelenting curiosity and enthusiasm that they bored their classmates to tears. Whether they first met in the library or at the lab, neither could recall. It was certain they had not met socially. As their friendship grew they developed the annoying habit of public jousting, to test if not display, as some suspected, each other's clinical knowledge. They would burst into spontaneous fusillades of symptoms and conditions, exchanging salvo after salvo of unpronounceable terminology in a cat-and-mouse game of wits. It was a practice as endearing as soiled bed pans that cleared a social gathering like burning oil clears rats. They were attractive and smart and engrossed in their work, which won them few followers among their highly competitive, maladjusted peers. In the years following medical school the envy of their colleagues did not so much fade as mutate, maturing into begrudging respect. Neither one was inspired by the profit motive which drew their classmates to lucrative specialty practices like moths to light. Astrid saw better than most how thinly veiled by the Hippocratic oath were the ambitions of her classmates. Some of them challenged common definitions of greed sufficiently to make a Wall Street sharpie blush in sheepish admiration. She was well enough acquainted with wealth to know it was a poor predictor of knowledge, which explained the frequency with which she and Katrine found themselves "consulted" in later life by medical school chums treating rare diseases.

With the pressing sensation of the Nama chief's death grip lingering in her throat, she seized at the opportunity to speak.

"Katrine! Katrine, thank God. Yes, I'm okay. What time is it?"

"It's really early, and I'm picking you up in fifteen minutes."

"Why?" she asked, thinking of sleep and a long hot bath. She ran her free hand through her dirty dense hair, her fingertips tarrying over the abrasive grains of African sand that had settled in her scalp transiting the Atlantic.

"No time to explain," Katrine chirped cheerfully. "See you in fifteen minutes," and she hung up.

In the air-conditioned emptiness of the generic hotel room in east Atlanta, more secure against the elements than any structure in Namaqualand, the full implication of Harry's death took hold. Like a commuted life sentence, Harry's dispatch left her standing at the open gates of life with long abandoned prospects. Perhaps that was why she had been less than forthcoming with Katrine about her unscheduled return to the U.S. She did not know herself where to begin. Not that Katrine would shed any tears. She had been unenthusiastic about Harry from the start.

Recent events came back to her now. Katrine had picked her up at Atlanta's Hartsfield International Airport the previous evening, and together they had driven the samples directly to the CDC for testing. She explained then that the surgical mask was purely precautionary, given the aggressive symptoms of the strain, and with the samples safely in Katrine's hands, she had checked herself into the closest national chain hotel and gone straight to sleep.

She saw Katrine pull into the hotel porte-cochere from the lobby where she was waiting. Katrine was driving the same old well-aged Japanese car, the white paint oxidized like desiccated bone by years beneath the hot Georgia sun. She marched through the sliding glass doors, nervous but excited to see her old friend. Her hair was still moist from a brief but revitalizing shower, and she landed in Katrine's passenger seat like a teenager on Friday night. Katrine floored the accelerator as Astrid pulled the door closed.

"What's the rush?" Astrid exclaimed, feeling mildly alarmed. There was something grave in her friend's demeanor, and she caught the familiar scent of Katrine's pungent body odor, an odor she had not smelled since medical school, and a sure sign Katrine had not left the labs at the CDC since they had parted company the night before.

"What did you find?" Astrid inquired, earnest as a crossing guard.

"Can't say until we get back to the office," Katrine replied, leaving her to puzzle why. What could she say at the office that she couldn't say in the car? Few were the clinicians whose professional judgment Astrid accepted unconditionally, and Katrine was among them. Katrine navigated the Atlanta dawn so aggressively that Astrid felt unnerved, her clinical poise decomposing by degrees until it was gone by the time they reached 1600 Clifton Road, the main offices of the Center for Disease Control. The CDC was directly across from the modern campus of Emory University, which was presently silhouetted against the smoggy first-light. Katrine slung the car to a stop in a reserved, covered parking place assigned too late, thought Astrid, to save the paint on her car.

"Astrid, come with me." It sounded like an order.

She followed Katrine through two sets of security card-controlled glass doors and into an elevator that descended far enough to make her ears pop. Katrine was out of the elevator and powering down the hall before the doors finished opening. It was long and antiseptic and the fluorescent lights were bright enough to make Astrid squint like an Inuit. She stutter-stepped to keep up as they passed through two more security card-controlled entries until Katrine eventually halted outside a numbered door that released with a swipe of her card and opened into an examination room that could have been any doctor's office in America. Compared to where she had been it looked to Astrid like an intensive care unit, neatly equipped with an examination table, wheeled stool, and articulated overhead exam light. Katrine held the door for her until she was inside the room and pulled it shut behind her.

"You need a shot, my friend."

"Wait a minute, Katrine. I'm sure you're right, but maybe you can tell me what's going on. I've been exposed to Ebola before, and I feel fine."

"Do you?" The doubt in Katrine's voice was disconcerting.

"I'm a little jet-lagged, but I'll feel better with something in my stomach."

"Astrid," Katrine began officiously, "I know what I'm talking about. There's no time." Katrine was telling her something. "We keep a little antidote locker down here... for accidents," she said flashing an unconvincing smile. "You know, sticking ourselves and such." Astrid felt her senses sharpen, as if she had taken a wrong turn into a bad neighborhood. Katrine took three steps into a small galley kitchenette that had not been visible from the door. At the end was a stainless steel refrigerator with a security card controlled lock. Katrine swiped her card again, punched in a code, and turned a heavy silver handle more suited to a bank vault than a household appliance. The steel door swung wide, frozen vapors spilling from the interior like spirits from a cauldron. She could hear Katrine sorting glass vials, and for a moment she was back in New York, her housekeeper dusting the crystal chandeliers. Katrine's brief search rewarded, she swung the steel door shut and drove the handle home like a sailor securing a bulkhead. She reached for a cabinet behind her and emerged from the kitchenette with a vial in one hand, and hermetically sealed package containing a syringe and rubber strap in the other.

"Come on, give me your right arm," she said routinely.

"Hold on, Katrine. Are you sure this is necessary? Are there any side effects? Is this going to knock me out, or make me nauseous or something?"

"Astrid," Katrine began, sober as an undertaker, "there might well be side effects. I just don't know. But I do know that if you've been exposed to what you carried in here last night, you're already sick. If you don't let me give you this shot, you'll be dead in a week, and you'll wish you died sooner." She felt another wave of nausea, possibly more pronounced than the last.

"Okay," she agreed reluctantly. Katrine strapped the rubber tourniquet around Astrid's upper right arm, twisted it until the veins on the inside of her forearm bulged, and delivered the contents of the vial directly into Astrid's bloodstream.

"Since when did you start mainlining antidote?"

"This is bad stuff," Katrine said. "USA prime," she mumbled to herself. Astrid was reflecting on what Katrine meant when she began to feel light-headed, and leaned against the examination table.

"Don't feel so good?" asked Katrine sympathetically. "Maybe you want to lie down for a minute. Take a rest. We have a lot to talk about." Astrid lifted herself on to the table and the room began to spin as she touched her head to the fresh disposable pillowcase.

She woke and felt rested, like she had slept for hours. Katrine straddled the wheeled stool beside her, a cardboard tray from a nearby coffee shop in her lap cradling tall black coffees and steroid-sized muffins.

"Want some? I bet you're hungry."

"How long was I out? And what was in that shot?"

"I probably should have warned you. There's a mild sedative in the antidote. We expected the victims' metabolisms to be in overdrive by the time they could be reached. I guess you were tired and it knocked you out," Katrine observed clinically.

"Katrine, who is 'we,' and what are you talking about?"

"Astrid," Katrine began, collecting herself. She looked tortured, anguish and guilt all in one.

".... I've been involved in some work here... work of which I'm not especially proud," she said, like a child thought Astrid, owning to an offense. "It involves things I'm not really supposed to talk about. Things that I got drawn into, that I was sure would never see daylight." She was sounding defensive.

"What kind of work?" said Astrid. Katrine held her breath as though doing so might contain regret.

"I wouldn't be telling you this if, if you weren't already involved," she insinuated carefully, "if I didn't think you could help."

"Involved in what?" Astrid demanded. There was implication in Katrine's tone of which she was sure she wanted no part.

"Those samples you brought in here last night, I need to know exactly where they came from, I need to know exactly what indications you saw in the victims."

"Of course," she said, wondering why Katrine would expect anything less, if that's what her tone was suggesting. She recounted the whole mission sparing no details. "It was the usual drill," she concluded, "took samples, documented the environment, treated the victims as best we could. It was the regular work-up in search of a clue...except this strain was tougher, much tougher, virulent, almost certainly Ebola, but maybe something else altogether, which is why I brought it here."

Katrine just stared at her, expressionless and unsurprised, as though nothing Astrid could say would change her mind about something she already knew. Astrid felt compelled to keep talking, to fill the void.

"Every measurable expression of the disease was aggravated, if that's possible. The time between fever and hemorrhaging was shorter, and the hemorrhaging more aggressive producing a faster, more ghastly death. Maybe the incubation period is longer, too; that, or a few individuals we tested were resistant or immune. We took dozens of blood samples and found the virus in every one. Some victims went a long time before developing symptoms, and once they became symptomatic there was no helping them. They were totally unresponsive to traditional intravenous hydration and antibiotics. Ebola is unmerciful, but there are always survivors - not many, but always some. The South African authorities were talking about shutting us down and I tried to explain that we had to stay, if for no other reason than to track the survivors. It's the only hope we have of triangulating on a cure. Someone will pull through and we need to know who."

"They won't," Katrine mumbled.

"What?"

"Not this bug."

"Bug?" Astrid despised the word. It was a glib if not egotistical term that genetic engineers used to describe their lab creations, and it had the desired and misleading effect of characterizing their work innocuously. The promise of bugs conceived by genetic engineering might be as modest as allergy relief and as ambitious as eternal life. Bugs could be the work of idealists or misanthropes, and accelerate natural selection, or pervert it.

"Katrine, what bug?"

"The bug in the samples you brought with you. Rest assured, my friend, you would be symptomatic in days, maybe even hours had you not come straight here. I need to give you a blood test to be sure," she said as she unwrapped a second package of syringes and vials.

"You're going to need white blood cell counts by the hour until at least tomorrow, just to be sure you're building immunity, and God forbid that you're already sick."

"Jesus, Katrine," she hissed as she presented her arm. Katrine reapplied the tourniquet and set about describing how she passed last evening after dropping Astrid at the hotel.

She had taken one of the Nama samples and run it through a gene sequencer. The sequencer's software cataloged DNA, comparing snippets of amino acid combinations from the famous double-helix formations and looking for matches to gene sequences in the database. The device was an expensive favorite of researchers who used it to build family trees of genetic mutation, mapping changes across time and space by tagging genetic sequences with the locations and carbon dates of their discovery. DNA was to the cellular world what stone tools and pottery were to archeologists, the common goal being evolutionary maps, patterns and timetables tracing life to its roots. The database was very new, but researchers imagined a day when it would become predictive, reliably forecasting the apparition of contagion the way weather forecasters predict rain. The promise of prediction hinged on capturing new mutations. Each new permutation of proteins could be the vital piece to a partially assembled jigsaw puzzle, with the power to bridge incomplete islands of understanding.

There was no such thing as a perfect genetic match between strains of tropical viruses, Katrine assured her, only permutations of more or less common sequences. Her years as a clinical researcher were not so far behind her that she had forgotten the velocity and volatility of mutation.

"Engineering viruses is like cooking a soufflé," Katrine said, "get the timing or temperature wrong and you might as well start again." Viral genetic instability had frustrated countless efforts throughout the clinical community, including her own, to develop prophylactic inoculations. The most common and public example were the vaccines that fail year after year to anticipate the strain of common flu that reliably lays low ten percent of humanity.

"How could I be so sure the antidote I gave you would be effective?" Katrine posed rhetorically. Because the gene sequencer had found a perfect match, a pattern with which Katrine was so familiar that she felt like a painter recognizing her own work; a pattern familiar to a select few assigned to government agencies with misleading names, where they're paid to imagine the unimaginable, to invent bugs that can be weaponized, and antidotes to counter them in an endless exchange of microbial strikes and counterstrikes. The pattern Katrine had found was without precedent in nature, a pattern whose antidote Katrine helped engineer, a pattern as familiar as the quilt on her childhood bed, and that's how she knew it was the antidote Astrid needed.

When Katrine described the pathology of the virus she spoke in the most even clinical terms: it was highly contagious with a long incubation period, to give it time to spread and become well-entrenched before the enemy could take measures to contain it. The bug was genetically stable, very little risk of mutation, so it would propagate indefinitely among the unprotected, and resist genetic dilution. It was engineered to achieve a hundred percent mortality, earning itself a catchy lab name – the genocide gene. The chances that such a pattern had mutated spontaneously without lineage or naturally occurring precedents were a trillion-to-one.

"It gives me no pleasure, Astrid, to say that I know what we're dealing with, and exactly what its effects will be."

The enormity of Katrine's words settled on her like a pall. She thought of Hammond and Botha and the rest of the Nama, and even of Sanderling. Depending how long he survived and where they took him the contagion could be carried deep into a dense population center. She herself had passed through Cape Town, London and Atlanta, aerosolizing the genocide gene in the water droplets in her breath. The surgical mask was a respectable precaution she was glad she took, but it was hardly foolproof. With every exhale she was crop dusting death in her contrails. She pictured a stone skipping across still water, the virus dispersing in concentric circles of perfect, even waves spreading at every point of contact. Everywhere she had been, everywhere Sanderling would go, the circles were widening, new circles endlessly forming until they collided in the chaos. She felt drunk with the unfolding tragedy, a tragedy in which she had played the lead. She, who had dedicated herself to relieving human suffering, now the pathogen for pestilence and agony of massive scale; made so by the death of Harry, which cut short her stay in Richtersveld, where she might have died alongside the Nama and kept Katrine's genocide gene contained. Even in death Harry's knack for spreading misery lived. The pernicious brew of fatigue and guilt, and anger and sorrow finally erupted, unleashing itself on the one available target of opportunity.

"How the hell could you be involved in something like this?" she demanded with the sort of disdain she reserved for Harry. "This is so wicked, so despicable, and you have made me the unknowing instrument of your... your depraved research. I guess you and your lab pals didn't think much of the Hippocratic oath," she seethed, outraged by the betrayal of it, and by a long-admired friend.

"How the hell did this thing get out? And what the hell do we do now?"

She felt nothing but scorn for the defenselessness on Katrine's face as she unleashed her fiery denunciation.

"Don't you think these are battles I've fought with myself before?" she heard Katrine say dejectedly. "Maybe I got lazy, or maybe, to justify my existence I fixated on a sort of self-serving rationale, a quaint resolve that goes something like this: I didn't choose my lot alongside the architects of Sodom and Gomorrah, these alchemists of evil. That's where I found myself, what life handed me. But what I *could* do is find ways to reverse whatever wickedness they devised. And I got good at it, very good if I may say so. That's what I've been doing here all these years, Astrid, as reprehensible as that may sound to you. There's not a darn thing they came up with that I haven't found a way to treat. And..." but she caught herself.

"And if I survive this thing, I'll owe it to you..." Astrid said, finishing the thought.

"Sort of, yes." It was worthy of consideration, perhaps even gratitude.

Katrine Burkhardt was raised in a sunny, lush, middle-class cul-de-sac in northern Virginia, on the outskirts of Washington, D.C., the eldest of two daughters born to a loving but bookish and overbearing German couple. Katrine was always murky on the circumstances of her parents' immigration to the U.S. but her big bones, fair hair and blue eyes meant there was no denying her German ancestry. Like many of her neighborhood friends, Katrine's parents worked at "the Agency." They left home early, in separate cars, and were generally home for dinner. Her father traveled often, leaving the country, and she abandoned inquiring of his destinations in childhood. Her mother was an archeological scholar of the Middle East, with an impressive personal collection of ancient artifacts that she displayed around the house in glass cases the way middle managers display monikered golf balls. Katrine could recall her mother being gone, too, in Egypt and Saudi Arabia, but that was before the Iranian revolution and the overthrow of the Shah. The U.S. government was generous to her parents and to the families of her neighborhood friends, so when the Center for Disease Control came calling during a brutal spell in Katrine's residency promising decent pay, good hours, and cutting edge work on immunology, Katrine's field of interest, her decision was easy. Astrid grew closer to her in the years during which they were both involved in research, the banality of life fading in the sympathetic glow of high minded research. But that was some years past, before Astrid devoted herself to relief work, and before Katrine pursued research beyond the pale.

For no better reason than duty Astrid felt obliged to indulge Katrine's half-hearted defense, of both herself and the institution she served.

"The CDC is never directly involved in developing anything," she began. It was, she said, quoting from a pamphlet she lifted from a neat little stack that could have been church service leaflets, *the sentinel for the health of people in the United States and throughout the world, striving to protect people's health and safety, providing reliable health information, and improving health through strong partnerships.*" She was an immunologist, and her focus for twenty years had been prevention.

"The way to think about us is we're the goalies," she said proudly. "We're here to keep things from happening, not to make things happen, but stopping things can sometimes mean anticipating, doing things to keep other things from starting," she said darkly. She said she had worked with partnerships in the private sector to develop antidotes for all kinds of diseases. A pharmaceutical or biotechnology company would target a particular disease, and Katrine used information collected by the CDC to inform the development and testing of remedies and vaccines. Yes, some of these partnerships involved government labs and some were engaged in developing military applications.

"It was all in the spirit of preparedness," she assured Astrid, "in the event the U.S. or one of its allies was attacked."

"Maybe I got used a little," Katrine conceded uncomfortably. "I'm a bit of a sleuth, it turns out, at decoding and preventing the expression of destructive genes. For every defense I devised they developed a countering offense in a game of molecular escalation that produced the super bugs we say we don't have." There was nothing about her work she could undo now, and there was solace in knowing that cooling in the basement of the CDC were countless variants of vaccines and antidotes for biological agents more destructive than any yet experienced by man or beast. To her knowledge there was no derivative of her work that could not be reversed, for which there was no antidote.

"It would be hard to imagine a bug for which we're unprepared and I played a little part in that I'm not embarrassed to say."

Astrid listened with growing curiosity as Katrine described how she had isolated the genocide gene carried by the Nama sometime before midnight. There was strict protocol around the identification of known *biologicals* and she had followed it. In the predawn hours she had alerted several government agencies, though she doubted the alerts would find their way through the bureaucracies any faster than a message in a bottle, certainly not before 9:30 a.m. Eastern Standard Time, after administrative assistants in office buildings dotting the Washington D. C. beltway had grazed basement cafeterias and traded gossip around the water cooler. The one exception, she expected, was the Office of Homeland Security. Katrine had spoken with a bio-terror specialist, and he had rousted a detail of special agents from their beds. They were already airborne. One was on his way to Atlanta to debrief Astrid while the others, organized in teams had been assigned to retrace Astrid's footsteps using airline databases and public surveillance cameras. They had probably already created a detailed track of her movements, starting at the CDC, back to the hotel where Katrine had picked her up, to Atlanta's Hartsfield International Airport, Heathrow Airport, Cape Town International Airport, and all the way back to Richtersveld.

After inoculating herself, Katrine had packaged every vial of antidote available at the CDC for shipping to pre-assigned distribution points in Atlanta, London, and Cape Town, and she had activated supply chains to produce more. Homeland Security would already be working with local authorities in the U.K. and South Africa to hunt down and quarantine individuals exposed to Astrid, and they would be held until the antidote reached them. The protocol had been well rehearsed but never activated. It was proceeding like clockwork, but there was no way to know whether it would be effective. The good news was that the extended incubation period gave them time.

Katrine made her feel naïve and self-absorbed as she listened to the escalation of events that took place while she slept. By the time

Katrine concluded, the fate of the Nama felt far beyond reach, the piteous parting look of the chief a parched postcard from a forgotten land; and like the Nama, Harry's death faded to insignificance with the thought of the genocide gene spreading unchecked across three continents.

"The road to hell," she said, reflecting on the irony of her mission to Richtersveld.

"You can't blame yourself," Katrine assured her. "How were you to know? Coming here was the best thing you could have done."

Astrid knew better than anybody she was a crisis junky, for the blessed distraction crises offered to lingering disappointments. Crises gave shape to a kind of frustrated energy that kept her semi-permanently agitated, like an incarcerated big cat wearing tracks in the perimeter of a cage, and she seized on every opportunity to join in desperate struggles against impossible odds.

"What can I do, Katrine? There has to be something I can do. Can you learn something studying me? Can I carry antidote to the Nama? Put me to work, Katrine."

"Astrid, my friend," said Katrine, sounding distant, "you've stepped into something bigger than you know. What you didn't hear from me is that Homeland Security has been tripping on itself like Keystone Cops to trace the theft of this bug. It was stolen, from a lab, not very long ago, and that makes you, in the defanged terminology of the U.S. government, *a person of interest*. I can't let you go anywhere. Those are my orders. Officially, you're quarantined. Ward of the U.S. government," Katrine said, cracking the door just enough to reveal the armed guard posted outside.

"You're kidding me," Astrid exclaimed involuntarily.

"Do I sound like I'm kidding? The Homeland bio-terror guys are on their way and they're going to want to spend some time with you talking about what you saw." Things were becoming preposterous, offensive. She risked her life to help the innocent, to serve the WHO and her nation, its largest benefactor, at their request for God's sake. And that earned her the privilege of being a suspect in the theft of some miserable engineered doomsday disease. Truly, the road to hell *was* paved with good intentions. She would have laughed had she the energy. Widowed, infected and implicated, all in one day. What were the alternatives to resignation?

"No. There's nothing for you to do. You're staying right here until you're not contagious. That could be a couple of weeks," she heard Katrine say as her mind raced. Whatever the conclusion of Homeland Security she was stuck, and knowing it exacerbated her frustration.

"I can't sit here for weeks. I've got to get to New York."

"I gather," Katrine replied, something knowing and suspicious in her voice. "But you'll be held here for observation until further notice," Katrine continued officiously.

"Do you know about Harry?" Astrid asked.

Chapter 7

Jack Whitaker could still see the stars as he guided his black sedan through the floodlight at the perimeter security gate at CIA headquarters in Langley, Virginia. By the time he reached his desk and the fluorescent glow of the overhead lights in his office flickered to life, the stars were fading, the night in retreat before the inky light advancing on the horizon. Whitaker suffered insomnia, the scourge of the aging, and arrived at work routinely before dawn. The peacefulness of his office so early in the day was his sanctuary, time reserved for bringing himself current on events transpiring overnight around the globe. The reports flowing through his email never failed to remind him of his good fortune and the good fortune of so many Americans. He took seriously the duty of protecting the United States citizenry, and fifteen-hour days were the least he felt he could give. He scoured his emails deliberately, absorbing countless details about people, places, and events. He read everything, even though the CIA rigorously prioritized electronic communications and précis were readily available, the background noise filtered out.

Like many in the intelligence community, he believed the events of September 11, 2001 could have been avoided with greater reliance on human intuition. The community was too dependent on automation and algorithms, too reliant on machines to see plots conceivable only by man. Informed intuition was the apogee of awareness and the key to intervention, as long as the courage to draw inference from uncorrelated information was not lacking. He had sensitized himself to inconspicuous detail, and encouraged his staff to do the same, pushing them relentlessly to consume and digest and filter and reconfigure more information, as much as they could physically ingest. He believed the subconscious was a tireless deciphering machine, running in the background like the autonomic nervous system, perpetually solving for extraneous data, trying to make it fit. He believed in hunches, which were primitive survival instincts, he told his people, in atrophied form, suppressed by centuries of higher learning. He believed in subtle cues lying dormant in the subconscious, like family secrets buried in the attic. He hounded his people to rifle their suspicions like grandchildren looting a hope chest, for the surprises they might find there. It was the liberal arts analog to hunting for unlikely events several standard deviations from the mean.

Whitaker's human information-gathering assets were as pervasive as ants on a playground, despite the oversights of 2001. They just got lazy, too secure in the overlapping complexities of the bureaucracy, too confident someone somewhere else was watching. The intelligence gathering apparatus had for decades reached into the private sector tapping thousands of U.S. citizens working and living overseas. These were men and women with no official association to the Agency, with normal families and inconspicuous careers, who dropped a dime now and then on notable events and curious circumstances. A few had the benefit of rudimentary surveillance training, but the balance never participated in any formal way in Agency operations. They were as ubiquitous and dark as phosphorus plankton, illuminating on contact with suspicious phenomena. They moved on the tide of business and social networks with relationships and confidences the CIA could never hope to cultivate using moles and spies operating under obvious covers. The CIA ingratiated itself to these expatriates as obsequiously as a Hollywood agent. It made no demands and applied no pressure, but did not disguise its curiosity either. It was a silent volunteer army that contributed willingly if passively to the CIA's global awareness, generating countless random pointillist observations, diverse but original compositions of common events, like studies of the same still life by an art class.

In a matter of urgency a local field agent reached out, discretely but deliberately. The request might be to clarify a publicly reported but vaguely described transaction, or to shed more light on an individual's personal habits, virtues and vices, no details spared. While laborious and painstaking, the process protected informers and obscured the Agency's interests. It was a low-tech solution pioneered by the once resource-constrained Chinese, and it had proved troublingly effective. The CIA gathered information this way perpetually. On some occasions the objective was specific, but not always. Listening passively, gathering useless information on a massive scale did on occasion materially inform the intelligence picture.

A few enthusiasts played marginally more active roles. Not rising to the level of field agents, but in positions to see rich streams of information, they maintained a steady commentary on current events, using coded phrases to raise concern. They accepted they might never know if or how they contributed to national security, but to a person they shared a fear, which was overlooking the one event, the defining outlier, that could have exposed an impending tragedy.

Elliot Schiller, whose name Whitaker was seeing for the first time, was such a sentinel. He addressed emails every second or third day to friends and colleagues at his company's headquarters, the *Washington Post* at 15th Street NW, in Washington, D.C., or so it appeared to anybody conducting internet surveillance. In fact, the emails landed in a non-descript office park in Chevy Chase, Maryland where they were downloaded to a zip drive by an Agency employee along with thousands of other emails just like his. The zip drive was disconnected from the public network, scanned and queried, and prodded and palpated like an emergency room patient, before it was reconnected to a separate, secure network. The physical separation or *air gap* in cyber security parlance, between the networks was the first of many obstacles to tracing the destination of the emails. Once on the secure network, the batched emails fed into the CIA's data gateway servers where algorithms parsed, recombined, time-sequenced, and filed by multiple references discrete events in each report. The theory ran that dormant in every piece of data lay a Rosetta Stone waiting for context to unlock meaning and make sense of chaos. It was a theory to which Jack Whitaker subscribed unwaveringly.

As Whitaker absorbed his daily deluge of dispatches, he came across a field report from Adam Woodcock. Woodcock had picked up a routine communiqué by this fellow, Elliot Schiller, which mentioned photographs of a man called Harry Achermann, a man once high on Woodcock's terror threats list. Schiller said he thought the photographs, which were delivered by hand to his door, were an attempt to compromise one of his reporters, or to blackmail his employer, the *Washington Post*. He thought the answer would come to light in the days ahead, and expected to issue an update soon.

Woodcock's report was succinct and thorough, as always, prompting Whitaker to reflect on the unorthodox path by which Woodcock came under his wing. Woodcock was on loan from British intelligence, and had been for almost three years. Born to a titled family with a long tradition of military service, he distinguished himself as an athlete throughout his five years at Eton College. He matriculated to Sandhurst, the storied British army officer training academy counting numerous royals among its distinguished graduates. That didn't mean anything to Whitaker, but he assumed it was important to Woodcock, or was once. Woodcock had been loyal to the family tradition, following his brother, father, and grandfather to Sandhurst after which they each received commissions in various branches of the British army. The youngest Woodcock, full of swagger according to his records, was posted to the Royal Green Jackets, a regiment famous for a number of military innovations including abandoning the traditional British army redcoat in favor of camouflage, or *Green Jacket*. The regiment was also the first to abandon concentrated musket shot in favor of accurate marksmanship, and the first to trade carefully choreographed battlefield maneuvers for spontaneous responses to enemy contact. The latter sat uneasily with the command bureaucracy, and came about only after brooding introspection. It sacrificed tightly held principles of battlefield command that mirrored basic tenants of British caste society to the initiative and self-reliance of the man on the front. Every Royal Green Jacket considered himself faster, more innovative, and decisively more creative and independent than soldiers anywhere else in the world, even though the regiment's practices had been widely adopted in militaries domestic and foreign. Woodcock was no exception.

Despite the wealth and high social standing of his family, to which he probably owed the distinction of attending Sandhurst, Woodcock made little if any impression on his military instructors. In fact the British military might have overlooked him entirely but for his keen personal interest in ancient languages which drew him to Middle Eastern studies, and to command of both Arabic and Farsi. Toward the end of the decade-long war between Iran and Iraq an irrelevant section of British intelligence monitoring the war called on Woodcock to interpret intercepted battlefield communications; and when Saddam Hussein invaded Kuwait in 1989, and Britain was called to join the coalition to free Kuwait, he was pressed into service again to question captured prisoners and decode enemy communications leading up to the Desert Storm counterstrike.

On the dawn of September 12, 2001, with unspecified terrorist groups of Middle Eastern origin claiming credit for the horrific events of the preceding day, the CIA found itself desperately short of Middle Eastern language experts, these having been sacrificed to a decade of intelligence budget cutting. America appealed to its allies for support until a domestic supply of new recruits could be trained and deployed, and this is how Woodcock had found his way to employ by Jack Whitaker.

As Whitaker soon found it was a welcome assignment insofar as it afforded Woodcock the opportunity to leave Britain, where his divorce had just been finalized. According to Woodcock, who kept a stiff upper lip about the whole thing, he left base early for home one afternoon to surprise his young wife, and found her with a surprise of her own in the form of another officer in his bed. It was a defining moment, or so Whitaker gathered, a crossroads in a life that had followed an honorable if unimaginative path. Dalliances were hardly unknown to decent British society, practically institutionalized by the royal family, and the randy behavior of British officers was legend, so it should have come as no surprise; but Woodcock had taken it hard, that much Whitaker knew, and the grip of newlywed idealism held tighter, and his battered pride haunted him longer than the average cuckold, and much longer than it should have a Green Jacket. According to his psychological assessment Woodcock fell into precipitous decline, losing faith in everything. There was, said the report, the potential for lingering anger, repressed rage that might vent inopportunely, like a geyser. Woodcock was a romantic, that much Whitaker knew. Language lovers were, and it was no surprise to him that betrayal turned everything on its head, that the polarity of Woodcock's world was reversed, which might serve his own purposes nicely. Woodcock said himself he was thrilled to throw-in with the Yanks. It was a chance to use his language skills to act out violently against the calculated incineration of innocents. It was a diversion bespoke for his wrath, and in time his wounds would heal. With the invasion of Iraq what began as a diversion became a trajectory, and Whitaker put him in perpetual motion between the Middle East, Washington, D.C., and the U.S. Navy Base at

Guantanamo Bay, Cuba, where the resident Islamic fundamentalists dreaded Woodcock's unannounced visits.

He once told Whitaker that he knew he was damaged goods, that he stalked the earth in an altered state. There had been a time when he found the brash willfulness and cocksure arrogance of the Americans unbearable, and now he envied the gun-slinging quality of the American national character, sympathizing with the American anger, the abiding reverence for self-determination, and the idealism that compelled Americans to right wrongs, and overturn and punish tyranny. He was not afraid to express embarrassment for superior British tolerance. He said working with the Americans brought him around to the view that tolerance was acquiescence by another name, and that England had lost her fiber; or worse yet, exported it two centuries past, the American frontier drawing the kingdom's pioneers and explorers like marrow sucked from a bone. The fighting traditions of the Royal Green Jackets resembled nothing so much as the American spirit, and when his regiment called him home he made his preference for serving Whitaker known. Whitaker prized the expression of loyalty and rewarded it with the weightiest assignments.

Woodcock's latest mission was to establish by whatever interrogative means necessary the progress of Al-Qaeda and related fanatical sects towards procuring weapons of mass destruction, including nuclear, radioactively "dirty," and biological weapons. In this capacity, he was leading a team at Homeland Security investigating unexplained inventory discrepancies at a handful of U.S. government research labs, a story recently carried by the *Washington Post*.

The mention of Harry Achermann in Woodcock's report had Whitaker's full attention. The email was sent about an hour ago, at 4 a.m. Woodcock would not speculate about whether it could be the same Harry Achermann who remained, despite his untimely death, the CIA's lead suspect in the disappearance of a highly classified biological agent from a government lab; however, Schiller, the Agency observer, had promised to scan and attach the photographs in his possession to his next report. Whitaker wanted them sooner. The trail was going cold along with Achermann's corpse, and Woodcock's report concluded by asking Whitaker to call.

He leaned back in his black leather chair, a contemporary throne the size of a backhoe bucket, applauding himself for the devotion to background noise he instilled in his subordinates. If the individual captured in the photographs were the same Achermann, the one he saw alive the morning he was shot, there was a chance the photographs contained contextual leads, including people or places connecting Achermann to his associates. Woodcock was already convinced, and Whitaker was inclined to agree, that the Harry Achermann they were hunting had been neutralized before they could apprehend him, silenced before his imprudent mouth and movements revealed the planners and the plan to use a biological weapon. Achermann's murder was to Woodcock long-sought affirmation that he was on the right trail, and felt confident the banker's accomplices were covering their tracks. It was not in Whitaker's heart to doubt Woodcock's theory, even though he understood its appeal, and he grinned at the prospect of Muslim ascetics sitting about the yurt reveling in the poetic justice of martyring a capitalist dog. The much less palatable explanation was that the CIA's surveillance had been detected and Achermann was sacrificed. Whitaker leaned forward and picked up the phone.

*****

"Commander Woodcock," he heard someone say. He cracked an eyelid and squinted into the rising sun, shards of brilliant orange reflecting off the wing and splashing the broken cloud cover over Atlanta with infernal color. His ears popped as the white, unnumbered Falcon business jet continued its descent into Hartsfield International Airport.

"Commander Woodcock," he heard again, this time from closer by, before he felt the weight of a hand on his shoulder. He looked up to see the copilot standing over him, his neck cocked in the confines of the cabin, like a spear-fishing egret.

"Commander Woodcock," he said for a third time, more insistently. Woodcock came to with a jolt, bracing the open folder in his lap to catch the papers that had already spilled in uneven sheets like spring ice to the cabin floor.

"Commander, you have a call from Langley. You may take it on the phone, there." The egret reached across his seat, his arm jutting out like a pike to impale a sleek handset cunningly recessed in the curvature of the cabin's skin, like a trinket in the naval of a belly dancer. He plucked the receiver from its rest, the accordion tether wriggling like a fish, and pushed the green blinking light on the cabin wall.

"Yes…yes," Woodcock began, groping for consciousness. "Thanks, old chap," he murmured, remembering his civility and not much more. He opened his eyes wide and blinked deliberately as the copilot stabbed the handset firmly in his palm and turned for the cockpit. "Buckle up, please sir," he said cordially over his shoulder, "we'll be landing soon."

"Hello?" Woodcock inquired tentatively.

"Good morning Commander Woodcock, this is the company operator, I have Mr. Elliot Schiller for you on the line," said a soothing female voice.

"Oh, jolly good," he declared enthusiastically. "Thank you, company operator, please put him through."

"Yes sir, have a good day," the voice replied indifferently.

"Not bloody likely," Woodcock muttered to himself, cupping the mouthpiece to guard the earnest American from offense. He heard a faint click and then silence, the sort of heavy silence that betrays a presence.

"Hello…Hello?" he inquired impatiently.

"Hey, good morning. I hope I'm not catching you too early, Mr. Woodcock," he heard a man say in that presumptuously friendly American way. "It's Elliot Schiller. I called as soon as I could, sounded like it might be important, like I might be able to help out."

"Yes… yes, well, quite," Woodcock acknowledged tentatively. "Yes…I don't know really, but I suppose you can, I mean I think you can."

"Well, Mr. Woodcock, besides the pictures, which you should have by now, and that are, I might add, a little steamy, what else about this character might it serve your purposes to know?" Schiller sounded like a school boy bursting with secrets he planned to keep unless he were asked just the right way.

"A bit steamy, you say?" Woodcock replied, following Schiller's lead.

"Yes, they include one of my young colleagues, in an unflattering way, if you get my meaning. She made a big mistake, and she's young, and it was a big mistake, so…ah…I would really appreciate it if these…" his voice trailed off as though his question would answer itself.

"Schiller," Woodcock began with uninspired sympathy, "with the greatest respect, and gratitude for sharing this information, I can assure you these photos will be treated with utmost discretion, as are all our investigative files." He hated pandering to the naïveté of the observers on whom he and his employer depended. How innocent were the flocks living beneath the projected power of the U.S., he mused. "But they will remain in the file," he added firmly. "Do you understand?"

"Sure, of course I understand, I just hate it to involve this girl. She's a kid, and she made a mistake, like any of us." Woodcock thought of his ex-wife. Between himself and her lover, he wondered which she considered the mistake.

"Schiller," he started, "if she's innocent, then you've nothing to worry about, do you? Nor does she, does she?" he offered, poorly disguising his skepticism. "Is now a good time to have a quick chat? I would be terribly grateful for anything more you can share, you know, the usual sort of thing, what you know, what you don't know, what you suspect."

Evidently this was not Schiller's first debriefing. He was measured and thorough, like a coroner at an autopsy, recounting every detail of the previous thirty-six hours. He noted Coco Stockton's research, sources, and contacts, and the series of articles she had penned for the DeBeer's exposé, copies of which were included with the photographs he had just sent to Langley.

Woodcock listened attentively, filling Schiller's pauses with encouragement, "quite…. yes…. emm…." Everything he was hearing was consistent with what he already knew about the Achermann that was the CIA's person of interest, except the association with DeBeers. Achermann was a womanizer. He traveled extensively, holding court with business leaders and socialites everywhere. To find him in London, meeting with the leaders of a powerful private global enterprise, and in the company of a young, attractive woman resonated with perfect pitch.

When he was quite sure Schiller had finished he said, "Ah, emm, Mr. Schiller? I wonder if you would be good enough to secure, ah, that, emm, that young lady's computer…Ms. Stockton's computer? And, emm, would you also be so kind as to secure her files? There's really nothing to do just yet, that is, until we see the photos and confirm this is the same fellow, do you see? But if it is in fact the same chap, then we're going to have to take a closer look, aren't we? I'd be terribly grateful if you would keep all this to yourself... I mean, you know, no point in frightening the poor creature if we don't have to; but of course, we may indeed need to have her in for a chat, and, emm, always best to keep these things spontaneous, don't you agree?"

He was glad Schiller understood him, for Ms. Stockton could well be involved, no matter how conflicted it left Schiller feeling, and he felt sorry for Schiller and his protectiveness. He had let barely more than a few hours pass between receiving Schiller's email and requesting he contact Langley. He had to remind himself that collapsing towers and ranting radicalized Muslims were still fresh on the minds of the populace, who felt the spread of insidious forces invisibly marshalling around them the same way McCarthy imagined communism advancing like locusts. The Agency was proud to be plucking suspects from foreign shores and rendering them for unmerciful interrogation to places where brutality was a badge of cultural pride, so Schiller's concern for Coco was understandable. Even Woodcock winced when he thought about how "having her in for a *chat*" must have sounded.

He hung up the phone as the plane touched down in Atlanta. Schiller's report raised two concerns. The first was the association with DeBeers. Woodcock and his team had missed this entirely. The relationship could be new, or possibly insignificant, or so important to Achermann that he had cultivated it discreetly. Why would an organization with the stature of DeBeers associate with the likes of Achermann? What could be its interest in a doomsday variety biological agent? Cold droplets of perspiration formed on his neck and ran down the middle of his back as he considered the uses to which the resources of DeBeers could be put by terrorists. He was paid to envision and undermine plots and he failed to see any benefit to DeBeers, especially of Muslim-sponsored terrorism. It was an organization with a profoundly Jewish legacy. It made no sense until he wondered if he had stumbled on the formative stages of a Jewish counter-offensive.

The cartel was renowned for unsavory business practices, outlawed in most of the free world, with a history of protecting its interests aggressively. He recalled Depression-era lore about the company stockpiling diamonds and dumping them in the sea to keep supplies tight while demand languished. But it was folly to taunt the free world powers which were madder than wet hornets and looking for bold strokes like asset seizures and crippling sanctions. Maybe he was reaching and the DeBeers connection was meaningless. Indeed it very likely was, but it would have to be investigated.

The second concern was the photographs. Someone was making a calculated effort to compromise the girl or Achermann. He was speculating on motives when the green light beside the phone resumed flashing, and he plucked the receiver from the cabin wall.

"Hello?" he said, depressing the green light.

"Morning Adam!" Whitaker's voice hailed from his desk phone at Langley. "You're on the road awfully early this morning."

"Ahh, good-morning, sir. Yes, it's bloody early, isn't it? You know, sir, anything for King, country and the colonies, that's what we say."

"Where the hell are you, anyway? I got your email about another Achermann lead. What do you think you have?"

"Yes, quite right, well sir, I just rung off with this chap in London who reported it in. One of our regular standbys I gather, very matter-of-fact sort of fellow. From the *Washington Post,* coincidentally." He paused to give Whitaker time, to appreciate the newspapers recurring role in the Achermann narrative.

"Should have much more information coming from him any minute now," he continued, "I left instructions for it to be sent on to you. Let's not jump to any conclusions, shall we? We don't even know if it's the same Achermann. We'll know soon. But you see, sir, that's not why I left word for you to call."

He felt the plane taxi to a halt in the hanger reserved for private aviation on the outskirts of Hartsfield International. The copilot reappeared to release the cabin door, the whine of the engines dissipating outside. Woodcock cupped the mouthpiece again, this time to address the copilot.

"I say, old chap, do you mind holding on a minute? Just need to finish this call, do you see? Be right with you." The copilot nodded and returned to the cockpit, dismissed like a courtier.

"Yes sir, so sorry, yes, emm, ah, where was I? Yes, the reason for my call. Yes, yes, you see I've come to Atlanta this morning because, well sir, we have a bit of a fast moving situation down here. CDC believes it has a case of our missing bug. Some woman walked in off the street carrying the virus in blood samples she had taken."

"Jesus Christ!" Whitaker exclaimed with uncharacteristic alarm, the buoyant charm of his greeting forgotten. "You mean the DRX?" he asked.

"Yes, sir. I'm afraid so. That's what CDC believes. Very credible report, perfect DNA match and all that."

"I'd say we *do* have a situation," said Whitaker, his tone darkening. "Have you…"

"Yes sir," Woodcock interrupted. "Everything was activated early this morning, as soon as the CDC confirmed the match. Rather a lot of moving parts though, sir. Apparently this woman flew in from Cape Town via London. Teams on their way to both places, sir, all the antidote on hand dispatched to meet them, sir."

"Cape Town? London? Whoever is behind this didn't waste any time."

"Yes… quite, sir." Woodcock caught his breath. Cape Town, South Africa, the historical seat of DeBeers' mining operations, and the largest point of departure for diamonds mined in South Africa; and London, the location of DeBeers' world headquarters. Perhaps there was more to the DeBeers connection than he supposed.

"Sir, I don't have any more than that just now, and I'm off to the CDC to have a chat with the woman in question. Let me be back to you directly the moment I finish with her."

Chapter 8

"Hey Jimmy, Tomato, would you two heroes join me for a minute?"
Guthrie called, summoning Jimmy Doolan and Franco D'Amato.
They were two very young trainees, officers technically, but only of
modest use so far. To Guthrie they looked like school boys in
detention, sitting one behind the other at two of a dozen otherwise
empty steel desks, arranged in rows on the dilapidated second floor
of the Poughkeepsie Town Police building. The lads rose briskly to
his voice, with pens and notebooks, and badges tucked with pride in
their elastic waist bands.

One day, he hoped, they would be as effective as they were
eager, and he smiled doubtfully as they reported to his office for
duty. It was not so much an office as a gesture of one, a ten-foot-
square corner of the second floor partitioned by eight-foot walls, half
glass, half grey steel casing that nicely complemented the steel
accents of all the other desks and filing cabinets at police
headquarters. The walls were open to the top, the whole enclosure
an uninspired nod to his authority. Contrary to affording him
privacy, the walls amplified voices and bounced them off the twelve
foot plaster ceiling overhead, which had its purposes when he felt
like being heard. Today his color-coded case files lay in sloppy piles,
randomly strewn between stained Styrofoam coffee cups. As Jimmy
and the Tomato alighted to his threshold, he was doing it again,
dragging the meaty surface of his stout thumb back and forth across
the edges of some papers he was holding, the abrasiveness of the
sound audibly expressing his frustration.

"You guys been through these files yet?" he inquired, his beady
blue eyes focused accusingly over the tops of his bifocals on Jimmy.

"No sir," said Jimmy. "We only got 'em yesterday."

"That's an excuse? And you, Tomato, you been through any of
this?" he continued, waving in the general direction of the cardboard
storage boxes settling like stone ruins along the partition walls.

"No sah," Tomato replied.

"You guys *do* wanna be detectives, right? Are you or aren't you trying to help me solve this murder?"

"I thought it was jus' annudder routine investigation," remarked the Tomato. Guthrie cut him a hopeless glance as Jimmy's eyes darted about the room. He liked watching Jimmy and his restless mind work, and he followed the kid's eyes around the room, first to the rifled boxes, then to the labels on his files. Apparently reading upside down still gave him trouble.

"Whatcha' got, sir?" he asked, forgoing a guess. "You want us to take a look?" Over the nine months Jimmy had spent in his care, Guthrie's opinion of the rookie had risen. At first he found the stocky, sharp-tongued Irishman from Long Island uncoachable. A full foot shorter than himself, but almost as thick, Jimmy reminded Guthrie of a college running back: low, powerful, easy to spot and hard to bring down. He walked with an arrogant strut, popping his shoulders forward and back in synchrony with the truncated stride of his chunky, muscle-bound legs. He cut his hair short, the line where the bristles of his crew cut became skin outlining the general vicinity of where his shoulders ended and his head began. Beneath his shirt, on his right bicep, was a tattoo, the simple black outline of a thresher shark with one oversized green eye. It was as short on symbolism as he said he was of money the evening he commissioned the unfinished masterpiece. True to his heritage he had a short hot temper and pasty rough skin that flushed with scarlet rage when he became irritated. He had steered clear of brawls since he joined the force, but he left the impression of spoiling for one when he failed to get his way.

Much to Guthrie's relief, Jimmy's appearance and idiosyncrasies masked a keen wit. Jimmy made him feel dry and Midwestern with his disarming magnetism, which worked like a truth serum on suspects and witnesses alike. And while his terse quips and coarse commentary were generally adolescent, they could lay the truth bare like a cowboy poet. Staying tuned to his perceptiveness was an acquired taste. The lad had navigated the public school system successfully enough, but he had no education. He spoke in boorish shorthand, peppered with street slang, the nuances of which Guthrie was still learning. But his instincts about people were unassailable. He could own your life story over a bottle of beer and discover your hang-ups and ambitions over the second.

The Tomato, dubbed so by Jimmy, held much less promise. He had played football somewhere on the offensive line. His nickname was a metaphor for the decay of his physique, an occupational hazard with which Guthrie was familiar. The Tomato, like Jimmy, was in his mid-thirties. He moved in a perpetual slouch, his shirt puckering like pie crusts around his button holes under the strain of his spongy belly. Guthrie had been surprised before by the Tomato's surviving athleticism. He could still move swiftly for a person of his proportions, and shown uncommon enthusiasm for running suspects down. But his wit was no match for Jimmy's, and he had learned to accept Jimmy's endless barbs as an awkward expression of affection. The Tomato parted his greasy black hair in the middle, and grew it down over his collar. It framed his olive face, prominent nose, and dull brown eyes with a sheeny indefinite outline, like heavy countershading in pastel.

Guthrie relied on him for an important and redeeming virtue which was his prominence in the town of Poughkeepsie. He had been co-captain of the Poughkeepsie High School football team the year the Pioneers brought home the state championship. Charlene, who was there, said the Tomato cleared the defense "like God's own wrecking ball," all but escorting the ball carrier to the end zone for the winning overtime touchdown. His family's cement business kept the D'Amato name in circulation, in bright red and yellow paint, on cement mixers and earth-moving equipment moving up and down the Hudson Valley. People in Poughkeepsie knew and liked the Tomato, and he was welcome where others were more skeptically received.

"What's that in your hand, boss?" Jimmy inquired, working his disarming charm.

"We'll get to that in a minute. You guys better get dialed-in here, know what I mean?"

"Yes, sir," they replied in unison.

"This fella, Achermann, he was a busy guy... real busy," Guthrie said waving the paper in his hand at the boxes again.

"That all come from his office, sir?" Jimmy shot back.

"No, that would take a subpoena, wouldn't it, Detective Doolan? These are public records, and this right here is an information package I obtained by calling his investor relations number. Amazing what you can learn by making a phone call," he observed, knowing Jimmy could be embarrassed into action. "This guy looks like he was everywhere: London, Munich, San Francisco, Hong Kong, Rio, Cape Town, or so these brochures suggest."

"What did he do?" droned the Tomato.

"Some kind of investment guy. Can't say as I understand much about it, but it would be easier to guess at what he didn't do. Here's a…" and he paused for effect, staring the lads down over the rims of his glasses before turning to his files. He set to rearranging them until he found the one he wanted, licked his powerful thumb like a lion cleaning its paw, and parted the flaps to reveal a dark blue brochure with gold embossed letters. The brochure fell open to a page he had visited before, and he broke the spine by inverting the centerfold before spinning it in place for Jimmy and the Tomato to read.

"Take a look."

The officers leaned forward to read the print. The Tomato's lips were still moving when Jimmy leaned back. "Stocks and bonds? Commodities and farmland, and a bunch of other stuff, too?" said Jimmy, cocking his head so his lazy eye peered out from beneath the furrows of his brow.

"What's a commodiddy?" droned the Tomato.

"It's anything real that you can trade, ding-dong, like wheat or cotton or metals, like gold and silver, copper and platinum," Jimmy shot back. "A bunch `a my buddies trade this stuff down in the city. They move big money, really big money."

"And so did this Achermann fella," Guthrie summarized. Jimmy leaned over the brochure again, squinting.

"What's this mean, boss?" he asked, stabbing a stubby index finger accusingly into the brochure, "private investments, other private investments." Guthrie righted the brochure and focused on the bottom of the page. He read aloud.

"Other private investments with a wide range of proven entrepreneurs and co-investors including," he flipped the page and continued reading, "investment banks, private equity funds, hedge funds, special investment vehicles, and family offices."

Jimmy's eyes brightened.

"Boss, my buddies in the city talk about this stuff. It won't take me more than a butt break…" he said, using a Jimmy euphemism for *short spell*. He didn't smoke himself and detested those who did, "and I'll tell you what this stuff means."

"Okay, Jimmy. Go see what you can get. There's a list here of, of, well, I don't know what they are exactly, but they look like other companies he was real proud to work with. See what you can find out about them, too."

"Okay, boss," Jimmy concluded enthusiastically, and he whisked away with missionary zeal, back to his desk where he began clattering away on his computer keyboard, searching for answers on the internet.

"As for you, Tomato, tell me what you know about Rick LeBeau and his brother Ron. Didn't they grow up around here? They look about your age," Guthrie speculated, girding himself for the sort of epistle for which the Tomato had a reputation.

"They sure did, sir. Rick played football wit' me. Great guy, de best. Split end, faster 'an all get-out, hands like a vice. Took big hits and nevah dropped the ball, nevah."

"Tomato," Guthrie interjected patiently, "let's not relive the glory days, shall we? What can you tell me about him? Is he mean? Did he drink, do drugs, run with a crowd?"

"No, Lieutenant Guthrie. He would nevah do that. His ol' man would a killed him first. I remember once…." the Tomato smirked, and Guthrie stared him down with fading tolerance. "It was one a those Jewish holidays, Yum whudd-eva-id-is or Roshahovah. Anyway, no school, middle a the week, an' we went to Rick's place, his parents both at work, to pound some beers. We was in middle school, seventh, eighth grade maybe, anyway, in walks Mr. LeBeau, outta nowhere, beer cans all over the kitchen, and Big Dirk starts passin' a bone. Jesus, God and Mother Mary, he kicked Rick's ass all over that house. Upstairs an' down. We cleared out faster than a fart from a duck. You could hear Big Dirk bellowing and breakin' furniture from down the street. From then on, Rick nevah did nothin,' and we wouldn'a let him if he'd a wanted to. I thought Big Dirk LeBeau would kill him, his own son. After that, when Big Dirk wanted one-a-dose boys home on time, we got 'em there. No messin' with Big Dirk. He put both those boys to work over there at Donner's Forge, no free time again, evah. We started callin' them Jeremiah and Johnson with all their huntin' and fishin' an' what not, you know, after that Robert Redman movie." Jimmy's keyboard, which had been taking a terrible beating, fell silent.

"Redford!" Jimmy shouted from his desk, "It's Robert Redford, you ding-dong."

"Whatevah," the Tomato concluded.

"You think Rick could be involved in this?" Guthrie inquired uncertainly.

"Rick LeBeau? Murder a member of Donner's Forge? Dat's crazy," the Tomato whispered, rolling his head from side to side like an elephant swaying its trunk.

"Is it?" shouted Jimmy from his desk. "Who the hell else would know where they were gonna be?" The pitter-patter of the hard plastic keys on Jimmy's computer keyboard resumed.

"There is that, Tomato," interjected Guthrie, noting the obvious. "He was right there, alone with Achermann," he continued, "who knows what really happened. No evidence recovered from anywhere nearby, and nothing up the mountain from where Rick alleges the shot was fired." The dialog between his protégés was worthy of encouragement, for the entertainment if not advancing the case.

"He knows more than he's telling!" yelled Jimmy, his fingers clattering away.

"Aw, I think you guys got this wrong," the Tomato replied.

"Jeez, look at these guys." Jimmy called from his desk. The brochure Guthrie supplied was pinned beneath his forearm. Jimmy was using it like a treasure map for digital forays into the badlands of Achermann's world. He could see Jimmy's screen, albeit at an angle, and he was clicking through websites like a kid with a Viewmaster.

"These guys make themselves sound like the freakin' National Geographic Society, listen to the names, Oak this and Sycamore that, Black Rocks, and Stone Mountains – I ask you, is there any other kind?"

"Jimmy, are you telling us anything we need to know?" said Guthrie, departing his enclosure for the coat stand by Jimmy's desk. It was then that the images crossing Jimmy's screen caught his eye. Each new website looked the same with brilliant images of impossibly clear skies over bustling modern cityscapes with reflective landmark skyscrapers in Manhattan and Seattle, and San Francisco and Boston. There were thumbnail graphics of stylized company logos, all with a common design scheme - an electron in orbit around a company name in what looked to Guthrie like a symbol of self-centeredness. They looked like cartoon versions of diagrams in a high school physics textbook, and they were hard to distinguish, every company trying to look different the same way.

"Pretty pictures, don't you think boss?" said Jimmy, sensing Guthrie nearby. "What does *deep domain expertise* mean anyway?" he said as he studied the thoughtful, smirking, youthful faces running in an endless loop of contrived expressions across the site where he was stalled. "Look at *him*, boss!" Jimmy exclaimed as a cherub face burdened by grave concern filled his screen. "You think *he* ever spent time in juvi, or seen a heroine O.D.?"

"What do *you* think, Jimmy?"

The Tomato materialized like a rain cloud.

"Who are dose guys?" he inquired as one face dissolved and a band of smiling young men came into focus. "Looks like a polo shirt convention," the Tomato pronounced.

"Yeah, check these guys out," Jimmy concurred. "Look at the schools, look at the… weird company names… I bet this guy Achermann is the same," said Jimmy, pulling up the website for Strategic Global Advisors, Achermann's holding company.

"Sure enough," he reported, sounding vindicated. "Check it out!" he said leaning back from his screen. "And look at the money, Tomato – not millions, but hundreds of millions, billions! How do they do that?" he said in awe.

Guthrie waited on the jibe Jimmy was bound to supply as he studied the headshot of Achermann in a corner of the screen. He looked feral with impenetrable eyes that looked like the ghastly glare of a cornered beast. Crow's feet bled across his temples in menacing black capillaries that looked like ink spreading on damp blotting paper. He had tight curly knots shorn close to his scalp, and acne pitted cheeks, and the scars on his chin were incongruous with any of the other faces to cross Jimmy's screen. Every bit of the man's success was hard fought and won, that much Guthrie could see.

"Tomato!" he barked, startling his trainee. "Let's go see Rick LeBeau." Guthrie was past the desks and entering the stairwell at the back of the room before the Tomato found the sleeves of his jacket. He stopped on the landing, impatience on his breath, which was audible over Jimmy's pounding finger tips. The Tomato was finally lurching for the stairwell when Jimmy cried out again.

"Hey! Don't go anywhere before you check this out." Guthrie groaned.

"This better be good, Jimmy," he said, directing the full force of his blue-eyed scowl over his bifocals. The Tomato relented in his drive toward the door, waiting on a cue.

"I mean it, look at this!" Jimmy fired over his shoulder. Guthrie reluctantly changed course, leaving the Tomato briefly adrift before he closed on Guthrie's heels, slouched his way around to Jimmy's left and deposited himself on the corner of the desk. With one foot on the floor, the opposing thigh occupied a considerable portion of Jimmy's desk top, and his meaty calf hung in mid-air like an aging side of beef.

"What's a matta, Tomato," Jimmy asked, looking up from his screen, "the walk tire you out?" Guthrie faced Jimmy from across his computer, leaning on his fists like a hostile primate. "Show me," he said.

Jimmy rotated his monitor to an angle they could all see.

"INN-QUE-TELL," the Tomato read aloud. "What's that?" Sultry eyes gazed on them with impersonal belligerence from the screen. A cross hair superimposed over the woman's left pupil converged with a blue geometric grid that hovered over the moon lit side of her face, while the side in shadow bled hauntingly into a ghostly colorless background that might have been the abyss. Overlaid on the grid, like course plots on a chart, and converging on the bridge of her nose, were dotted lines that intersected with technical looking blueprints bordering the screen. To the right of the face, in bold blue letters, appeared the phrase *Investing in Our Nation's Security*. Jimmy leaped at the opportunity to read the small print aloud:

Our mission is to deliver leading edge technologies to the CIA and the intelligence community. We're a critical link between the Agency's users and the most promising technologies in the marketplace.

The magnetic eyes cast a silent spell, like a swirling vortex, that drew all three men closer to the screen.

"Scroll down," Guthrie whispered apprehensively.

"Areas of Focus," Jimmy read, skimming the paragraph headers and bullet points "Software... Infrastructure... Physical Sciences..."

"No shit," said Tomato. "What does that mean?"

"Read it, you bozo!" Jimmy offered encouragingly.

"Physical Sciences: Biological and Chemical Technology, Functional Materials, Power," the Tomato read aloud.

"Hey boss," Jimmy interjected, "Wasn't that guy who bolted before we got there, the one in the book with the pussy duck suspenders, in the CIA? Maybe he could tell us something about Achermann's business dealings."

"Whitaker?" Guthrie replied spontaneously, caught off guard. What were the chances? Were the CIA and Whitaker and Strategic Global Advisors and Achermann connected?

"Yeah. Whitaker, who split before we could talk to 'em." Guthrie was no actor and he felt his anxiety show.

"What do you think, boss?" Jimmy speculated, more than a little proud of his handy work. "You think they were mixing business with pleasure?"

"Did you find In-Q-Tel in that book?" Guthrie countered, pointing at the glossy company brochure with the broken spine.

"Yeah, why else would I be showing you this? It's right here," Jimmy said, pointing out the name in the middle of a neat column.

"Look, Jimmy," Guthrie cautioned, "this guy had hundreds of investments. This is just one name in his brochure. You can't tell anything from this. I want you to dig through everything here," he said, gesturing at the boxes again where they were settling under their own weight. "Get as smart as you can on *all* of Achermann's business dealings. Then I want you to go down to the city, to his office, and see what you can find out from his people." He could feel Jimmy read him, sensing his alarm.

"You're thinkin' something, boss," he said suspiciously.

"You're wrong, Jimmy. Not yet. There's procedure to follow."

"Yes you are, boss," he replied, his voice building with conviction.

"What you're thinking, boss, is that you're hoping like hell this hit didn't have nothin' to do with the CIA, which would leave you, I mean, would leave *us*, in a bit of a pickle, am I right?"

"Yeah, Jimmy, that's right," he conceded with lackluster resolve, knowing the effort to mislead Jimmy would be wasted.

"Now finish going through this stuff, go down to Achermann's office, and figure out what this guy does. When you've done all that come back and tell me something new. Tomato, let's go find Rick LeBeau," and he started for the stairwell afresh, Tomato on his heels. As he turned he saw Jimmy lock eyes with the featureless cold face of In-Q-Tel. Superstitious, maybe, but mystical, no; he was no believer in paranormal experiences and certainly not in premonitions, but there was no denying the foreshadowing shiver that ran down his spine.

Chapter 9

Schiller reached into his overcoat for the ungainly clump of keys
cutting at his thigh deep in his pocket. He craned his neck as he
groped to keep the shoulder strap of his satchel from falling and felt
a small channel of rainwater from another saturating commute
trickle down his collar. The *Washington Post* offices behind the
glass door looked peaceful and inviting, the darkness accentuated by
the small green lights of computer peripherals blinking like dazed
forest animals in the night. The windows separating the offices from
the deluge outdoors looked like tapestries bubbling with reflections
of the city night. He had made arrangements to have Coco's files and
hard drive collected at 5:00 a.m. and replaced by an identical unit.
Nobody at the *Washington Post* but Schiller knew.

He turned the key and shoved his way through the door, the
drenched epaulette of his overcoat smearing the clear glass door
before threading his way through the darkness to his office where he
dumped his satchel and hung his dripping coat. The message-waiting
light on his phone flashed impertinently in the darkness, and as he
reached out of habit for the phone he saw two men standing outside
the door through which he had just entered. They were small and
well-dressed, business suits and silk ties, obscure but visible beneath
the buckle and button crusted overcoats that were the fashion of the
hour in the financial district. The Agency spared no detail. One
carried a large cardboard box. They were studying the features of the
door and the offices beyond. The one without the box cupped his
hands around his eyes to peer into the darkness, and rapped
impatiently on the glass as soon as he spotted Schiller. He
suppressed a curious urge to duck behind his desk before leaving his
office for the door.

"Come in, fellas," he said cordially. The men entered without a
word, the door swinging shut behind them. Schiller wheeled on his
toes to reach for the main lights, and found his wrist pinned to his
waist.

"No offense, Mr. Schiller," murmured the distinctly American voice, soft and low, with a twinge of Brooklyn. "Let's keep the lights off and we'll be in and out of here in a jiffy," the man said sounding good-natured and well-intentioned like an authority figure from a black and white television series.

"Where's Ms. Stockton's desk?"

"Right this way," he blurted, having second thoughts, and he led them through the shadowy obstacle course of cubicles to Coco's desk. Luminescent red headlamps broke the darkness. Each man must have donned his light on the way through the office because there was no evidence of the lights when they came through the door. Without warning they were down on their knees, like plumbers beneath the sink, pulling cables, disconnecting peripherals and replacing the hard drive like they had done it a thousand times before.

"Isn't she going to notice?" he inquired, his complicity in the deceit weighing on him.

"Not a chance," the voice from Brooklyn replied. "We mirrored it online, Mr. Schiller. She'll never know the difference." A beam of red from his partner's lamp caught his face, and he looked like a gargoyle in the fires of Hell. It was the same man who had pinned Schiller's wrist coming through the door, the one with the authority to speak.

"Well, if you mirrored it online, and you already have the files," Schiller countered, "why do you need the hard drive?" The newsman in him wanted to know.

"In case it takes a walk," said the gargoyle from Brooklyn. "Wouldn't it be nice to know where it goes? This one phones home. We'll see every file that's opened, who's looking at it, and where that file goes."

"You couldn't have loaded your sniffers and Trojans when you mirrored the files?" Schiller shot back, demonstrating with pride his knowledge of cyber tactics, acquired researching a story on cyber war.

"Yes," the gargoyle said defiantly, "we could have, but software only takes you so far. We can find the major components of this box anywhere in the world. Maybe this box finds its way to some bad guys, bad guys we want to target, know what I mean?" Schiller imagined him winking in the dark. The men connected the new unit, slid it beneath the desk, and packed the old unit in the Styrofoam forms in which the new unit arrived. Then they emptied two drawers full of Coco's hanging files into zippered canvas travel cases, taking care to preserve the order in which she kept them, and extinguished their headlamps.

"We'll get these back to you same time tomorrow," said the gargoyle. "Keep her out of the office until then," he said before leading his mute partner out the office door. Seven minutes and twelve seconds after the two men arrived, Schiller stood alone in the dark, rain cascading down the outside of his windows, hanging on the improbable hope that this would be the last of his involvement with Coco's troubles. He dumped himself into the chair behind his desk and listened to the rain run in soothing fitful rivulets down his windows. He felt rattled, deep in his core, uneasy with the devolution of events, haunted by the specter of betrayal.

He succumbed quickly to drowsiness, the anxiety of his predawn rendezvous dissolving with the city grime in the rain on his office windows, and when he opened his eyes the rain had ceased and daylight was advancing on the city outside. The cubicles outside his door remained in empty shadow, like precinct holding pens waiting on fresh perps. He rubbed his eyes and reached for the phone where the message light was still flashing, and navigated the voicemail tree with such habitual impatience that he blew right through the message header.

"Hey," said Coco's voice, distant and fearful, dashing the tranquility. "Elliot, I'm, ah, there's someone, ah, can you give me a call as soon as you get this? Really, as soon as you get this, *please*? Thanks." Schiller instantly pressed three to replay the message header. She called at 3:17 a.m., less than two hours before he arrived at the office. He dialed her home phone and she answered on the first ring. She sounded shaken and pathetic, and wanted him to come to her apartment as soon as possible, right away if he could manage it. His coat was on his arm before he hung up the phone, and he was across the threshold of his office before he hesitated. Was he completely nuts? Where this would lead was anybody's guess, and he had plenty to lose and little gain. While caution wasn't his nature, this was different, even though hesitating made him feel like a coward.

On the other hand the situation had grown considerably more complex since he ordered Coco home. There was the debriefing by a faceless Englishman in the employ of the CIA, and the agency's obvious interest in Coco's acquaintance, or whatever he was; and as of an hour ago, the agency expected the contents of Coco's hard drive to find their way to places that warranted *targeting*, whatever that meant. The notion that Coco was anything but an innocent bystander was losing credibility fast, and there was no shaking the thought that he would soon be implicating himself.

He gazed around his office at the jumble of pictures that crowded his shelves like collectibles in a gift store - his wife and children, on talcum beaches, beneath cerulean skies, in turquoise seas, and among ancient ruins. In the sun addled glow of his children's joyful faces, Coco Stockton's fate dimmed to a piteously faint light. The instinct to put his coat down and return to his desk where he belonged was strong; and yet, against his better judgment, the indignant newspaperman in him rose up, righteous beyond reason like an imprudent journalism student. He pressed on through the door leaving the sanctuary of his sunlit office for the curb below his window, and hailed a cab from the rain-washed street for the ride to Coco's apartment.

It was a long and expensive ride to Old Church Street off the Fulham Road in South Kensington, a posh neighborhood by journalism standards, where Coco rented a fourth-floor, walk-up flat. Long rows of uninspired three- and four-story London townhouses loomed over the quiet street, each abode running indistinguishably into the next. But for the low wrought-iron fences enclosing identically diminutive gardens in front of each home, the boundary between them was invisible. The exterior façade of weathered, whitewashed plaster ran the full length of the block, as if applied by one sweep of the trowel. A few small gardens showed evidence of care and only a Londoner would know such modest lodgings commanded millions.

He made the easy mistake of passing her door, and when he reversed direction to retrace his steps the swaying drapes in a pair of full length windows on the fourth floor of a town home up the street caught his eye. The drapes fell quickly back into place like a hedgerow stirring stiffly in a breeze.

He found the door beneath the windows and the buzzer releasing the lock activated before he reached the crumbling stoop. He entered and began mounting the steps by twos until he landed on the fourth floor out of breath. Coco was hard to miss, peering at him from behind the security chain of the only door on the landing. She shut the door, disengaged the chain, and swung it wide, concealing herself behind it until he stepped fully inside, whereupon she closed it abruptly and reengaged the security chain and two deadbolt locks.

"Thanks for coming," she said and led the way into the little apartment. Her arms were crossed and she clung to herself as if she were frightfully cold.

"Want some tea?" she asked from inside the cramped kitchenette. "The water's on," she continued, busying herself with cups and saucers to avoid making eye contact.

"Sure. That would be nice, anything is fine," he replied, throwing his coat over a small wicker chair and taking in her circumstances. With its all-purpose functionality the main room was a modern throwback to the great halls of the earliest manor houses, serving as greeting hall, living room, sitting room, and dining room all in one. There was a line of sight between the main room and the kitchenette, but only by stooping below the kitchen cabinets to peer through a low pass-through counter. The room was small and dark and sparsely decorated, but he could imagine it was pleasant filled by natural light which was presently blocked by the drapes. An overstuffed loveseat and table occupied most of the floor space, and a short, close hallway led off to where the bedroom and bath must be.

"Nice place," he remarked.

"I could be in a penthouse on Park Avenue for what I pay for this."

He approached the window and drew back the curtains, curious to see the view. He felt Coco watching him as he looked up and down the street, and heard her place two cups of tea on the pass through counter.

"Milk or lemon?"

"Lemon, please," he replied, gazing out over the chimney pots rising in clusters like thickets on the urban landscape.

As he looked down the street to his left, Coco said, "Do you see the antiques store just beyond the pedestrian crossing on the Fulham Road?"

"Yes."

"Now, look up the block two or three houses. Do you see an old cream colored Mini?"

"Yes."

"Can you see the man in the front seat, green cable cardigan, newspaper open on the passenger seat, unshaven? Looks like a pensioner?"

"I see the car, and there's someone in it," he said, straining to confirm the detail. "I'll take your word on what he's wearing."

"He followed me home yesterday morning," she said trying to sound indifferent, "after our enjoyable little rendez-vous at the Café Paris. I noticed him for no particular reason on the platform waiting for the tube. I felt like someone was following me all the way home from South Ken, and when I turned around for a look, just before crossing the Fulham Road, down at the end of the block, there he was. I ducked into the antiques shop and he kept going. But yesterday evening I went for a walk up to Hyde Park and noticed him sitting in the car hiding behind his newspaper. I was up all night watching to see if he would leave. He never did."

"Have you noticed him before?"

"No, but I've never been so paranoid before." Coco was stirring her tea to distraction, the quiet clink of her spoon filling the empty pauses like whispers in church.

"Those pictures," she started, drawing his attention from the window.

"Yes?" he replied, looking her in the eye.

"The guy," she said, gathering herself and starting again. "The guy in those pictures… with me, Harry Achermann. Did you know he's dead?" she inquired. There was little to gain by confirming or denying so he mugged like a Queen's guard, cold and opaque. "Shot in a supposed hunting accident a few days ago in the States," she continued.

For a split second her composure cracked, like a bird catching its balance, and then her professional persona reasserted itself. She wasn't the sort to seek sympathy and he knew she would be good for the facts, just the facts, whatever her emotional state.

"The story wasn't carried by anybody but the *Poughkeepsie Journal*, a small-town rag, which is a bit suspicious if you ask me," she noted. "He was a big wheel in financial circles, apparently. Did you know that?" she asked, as though his mind might be wandering. "I certainly didn't," she continued. "He was," she said, pausing to choose her words carefully, "prolific. In many ways, I've discovered, and now that I think of it, a bit of a star-fucker, if you'll pardon my French. Heads of state, charity balls, society section pictures, you name it," she said staring at him. He excelled at staring contests, but he turned his back under the guise of giving the man in the Mini down the street a second look. "You're not surprised because you already knew, didn't you?"

"I run the largest foreign newsroom of America's most important newspaper, Coco," he began, talking into the window, "and someone connected to this guy is trying to compromise you or me. Of course I knew," he replied calmly, his eyes fixed on the street below. What troubled him much more than being scolded by Coco was that Woodcock had failed to mention Achermann was dead. It was occurring to him that he and Coco could both be pawns, perhaps he more than she. It was better than even odds, he guessed, that the fellow in the car was CIA, and they were both under surveillance for Coco's transgressions, whatever they might be.

"Well? Don't you think it's suspicious that his death hasn't gotten more coverage?" she continued.

"Why did you ask me to come here, Coco?"

"I don't feel safe leaving the apartment." It was a concession unbefitting the invincible Coco Stockton. "Achermann is dead, and there's a guy out there who's been watching me since you sent me home. Maybe I'm next," she stated matter-of-factly. He turned away from the window, letting the drapes fall, and cocked his left eyebrow.

"And why would you think that, Coco?" He wasn't surprised to provoke the Stockton stare, a staple of the newsroom, and he let the question hang in undaunted suspense like his eye brow.

What was she concealing? She continued to stare, with animus now. The first time she stared at him that way was early in her career, when she had come to him with an improbable story that he doubted. It was about large pharmaceutical companies generating gargantuan profits by selling expired product into developing world markets desperate for medicines of any kind. It sounded too dark to be true, but she was vindicated, and the series of stories she wrote became the impetus for legislation, that never passed over stiff lobbying by the pharmaceutical industry, for *pedigree tracking*, a euphemism for tracing the origin and route of expired pharmaceuticals that found their way, against the law, and contrary to the most modest of ethical standards, for sale to the poorest and most desperate consumers.

"It's embarrassing, Elliot, I know... and I'm sorry if it's offensive... to you. Call it a bad boy attraction or maybe a conquest complex, it doesn't really matter, but the truth is I didn't know Harry Achermann very well. And that was that. Never thought about it again until... until your pictures, and then last night I remembered something that didn't seem important at the time, but now I'm not so sure."

"And what was that?"

"It was at a meeting with Sam, and Harry was there when I showed up. This was a couple of years ago. They didn't seem to know each other so well either, and maybe there was a little tension between them. Anyway, Sam seemed uneasy and left me there at the restaurant with him, and well, you know the rest." Coco gazed into her tea like she was staring at the ocean. He could see she was puzzling through her recollection of events.

"You said you remembered something," Schiller prodded.

"Yes, I remembered asking Harry how he had gotten to know Sam, and Harry said he was helping DeBeers with a problem. He seemed quite pleased with himself to be engaged by DeBeers, and even more pleased to tell me he couldn't say more."

"Couldn't say more about what?" Schiller demanded.

"The problem. Harry made a few cloak and daggery references to some kind of supply problem. I just assumed it had something to do with logistics or mining operations. Whatever he was doing for Sam didn't sound like it had anything to do with the U.S. price-fixing case, and I figured out pretty fast I wanted nothing more to do with him. Not fast enough, it now seems," she added. Was it her promiscuity she regretted or the inconvenience it was causing her, he wondered.

"He must have told you something important, Coco," he finally said. "The pictures are a threat."

"You don't say. And what should I make of the fellow down the block? The paparazzi?"

"So you think this is connected to the DeBeers stories? Did you unearth anything more sensitive than it may appear? or..." and he paused, to avoid sounding ironic, for it was not the sort of question one expected from a hard-nosed newspaper man, "...break any confidences?"

"And cross Sam? Don't be daft Elliot. Besides, retaliation isn't his style, and he's not naïve enough to think a few intimate photographs would intimidate a news organization. He knows threatening me would be about as effective as prohibition was on drinking. He wasn't looking to encourage me." Schiller was well aware of their understanding. Sam gave her more access to the inner workings of DeBeers than had ever been granted before, and she reviewed her stories with him in advance of deadlines, contrary to Schiller's express instructions. Sam didn't quite have editorial control but he did have sufficient warning to spin the news as it came out, which drove Schiller nuts by muffling the paper's voice. But it was a highly practical symbiotic arrangement, Sam the revisionist biographer, reinterpreting past misunderstandings about a much maligned family dynasty, while the *Washington Post* delved deep inside a company the inner workings of which rivaled Kremlin-grade mystery and intrigue.

She said Sam delighted in saying things like the market-making mechanism for diamonds was nothing so boorish or crude as a cartel like OPEC, or as heavy-handed as the Medellin drug gangs, as she had once alleged; and even Schiller came to appreciate that the DeBeers endeavor was a far more sophisticated and even-handed creation than a simple cartel. Its longevity, now approaching a century, seemed to validate the important role the company had played in balancing an otherwise volatile and lawless market, renowned for unsavory interlopers, from Third World strong men to Asian drug barons.

In truth her reporting had been masterful. The world had learned that the DeBeers system consisted of six integral mechanisms, carefully managed to serve all the constituents of the global diamond industry. The first mechanism, producer quotas, were exclusive long-term contracts between the company and designated producers to supply stipulated percentages of DeBeers' annual sales. Each producer was guaranteed sufficient market share to ensure a minimum level of cash flow, the commercial equivalent of *give us this day our daily bread*. Knowing there would be demand gave producers the confidence to maintain production, which guaranteed DeBeers a healthy, reasonably priced supply of rough diamonds. The market for cut diamonds had the potential to swing wildly, hanging any moment on a composite index of global romantic and economic sentiment, which were highly correlated, to no one's surprise. Because demand could be fickle producer quotas never guaranteed absolute volume, only a defined share of volume over all, a seat at the table, feast or famine, which insulated DeBeers from demand shocks in times of depression or war.

But the company had proven its commitment to producers by preserving purchasing patterns even during periods of weak demand, investing formidable sums in buffer stock, the second vital mechanism in the DeBeers system. Buffer stock was acquired to soak up supply and keep prices high when demand waned, and was released when demand recovered, the result being stable prices at both ends of the economic cycle. It was good politics and good business, for the company enjoyed stupendous windfalls when buffer stock, accumulated at attractive prices during periods of slack demand, reentered the market at higher prices when demand recovered. Sam convinced Coco that price stability was not achieved without huge, risky investments for which producers were grateful, and for which the company had been well rewarded time and again.

Sam had also stressed, and Coco dutifully reported, that buffer stock did not always result in cyclical windfalls. Indeed, the investment in buffer stock existed as much to punish cheaters as it did to absorb excess production, and the company had, on a few rare occasions, dumped diamonds on the market to discipline producers trying to operate outside the DeBeers system. Even at low prices, diamonds did not experience sharp increases in demand, which meant cheaters found themselves selling at very low prices for extended periods of time, if they could find buyers at all. If cheaters survived the disciplinary action, and very few did, they did so by enlightenment, which meant dealing through DeBeers, which would *forgive us our trespasses as we forgive those who trespass against us*.

The third mechanism of the system was vertical integration. The company owned and operated the lowest-cost diamond mines in the world, making it a vital swing producer during periods when buffer stock alone was insufficient to stabilize the market. Mirroring its production capacity was the fourth mechanism of the system – a network of external buying offices or diamond brokers that bought in the open market when demand was weak, and remained neutral or sold as prices rose. The company's market-making mechanisms, said Sam, were no different than interventions by the U.S. Treasury, lowering rates to boost liquidity during credit shocks, and raising interest rates to tighten liquidity in times of speculative excess, with all the collateral winners and losers one would expect in any liquid market, of course.

The fifth and perhaps most celebrated mechanism was the community of rough diamond cutters who dealt directly with DeBeers, the centuries-old guild that turned rough diamonds into gems sold at retail. On the fifth Monday of each new year an exclusive community of diamond dealers, or *sight-holders* in company parlance, were invited to DeBeers headquarters in London. The dealers participated as a group in a ritual known as a *sight* during which each sight-holder received a sack tied with a ribbon containing a selection of rough stones corresponding to demand the sight-holder registered in advance of the meeting. Each sack was valued at several million dollars and the price was non-negotiable. *Thy will be done*. Dealers could take or leave the sack – there was no obligation to buy, but participating in the sight was a coveted industry privilege, and declining to purchase put the following year's invitation at risk. The sixth and final mechanism of the system was demand management: highly effective, worldwide retail advertising campaigns reserved exclusively for periods of lackluster demand.

From mining to retail, the stability and profitability of the diamond trade were almost without precedent, and the health and vitality of the global diamond market was due in no small part to the company's well-managed market-making mechanisms. Few long-term industry players would dispute its value or have it any other way, Sam contended. The U.S. Justice Department did not share that view, and neither did the federal judge presiding over the court case in Columbus, Ohio, it appeared.

"Are we leaping to conclusions?" Coco posed. "Why does it follow that DeBeers is behind all this? Maybe someone wants us to dig into Harry Achermann, and the pictures are the bait."

"It's possible, Coco, but what's your gut tell you?"

"DeBeers isn't the source, not least because the exposé is over. There's nothing new coming out." She had a point. There was nothing left to silence, and the U.S. price fixing case had gone to trial.

"There had been no hard news, no revelations, for a long time, and we're still friends, I think," she said.

"But you said yourself something changed when he called you the day before yesterday."

"Sure, but not blackmail kind of change, and for what? No, Elliot, the story is behind Achermann. Gotta be."

"There are probably lots of stories behind Achermann, Coco, but those pictures were delivered to my house for a reason. Why me? What's the reason? Anything else you've got cooking I ought to know about?" He caught the stare again. It was the distrust she couldn't stand.

"I don't know, Elliot," she finally said, "I really don't know."

"Does this change anything?" he said like a prosecutor introducing new evidence. He pulled a single page, neatly folded in thirds, from his breast pocket and deposited it on the pass-through counter to the kitchen. She looked at the paper as though it might be contaminated.

"What's that?"

"Nothing implicating," he replied, reading her mind, "but I think it will surprise you. Dateline, last night." Coco reached for the paper and unfolded it suspiciously. Her eyes widened as she read the *Washington Post* headline: "DeBeers Pleads to Price-Fixing." She read on.

DeBeers SA, the huge diamond company, pleaded guilty yesterday to price fixing and agreed to pay $10 million to settle a 10-year-old indictment, which paves the way for the company to start doing business directly with the American market. Based in London and South Africa, DeBeers controls 60 per cent of all rough, uncut diamonds sold worldwide. It already reaches U.S. consumers through intermediaries, including diamond distributors and *marketing firms, so yesterday's action in federal court in Columbus, Ohio, may have little impact on diamond prices and market share here. But the settlement will give DeBeers a bigger marketing presence and greater legitimacy with U.S. consumers.*

"Elliot. This is crazy. They would never do this. And the government settled for such a small sum? After ten years? Something stinks," Coco cautioned, her passions ignited.

"I expected that would be your reaction," he said, reasonably pleased with himself. "Read on," he instructed. She scanned the article quickly, recognizing many facts and figures restated from articles she had filed months before. Her eyes settled on a short, conspicuous paragraph towards the end of the article.

[Lynette] Hori, a spokeswoman for DeBeers in London, said there is "absolutely no connection" between the settlement and the growing competition from mined and synthetic diamonds. She said it is part of DeBeers' strategy of "total legal compliance around the world" and "our drive to create a new, modern DeBeers."

Coco shook her head incredulously and caught him smirking. "That last line? About a new, modern DeBeers? That's right from Sam's playbook."

"No kidding," he remarked unimpressed. "So now what do you think?"

"I don't know what I think. Except there's a rat."

"That's what I think, Coco. And I think you know what it is. You just don't know you know. Whatever it is, it's got DeBeers and the U.S. government worried enough to want to make it go away, quickly. I suggest you start reviewing your notes, and I need to make a phone call."

Chapter 10

Jimmy was counting the seconds. He felt like a bumpkin in his scuffed black gum shoes, polyester slacks, and police department issue knit tie. He was squashed in the corner of a high-ceiling elevator with polished brass walls and crystal clear buttons. Thank God for the women, their svelte tailored suits, and intoxicating perfume. They were taller than he, even in bare feet, and their pouting cold expressions were growing on him, never mind their straying attentions to the male specimens towering around him. The gleaming brass doors finally swept open and disgorged them like a fist full of jacks into the expanse of the three-story marble and glass atrium. He marched across the lobby and exited by the revolving door onto 45th Street, threading his way through a volley of careening yellow cabs before ducking into a basement garage where he had parked his car for twenty dollars an hour. A few minutes later he pulled the aging unmarked Crown Victoria cruiser on to the street. He had just turned north on the West Side Drive in the direction of Poughkeepsie when his cell phone rang. It was Anita, from the police research library in Albany, responding to his request for background on the three company names he texted her from Harry Achermann's plush midtown offices. He had read the names off Lucite blocks, financial transaction mementos or *tombstones*, that were stacked like animal crackers on the cookie aisle throughout the office. Jimmy had noticed other things, too, like the paternal looking face of a celebrated executive captured in a photograph with Achermann. It was in an inlaid lacquered frame that matched a nearby humidor, and the photograph had a personal inscription scribbled in heavy black ink across the bottom. The man had been in the news, he couldn't recall why, and the distraction of other Achermann portraits, including some with political figures, drew his attention away. The photographs looked like others he had seen in overrated Italian restaurants of the proprietor mugging with celebrities.

The elder of Achermann's assistants had shown him around the office, escorting him to Achermann's chambers like a rare exhibit docent. It was there that a framed reprint of a *New York Times* society page had caught his attention, or more correctly, the woman in it. She had all the presentation of the girls in the elevator, only softer, less contrived, without the attitude, which made her elegant. She was standing with Achermann, of course, exquisitely dressed, and surrounded by self-absorbed party-goers.

"The Mrs.," the assistant assured him dimly on seeing the picture catch his eye. Jimmy was smitten by the primitive beauty in the expanse between her eyes, and the carnal magnetism of her pouting lips. She looked like an unpretentious field hound among heartless show dogs, though it was hard to be sure from the newsprint quality photograph. There were also around the office pictures of a graceful sailing yacht under a full press of canvass, and distinguished looking gentlemen in matching blue blazers and striped ties, standing in a jovial pack around a polished brass binnacle. Where there weren't photographs or Lucite blocks there were leather bound volumes with gold embossed letters, rows upon rows of them like the legal reference books in the prosecutor's office. On closer inspection they turned out to be transaction binders, ceremonial tomes marking companies bought and sold, investments reaped and sewed with lives and careers traded like ship's cargo.

Anita had preliminary information on all three companies, two of which had been liquidated in bankruptcy. Executives had gone to jail, and the circumstances of one of them helped Jimmy place the face he recognized in the frame by the humidor. It was *Jimmy Boy* DuGary, the CEO of now defunct GasTel, a global energy and telecommunications company. DuGary had once been a candidate for Secretary of Energy, and made himself infamous by manipulating energy markets and selling his shares while promoting them to his own employees. His henchmen were all doing time in the big house, but DuGary had a heart attack on the eve of his trial and died. Jimmy remembered the scandal and that DuGary's timely death got less media coverage than a prize pig at a state fair. It struck him at the time that DuGary had obviously staged his own death and used his prodigious wealth to suppress curiosity and escape the country. He would lay odds that DuGary turned up sooner or later living in luxury somewhere down in Central America on the millions he would have forfeited on conviction, which was never in doubt.

As Jimmy drove north on the West Side Drive, he recorded his impressions of Achermann's staff on a vintage miniature tape recorder that were popular about the time he was born. He spoke in a hushed conspiratorial tone, like a golf sportscaster, because it made him feel like the narrator in a crime series, and he knew it amused the likable transcriptionist. He had questioned all four of Achermann's staff - his two assistants, a young associate, and a gentleman in his late fifties, Stan Benedek, and he was capturing his thoughts while they were fresh.

The young associate harbored thinly disguised contempt for Achermann, and appeared both relieved and delighted he was already leaving for a graduate studies program in economics. Benedek called himself Achermann's partner and was both inscrutable and rude. It was a curiously light staff, Jimmy thought, for managing so much money, and he discovered a common misconception about the entourage of the rich, which was that they shared to some degree in the spoils. The associate was bitter and overweight with grand aspirations and no prospect of washing the blue from his collar. "A reacher," Jimmy's father would have said, "and a disgrace to his roots." He resented his life in a tiny Lower East Side studio apartment. He had kind words for no one, especially Achermann, and Jimmy pegged his dripping contempt for the assistants as envy for their better access to the boss.

He was scornful of Benedek, whom he called "Achermann's butt boy… an inveterate yes-man who can't see beyond his own big nose that he's no closer to the big pay-off than he was twenty years ago when he started," and he gleefully sneered at Benedek's circumstances, "in a wannabe town a couple stops short of the gold coast across the Connecticut State line." Jimmy understood: geographically close, but as socio-economically distant as the far side of the moon. The "girls," the associate said, lived in the outlying boroughs, "where they belonged." He was a malformed spirit, thought Jimmy – he had seen them before - and Achermann had given him no reason to heal.

He called Achermann "a lone wolf," restless and cunning, who circumnavigated the globe in an endless hunt for money, new or old, it made no difference. "The philanthropies?" he replied, "they're a joke, a cover for elephant bumping," for hunting kingpins with cash who dream of wealth multiplying like popcorn.

"You ever been to one of those things, those charity balls?" the associate had asked Jimmy. "It's a male organ marathon," he said, answering himself before Jimmy could expose his unworldliness.

"Everyone trying to figure how the other guy made his," the porcine associate said, his beady little eyes flickering covetously.

"And how *did* Achermann make his money?" Jimmy had inquired, stumbling for the first time on a subject for which the associate had no ready opinion.

"I'm not exactly sure… but his results are very, very good," he recovered quickly, invoking a refrain that sounded borrowed and parroted repeatedly.

"What about Benedek?" Jimmy had asked. "Does *he* know how Achermann gets his results?"

"He'll tell you he does, but he's a liar," the associate said. "You can't trust anything he tells you. It's all about sucking up to Achermann for Stan. There's nothing he wouldn't say or do. Who knows what he'll do now," he gloated.

"How far exactly would Benedek go?" Jimmy asked. "Would he break the law?"

"Stan wouldn't know it if he did. I'm tellin' yah, the guy's a mindless sycophant, desperate to be in the big leagues."

"Would he cover up a crime?"

"No problem. He's all about loyalty to Achermann. Anything Achermann wanted."

"What about murder? Is he up to murder?"

"You mean Achermann's murder?" the associate asked.

"Yeah, Achermann's murder. If he's as bad as you say, you think maybe ol' Stan just had enough?"

"No way. Doesn't have the balls. Or the imagination. And besides, what's he gonna do without Achermann?"

"So what did *you* do for Achermann?" Jimmy persisted.

"My job was to research people, to find out what they were worth and how they made it. Harry had a nose for deep pockets. He would send me files overnight from all over the world: Brazil, Taiwan, London, Zurich, wherever the money goes. It was usually about a family business, and there was a consistent pattern, second-generation wealth, if you know what I mean."

"No, I don't," Jimmy replied.

"Widows, first wives, and spoiled rich kids. Harry opened my eyes to the scratch out there in the hands of losers. He could spot them across a room," the associate said, unable to conceal his admiration.

Jimmy wondered if he were all bitterness all the time, just a punk frustrated by working for the man, or if there was more to his anger. There was a hard-scrabble part of himself that he recognized, a deviant on the mend with subdued but not banished indignation capable of justifying almost anything. If he were keeping secrets Jimmy guessed they could be bought, or very hard to pry loose.

"And that's what you did – find out about people?" Jimmy concluded.

"Yep. That's about it. After that Harry did the courting and Benedek did the collecting, and off the money went to the placement agents." It was a world so abstract, thought Jimmy, it might as well be time travel.

"What about his wife? She ever meet him here? Did they socialize with his clients? Did they ever have you over?"

"No," said the associate, making the suggestion sound absurd. "Never laid eyes on her. She's never been here and I've never seen them together."

"Did he do anything for fun? Didn't he like to hunt? And what about all the pictures of boats and sailors?"

"You're not gettin' it, are you?" said the associate, losing patience. "It was all about the money, putting himself near the money. Everything he did, everywhere he went, he was on the prowl. That *was* the fun."

"I see," said Jimmy, reflecting on the portrait of Achermann and the profile of Donner's Forge members emerging back in Poughkeepsie police headquarters. The pattern the associate described was plainly visible at the club where new money outnumbered old three to one. He wondered how many Donner's Forge members were already cataloged, how many had already slid beneath the door of the run-down building on the Lower East Side?

Jimmy had listened patiently as the punk had mused like a two-beer philosopher on Achermann's motives. No thing, no object of desire was out of Achermann's reach, but he didn't covet what he did not have, "as the wealthy often do," he had assured Jimmy.

Achermann indulged a single passion, which he exercised like a thoroughbred, and that was separating the wealthy from their wealth.

The elder of Achermann's assistants had been more guarded than the associate. She counted her time in Achermann's service back to the day he opened his doors, "longer than he's been married," it seemed important for her to say. She wore too much powder on her face, perhaps to mask the translucence of her skin, which stretched like cellophane over the tendons of her emaciated hands. She dyed her hair an impossible shade of blond, which she whirled into a bun like a French fashion model. Her scalding red business suit flattered her fetching if lapsing figure, and glinted with brass buttons the size of silver dollars as she sauntered with studied sultriness through the office. She spoke of Achermann admiringly, even wistfully Jimmy thought.

"The poor thing loved him, I think," he said softly into his tape recorder.

Jimmy had observed before the curious tendency of long-tenured employees to confuse bosses for father figures, turning veneration to a need. It reminded him of Stockholm Syndrome. This was the elder assistant's pattern, except in the presence of the younger assistant, who was young and dark and voluptuous. Jimmy was not immune to the younger one's brooding femininity which lurked beneath her conservative dress as subtly as a downpour in a thunderhead. She had docile innocent eyes like a farm animal, except in the presence of her superior, when they became anxious and dispossessed like a panicked doe.

She had interrupted Jimmy's interview to report somewhat fearfully that her colleague was needed on the phone.

"Take a message," Jimmy's subject hissed, crossing her legs and readjusting her hemline. She wore her animosity like a medal, and her sentimentality for Achermann was usurped by a primitive Amazonian quality every time her subordinate was nearby. No sooner had the younger retreated to her desk than the elder spoke her mind.

"Men as shrewd as Harry have enemies, don't they," she said as if to suggest she could be helpful.

"Who do *you* suspect?" Jimmy replied.

"Anybody. Everybody."

"Like who?" he persisted. It seemed to Jimmy that murder titillated her and that she wanted his attention, but not for the reasons he hoped. She ran him in circles before conceding she had nothing to tell. Achermann was no closer to any one acquaintance or business partner than he was to any other, and of disputes or misdeeds she knew none. Indeed her statements were nothing if not an endorsement of the associate's lone wolf characterization, a portrait that acquired depth with each new discovery.

"What about his marriage?" Jimmy asked, trying to complete the picture.

"What about it?" she replied in the same tone she used when her subordinate was nearby.

"Was it a good marriage, bad marriage, did they get along?"

"I really couldn't tell you."

"Did you have a thing for him?" Jimmy asked, wondering only whether she had acted on it.

"What does that mean?"

"Were you involved? You and Achermann." She cut him a look that hit him like a nail gun, and narrowed her mottled hazel eyes like a falcon.

"Yes," she finally said, "but that was a long time ago, before they were married."

"No relapses?" he persisted.

"Not recently," she said, casting her eye at the door, "and not with me."

"You mean he jilted you for his wife, and then for her," he had said, perhaps a bit insensitively now that he thought about it. The unforgettable stare had removed all doubt.

"I think I've said enough," she concluded, pulling on her hemline again before uncrossing her legs and taking her leave.

"I suppose you'll want to speak to Benedek and that other one, too. They're both here. You'll have no trouble finding them," she said as she walked out. Jimmy felt sorry for her. She had "waited for Achermann longer than Moneypenny had for Bond," he remarked unsentimentally into his tape recorder.

The younger assistant was useless, confessing to loving Achermann despite knowing of his infidelities. There was a stray dog begging for scraps quality in her indifference to Achermann's betrayals. She was "roadkill," he noted for the transcriptionist, "even before Achermann's murder." The purpose she served, he was sad to say, was to demonstrate the relentlessness of Achermann's appetite for feasting on the weak.

Jimmy hoped Benedek would break the pattern of exploitation, if for no other reason than his growing disdain for Achermann. He was a coarse, inscrutable Hungarian with an expressionless face and dyed black hair that he combed like a motor head straight back over his crown. His awkward, staccato speech begged the question of his fluency, even though he had no discernable accent. He made a respectable effort to convince Jimmy he would help the investigation, expounding in turbulent, long-winded responses that Jimmy failed often to follow. He said a pole-vaulting accident in his youth had left several neck vertebrae fused and limited the mobility of his head, which he subsequently proved under questioning. Subjects averted their eyes, especially under duress, and most accomplished it subtly. But Benedek looked with his torso, his eyes pinioned to his body by the neck, which meant he broadcast his lies in great spasms as if deflecting glancing blows. In the end he was useless, too. Yes, he had worked with Achermann for almost as long as the elder assistant. No, he was not aware of unhappy personal or professional relationships, and no, there were no disgruntled investors. Why would there be? Investors had never lost money. Achermann's death, he told Jimmy, "was simply tragic… not in the least bit suspicious, a man taken in his prime in a terrible accident." There was something sad to Jimmy about Benedek, a proud if intellectually unlucky henchman, reduced to parroting throw away lines like an over-rehearsed public relations agent.

The Hudson River was flowing south outside Jimmy's driver's side window as he powered up the West Side Drive against the current in the direction of Poughkeepsie. His journey into the heart of Achermann's enterprise had been a bust, discovering little more than a predictably dysfunctional office environment, and very little about what the man did or how his business worked. Benedek gave uninspired lip service to investment strategies with asset classes too numerous and arcane for Jimmy to recall accurately, and nobody could describe where and how investments were made. Benedek renounced all know-how besides "moving the money," and would not or could not reveal what happened thereafter. He spoke in wonder and dread of ingenious trades devised exclusively in

Achermann's head, and repeated as though for posterity that Achermann never ever lost money. That was the dead giveaway something was amiss. He knew from his trading pals that everybody lost money some of the time, even the ones with the best information, however they came by it. It made him wonder if Global Strategy Advisors invested by any traditional meaning of the word at all. References to performance were conspicuously absent, beyond general claims of success without loss, and this begged the question of Achermann's investments, of where the money actually went.

Chapter 11

He felt like a Tennessee bootlegger barreling through the Atlanta dawn in the back of a black Ford with government plates, and he had no stomach for the breakneck speed at which the vehicle was traveling north on I-75, from Hartsfield International airport, past the Braves' stadium, and into downtown Atlanta where the driver veered on to the Freedom Parkway and careened northeast toward the CDC. Only after the car rolled to a full stop did he release his grip on the dome-mounted passenger handle. He realized how exhausted and disheveled he must look as the car pulled away and left him standing in the crisp dawn, unshaven and sticking to his clothes. As he approached the door, Katrine Burkhardt materialized on the opposite side of the glass.

"You must be Woodcock," she said reasonably nicely as the doors parted and he was met by a blast of super-cooled air. The bloody southerners ran the air conditioning whether they needed to or not, he thought to himself.

"Indeed," he replied courteously.

"Can I get you a coffee or something?" she said.

"Black," he replied, following her to a tired coffee machine that was laboring like a farm tool to spit a thin spew of dark water into a cloudy carafe.

"Help yourself." He detected something curt and inhospitable in her voice.

"This must be quite a serious thing, this virus or whatever it is," Woodcock began, trying to sound uninformed.

"Oh for goodness sake!" she erupted, "You mean you don't know?"

"I'm not following you," he replied.

"Nobody told you this is one of ours? That this came from one of your labs?" He felt her study him like a serpent thinking of swallowing its prey whole.

"Yes, quite," he finally acknowledged, abandoning the charade. "You're sure," he said, blurring the distinction between query and assertion.

"Yes. I worked on the antidote."

"We received all the clinical data. Thank you. It's in the hands of the teams, who are briefed. Please tell me the symptoms are exaggerated in the tradition of all well-marketed weapons systems," he said.

"No, the indications are accurate," she countered, "according to the lady locked down in quarantine in the basement. It's working the way it was supposed to."

"I don't suppose you have any theories on how it got out?" he inquired with blunt insinuation.

"No, actually," Katrine replied, "I expected *you* would." He didn't mean to shift uncomfortably. She was a colleague in some respects, as knowledgeable about the disease as he, if not more, but a stranger, too.

"And why would you think that?"

"Because your labs are notoriously lax – it's no secret. What you should be worried about is where it went, and how many places it's been. You," she started, pausing for effect, "*We* have a very big problem Mr. Woodcock." Her irritation was evolving, building like a wave barreling for shore.

"Oh?" he replied, with nothing to lose by playing possum.

"Yes, as soon as I matched the DNA the casework came back to me, an interesting case, too, if you like the idea of doctor doom all-star teams."

"How do you mean?"

"The scientists were this weird combination of Russians and Americans. They had been organized by an investor group in Silicon Valley, I think. It was the early nineties. I guess the Wall had just come down and there was a rush to commercialize some of the science bottled up in the old Soviet research system." She paused, adjusting to the intensity of his stare.

"Go on," he said.

"This was back in the dawn of genetic discovery when DNA replication was hard. It took time, and we could only culture and harvest minute amounts. Whoever broke the code on replicating DNA sequences in large quantities would be sitting on a goldmine.

Every lab in America was clamoring for it." She sounded like an historian recalling the golden age of railways.

"And?" he prodded.

"Well, the Russians had come up with something that was way ahead of anything we had. That wasn't so unusual," she noted. "They were so resource-constrained that they had a knack for devising simple and elegant solutions to problems we spent millions trying to solve. Everybody knew ribosomes were the locus of protein replication in cells, sort of a cell level hot-house for growing the component parts of DNA, but the Russians figured out how to concentrate ribosomes in large numbers, accelerate their protein replicating processes, and then harvest the resulting crop. Anybody could have done it in a batch process, but the Russians devised a continuous process." He must have looked lost and perplexed because she launched into an explanation. "Not that it matters, but the batch process was inefficient and slow. You had to culture cells, sacrifice them and then harvest the protein. You were lucky if fifty percent survived harvesting. The Russians had developed what they called 'continuous flow, cell-free, protein synthesis.' CFCF they called it. They induced ribosomes outside the cell to pump out pristine protein in high quantity for DNA engineering. Talk about necessity being the mother of invention," she concluded breathlessly, the significance of the accomplishment apparently magnified by the lens of time. "The rate of replication was astonishing."

"I don't follow," he said again.

"You don't follow what?" she said, clearly irritated by his inability to keep up.

"How that places the origin of this strain of virus in a CIA lab, as you just alleged."

"Oh, right. Well this team of scientists had formed a company. Can't remember the name. Doesn't matter." She started speaking fast, in clipped, condensed phrases, to get back to the point. "The company struggled. Someone came up with a better way than CFCF, and they got desperate for a new breakthrough, something new to sell. The scientists had this intense period of collaboration where they came up with some crazy stuff, probably among the first to experiment with designer DNA." She paused.

"For a moment in time," she started, her voice growing dark, "it was the very best of science for the very worst of applications," she mumbled softly. "Ironic, isn't it, that they tried to save their company by turning out a plague they had been saving for each other."

"Yes," he acknowledged diplomatically. "I do admire your taste for irony, Ms. Burkhardt, but that doesn't get us back to your allegation, does it?" Katrine was gazing at the floor.

"DecimRiboX," she mumbled. "DRX they called it. It's lethal, as you know, with all the fast replication properties of CFCF. I couldn't remember the name of the company, but I remembered that. And I remembered how quickly it got the attention of the CIA," she said through fatigue that was taking its toll.

"And why is that?"

"In-Q-Tel," she replied.

"Say again."

"You've never heard of In-Q-Tel?"

"No, should I have?"

"Yes," she said angrily. "It's a CIA investment company. They funnel money into technologies that catch their eye, and apparently CFCF did. As the company was folding, In-Q-Tel bought the scraps and ended up with the intellectual property. DRX and the code for making it is under your roof somewhere," she said accusingly. "You're just lucky we kept some antidote."

"Who is the woman in quarantine, and what possessed her to come straight here?"

"She's a very good friend from medical school. Lucky for you she knew she was dealing with something unusual and brought it to me." Katrine continued at some length boring him with Astrid's virtues, and filling in the blanks relevant to her work and travels with the World Health Organization. These were important details he came unprepared to record so he scrounged a three-by-five note pad from his jacket pocket and began scribbling like a portrait artist.

"Where does she live? With whom does she affiliate? Is she married, and to whom?" he asked before reminding himself this was not an interrogation.

"Her home is in New York when she's not in some God-forsaken place tending to the ill." Katrine said. "She's married to a banker... or was..." It must have been a slip for she wouldn't say more.

"And who is the banker? What's his name?" he continued.

"Harry Achermann."

"Achermann you say?"

"Yes, so you've heard of him," she said. He wasn't sure what that meant.

"No, actually," he replied. "Should I have heard of him?"

"You're not a very good liar, Mr. Woodcock. He was killed a few days ago. There's been very little information." She seemed to be insinuating foul play. If she thought she could get him to talk she was wrong. His possum routine was working, and he intended to keep the silence so long as she insisted on filling it.

"Even his wife doesn't know the details," she resumed, "but with what's waiting for her in New York, quarantine may suit her for a while."

"And what *is* waiting for her?" He asked.

"Harry was quite a successful, well-known guy..."

Woodcock didn't believe in luck or coincidences. He had been on Achermann's trail like a bloodhound, and Harry's murder, while inconvenient, was not altogether surprising given the company he kept. However, the position in which he now found himself was propitious, almost too good to be true. In a few short hours evidence was accumulating like vowels in Hangman. Unconfirmed but racy images of Achermann had surfaced, forwarded by a *Washington Post* journalist stationed in London, who thought they were a threat; and a woman, allegedly Achermann's wife, had walked straight off a plane from Cape Town via London, and into the CDC carrying the biological agent in which the CIA suspected Achermann of trading. For the first time in his intelligence career, he reflected, the evidence was coming to him and all he had to do was make sense of it. He didn't much care who killed Achermann or why. He was after the buyers of DRX, and in a race to control a pandemic.

"Do you have a clearance?" he asked.

"Top Secret," she replied, yawning. "Excuse me, it's been a long night."

"For us both," Woodcock acknowledged. "I would be grateful if..." he began with affected charm before dropping the pretense. "This is classified and should be treated as such, do you understand?" he said. She nodded indifferently. Harry Achermann, he told her, had been under surveillance, suspected for some time of attempting to trade in biological agents.

"Do you suppose his wife is an accomplice?"

"No," she snapped.

"You're certain they had no shared agenda?"

"Absolutely certain," she replied. "Sounds to me like the CIA needs a scapegoat for its own lax controls. That's what it sounds like to me, Woodcock." He gave her a withering glare.

"You said they had a bad marriage," he said.

"Did I?"

"What if it's a cover? What if they've been sleepers?" he suggested. "This is what the lives of sleepers look like."

"Spies?" she replied. "You're reaching."

"Am I? Achermann's background is pure fiction. None of his schooling or residences or former employers check out. We don't know where he's from and he spends a lot of time outside the country," he added. "Don't you think it's quite a coincidence that his wife walks in from the South African wilderness with the very thing we suspect him of taking?" He could tell by her expression it was a fair if galling question, and he watched her grope through her exhaustion for clues from the past. The seeds of doubt had been planted and she was wondering if he could be right. She would be questioning her old friend's intentions and picturing their friendship as a ruse.

"Why bring it here?" she finally said, trying to trump his theory.

"Yes. A bit of a fly in the ointment, that," he conceded. "Maybe she got cold feet," he speculated. "Was she a zealot, a fanatic, a political or religious acolyte?"

"Hardly," Katrine responded. "For Astrid it was all about the science, before compassion became... well, her life."

"What did she read? Where did she worship? Did she ever go through a period of radical thought?" They were disorienting questions designed to sow doubt, for who did not read or worship or have dark spells of uncertainty and doubt, especially people with energy and education, people just like Astrid Achermann. No doubt she read voraciously and waded into life, encountering the highs and lows that strivers always meet, propelled by faith today and disillusionment tomorrow. He was forcing Katrine to question her assumptions, to reexamine the premises of their relationship, and perhaps surprise herself with how the good doctor's ambitions appeared in a different light.

"No, Woodcock," she finally declared. "Her maiden name is Taylor, born and raised in a big house in the Garden District in New Orleans. Nothing about your theory fits, and it's not such a coincidence either. She's a tropical disease epidemiologist. You would find Astrid wherever diseases like DRX appear."

"And her husband?" he continued.

"What about him?" Katrine snapped.

"How well did you know him?"

"Not very well. I was already here, in Atlanta, when they met. I came to the wedding. Astrid and I stayed in touch. He seemed charming enough, but we were in different places, on different paths."

"That all?" he persisted. He could feel her withholding.

"I don't think they were in love, if that's what you mean, at least he wasn't." There was something in her voice, contempt, or possibly envy, maybe disillusionment. He glanced at her hands. She wore no rings.

"Did you feel betrayed… when they got married?"

"I beg your pardon?"

"You know what I mean," he said.

"No, I'm quite sure I don't. You people really are…"

"What?"

"…twisted. I never understood the attraction, if that's what you mean. He was a soulless, self-absorbed sort. If he's been under surveillance I'm sure you know more about him than I do." He kept staring unsatisfactorily.

"I'll tell you this," she began, "Astrid was a feather in his cap. She would have been a catch for anybody, but to Harry she was a breakthrough, a milestone, tangible proof of his destiny."

"Oh?"

"He was superficial that way. Did things, bought things, said things for appearances. And he was manipulative. But you don't say that to a friend who thinks she's in love. He wanted Astrid for the world she came from, like another collector's trophy for his rendezvous with greatness. But she never saw it, or not until it was much too late. Who knows, Mr. Woodcock, he could have been up to anything, or maybe nothing, but if there really was a plan you can be sure it was all about money. You could ask his wife, but I doubt she knows any more than I do." He had come to do just that. The friendship between Katrine and Achermann's wife was an unexpected bounty, another fortuitous discovery.

"Was Harry's death suspicious?" she asked him unexpectedly. He gave her a calculated smile.

"I don't know," he finally said. "Not my end of the problem, really. My end is who has DecimRiboX, how did they get it, and how will they use it? Perhaps Mrs. Achermann has some ideas."

"Dr. Achermann," she corrected him. "Come with me," she said, and started in the direction of quarantine in the basement.

They found Astrid sitting quietly in a spare white room with a hospital bed and an adjoining bathroom. She wore comfortable looking, loose fitting turquoise scrubs, and she was reading intently. Her curls spilled in a tightly textured vortex around the back of her head, leaving the opposite side of her neck exposed, and he noticed her skin glowing bright in the cold antiseptic light. She had her back to a large observation window, and she was unaware of their presence until Katrine approached the voice activated microphone and said "Astrid, this is Adam Woodcock from Homeland Security."

She continued to read as still as a mannequin, hunched unresponsively over a large heavy book in her lap.

"Astrid?" Katrine persisted. This time Astrid raised her hand, begging forbearance, and continued to read unapologetically. Woodcock was not accustomed to cooling his heels and approached the glass until his breath condensed on its surface.

"Hello Mrs. Achermann, I'm Adam Woodcock from Homeland Security," he said in his most authoritative Etonian. Astrid uncoiled like a swing dancer from her wheeled swivel chair, and approached the glass until she came face-to-face with Woodcock and Katrine.

"You don't *sound* like you're from Homeland Security, at least not this homeland, Mr. Woodcock."

"Yes, quite. I'm sort of on loan, as it were, from one homeland to another, do you see, Mrs. Achermann?"

"Yes, I see. Please call me Astrid, or Dr. Achermann. Mrs. Achermann sounds so, I don't know, dowdy, do you see, Mr. Woodcock?" They were off on the wrong foot and the contempt in her voice boded poorly for prying loose information.

"Dr. Achermann, this is not your typical sort of naturally occurring Ebola virus, is it? And that's why you brought it here to Ms. Burkhardt, is that right?"

"You know exactly what it is, Mr. Woodcock. It's DecimRiboX, still in existence in blatant violation of treaties banning biological warfare agents, for reasons only a nihilist such as yourself could understand," she said. "It's now spreading contagion among an innocent people in a remote desert in South Africa. You'll have to explain to me sometime how this advances the security of our homeland," she seethed, pronouncing her words in measured enunciated phrases, as though she were practiced at containing lurking rage.

"Dr. Achermann, if you please, I'm not here to make excuses or to answer to you. I'm here to find out how DecimRiboX got loose. It seems unlikely it was an accident, and I would be grateful, if it's no imposition, that is, if you would help me." Being conciliatory caught her by surprise, just as he intended, and earned him a reprieve, like the eye of a storm, as she weighed his appreciation of the crisis.

"I think you can be sure it's no accident, nor a freak mutation," she finally said. "Ebola and diseases like it don't propagate in deserts, at least they never have before. They need warm, wet environments where temperatures hold steady. It's far too dry and the nights too cold for this to have found its way by accident, or to have originated where we found it," she said.

"Let's assume you're right, Dr. Achermann, that it's not an accident," he stipulated, sensing an opening. "Why South Africa, and why amongst such a..." and he caught himself before using the derogatory term that first came to mind, "isolated population?"

"Maybe it's the thoughtful Homeland's idea of a safe place for an experiment," Astrid replied, her anger stirring afresh.

"How do you mean?"

"Well, it's Africa, so Ebola-like symptoms would not raise eyebrows. It's in a remote locale among a virtually unknown population in an environment so arid they may have the false impression the spread could be contained, eventually, after eradicating the population." He had to admit, the idea held water, the logic of the location, the subjects and their circumstances, it all hung together, as good conspiracy theories do.

"That's pretty compelling conjecture," he said. "Is that where *you* would conduct this kind of experiment? Dr. Achermann?"

"Nice," said Astrid, turning to Katrine. "Nothing like leading the witness. Does this ignoramus have any idea of what I do, or how long I've been doing it?"

"The problem is," he interrupted, choosing his words carefully, but Katrine cut him off.

"What Mr. Woodcock is trying to say, Astrid, is that the CIA thinks Harry was involved in stealing DRX."

"I'm sorry," he said. "It is a remarkable coincidence, is it not?"

"Isn't what?"

"That you should walk out of a remote part of the world with DRX, which has been under lock and key for more than a decade, and that," he paused again, savoring the moment like an executioner, "and that your husband is suspected of a keen interest in acquiring it."

He watched her defenses crumble, as they often do under irrefutable circumstances.

"How do you know?" she asked.

"I don't know, do you?" he replied.

"And you suspect *me* of being involved? Of working with *him*?"

"Were you? Did you?" Woodcock replied. He felt doubt take root in Katrine, a kernel of suspicion, sprouting like a jonquil in March. Dr. Achermann's humanitarian exploits were hard to impugn, which made them suspiciously good cover, especially for traveling to places notorious for harboring the unsavory characters who wouldn't hesitate to put DRX to use. This is what he hoped Katrine was thinking, the easier to enlist her in exposing Dr. Achermann's mission; but that hope was promptly dashed.

"This has the smell of an experiment gone wrong, and I make a convenient scapegoat, don't I? A target of opportunity, isn't that what you intelligence types call it?" Touché, he thought. "Surely you have more imagination than that, Mr. Woodcock. Perhaps your ham-handed Homeland Security found the remoteness of Namaqueland ideal for testing DRX, a place for the disease to run its course and disappear." Even though he knew better, or thought he did, it had the makings of a devastating headline, and he could scarcely imagine the damage control required to contain such an allegation if she made it publically. Message received. Two could play at games of reckless insinuation, and she held the moral high ground, this militant Mother Theresa with advanced degrees and no burden of patriotism. She appeared to taste victory, because he was hesitating, and she squared her shoulders, holding her ground as she opposed him through the glass; but the truth was less grand. He was simply reloading for a new line of inquiry, an idea that had been percolating since he rung off with Whitaker back at the plane.

"Dr. Achermann," he began carefully, "this may seem off the subject, but do you know if there are mining operations in Namaqueland?" She gave him a puzzled look.

"Why is that relevant?"

"Quite," he acknowledged. "Probably isn't," he conceded, deflecting her ire, and deciding she needed more softening. "Tell me about your husband," he proceeded. She turned her back on the glass and set to pacing the perimeter of the cramped chamber in close careful steps, one hand on her neck beneath her thick black tresses, floating like a sleepwalker between the furnishings.

"What do you want to know?"

"It was not a personal question, Dr. Achermann," he replied, intent on explaining himself, but she interrupted.

"Then what are you asking?"

"What do you know about his work, and what were his dealings in South Africa?"

"South Africa?" she said, "none, as far as I know… but the truth is I wouldn't know. I really don't know what he did. Do you see, Mr. Woodcock?" she said, using his barbed turn of phrase again, but this time for surrender. She glanced at Katrine for encouragement, like a dancer checking her balance.

"It's no secret, really, is it Katrine," she continued. "I don't keep track of him." It was the plain truth pronounced like a verdict, but unnerving nonetheless, the way she thinly masked the pain.

"Yes, quite," he said, no stranger to her plight. He was going to need a cleaner line on Achermann, and time was passing. On to London, he thought, where this bloke Schiller might be of use, when Astrid began to speak.

"We travel, a lot, separately, on our own. We're home together, under the same roof, by accident. It's like that."

"I see," he said quietly. "I'm sorry."

"No need. These things happen." She began pacing again, her eyes bent to the floor by the hand on her neck, as if bowed to compromises she never agreed to make.

"Yes. I suppose they do," he acknowledged, and then he watched with surprise as she transitioned to a susceptible psychological state, a frame of mind interrogators labor to induce, and train to recognize, in which emotions blossom like ocean upwellings, and the truth floats on its own buoyancy to the surface. The *inner child*, so-called by practitioners, was elusive and prized by romantics and interrogators alike.

Evoking the *inner child* the way he had been trained called for tireless investment in bonding, and with time the formation of trust, set down in careful even layers, and fused like sedimentary rock under the stress of incarceration. On the foundations of trust the interrogator sprinkled charged words and loaded catch-phrases, common to every language, for expressing deeply felt and universally held emotions like love and hate, fear and greed, seasoning the patter of day-to-day interrogation with passion-stirring sentiments, like spices to awaken the emotional palate. Interrogators like Woodcock knew they held the upper hand when subjects entrusted their feelings, and he had proven to himself time and again that everybody carried an unhealed inner child, even hardened criminals, even fanatical terrorists.

But his experience was limited to hostile witnesses, often foreign, always angry, and disoriented by design, plucked from far-off, war-torn lands and deposited and deprived in depressing conditions to exploit their vulnerabilities. The bonding phase could take months, and trust much longer, time he did not have with Astrid. So her spontaneous willingness to confide was surprising, even disarming to the degree that he had to remind himself of the next stage in the process: the part where he reversed roles to make himself emotionally accessible, and this could take time because it meant getting past his own hostility toward an adversary, which was its own challenge. But Astrid had jumped to the end before he was ready.

"He must have been driven," he said gently, to acknowledge Harry's death with the past tense.

"He was needy, in ways I couldn't help him, in ways I didn't want to help him," she said. He waited. He would know when she needed coaxing.

"And classically abusive," she added calmly. He could feel Katrine squirm in the awkward silence, dreading what came next.

"Oh, not like that," she said, sensing Katrine's distress and unburdening her guests with a smile. "I wouldn't put up with that. No, I meant he was classically self-defeating, self-destructive. He craved things to fill the void, to achieve acceptance, and when these things failed him the hole got bigger. Achievement aggravated the problem, and being happy was always just out of reach," she mused. "I think *we* were just another of his Quixotic quests that failed to ease the torment," she said without pity or remorse.

"I suppose he thought our marriage would get him to the right side of the tracks. But he never understood himself, never relinquished a sort of shame from somewhere in the past that haunted the present." It was candid and clinical and articulate, considered and reexamined so many times and from so many angles that the analysis was a well-worn path.

"When marrying me was not the balm, he hunted for it socially and professionally, and that was doomed from the start. But you know about this stuff, Katrine," she said, "it's Psych 101." Woodcock knew about it, too, a doom loop to which he was susceptible in periods of boredom and melancholy. "He fabricated the obstacles he imagined," she continued, "to play out the self-fulfilling prophecy of low self-esteem." Apparently Harry was everywhere and anywhere but relegated to her past.

"I'm afraid you clinical types are getting ahead of me," Woodcock interjected. "This is all foreign ground to me. I haven't the slightest idea what you mean." She glanced at him skeptically, rightly questioning his sincerity. He was employing a tactic called *rescue me*, feigning ignorance on a subject she could explain to him in a way that would build her power and confidence in the relationship and so her desire to trust. And it worked.

"He believed there was an inner circle from which he was excluded," she continued unguarded, her eyes widening, the inner child resurgent.

"Who?" he inquired. He didn't mean to ask so tenderly and wondered if they noticed. It didn't seem to matter for there was something she needed to say, and proceeded without hesitation.

"I don't know. Titans of finance and industry? The harder he tried, the more futile his effort, just like Sysiphus," she said. It sounded like a pent-up confession, a long stifled embarrassment. "Oh, the usual sycophants and pretenders came around, leading him further astray, but the paradox made him a cliché: driven to succeed, undermined by success, the price of insatiable appetites. Eventually I got tired of explaining it to him." He heard the longing in her voice, the sound of heartache entombed in plain sight, like first love's letter in the front of a dusty scrapbook.

"Was it for pity, or fear, or money that you stayed with him?" he asked, bearing down.

"In a way, for a time, I suppose all of them, some of them, and then none of them, for a very long time now," she said, looking him sternly in the eye. They were promenading through the recesses of her soul, strangers separated by glass, and he saw Katrine shift self-consciously. She must be feeling like a voyeur, he thought, trapped between attracting forces, oppositely charged and inexorably entwined.

"He became one of those people who got what he wanted: clubs, houses, collections, secretaries, no material or carnal desire was beyond his grasp," she continued, covering well-worn and plainly unconquered ground. "The wanting never satisfied by having, and having begetting more wanting. And so it went," she recalled, "until the person you once knew is gone," she murmured, her thoughts trailing off like the hopeless last line of an epilogue.

"I don't suppose you have any inkling of what I'm talking about, Mr. Woodcock, do you?" she said as she recovered her bearings. "Not that it matters now, I suppose. He didn't interfere, and I had all the freedom and wherewithal to live my own life, to indulge my own convictions. The arrangement was convenient enough, wouldn't you agree, Mr. Woodcock?" The inner child was gone and she sounded acerbic and defensive, enough to make Katrine recoil.

"And what *are* your convictions?" he persisted, to which she simply rolled her eyes.

"I like taking care of people, Mr. Woodcock. And since I haven't children or a husband to mind, I tend to the unfortunate, do you see?" she replied, reasserting the gulf between them. He realized then they could scarcely be more different, her compassion the spiritual antithesis of his cruel dedication to purging the earth of depravity. He entertained a notion, as optimistic as it was brief, that they served the same God, she by healing and he by cleansing. He was washing the world clean of designs unimaginable to her compassion, and this helped him lose sight of their differences.

Chapter 12

Guthrie rose early. He had twice before tried and failed to drop in
unannounced on Rick LeBeau, who could have been summoned to
the stationhouse for questioning, or invited to meet at any number of
familiar venues. But Guthrie wanted to visit him in his own home,
where he would be comfortable and unprepared, and his answers
spontaneous and unrehearsed. Rick lived twenty-five miles east of
Poughkeepsie, in Highrock, a small knot of slumping single story
homes clustered around a small rural route crossroads with a stop
light, a gas station and a convenience store. He figured on arriving
early, before Rick left for work. A cold rain had just relented as the
Poughkeepsie city limits faded like a mirage in his rearview mirror.
A dense mist shrouded the silent woods bordering the narrow two-
lane road that wound its way east through the quilted patchwork of
wetlands and pastures and new-growth forests. The road was
bordered on both sides by meandering stone walls and decrepit
barbed wire fences, a testament to the hardy few still scratching a
living from the landscape. Outside Poughkeepsie, Dutchess County
subsisted on timber cutting, dairy farming, and caretaking for
wealthy second-homeowners from New York City, who sought
refuge on weekends in the unspoiled serenity of the Hudson Valley.

Rick had been the only witness to Achermann's death, and spent
the last two hours of Achermann's life by his side. Guthrie's
questions for him were routine: what did Achermann say in the
hours before his death? Did Rick see or hear anything in the woods
before the shooting? and after? Had he been a guide for Achermann
before? Guthrie was not in search of anything so specific as a lead or
a clue. Those would come. He was hunting for context, a feeling for
the scene in which to place a portrait of Achermann, a portrait that
would come into focus in the course of triangulating answers from
dozens of interviews he and his team would conduct with people
who knew Achermann better than Rick. There were easier, less
conspicuous places to stage a murder than Donner's Forge, which

fed Guthrie's confidence in a compelling motive for the location. For the time being he was just groping, playing pin the tail on the donkey.

He eased through the flashing red traffic light at the center of Highrock and slowed his car's descent into a small depression where the mist grew especially dense. Along the road a series of mailboxes stepped out of the mist, ghostly traces of civilization materializing in a deserted landscape. The number fifty-three reflected suddenly and dazzlingly in his headlights, the luminescing lenses of the old plastic numbers still as brilliant and clear as crown jewels. The mail box was especially distressed, askew on a knotted, cockeyed fence post. He steered into a rutted gravel drive that vanished through his headlights into the pall. The car rose and fell between balding ridges and flooded troughs, the hub caps spilling water as the chassis bottomed out. He traveled fifty yards before illuminating a modest single-story home floating like an optical illusion in the fog. Frenzied barking erupted from a chain-linked dog pen nestled to the right against a brooding silent forest that loomed over a neatly kept yard.

He was surprised to see three vehicles pulled up to the house, one of which he recognized by its dents. It was Dirk LeBeau's pick-up truck. A light from the back of the house bled through two glass panes in the top panel of the front door, and the blinds were pulled on the front facing windows. Guthrie checked his watch. It was almost 6:00 a.m., early by most measures, but not a surprising time to find men like the LeBeaus gathered around rural kitchen tables for fellowship and a grumble before heading out to work. He assumed the dogs and headlights had alerted the occupants to his arrival, and he strode to the front steps where he rapped on the door and waited in the moss accumulating in the loose mortar between the bricks. The front door was protected from the elements by a stamped metal storm door with thin glass panels that winced in the vacuum as the main door swung open. There stood Rick LeBeau in his heavy wool socks, coarse canvas work trousers, and a checked flannel shirt. The low rumble of his father's voice drifted on the dead air from the back of the house.

"Well, good morning, Detective," Rick hailed. "You're up early," he said with a smile as he stood aside to welcome Guthrie in.

"Sure didn't expect you. Care for a cup of coffee? Ron and Daddy are back there too."

"Don't mind if I do," he said, and proceeded down the narrow hall toward Dirk's voice and the light. He found himself on the threshold of a cramped, dated kitchen where Dirk and Ron LeBeau were hunched at a small table dressed in heavy camouflage pants and worn canvas work jackets.

"Morning, fellas, sorry to intrude," said Guthrie, taking three baby steps to the far side of the room so Rick could enter behind him.

"Why, Detective Guthrie, welcome," said Dirk pleasantly enough. Ron just stared in steely silence.

"Grab yourself a cup," Dirk ordered, taking command of the room.

"Thank you," said Guthrie as Rick pulled a discolored mug from a sagging cabinet and placed it by the thick black brew steeping on the hotplate.

"What can we do for you this fine morning?" Dirk inquired.

"Look boys, I don't mean to interrupt but I came to see Rick, and I can come back another time," he began, trading the element of surprise for disarming honesty. He saw Rick glance at his father, then his brother.

"You won't be in our way," Dirk assured him. "But it's up to Rick," he said. It sounded like a concession. "What time you have to be at work, boy?"

"I'm good, good for a while, Popps." Battle-hardened maybe, thought Guthrie, but no stomach for facing questions alone, and his father and brother had gotten the message. They visibly closed ranks around the table.

"Pull up a chair," Rick said.

"Thanks, boys," Guthrie replied, pouring himself a mug. The four men filled the room, their proximity destabilizing the air.

"I want to ask Rick a few questions about the last couple hours of Achermann's life," Guthrie explained.

"Don't mind us," Dirk replied. "Fire away."

"All right then," he started. "Let's begin with what you knew about Achermann before the morning he was killed."

"Nothin'," said Rick. "I didn't know nothin' about him."
Guthrie's peripheral vision caught the corner of Dirk's face, which

became furrowed and anxious the moment Rick spoke. Was it the natural response of a protective father, or was Rick lying, and Dirk knew it. He paused, waiting for Rick to say more, but he never got the chance.

"Nobody knew much about Achermann," Dirk interjected. "He was a new member. Shot a few times last fall, as a guest," Dirk snorted. Guests were outsiders, pretenders apparently. "He hadn't been around long." He seemed anxious to do his son's talking.

"Thank you, Dirk," said Guthrie.

"Like I said, I didn' know nuttin' …about Achermann," Rick repeated.

"No obvious friends or acquaintances among the members? Didn't come or go with anybody?"

"Don' know," Rick offered, "I jus' met him at the club house an' took him out. Never saw who he was with."

"And that was the first time you were his guide?"

"Yes sir," he replied. Dirk began to work at showing his impatience, staring maniacally at his hands which were clenched in a tight-fisted knot.

"And what did you talk about, on the way into the woods?" Guthrie persisted. Rick hesitated, to gather his thoughts.

"Not much of anything," he finally replied. "Maybe small talk, but nothin' special that I can remember, except what to do when we got on a bird." Guthrie produced a small dog-eared notepad and scratched something brief on it.

"Did you know where you were taking him?" Guthrie asked, "Where you planned to sit?" he specified, "before going out?" Rick shifted uncomfortably in the little kitchen chair. He didn't like the notepad, Guthrie could tell, and he glanced at his aspiring law enforcement agent brother.

"Detective Guthrie, sir," Ron interjected, "if my brother's a suspect he should have a lawyer, and if he isn't, he should know his rights. You're askin' him some pretty specific questions, aren't you?" He felt the room turn cold, his initial gambit foiled.

"I suppose that's right," he conceded, "and this isn't going strictly by the book, which we can do if that's your preference," Guthrie replied, "though I wonder," he speculated, "that you should risk the appearance of hiding something."

"We ain't got nothin' to hide," Dirk growled. "What do you wanna know? Jus' ask and we'll tell you."

"Thank you, Dirk," Guthrie acknowledged, "and you sing out, Ron, if I cross the line," Guthrie offered.

"Count on it, Detective Guthrie," Ron said.

Guthrie backtracked. "As a rule," he began, "beyond the general vicinity of each guide's assignment, would anyone have known, or been able to guess at where you would be sitting?" There was no diffusing the question, however he rephrased it. He knew by the way they shifted the answer was *yes*. After so many years stalking the same grounds together it stood to reason they knew each other's habits. He could imagine that hides and sweet spots were something of a preoccupation, as much as guns and dogs and possibly as much as women; a chance to brag and scheme and banter ad nauseam, which is why his question met with silence.

"Yeah," Rick finally said. "Most all of 'em coulda guessed at where we would set up. We know each other's spots. Everybody knows the places that pay." He saw Dirk's eyes narrow, and his sons ease back from the table as if they felt something coming that might catch him by surprise. Maybe Dirk objected to his casting about and widening the circle of suspicion. In any event, Dirk's brooding hostility looked ready to erupt.

"Did you want to add something, Dirk," Guthrie said, trying to sound amenable. Dirk heaved with restraint.

"Look Guthrie," Dirk began, his guttural voice trembling, "nobody here had nothin' to do with this, see? We ain't got no dog in the fight, see. We wanna help, an' we will help. But you sound like you're trying to put it on Rick, or maybe on one 'a the other guys, an' I ain't gonna let ya 'cause it ain't right, see? You wanna know about Achermann, we can tell you what we know, which ain't much. You wanna start trouble for my guides? That's a whole 'nother shootin' match," he said, his eyes turning bloodshot. "I know 'em good. None 'a them would care enough about a guy like Achermann to go to the trouble, see?" he continued, sucking the air from the room. Rick looked dazed and vulnerable while Ron sat sternly by, nodding with righteous affirmation for the long and principled arm of Dirk LeBeau law. Guthrie's reliance on spontaneity, for catching Rick off guard, had utterly failed.

And then, quite unexpectedly, he caught Dirk steal a glance past his left ear. There was something over his shoulder, a more blatant tell than he'd ever witnessed, something powerful enough to distract him from the moment. It lasted just an instant before Dirk glared at him again.

"Look boys," Guthrie began, talking like a family therapist, "we're going to ask a lot of questions, understand? And if it's like you say, nobody has anything to worry about. It's when you don't answer questions that I worry. That's the way it is. So you can talk to me now, and we can start ruling out suspects, or you can leave me wondering if you're all suspects. He rose to his feet, tipped the remnants of his mug down his throat, and placed it routinely in the sink behind his chair. It was a considerate gesture on its face, choreographed to inspect whatever diverted Dirk's attention.

On a bowed shelf suspended precariously over the sink he saw a photograph of the girl from the Mad Hatter, Kelley Sutton. She looked younger than he recalled, and radiant and reserved with a preternatural innocence like the pale light of dawn. Her youthful gleam matched a cheerful corsage she had used on a swirl of her ebony hair, and she was standing arm-in-arm with Rick LeBeau. He was young and awkward, his hair parted down the middle, and he looked uncomfortable in an ill-fitting tuxedo. There was no ignoring the contrast to the episode he had witnessed in the tavern, and he resisted the temptation to study the photograph longer. As soon as he turned the eyes of all three LeBeaus were on him.

"I'll be on my way," he said, "and I'd be grateful, Dirk, for you to send me a list of all the club staff and their addresses. We'll need to question everyone."

"Ah' course," Dirk replied. "Dey all live 'round here. Let me know when you wanna talk to 'em and I'll see dat dere available," he said, reminding Guthrie who called the shots.

"Actually, Dirk, we'll be contacting and meeting them on our own schedule."

In truth he admired Dirk's territoriality, his fealty to his staff. Governing documents and legal jurisdictions aside, Donner's Forge was his turf, these people his life-blood, and he ruled alone, a firm but benevolent dictator. Or was there more to Dirk's vigilance than protecting his people?

"I'll find my way out," Guthrie said excusing himself, and ambled away down the narrow hall. When he arrived outside the dawn had taken hold in earnest. The sun was scaling the foothills surrounding the valley, grazing the peaks and thinning the mist in the waking forest.

As he pulled away he glanced in his rear view mirror. There were the LeBeaus, standing shoulder-to-shoulder on the steps outside the front door. In their earth tones and camouflage they looked like partisan militia guarding a clandestine war council. He was leaving an untamed borderland, he thought, where natural law presided, and the justice he came to enforce was a fragile conceit. When he looked again the LeBeaus were gone, swallowed by a plume of mist that ushered him back to the road.

Perhaps he was quitting too soon. Instead of turning right in the direction of Highrock center and returning to Poughkeepsie as he had planned, he turned left in the direction of Donner's Forge. The club would be deserted so early on a week day and he should seize the opportunity to walk the grounds alone, at his own pace, and revisit the scene of the shooting. It might divulge something obvious and overlooked in the rush to get Achermann off the mountain, and in the frenzied search for the gunman that followed. He drove another three miles east on the winding two lane road, distracted by the landscape from decoding the gathering at Rick's kitchen table. Was it routine, a regularly scheduled event, or a meeting of graver significance? He hadn't come to implicate Rick, but the family's defensiveness could not be overlooked. The encounter had raised more questions than it answered.

He drove on in shadow along the southern border of the valley before navigating a long curve that brought the Donner's Forge farmhouse into view. It was sited on a low rise about a half mile north of the road, and he crossed the oncoming lane into a rough gravel track that fell before it rose to the right on its final approach to the club. He proceeded gingerly as much in respect of the stillness as fear of setting the car to rocking again. Sunlight clearing the peaks to the south vividly illuminated the foothills to the north making a fiery backdrop of the new foliage behind the farmhouse, the stark divide between sunlight and shadow moving across the slope like a stage curtain opening on the valley. He pictured the farmhouse in sunlight, resplendent in golds and oranges like a sanctuary on a hill, even though it remained in shadow, and it was through the persistent gloom that he saw a dim light smoldering from a window on the ground floor.

He pulled to the grass shoulder on the gravel track and cut the engine. The light he had spotted was flickering like a hurricane lantern, and he soon became aware of a figure passing back and forth in the window. It wasn't strictly procedure to sneak around spying like a peeping tom, but he had a premonition of discovery, of happening on something important, and he exited the car and moved toward the light in the window.

The gravel drive tracked north a hundred yards past a shallow, slow-moving brook before turning east up the rise to the farmhouse. It would lead him conveniently out of view from the window in which the figure was moving, before squaring on its final approach to the building. As he made the turn east he was relieved to find he could still see the light through the corner window of an adjacent room, though the light was now burning steadily, uninterrupted by the movements inside. As he closed on the house he heard the faint but familiar bars of a song on the radio, joined in mournful harmony by an accompanying voice, shattered intermittently by the clatter of cold metal cutlery thrown carelessly in a drawer.

He was standing still in the long shadows of a large maple near the house when a figure silhouetted by the filmy inside light appeared in the west-facing corner window. From where he was standing, below grade of the farmhouse, only the head and shoulders were visible above a vanity curtain masking the bottom half of the window. The silhouette appeared for just an instant, but long enough for him to see it was a woman, who lunged for something behind the curtain. For a moment he thought she had seen him, and she had ducked in surprise for cover. But then came the inglorious sounds of nausea, the violent heaves and soothing moans and quiet gasps coming in waves. The poor woman wasn't hiding, she was violently ill, and he felt guilty for spying on her suffering. She was distracted enough by her condition for him to make an unhurried withdrawal to the car, and it was not long before the rushing sound of a vacating privy carried over the trickle of the meandering brook and the mournful harmony of the woman's voice accompanied the radio again.

He had pulled off the shoulder and was half way up the drive to the farmhouse when headlights appeared in his mirrors. The raised vehicle behind him pulled to within inches of his rear fender, dousing the interior of his car with direct light as it tailed him to the parking area outside the building. He pulled to a measured stop as Dirk LeBeau roared up beside him and skidded his beaten-up truck to a halt. Guthrie was barely out of the car before Dirk leaned out his window and rumbled.

"Twice in one morning. What a nice surprise, Detective Guthrie."

"Well, I figured I was out here, it couldn't hurt to take another look around. That okay with you, Dirk?"

"You gotta warrant?" said Dirk. Guthrie loved that question. Standby vernacular among the general populace thanks to too many cop shows. He grinned and leaned toward Dirk over the roof of his car.

"You tell me I need one, Dirk, and I'll get it, and when I come back it will be in a way that you and your members won't like." He beamed as Dirk stared him down.

"Or, you can let me take a look around. Suit yourself."

Dirk's constitutional aversion to backing down weighed the merits of calling Guthrie's bluff, and Guthrie sincerely hoped he would so he could demonstrate this was no test of wills. He wanted to show he would have his way with or without cooperation.

"Yeah, all right," Dirk finally conceded, dismounting his truck. It winced under Dirk's shifting weight, springing back to center like a totter toy as Dirk landed on his feet.

"I guess we'll be seein' a lot of you 'til you get this thing solved, hunh?" Dirk remarked.

"You may not be that lucky, Dirk. I'm going to look around a little, and we're going to talk to a few folks. But we won't find the answer here. At best we might find a clue," Guthrie assured him. Dirk looked relieved.

"You mind if I use the john?" Guthrie asked.

"Sure. Follow me."

Dirk led the way through the front door of the farmhouse into an unassuming entryway lined left and right like a Hollywood jailhouse with gun racks. They made an odd pair, Guthrie thought, Dirk dressed in camouflage including a camouflage baseball cap that mashed the bristles of his scalp that were barely longer than the stubble of his beard; and he in his khaki overcoat, white button-down oxford and grey wool trousers.

Dirk turned right at the end of the entryway into a darkened doorway, flipping a switch on his way through. Warm, honeyed light poured from the adjoining room into the entryway. Before he could make the turn himself he heard the distinctive creak of a spring-loaded door from the far end of the room.

"Oh Dirk, thank goodness. I've been waiting for you," said the girl, in a way that could have been mistaken for intimacy. He followed uncomfortably on Dirk's heels. Standing at the far end of the room, where she had entered from the kitchen, stood Kelley Sutton. When he entered the room he caught her off guard and she reached for her throat in surprise.

"I'm sorry. I didn't realize you had company," she stuttered.

"Kelley, this is Detective Guthrie."

"Hello," she whispered.

"Please call me Wayne," he said, trying to put her at ease. "May I use your rest room?"

Moments later he was back in the parking lot trading his street shoes for a pair of lightly used boots. Dirk appeared in the doorway of the farmhouse, a fluorescent orange baseball cap rolled like a newspaper in one hand.

"Might oughtta wear this if you're going any distance," he instructed. "Ain't nobody supposed to be out there, but you never know," he said, rifling the hat through the air like a touchdown pass. "You know your way up to where they was at?" Dirk inquired, looking off in the direction of the hillside.

"I think so," Guthrie replied, feeling for the snub-nosed .38 he kept snapped in a holster on his belt.

"You're welcome to ride the Gator out to the hill. Key's in the ignition," Dirk offered.

"I think I'll walk. I like to walk," he replied, and started off in the direction of the hillside. He took a few steps and then wheeled like a weathervane on his heels.

"By the way," he began, "does she work here?"

"Yeah," Dirk said. "Since she were a kid."

"Thanks," he said and resumed course, descending over the lip of the parking area and into the field beyond. He was trying with passing success to organize his hair before putting on the orange hat when he wondered how visible he really wanted to be. The hat would make him easy to see, as easily seen by a ne'er do well as an over-zealous sportsman, but he put it on anyway, despite his misgivings.

The sound of his heavy boots trudging through the dew-soaked grass ignited impassioned protests from songbirds whose furious chatter echoed listlessly through the dense woods ahead. There was a vague and perfect balance in the valley, a balance he had felt before in the wilds of Dutchess County, an intangible harmony he found hard to ignore as he moved north into the sunlight from the swirling shadows lingering about the farmhouse.

The entrance to the trail that led to where Achermann was shot might once have been discrete, but the frantic movements of guides and emergency personnel on and off the mountain in the hours following the killing had left an apron of scarred and rutted earth around the mouth of the trail. If Rick and Achermann had been followed, all evidence of their pursuer had been lost, ground like chaff back into the soil by the heavy treads of boots and all-terrain vehicles.

He paused in the middle of the field to survey the sweep of the landscape. There was no alternate route to the crime scene, no obvious substitute for the path used by Rick and Achermann. The gunman must have traveled the same path, before or after the hunters, or possessed intimate knowledge of the territory and known where to find Achermann and Rick. To the right he saw a roadbed, lightly used judging by the healthy grass cover. It ran from the farmhouse across the edge of the field into a shallow gorge where two foothills intersected, before bearing right at the tree line, away from where he was standing near the trail.

With declining optimism for finding a clue on the trail, and his curiosity piqued by the road, he altered course to pick up the tree line where the road entered the wood. He followed it into the wood where it became a dirt lane that curved slowly away from the hillside before opening on a straight-away and vanishing over a tree-lined rise. He followed the road longer than necessary to conclude it would never lead back to his destination. Unrewarded persistence was an occupational hazard of thoroughness, a symptom of his obsession with procedure. When he finally turned around he faced the shady backside of the same low foothill where Achermann was shot. It was dark and steep, much steeper than the trail side, and far less densely forested, and there were great discolored expanses of exposed granite too sheer to scale easily on foot. Sparse stunted trees clung like fall leaves to the precipitous hillside, and they swayed in the light air like currents in a stream.

As he retraced his footsteps through the curve the field came back into view and he quickened his pace to rejoin the trail. And then, by the side of the lane, the outline of a boot print caught his eye. It was sufficiently immersed in standing water for the tread to have dissolved, but fresh enough in its outlines to be no more than a few days old. A dense and lively stand of saplings surrounded the roadside depression like herd animals at a watering hole. He abandoned the road and waded into the small trees, parting sprigs like the doors of a saloon until he found himself in an opening amid towering old-growth trees. There was a natural approach to a sheer granite slab where the forest floor ended abruptly, and the leaves at the base of the sheer rock wall were matted. There was no way to tell if they were heavily trafficked or compressed by snowpack that collected there in the winter, and he concluded the latter lacking evidence for the former. It was a dead end.

As he turned to retake the road, a beam of sunlight refracted from a film of moisture high above, a rivulet of ground water that had found its way by a seam to the surface. The water was weeping from high above the granite slab, like stoic tears in stony silence shed. There was barely enough flow to wet a modest channel that meandered down the rock face, and then it stopped inexplicably midstream before resuming a few feet to the left and continuing its journey to the forest floor.

He studied the reflection, perplexed by the water's path. The explanation had to be a ledge, imperceptible from where he stood. He approached the granite wall, standing close to survey its rough, lichen-encrusted contours. At exactly eye level a ledge materialized, barely a few inches wide at its origin, but widening comfortably as it rose and circumscribed the stone face, forming a smooth, spiral route across the granite wall. He took to the ledge and started to climb. He was soon atop the forest canopy with a spectacular view down the valley, and of the farmhouse at the end of the road emerging from the woods below. He rose quickly, impeded only by the thought of losing his footing. The incline of the ledge eventually moderated, giving way to scrub, and then to forest near the rounded peak of the mountain. He estimated the traverse of less than half a mile ought to put him in the vicinity of where Achermann was shot.

Down to the left was the field between the farmhouse and the mountain, which he kept in view as a point of reference as he moved west in the direction of the crime scene. He was halfway to his destination when he detected motion near the parking area. It was Dirk, departing the clubhouse, marching across the parking lot, and heading in the same direction in which he had himself embarked before diverting to the road into the woods. Dirk was moving with purpose, his arms and legs swinging like a staff sergeant as if gaining equal purchase in the air as on the land. Guthrie kept moving along the ridge, trying to match Dirk's pace. He assumed Dirk was coming to find him, and they would converge near the crime scene. He was soon dashing to keep up, gasping for air, and stumbling over rocks and fallen limbs. Surely Dirk's pace was unsustainable, especially climbing the mountain.

Dirk vanished near the opening to the trail at the tree line. The mountain peaked a hundred yards ahead, and he guessed it would be a short descent on the far side before he intercepted Dirk. When he crested the rise he found himself peering over a sun-dappled slope that the burgeoning canopy would soon eclipse. But for imposing stands of oak and maple and birch, he had an unobstructed view of the area cordoned off by yellow crime scene tape.

Dirk emerged from the logging road just beyond, arriving even sooner than Guthrie expected, and he set to pacing the perimeter of the tape, scanning the surroundings as he went. He eventually cocked his head and bellowed.

"Guthrie!" he roared from down the slope. Guthrie stood still.

"Guthrie!" Dirk thundered again. His voice carried through the wood, chased by an echo that ran eerily down the valley. Guthrie stepped from the shadows on the knoll.

"Up here!" he yelled back. Dirk turned on his heels and closed the ground between them in double-time. He was a practiced conqueror of the Donner's Forge topography, uncompromised by his proportions, and he reached Guthrie on the mount breathing easily.

"What brings you all the way up here?" Guthrie asked.

"You," Dirk replied. "Truth is, Guthrie, I don' have no problem with you lookin' round, see. I really don't. But we all got our bosses. Mine's the club president, and he don' want you here without a warrant. I'm sorry, but I gotta ask you to leave." Dirk wasn't trying to contain his delight.

"I wonder how he knew I was here?" Guthrie said, realizing that biting sarcasm had become an acquired taste since working with Jimmy Doolan.

"He called a few minutes ago. I told him you was here and he said for me to run you off. Come on, let's go."

"Okay, I'll go," said Guthrie. He took a last look up and down the ridge.

"You figure this is where the shot came from?"

"How do I know?" Dirk replied. "Coulda come from anywhere I s'pose."

"Well," Guthrie started, "not anywhere, if you think about how Rick said Achermann was sitting. He was shot from somewhere up here, or out there," Guthrie said, sweeping his arm across the slope. "Could someone have made that shot from up here, or is this too far away?" he asked, as if calling on Dirk for an expert opinion. Dirk studied the slope.

"This would 'a been perfect," he said looking in both directions. "Anywhere along here. Would 'a had to been a decent shot though." Guthrie scanned the surroundings.

"Is there another way on and off this mountain, Dirk, besides the way you came up?" Dirk looked confused.

"A' course. It ain't as easy as takin' de path, but I s'pose you could get up here any ol' way you want. Now come on Guthrie, let's go." He ignored Dirk's order and began walking the ridge where the slope rose up to meet it, studying the vantage points from trees, fallen logs and stone outcroppings.

"What do you think?" he posed. "Any place along here strike your fancy?" It was intentionally leading and he could feel Dirk's ire.

"This tree would cast a shadow, at sunrise I mean, wouldn't it," Guthrie observed, approaching a huge oak. He moved in close and took a bearing on the crime scene. Then he looked at the ground. The starburst of roots spreading from the base of the trunk clutched at the mountainside like muscular tentacles. The fallen leaves looked undisturbed, and the bark on the roots unblemished. He took a turn of the tree and that's when he noticed a small, fresh abrasion on the trunk about shoulder height. The new scar was between two and three inches in length and ran horizontally across the bark.

"What do you make of this?" he asked, peering at the trunk. He heard Dirk approach from behind until they were close enough to be standing in line. He peered over Guthrie's shoulder at the bark, his hot breath stirring the hair on Guthrie's temples; and then he reached around and brushed the indentation with his hand, which caused more bark to fall away, and left a deeper more distinct channel in the trunk, about two inches in height and four inches long.

"Would an animal have made that?" Guthrie asked. Dirk looked perplexed.

"Nope," he finally said. "Never seen a mark like dat," he concluded slightly bewildered. They stood in uneasy proximity, staring at the small puzzling gouge in the tree.

"That had to have been made by a person, it's too geometric, isn't it?" he asked Dirk, "and who else could it have been if not our shooter?" He rustled in his coat pocket and produced a disintegrating piece of yellow chalk. Then he squatted and etched a heavy "X" at the base of the tree, retracing his strokes to grind the chalk into the crusty, uneven bark.

"I guess I will get a warrant, Dirk. You leave me no choice," he added.

"You do what you gotta' do," Dirk replied. "Dat's all I'm doin'."

Guthrie backed away from the tree. He was all but certain he was standing in the very place from which the murderer took Achermann's life, and it never got easier, understanding how humans pulled the trigger on each other. Dirk was unphased, anxious to go. They descended the slope and rejoined the trail down the front of the mountain, avoiding more talk until they emerged from the trees at the edge of the field.

"It gives me no pleasure to ask you this, Dirk, but I have to," Guthrie began.

"Ask whatever you want, Detective."

"Do you think Rick was involved in this?" He studied Dirk's face.

"You sayin' you think he shot him through the neck at point-blank range?" Dirk said. It was contempt in his voice, for the messiness of the job, as if that alone disqualified his son.

"No," Guthrie replied, "I don't. I'm asking if he had a reason to collaborate in Achermann's murder?"

This time Dirk came alive, a menacing shadow lengthening beneath his occipital lobe, more pronounced than the natural scowl of his face in repose. His eyes flashed with anger like the muzzle of a gun. Now was the time to press him, to see what he might say.

"Is it out of the question?" Guthrie goaded.

"Yes," Dirk finally hissed. "It's outta da question."

"And why is that?" he persisted. "He's a decorated vet, isn't he? A sniper, right? He's killed people before," he pressed, "right?" Dirk stood still-life still, austere and immovable and cold like a monument in winter.

"I have to ask the question, Dirk. Sooner I have a good answer, sooner I can cross him off."

Dirk finally spoke, his words forming slowly, so low on the sound spectrum that Guthrie felt the words in his chest.

"You're as bad as da rest of them, Guthrie," he began. "Whatta you know about us? Sittin' in your easy chair in Poughkeepsie, pushin' papers around, playin' games with people's lives. My boy volunteered, put 'is life at risk. More than piss ants like Achermann ever done. Then they drag 'im into somethin' like this. I always told him, can't spen' too much time 'round shit 'fore some rubs off on ya," Dirk said.

"You didn't answer my question," Guthrie replied. "Why shouldn't Rick be a suspect?" Dirk was doing better than he expected keeping himself under control.

"Why?" he repeated.

"'Cause he ain't the kind," Dirk rumbled. "He don' go murderin' people, no matter how low," Dirk muttered. Guthrie studied him and saw nothing but venom. Finally he turned and moved in the direction of the farmhouse, speaking over his shoulder as he went.

"Didn't mean to make you angry, Dirk. I had to ask."

He had traded his boots for street shoes and was closing the trunk of his car when the farmhouse door slammed and he saw Dirk vanish inside. There was nothing disingenuous about Dirk, he thought. He wore his contempt with pride; and there was no mistaking his feelings, no reason to suspect deception, or the sort of insincerity he came to expect from people with something to hide. But Dirk knew something and it implicated his son, and he was behaving the way concerned parents do. The question he was weighing was the role of Dirk's anger, and whether it rose to having a motive of its own.

Chapter 13

Schiller realized he was skulking like Mr. Hyde as he emerged from
the front door of Coco's apartment townhouse. He was down the
path and through the gate in the iron railing before deciding his best
bet was the tube. South Kensington station was left, down Old
Church Street, across the Fulham Road, and directly past the old
Mini to which Coco had drawn his attention. It was a good excuse to
see if Coco were completely mad, and he felt his blood pressure rise
as he crossed the street a half block before the Fulham Road. It was a
frenzy of traffic as usual, and he stood for an eternity at the
crosswalk, the Mini in plain sight only a few parking spaces down
on Selwood Terrace. His heart was pounding, and his breath grew
short in the swirling fumes of the passing city buses. The pause in
traffic he was dreading materialized and he willed himself into the
street.

On the far side curb he was in plain view of the man in the Mini,
and he dared not steal a glance until he was close enough to see the
man's face. He was already regretting his curiosity when the report
of his footfalls on the cold slate sidewalk alerted the Mini's occupant
to his approach. Abreast of the Mini he met the man's stare. He
looked caged and heartless from the vehicle's confines, with ruthless
taught cheekbones and a Neolithic brow that quickened Schiller's
stride. By Onslow Gardens curiosity turned to fear that stayed with
him until he turned out of sight on the Old Brompton Road, and then
he crumpled with the exhilaration of escape. He stopped in a
doorway and fumbled for his cell phone. His fingers fluttered with so
much adrenalin that he abandoned the key pad for the recent calls
register, and mashed the only unattributed number on the list.

"Hello?" came the familiar British voice of the operator.

Schiller had been reporting to the CIA for a decade. His
unexceptional missives were condensed, he assumed, into subatomic
particles and packed like Carolina chickens in the crypts of
unremarkable buildings throughout northern Virginia, the places and

names, and dates and faces forever entombed, waiting on a wake-up call from an omniscient computer algorithm. He performed the duty without reward, the way the faithful observe the Sabbath, and he had doubted the relevance of his reports for years, until his call with Woodcock.

Everything had changed now. Things were getting crazy, over the top, he thought as he heard his call click through a series of digital switches.

"Woodcock?" he inquired when he thought he heard another party join the line.

"Yes?" The voice was crisp and calming and his panic eased.

"Schiller here." He tried not to sound rattled.

"Yes, yes, my good man, so glad you called," Woodcock crooned.

"Begging your pardon, sir, but this is no time to chat," he said. "Is Coco Stockton, the woman in the pictures, being followed?"

"Calm down," Woodcock replied. "Whatever do you mean?"

"Do you have her under surveillance? Did-you-send-someone-to-follow-her?" he said, enunciating as he went. He was tired of being treated like a moron.

"Don't be silly," Woodcock replied, "why on earth would we do that?" He waited, and in the silence the mystery solved itself. Coco had a stalker.

"This is not a nice looking guy, Woodcock, and he's been following her for twenty-four hours. Is she in danger?" He was scared and he couldn't hide it.

"Couldn't tell you I'm afraid, old chap. But let's not wait to find out, shall we?"

"I just left her apartment in Chelsea. This guy is in a car down the block," he said as Woodcock's last remark registered. "I'm turning around and going back."

"Slow-down old chap," Woodcock replied. "You don't want to alert this bloke and cause a drama, do you? Where are you now? I'll come to you."

"You're in London?"

"Yes, old boy. On my way in from the airport. Where are you?"

"Old Brompton Road, about three blocks from South Ken."

"Right. I'm about five minutes away, I should expect. How shall I recognize you?"

In moments a Teutonic black car with impenetrable windows swept to the curb in front of him. A voice came through a slit in the rear window. It was even more stilted than it sounded over the phone.

"Schiller, old boy, do get in, won't you?" He broke stride, reached for the door, and bundled himself ungraciously into the back. The car started moving again and the door thudded shut like a bank vault behind him.

"Where to, sir?" came the driver's voice through the insulated silence.

"Not sure yet, Harold. Let's find out. Hello, Schiller. Pleasure. I'm Woodcock, United States Homeland Security," he said with an ironic smile.

"Elliot Schiller, *Washington Post*. Good to see you, too. I don't suppose this is a coincidence."

"No, not really, I'm afraid," said Woodcock. "Now where can this Ms. Stockton be found?"

"Next left," he said as he felt himself sink into his contoured leather seat and the car accelerate like a fighter jet. Harold carved a smooth stirring turn on to Onslow Gardens and took the vehicle to terminal velocity before passing the parked Mini and its menacing occupant. Schiller pointed out the car just as Harold decelerated to a stop at the intersection with the Fulham Road.

"Don't look now, Gov," said Harold studying the passenger side rearview mirror, "but your man on stake-out has left his car and he's walking this way."

"Right," said Woodcock. "Schiller, call Ms. Stockton and tell her to collect her things promptly and come to the door. We shall be waiting for her." Coco answered her phone just as the man drew even with the car. The traffic across the intersection looked interminable as Schiller gave Coco her instructions.

"There he is," Schiller said after hanging up with Coco. The man was staring at the car and Schiller looked straight ahead to avoid eye contact. Woodcock leaned over his lap to get a good look.

"Don't worry, old boy. He can't see us in here."

The car shot across the Fulham Road without warning and on to Old Church Street, Woodcock's shoulder crunching Schiller's sternum.

"Sorry, old chap," Woodcock quipped. "Harold's quite an enthusiast, aren't you Harold?" The car glided to a stop in front of Coco's townhouse. She was already at the front door. He turned and peered through the rear window to see if the man was still moving in their direction.

"Jesus Christ!" Schiller exclaimed, "the guy's running!"

"He is, you know," Harold observed, looking in the rearview mirror. Schiller was stunned by how swiftly Woodcock left the car, leaving the back door ajar while he assumed a position on the sidewalk between the open car door and the wrought iron railing. He could see Coco from the car, frozen on the front steps. He could only imagine her panic – the ominous black car with tinted windows waiting at the curb, an unfamiliar man guarding the open door, and the man who had been following her sprinting towards her.

"Please get in the car, Ms. Stockton," he heard Woodcock say.

"Get in, Coco!" Schiller bellowed from the back seat. It was then that he saw the dagger in Woodcock's hand. It was a serrated model with more sharp angles than a lightning bolt, and he held it inverted to conceal it behind his wrist.

"Get in!" he barked again. Coco bounded for the car, her flailing shoulder bag and loose fitting overcoat threatening to entangle her and bring her to the ground. She dove headlong into the back seat and Woodcock slammed the door behind her, circling the rear of the car and joining Harold in the front seat before gauging the pursuer's advance in the passenger side mirror. The man had reversed course and was sprinting back across the Fulham Road toward the mini. Harold guided the sleek sedan into the street, the terror of the moment subsiding until Harold said, "He's following us, sir."

"Let's go in circles for a bit, Harold, test his resolve," Woodcock replied. The car accelerated again and commenced to weave through traffic. Schiller felt sick as Harold made sudden gravity defying turns.

"Elliot, what is going on?" Coco hissed. "Who are these people?" What could he say, where should he begin, he was asking himself as Woodcock produced a cell phone.

"Yes, hello, Beatrice? Woodcock here." Schiller felt Coco staring at him as he assiduously ignored her and peered out the window as another city block whizzed silently by.

"Oh yes, quite all right, thank you. Back in town for a few days. Yes, riding with Harold just now as a matter of fact."

"Riding?" Coco asked to no one in particular. "How about screaming or tearing or hurtling through traffic. Someone please tell me what the hell is going on!" He saw Harold smirk as she raised her voice.

"I say, could you be a dear and have Max intercept a chap following us?" Woodcock continued. "Bloody nuisance, really." Woodcock cupped the phone. "Explain in a minute, Ms Stockton."

"How the hell does he know my name?"

"He's in an old cream-colored Mini, plate number JGK 928K," he continued. "We're sort of driving in circles."

"I'll tell you when I can," Schiller finally said to Coco.

"Have him sit in the parking lot at the Serpentine," Woodcock continued, "and we'll bring him 'round....in about 10 minutes?" Woodcock paused, while Beatrice contacted Max, Schiller presumed.

"Jolly good," Woodcock said. "Thanks, Bea."

"He's quite determined, this chap," Harold reported.

"We'll know who this bloke is within the hour. Max won't take any guff," said Woodcock. "Apologies for the rushed introduction, Ms. Stockton. I'm Adam Woodcock, U.S. Department of Homeland Security, and this is Harold." Even in a high speed chase he sounded courtly.

"Ma'am," Harold acknowledged, touching the brim of his cap, and throwing the car with his free hand into a diving left turn.

"Thank you, guys," she blurted. "I don't know why you're here, but I'm glad you are."

We should do a story on agency drivers, Schiller thought, as his confidence in Harold grew. There was no letup in the invigorating pace. They raced through Hammersmith, up the King's Road, through Sloan Square, north to Knightsbridge, north on Park Lane, around Speaker's Corner and then west on Bayswater before turning left into Hyde Park. He was sure the overpowered black sedan would have quickly outpaced the Mini if there had been less traffic, but the Mini had the advantage in city gridlock and stayed disconcertingly close. It wasn't until Hyde Park that Harold extended his lead.

Schiller felt weightless as the car cleared a rise into a curve around the Serpentine, and Harold accelerated into the turn leaving the Serpentine parking lot behind. He saw an unusual vehicle idling there, a threatening looking British Army Land Rover with a large metal brush bar on the grill, and a retractable windshield riot screen perched on the roof. He had seen them before, but in Brixton, not Hyde Park. It seemed to idle forward before passing from view. An oncoming car came barreling out of the approaching turn and vanished as quickly as it appeared. The whoosh as it passed was followed by a pop and then a roar like nearby artillery. He felt the compression of the shock wave in the cabin and then a brutal metallic sound like a train crash.

"Bloody hell, Max," Harold murmured as he stopped at a red traffic light exiting the park. Woodcock adjusted his side mirror with a Q-tip sized joy stick, calmly eyeing the scene.

"Bloody hell," Woodcock repeated. "Will there be anything left of that poor sod to question?" Harold shook his head.

"Not likely," he said as the light turned green. "He pushed the mini straight into the oncoming traffic," said Harold as the car glided east like a bird of prey.

Schiller felt his body uncoil as the adrenaline saturating his nervous system dissipated, and he began to feel himself shake. Coco looked even worse, hunched over her knees in textbook airline crash position. And why wouldn't she. It was appalling premeditated violence the likes of which neither had ever seen. Not so, apparently, for Woodcock and Harold who were carrying on, a man and his driver. He didn't know quite what to do until Woodcock turned around and grasped the condition of his passengers.

"Sorry chaps," Woodcock said. "These things happen, I'm afraid," he reassured them. There was nothing to say. Coco looked in danger of vomiting.

"Look," Woodcock finally said, "I'm taking you back to your offices. It's been an upsetting start to the day, I know, but we need to discuss this fellow Achermann." Coco sat up and ran her hands through her hair like she was waking on a new day.

"There, there," said Woodcock addressing himself to her. "You're safe."

"Who is this clown?" she said to Schiller.

Schiller led them through the glass doors of the office, Coco and Woodcock following in single file. He was rattled, no hiding it, and he handled crisis as well as Lady Macbeth so his staff was certain to be suspicious. On his way past Coco's cubicle he spotted a careless tangle of orphaned network cables. The replica hard drive was already gone.

"Jesus Christ," he muttered beneath his breath without breaking stride, "this is getting out of control." He led Woodcock and Coco to the conference room adjoining his office, closed the door and feathered the blinds on the inside glass wall. The naturally prying eyes of the news organization just outside needed no encouragement.

"Do you want to tell me what is going on, Woodcock?" he demanded. Woodcock had already positioned himself by the window where he was studying the street below, looking in both directions. He ignored the question entirely.

"So you two know each other?" Coco concluded. Schiller in turn ignored her, and watched Woodcock shift his attention from the street to the windows in the building across the street.

"Ms. Stockton," Woodcock began without turning, "Would it interest you to know that your friend Achermann has been a person of interest to the United States for some time?" he inquired ceremonially.

"Please, Mr. whoever you are, until someone tells me what's going on, I don't give a damn. Really."

"Yes, my dear, but you will when he's connected to the next great act of terrorism, and your….what shall I call them….associations with him become a subject of scrutiny."

"How much does he know?" she barked at Schiller.

"Everything, I'm afraid," he replied.

"Thanks," she shot back. "So much for professional courtesy, Elliot."

"I'm sorry," he said. He was genuinely disappointed in himself. "Not as sorry as I am."

"Right," Woodcock intervened cheerfully, "Never you mind, Ms. Stockton. Achermann can't hurt you now, can he, and with your cooperation, nor will the source of the, emm, photographs," he added. "Perhaps you can start at the beginning, spare no detail, if you don't mind." Schiller leaned back and let her go. It was a relief to be out from in between.

Coco recounted her coverage of the price fixing case. The court case became the backdrop for the real story, she said, a serial exposé on the history of DeBeers. A company executive, a direct descendent of a founding family, had been unexpectedly obliging and supplied fascinating historical context, including details of the family intrigue that gave birth to the cartel. She was probably guilty of reporting the sanitized version of events, but it was great journalism and irresistible story-telling, if she didn't mind saying so herself. Readers loved it, hanging on every installment. "Circulation spiked, didn't it," she said to Schiller. He couldn't help but smile like a proud parent.

"Achermann was regrettable," she conceded, one of many colorful characters she encountered in Sam Dunkelsbuhler's circle, though none other so intimately as Harry, she added hastily. Sam tolerated Harry's company, but not easily, for there was something Harry wanted. Their parting was tense and Harry turned brooding and mean; but she remained on good terms with Sam, which seemed to keep Harry at a distance until he vanished altogether, about a year ago. It was only when Schiller produced the photographs that she became curious about him and discovered he was married to a doctor of some notoriety.

"So he was a scumbag. That's about par for me, as my boss can attest. But terrorist is new, murder victim, too. Both firsts for me."

"I'm glad to see you're taking this all in stride, Ms. Stockton."

"Speak for yourself, Mr......,"

"Woodcock. Adam Woodcock," he said.

"Woodcock? You're joking. Really?" Irrepressible as ever, thought Schiller, as she made the first dent in Woodcock's impermeable façade.

"I've told you what I know. Perhaps you can tell me how you and Elliot arrived at my door just as that hoodlum, who is now most likely dead, along with the other driver, came running down my street?" She looked back and forth between them.

"Should I assume the *Washington Post* is not only reporting to the general public, but to the U.S. intelligence community as well?" she inquired.

"Not the *Washington Post*, Coco, just me," he confessed.

"It's a valuable service, Ms. Stockton, and you may owe your life to it," Woodcock added.

"Coco," Schiller began, "you're hardly clean in this thing," he cautioned. "Getting involved with an associate of a source like Sam breaches every journalistic professional ethic in the book. That's why I sent you home. Pictures through my mail slot? That's way beyond bad judgment."

"Hmme," Woodcock affirmed unsolicited. "What do you suppose they were after?" he added.

"Who?" Coco replied.

"Quite," Woodcock answered. "Who took the pictures? Who delivered them? And what were they after?"

Chapter 14

"Do you suppose the intention was to blackmail Achermann?" she suggested, "to extract information, or obtain a commitment in exchange for concealing his adultery?"

"I doubt it," Woodcock countered. "Achermann was already dead. He wasn't much good for anything by the time the pictures were delivered. No, I'm all but certain that, you, Ms. Stockton, are the target. You know something. Or someone is afraid you know something, possibly something you learned from Mr. Achermann." She looked at her boss disconcertingly. He had drawn the same conclusion in her apartment that morning and the consensus was unnerving.

"Make no mistake, Ms. Stockton," Woodcock persevered, "the photos are a threat from someone who has already killed."

"For Chrissake!" Schiller exclaimed, gulping air by the window like a goldfish. "You mean you knew all along Achermann was murdered?"

"Well, yes, sort of…" Woodcock replied. "My good man," he finally continued "you didn't really think it was an accident, did you?"

"You mean the hunting accident," she confirmed.

"Yes, quite," Woodcock replied.

Schiller began to pace, muttering to himself like a madman.

"So is now a good time to tell you the computer you exchanged for Coco's is already gone?" Schiller said, taking her by surprise. Suddenly she felt naked, like a shorn lamb.

"Oh, jolly good," said Woodcock. "Let's see where it went. Maybe that will give us a clue." Woodcock reached for his cell phone and was speaking distractedly with "Bea" about activating a GPS something-or-other when she finally gathered herself enough to think clearly about what Woodcock said. It was unlikely she missed an indiscretion by Harry that was important enough to silence her. Were Achermann British or South African it was possible, with all their nuanced, backward syntax. But he was American, in all his blunt vulgarity, and rough and ready vitality. These were the familiar qualities about him that she liked, an island of self-centered American illustriousness in a sea of affectations and false modesty.

The allure of common customs was strong so far from home, even the shared conventions of language seductive as siren songs. These were the risks of forsaking one's roots, of leaving the people and places one knew, and venturing forth in foreign lands to dabble in strange customs. She was drawn like so many young singles to the novelties of expatriate life - conceits that excite the senses and shipwreck the soul, making her easy pickings for men like Achermann. But he was nothing, a reminiscence, a taste of home, and a disappointing one at that, whose single-minded interest barely tolerated her curiosity. He never disclosed his marriage and never engaged in shop talk, which left her reasonably certain she knew nothing of significance about him: but someone disagreed, or so thought Schiller and Woodcock.

If Harry's murder, the photographs, and her exposé were connected the first place to look was her reference materials and notes.

"I'm getting some files," she announced over her shoulder as she bolted through the conference room door. Woodcock was hanging up with Bea as she returned clutching a large neat stack of paper laden folders.

"I don't suppose I should be surprised that someone has been through my files," she observed, dumping the stack like a brick layer. "The one thing that stands out right away," she said to Woodcock, "is the settlement."

"What settlement?" asked Woodcock. She summarized the news Schiller brought her that morning.

"It's not just anticlimactic," she concluded, "it's conspicuous. So sudden, such a small amount of money, and for no reason. Nothing had changed, no new evidence, no reason for either side to settle."

"Have you heard of a place called Namaqueland?" Woodcock posed. She looked at her boss again. He had achieved a new milestone in the art of looking confused.

"Gosh," she remarked, "that does ring a bell." She spread the stack of files like a card dealer across the table and chose one.

"It's in northwestern South Africa, near the border with Namibia," Woodcock prompted. "Home to an indigenous people known as the Nama, not too surprisingly, I suppose."

"Yes, of course," she said. "Remember, Elliot? The beach covered in diamonds I was telling you about."

Woodcock approached the table across from her and leaned forward, spreading his fingers in conical frames to support his weight. He peered at the file in her hands and then looked up into her eyes.

"Do tell," he said. He was standing close, despite the table between them.

"Another colorful chapter in the story of tightening the noose on the South African diamond industry," she said, a bit too familiarly she supposed, but he seemed to be dropping the formalities.

"And what happened in Namaqueland?" Woodcock persisted.

"The Orange River runs down from the coastal plateau through Namaqueland. For centuries, maybe eons, it carried diamonds, and deposited them into the sea at the mouth of the river where the surf washed them ashore," she said, enjoying the power of her knowledge and the rapt attention of her audience. "Oppenheimer used local political influence to have the beach expropriated by South African troops, and traded to his Consolidated Diamond Mines. But that was a long time ago. Namaqueland has been in the news more recently," she said, letting a leaf of her tousled blond hair fall across her face.

"I just can't remember why," she said as she spread a sheaf of newspaper clippings from the file across the table.

"Yes," she said, selecting a ragged strip of newsprint. "Here it is," and she read aloud.

The Guardian –

London, October 15th 2003. Johannesburg. A South African tribal community robbed of its land in the 19th century yesterday won a court battle to regain land and mineral rights to diamonds that could be worth billions of pounds.

"Jesus Christ," Schiller interjected. She saw him turn back the years by pulling on his hair, which flattened the wrinkles in his forehead. She continued to read:

The Nama community in Richtersveld are former goat herders who today mostly live in tin shacks without electricity. The Constitutional Court in Johannesburg ruled that the Nama had been cleared from their land under racist laws and had a legitimate claim to ownership – including the mineral rights to the lucrative diamond mines at Alexander Bay on the northwest coast.

She paused, returning Woodcock's gaze.

"Whatever possessed you to inquire about Namaqueland?" she asked. He stepped back from the table.

"Tell you in a minute," he replied. "You know as much as anybody about the modern day DeBeers, don't you, Coco," he said, dropping her surname for the first time.

"Will this verdict affect the company?" There was intimacy in his voice and it caught her off guard, one old friend to another, but more, attracted to her to no surprise, but it disturbed her to think about why.

"Hard to say," she replied, gauging his attentions.

"Let me ask it another way," he countered. "Assuming Namaqueland could become a competitive source of diamonds, how would you expect DeBeers to react?" There it was again, the softening tone, the sympathetic redirect, like a teacher encouraging a student.

"I don't know," she said.

"Did Achermann ever mention Namaqueland to you?" he persisted gently.

"No, he never did," she replied, faintly aware of the flush on her neck. He was casting some kind of spell, and she distracted herself by reading the conclusion to the article.

The Nama lost ownership of their land when the Cape Colony annexed the area in 1847. When alluvial diamonds were found in the 1920s the government cleared the community from around 85,000 hectares (210,000 acres) around the Orange River...

"Alluvial?" Woodcock interrupted.

"Yes, the most prized," Coco replied with a concocted smile. "Refers to the alluvial plain at the base of a river where they settle. Only the biggest diamonds make it that far, and they get polished along the way, too, making them easy to pick out from the loose gravel in the sediment. No mining required, at least there didn't used to be. You just sifted the sand and picked them out. Now they use earthmovers the size of buildings to gather the sand for sifting."

"There must be a lot left," Woodcock murmured. She studied him from a distance and cocked her head just enough to loose another tress of hair, which fell like a veil across her eyes.

"I don't suppose the Nama would have sued if there weren't," she acknowledged.

"Quite."

"So you discovered after the fact that Achermann was married, did you?" It was a rotten, gratuitous question, she thought, contrary to the spirit in which she was helping him, and proof he was drawn to her. Another disillusioned romantic, vulnerable to the conquests of his predecessors.

"Yes, after the fact," she emphasized.

"You're a nosy journalist," he began, "what did you discover about his wife?"

"It's not the sort of thing you want to know more about once you discover it," she replied.

"Pardon my persistence," he said, "but after Achermann vanished, and you learned about his wife, did you ever discuss her with your source at DeBeers, this fellow Sam?" It was such a specific question about such a peripheral figure that it raised her suspicions immediately. Schiller appeared to dial in, too.

"Why?" he demanded from the end of the table.

"Well," Woodcock started, turning on his heels, "and this is, as you journalists like to say, strictly off the record, I just came from visiting her at the Center for Disease Control in Atlanta. She's in quarantine. Quite likely very sick with an Ebola infection she picked up last week, in Namaqueland, of all places. And not any Ebola virus, mind you, an exact match…"

"…to the one our U.S. edition reported missing," Schiller interjected. "Jesus Christ!" he exclaimed again. "Where does this end?"

"Now then, you're sure Sam never mentioned someone named Dr. Astrid Taylor or Dr. Achermann?"

"Yes. I'm quite sure. He barely knew Harry and didn't like him. Probably didn't even know he had a wife, like me." Woodcock continued to pace.

"It's quite a coincidence, don't you think," he said in that self-important Socratic style that was downright annoying, "that you, Coco, should have come across Achermann through this fellow Sam, and that Achermann's wife just came from Namaqueland where an indigenous tribe just won vast mineral rights denied them a century ago by a government sympathetic to Sam's progenitors. The world is small, I grant you," Woodcock noted, "but is it that small?"

She began to feel the shape of Woodcock's suspicion, to see why he thought the people and places fit neatly together. Had Achermann schemed with Sam to keep the diamonds from Namaqueland off the market? It was an appalling scheme and sadly consistent with the age old allegations about the company's unscrupulous practices. If he were right then Schiller was, too, and she had been played. Sam had scored a public relations coup on the pages of the *Washington Post* while plumbing new depths of moral depravity to keep a fresh source of diamonds off the market.

"Knowing what you know now, do you see the association between Achermann and Sam in a different light?" Woodcock said.

"I wish I did," she murmured, "but the truth is I never knew anything about their association. If it's what I think you suspect, I'm an even bigger fool than I thought, and Sam had a very good reason to be clearing the company name in the court of world opinion. But none of that explains the settlement in the U.S. case," she concluded.

"Why would Sam want to intimidate you, Coco?" Woodcock inquired warily.

"You mean, am I hiding something? Have they succeeded in intimidating me?"

"Sort of, yes," Woodcock conceded.

"No. The exposé is over, published, no more installments, unless, I suppose, all this changes that and we feel compelled to correct the record," she floated, looking at Schiller.

"Very well, then," said Woodcock. "Does the settlement, or Harry's murder, or the presence of a bio-warfare agent among the Nama change that?"

She wasn't sure and she began piecing together a process for redeeming herself and the paper's reputation. Substantiating

Woodcock's suspicions required digging deeply into Harry's life, a job for which she was ill-suited, conflicted in a strictly journalistic sense; and understanding the cross-currents leading to the settlement, required access to the legal teams, and to the judge, if he would talk. She would also be turning on Sam. Reversing the exposé's sympathetic view of the company was risky. There would be allegations of sour grapes for the paper's gullibility, for its incompetence.

"I should have thought you could well predict the cartel's reaction to this new source of diamonds worth '*billions of pounds*,'" Woodcock added, "given everything you know."

She barely heard him, off in another world, to plan her professional comeback, when Woodcock's cell phone chimed.

"Oh hello, Bea. Yes, go ahead…Oh bloody hell. Well that's bloody inconvenient isn't it? Yes. Please have him give me a ring. Yes, thanks. Tah."

He slipped the phone back in his pocket. "You won't have to worry about being followed by that bloke anymore," he reported. "Not expected to survive, I'm afraid. Max can go too far sometimes. Problem now is the one person who might have told us something is gone, or soon will be. Bloody shame."

"Jesus Christ," Schiller whispered. "Will there be more where he came from?" he asked.

"Coco," Woodcock began, jolting her back from the rescue of her professional demise, "can you get me a meeting with Sam? Make it sound like one of your routine get-togethers, and I shall turn up instead of you?"

Chapter 15

D'Amato stood by the second floor window of Poughkeepsie police headquarters like a teenager waiting for a ride. He wasn't excited about his assignment, but he accepted it willingly because he was a good soldier. Guthrie had asked him to question a lifelong friend, a person with whom he shared all the raptures and embarrassments of youth in a close-knit community that kept no secrets. D'Amato and Kelley Sutton met in primary school. She was his first true confidant of the opposite sex, and she remained an unfailing friend. Their physical appearances diverged so strikingly in adolescence that it couldn't have been easy. Kelley's nubile, Ivory-soap allure became as irresistible to men as it was galling to women, while D'Amato grew large and awkward and oily like a bottom fish. Kelley never forsook their friendship, even in high school, when she was voted most popular three years running and became captain of the football cheerleading squad. As D'Amato and Rick and Ron LeBeau took to the gridiron on crisp fall Saturday afternoons, she and her squad poured their hearts into the sparse but unflagging crowd that came to root for the Pioneers. When she fell for his best friend, Rick LeBeau, she stayed true to their friendship, affording no less time for his confidences. They were to their classmates one of those inseparable trios where the lines between friendship and intimacy were never clear to the outsider.

When D'Amato called Kelley to suggest they meet she never hesitated, as old friends don't. He said upfront it was "police work." She was a long-time employee of Donner's Forge, present on the morning of the shooting, and he needed to ask her some questions. She could talk to him or another officer. The choice was hers.

She was right on time, her aging, oxidized sedan creaking to a halt at the station steps below the window, a torrent of her ebony hair glistening on her shoulders in the afternoon sun.

"Go on, Tomato," he heard Guthrie say.

"Yeah, boss," The Tomato replied with resignation. "This is jus' routine, right? She's not gonna know nothin' right?" He swung by his desk to collect his jacket before exiting to the landing, and loping down the stairs in heavy unenthusiastic strides.

It was an uncomfortable feeling, knowing Guthrie was using his friendship to develop a picture of the inner-workings of Donner's Forge. He just hoped she had nothing to hide.

"Hey, Frankie," she chortled as he descended the station steps.

"Hey Kel," he droned. He walked around to the passenger door, climbed in, and was barely in his seat before she gunned the engine and the car lurched ahead. She accelerated across the parking lot and veered in a jolting clatter on to the street beyond. Kelley was a study in sound and fury, but she was all bark and no bite. That's what he liked about her. She was never the risk-taker she pretended or wanted to be, which was easy to see by how she stopped on amber at the first traffic light when he would have gunned it through the intersection.

He noticed a twitchy, cornered-squirrel energy about her that subsided without warning into uncharacteristic reserve. She looked older, too, and perhaps a bit heavier, though it was hard to tell from her thick wool sweater. Perhaps it was the sweater that made her look frumpy. She had never worn anything like it.

"How you been, Frankie?" she asked.

"Yeah, okay," he said.

"Work still good?"

"Yeah, yeah, you know, de same," he said as the light turned green. "How 'bout you?"

"Weird," she said. D'Amato felt uncomfortable. To the extent he ever had a plan for questioning it relied on small talk, patience, and a good deal of reassurance. Thoughts and feelings came easily when people were comfortable and calm.

"Where we goin'?" he asked.

"I don' know. Where you wanna go?"

"It don't matter. We could drive 'round a while, go for a beer, whatevah you want," he suggested. They drove an aimless route through Poughkeepsie, drifting like castaways, trading immaterial gossip about friends and classmates, and reminiscing as they passed old haunts. She seemed grateful for his company, and relieved.

"Your family good?" he asked.

"Yeah, they're good," she replied. "Mom and Dad still don' talk, but that's good, right?"

"Sorry," he said. "You still go huntin' with your old man? You wasn't too bad a shot back in the day."

"You mean for a *girl*," she replied. "Yeah, we went last fall, I got a six-pointer. It was a long shot, too," she said proudly, "what about you?"

"Nah, I ain't been anywhere with anything but this pea shooter," he said placing his hand on the cover flap of his holster, "'cept the police shooting range… Hey, I gotta an idea. Let's go to the park. We could walk over the bridge and watch the sun go down."

"Jus' like old times?" she said nostalgically. He always liked it when she made fun of him.

"Yeah, jus' like old times."

Kelley changed course, steering the decrepit car toward the Franklin D. Roosevelt Mid-Hudson suspension bridge, a diminished but more elegant cousin of the famous George Washington Bridge downstream. The bridge linked Poughkeepsie to Highland on the west side of the Hudson River, and their destination was Kaal Rock Park, an unremarkable but tranquil sanctuary with a slightly urban feel, lying in the shadow of the span connecting Poughkeepsie to the east suspension tower of the bridge. They were once among the city's youth who prized it for parking and partying after dark, and until it lay in shadow beneath the western hills they could watch the river collide with the massive foundations of the suspension towers. The strife in the shadows of the bridge was a spectacle of untamed forces attracting poets and deviants and alike.

Kelley pulled to a stop in a parking lot facing the river, the chipped and smoky windshield filtering the receding sunlight like a frosty window. A large boulder separating the car from a scruffy patch of grass between the lot and the river was one of a dozen forming a man-made barrier to keep vehicles from finding their way into the river. They sat in silence, humbled by the expanse of water rolling by. The remnants of a rusty chain-link fence on the riverbank had been all but consumed by dense thickets of scrub, and the water welled up along the shoreline in turbid plumes, debris and flotsam circling in endless whirlpools while the current offshore rushed impatiently downstream.

"So what do you want to know?" Kelley started, sounding like the confidante he remembered.

"Kel..." he began, "we're wonderin' if this guy Achermann could'a been murdered?"

"I'd say he *was* murdered," she said, "wouldn't you say?" For a moment he wasn't sure if she was teasing him again.

"Oh, I get it. Funny Kel. No. I mean a planned murder, not an accident de way it was reported," he said. She gave him a strange sort of look, vacant and indifferent. "Rick was the last guy to see him alive," he continued, "and they was alone for some time before Achermann was shot. So if it wasn't an accident, everything's gonna start with Rick." She sat perfectly still, staring at him blankly, like he was talking about the weather.

"Why don't you ask him?" she finally replied.

"We will, but I'm asking you. You don't have to say nothin' if you don't want to, but you know him better than anybody. It makes no sense that Rick would be mixed up in a thing like this, but I gotta ask. Did he have anything against Achermann?" He had never seen her so utterly still. It was eerie. She looked like a wax statue, her color, vitality, life energy drained like a riverbed parched by drought.

"Let's walk," she finally said, driving her shoulder hard into the car door.

It was cold, a trace of winter in the air, as they strolled toward the footpath from the park through the ramparts anchoring the suspension cables. The alchemy of sun and cool river vapor released a musty torpid odor that reminded him of summer, and teenage rendezvous in the park.

"I really don't know, Frankie. We haven't been seeing each other for months now. Things haven't been so good between us," she confided.

"Awe, come on Kel. Not again. When are you guys gonna stop? You been doin' this forevah."

"No, Frankie, it's different this time." He had heard her say it before, but never with such defeat. She sounded like a stranger speaking in a familiar voice. They walked into the shadows of the ramparts bracing themselves against the chill, and he thrust his hands deep in his pockets. He felt her fingers, slender and determined, probe for an opening at his elbow, and she slid her arm through his.

The path turned slowly to the right, into a dark stone tunnel beneath the ramparts and he glimpsed her desperation before shadow obscured her face. She was about to tell him something. The tunnel walls were damp, streaked and stained by petrified webs of glistening calcium and road salt. They drew closer in the cold tunnel air and her arm relaxed, and the turmoil passed.

"Okay," he finally said, "let's talk about Achermann. What do you know about him?" The opening at the end of the tunnel was coming into view, a brilliant beam of sunlight cutting a geometric shadow across the path and up the furrowed stone face of the adjoining tunnel wall. A draft of warm air reached them as they emerged into the sunlight, and followed the path through a steep incline that landed them on the deck of the span. She had withdrawn again by the time they reached the walkway high above the river. The traffic stirred the afternoon air, a strange and misplaced manmade chaos amidst muted sunset hillside splendor and swirling silent water below. They walked west across the bridge into the raging scarlet sky and she gulped the evening air, taking it in like a fortifying elixir before letting go his arm and recounting events of last winter.

She met Achermann for the first time working the New Year's Eve party at Donner's Forge. It was not an especially lively affair, a dozen or so couples to whom she served cocktails and hors d'oeuvres, a staid, formal dinner, and after-dinner drinks. The older set retired upstairs before midnight, while the next generation stoked their buoyant spirits with cigars and brandy, becoming raucous and familiar, even randy in a way she found heartening, a welcome change from the usual formality of relations between the members. She had been on her feet all evening by the time the hard core revelers came to roost around a blistering fire just before midnight. They had moved an ancient television from an adjoining room to a small table beside the imposing stone fireplace, which they monitored periodically between hunting stories and tall tales of scandal and intrigue. A fully extended set of drooping rabbit ears strained to capture fuzzy images of Times Square that faded in and out on the intermittent signal bouncing down the valley walls, boosted from Poughkeepsie.

Despite her amusement at the divergence of wardrobe between first wives, and second wives and girlfriends, underneath it all she felt a sympathetic kinship, especially with the younger women who could just as easily run with the crowd that frequented the Mad Hatter, she supposed.

"A few pops with friends, and we're all the same," she told D'Amato, "and you can bet the old timers would `a been right there with `em if they'd left their Betties at home," she snorted mischievously, but something in the pleasure of her recollection rang hollow.

One of the women had become flirtatious and uncomfortably forward, which aroused and incited the whole gathering. The woman divided her attentions evenly between her companion and Achermann, the only man to come stag. The atmosphere grew tense, even combustible, "like there was gonna be a fight," she said.

Achermann had showed interest in her early in the evening, engaging her in small talk while she served the party-goers dinner, and leering at her as she moved between the kitchen and the dining room. She was practiced at deflecting unwanted attention, and she handled him politely, with professional distance. Approaching midnight, the senior member and his wife encouraged her to abandon the kitchen and join the nighthawks around the fire, and Dorris Farragut, the dour cook, released her from dish duty to join the party. It was the sort of invitation she would have been disrespectful to decline, and Achermann wasn't taking the hint.

"I thought he kept after me to get the other one off his back," she said, "and I just ignored him. Some of the others I probably served a thousand times, and they were being so nice. And you know what Frankie? I just never thought.... I never saw it coming." She grew tense and confused as she tried to remember what happened after midnight, sounding detached and unresolved, like an unconsenting visitor to a stranger's nightmare.

The party carried on, she wasn't sure how long, and she withdrew to the kitchen when she realized she was drunk. She vaguely remembered speaking to Dorris, who had closed the kitchen and was on her way out. It was saying Doris' name that sent her into a trance, and she became somber and brooding like a sorceress conjuring a spell. He had followed her into the kitchen, he was not to be deterred, and she wished she had screamed. But she was embarrassed, or scared, or maybe he had threatened to hurt her.

"Anyway, who would believe me? I'm just the washer girl," she said, stoic as an undertaker. She was fearless, he thought, as his emotions towered like a thunderhead, and his temples throbbed, and his vision narrowed, and adrenaline marinated his nervous system.

"You mean he raped…" he began, but she reached with her fingers and stilled his lips, and a glistening tear sparkled in the sun on her cheek. He thought he was ready for the worst, to hear one friend implicate another, but never this. It cost him what little impartiality he had left. Good riddance to Harry Achermann and God bless his murderer. Guthrie was wrong to have him question a friend.

"I thought it would go away, Frankie. I thought I could make it go away, but it's never going away, Frankie," she said.

"Why didn't you tell nobody, Kel?" he implored.

"I didn't need to. Dorris took care of that. Who knows what she heard or saw, but next thing I know Rick wants me dead. Only Big Dirk keeps him from giving me trouble."

They walked on in silence the sun low in the west, shimmering on the upwellings in the coursing current below. She stopped at the center where the cables licked the span and parted with purpose in opposite directions. With her back to the guardrail and him by her side she closed her eyes and faced the sun. The light seemed to revitalize her blameless unblemished beauty, and to paint her swollen figure in a fiery, glazed-apple ruby red mantle. He leaned beside her and gazed downstream, as they had countless times before, the sun and the hills and the water converging on a hazy vanishing point near Newburgh, and they stood there in silence until she turned to look upstream. He saw her stare at the vast creeping silence as it flowed from the deepening darkness in the north.

"Frankie," she said, peering over the rail. "You ever think of jumping?"

"No, never," he replied. "And you ain't gonna either. Dat bastard is dead now. You got nothin' to worry about from him no more." The next time he looked there were tears in the shadows of her contorted cheeks. She forced a lifeless smile from her desperate eyes, which spoke like a wounded animal inarticulately of suffering.

"What else, Kel?" he asked. A gentle breeze laid a wisp of her hair on the moist outcropping of her chin.

"Are you in trouble, Kel?" he finally asked. She reached for his hand and dipped her chin, and nodded with ghastly restraint.

"Jesus, God and Mother Mary," he whispered, turning beside her away from the light. He cradled her hand, with new appreciation for the abyss, pulled her back from the rail, and led her quietly off the bridge. Again they walked in silence, more than ever unwilling conspirators.

They reached the ramparts, turned off the bridge, and descended into Kaal Rock Park as the western foothills eclipsed the sun. He felt chilled and exposed by the time they reached the car, where they sat in the darkness, their breath condensing on the air.

"Kel," he began, "I gotta ask you a few more questions."

"I know, Frankie," she said, breathing and wiping her cheekbones clean.

"It's the only way, you understand?" he explained. He imagined her nodding in the darkness.

"The way it looks right now, Rick's the prime suspect, unless there's more than meets de eye, Kel. Ya see?" He waited in silence.

"I'm ready," she finally said.

"Okay, then," he acknowledged, vowing never again to mix friendship and police work.

"So, at the New Year's Eve party, did Achermann piss off the guy wit' de bimbo?" he started, broadening the search for Achermann's enemies.

"Enough to shoot him five months later?" she replied. "She didn't get him in the end, did she?" Kelley snuffled.

"Yeah," he conceded, seeing the weakness to his angle. "And nothin' else was weird?" he asked, "outta the ordinary, like."

"I don' know, Frankie. We were just having fun 'til things got bad, and now it's all mixed up, and I'm trying to forget."

"Yeah," he said again.

"Except now you ask, he sat next to Whitaker, at dinner I mean," she recalled.

"Who? Achermann?" he asked trying not to sound bewildered.

"Yes."

"So what?"

"So it's sort of against the rules," she said.

"They have rules about where you sit?"

"Well, not really rules, but they're supposed to sit by seniority. Whitaker is senior, Achermann was new."

"Maybe Achermann didn't know," he suggested.

"Yeah, maybe. It was noticeable, that's all. You asked if anything was weird," she replied, sounding prissy. Nothing else she could remember stood out.

"So what happened the morning Achermann was killed?" he continued. She arrived, she said, as she always did for turkey hunts, about 3:00 a.m., to lay out breakfast and feed the guides. The food was out and she was back in the kitchen by the time the Guns came down.

"And what did you do after they went out?"

"What I always do. I slept in my car. I can usually catch an hour or two before anyone comes back for coffee." He wished she had a better answer.

"Did anyone see you in your car, Kel'? …Can anyone place you there, in your car, while you was sleepin'?" he asked.

"No. Who would see me there?" she said. It took her a moment but he saw her read his mind – that reconstituting love by avenging her defiler was a legitimate if not honorable motive.

"You think *I* could have done it?" she asked, "Frankie!" He felt it tear, their invisible seam, frayed and patched, and stitched and repaired through the ignoble travails of youth. All at once it was clear, beyond a reasonable doubt, that she was the more perfect suspect - in the right place at the right time, with the motive and the skills, and no alibi.

"I didn't do it," she said. "I wish I had, but I didn't. He would have died slower if I had," she said gruesomely.

"Who was de first person to see you aftah you went to the cah?" he resumed.

"It was Dirk," she replied. "He drove right past me in the Gator and woke me up. It must have just happened. He was hurrying. A couple of guides were right behind him in their trucks. They kept going, drove across the circle, into the field and straight to the base of the mountain. I knew something was wrong."

"How do you know he saw you?"

"Because he pulled up to the house and came out with the med kit when I got to the door to find out what was going on. There was a whistle blowing, up on the mountain. He told me to stay inside and listen to the walkie-talkie at the desk. I was the one who called 911 after Ron radioed someone was shot."

"Was Ron the first person to get to Rick?"

"Don't know," she replied. "He called for the ambulance as I got to the desk. No telling who else was with him." That put Ron nearby too, he realized.

She delivered him back to the stationhouse long past dinner time, his simple plodding life upended like a tea tray. His three best friends were suspects, one or all, in a murder he could well understand - the beastly, insatiable appetite of the man avenged by just and well-executed retribution. Just, perhaps, but in the eyes of the law and in the jurisdiction of Detective Wayne Guthrie it was a criminal conspiracy, a crime of passion he could never withhold from his boss.

Chapter 16

On Saturday at 6:45 a.m., a week to the day after the murder,
Guthrie crossed the threshold of Poughkeepsie police headquarters
looking disheveled. Jack Whitaker woke him late Friday night to say
he was coming to town for some fishing and would make himself
available for an interview, per Guthrie's request. Whitaker looked a
might overdressed waiting near the intake counter in a plaid cotton
shirt and crimson silk ascot. He was sitting in a long line of chairs,
backs against the wall as if they'd been cleared for a dance in the
gym, except the room was too cramped and clinical in the
fluorescent lighting to be festive. A donut fattened duty officer
slouched behind the high oak desk guarding the entry to the
stationhouse.

"Morning, Donald," said Guthrie.

"Morning, sir," Donald replied.

"Mr. Whitaker?" Guthrie continued, recognizing his face from
the Donner's Forge membership book.

"Why, yes," said Whitaker. "And you must be Detective
Guthrie."

He led Whitaker through the wire reinforced security door by
the intake desk and down a long hall on the first floor of the two-
story building. They passed a string of messy, darkened offices that
always reminded Guthrie of carnival stalls. To the left was an open
cubicle farm, the personal effects of its denizens, from colorful
family portraits to authentic children's art, brightening the drab
institutional decor. The faint buzz of lighting stirred the air.

A door was open at the end of the hall and the light was on
inside. He showed Whitaker to the room where Jimmy Doolan was
waiting. Jimmy was clear-eyed and unshaven, like a mariner just put
to sea, and he sat at the end of a long metal table. The walls were a
collage of material, from Polaroids of the club staff to the black and
white headshots of the Guns from the membership book, and the
pictures were connected by strands of colorful yarn and adhesive

correction tape making a rainbow web of known or suspected affiliations. There was meaning to the colors, but only to Jimmy.

He saw Whitaker locate himself among the member photographs and note his prominence at the hub of a colorful and prolific pinwheel. There was an easel in the corner with a large paper writing tablet, divided down the middle by an imprecise vertical line, the left column labeled *motives*, and the right *suspects*. The left column was blank and the right listed four names: Rick LeBeau, Ron LeBeau, Kelley Sutton, and Dr. Astrid Taylor Achermann, who was noted parenthetically because she was running a distant fourth. An aerial photograph of the club grounds was centered on the adjoining wall. Whitaker lingered in the doorway like a house tour tag-along until his gaze fell on Jimmy. Irreverent yes, but disrespectful, no. Guthrie could count on Jimmy to handle himself, and he stood on cue as Whitaker passed through the door.

"Thank you for paying us a visit, Mr. Whitaker," Guthrie began. "We have attempted to contact everyone on the premises that day, as well as a few others, like Mrs. Achermann, or rather Dr. Achermann, the victim's wife. As you might expect, some members are being more helpful than others. We appreciate you coming to talk to us."

"Don't mention it," Whitaker replied. "It was easy to come by as long as you don't keep me so long the fish stop biting."

"Oh, we won't need that long, Mr. Whitaker," Guthrie assured him.

"How can I help?" Whitaker inquired.

"We're still piecing together events of that morning," Guthrie began. "Can you give us a timeline, as best you can remember, from the moment you arrived until the moment you left?" Whitaker looked pleased to comply.

The day before the shooting Whitaker had traveled to Donner's Forge from his home in Washington, D.C., his security detail in tow. He arrived, as usual, early in the evening before opening day, joining a handful of early arrivals for dinner at the club, and retiring to bed early while his security detail ate in the kitchen and slept in an adjoining room on the second floor. Achermann must have arrived later that evening as Whitaker first saw him at breakfast. That wasn't so unusual. Members living nearby frequently arrived after dinner, coming for the shooting, more than the company. Whitaker had risen at about 4 a.m., roused with the other Guns by Dirk LeBeau. He ate breakfast and departed with his guide, his security team shadowing him, Guthrie imagined, like Bedouin wives.

"Who was your guide?" Guthrie asked.

"Ron LeBeau. Ron has been my guide for years," Whitaker replied before eyeing the easel skeptically.

"You can take him off your list because he was with me," he instructed.

"Sure. Okay. Let's get to that in a minute," Guthrie said. "Please keep going, what happened next?"

"We drove to the edge of the woods at Westbrook," he continued, rising like a mission commander to address the aerial photograph. He found the farmhouse and jabbed it with his finger, tracing his party's route from the front door, out the driveway, and left down Pine Valley Lane which bisected the club grounds. He guessed it was less than a mile to the clearing where they pulled to the edge of the road.

"We parked here, and walked through the woods to this field, here. We positioned ourselves in this hedgerow, here. Great hide," he editorialized. "We had a beautiful field of fire," he added. Guthrie grew nervous as Jimmy approached Whitaker from behind, studying the aerial photograph over Whitaker's shoulder. The hedgerow in which Whitaker had placed himself was less than a mile as the crow flies from where Rick LeBeau and Harry Achermann were sitting, their location marked on the aerial photograph by an adhesive red dot like a bombing target.

"Isn't that pretty close to where Achermann was shot?" Jimmy asked alluding to the red dot.

"It's not unsafe, if that's what you mean, son," Whitaker replied. Just as Guthrie feared, his protégé's distaste for being patronized showed.

"Would anyone else have been as close, or closer to Achermann and LeBeau?" Jimmy persisted. He saw Whitaker study Jimmy in a new light, his eyes narrowing as he took the Irishman's measure.

"I can't say, son. Pretty unlikely though, just looking at this picture," he said. His defenses were up, like pricked ears on a wolf, so Guthrie interceded and backpedaled.

"Was your security detail nearby?" he interjected.

"One was probably close by, behind me in the hedgerow somewhere, and the other may have been further out, at the corner of the field with a better view of the approaches."

"Probably?" Guthrie countered. "Are you not sure?" It sounded more antagonistic than he intended, and he was relieved when Whitaker took it in stride.

"No, I'm not sure. Once I was backed into the hedgerow I had about a 90-degree field of view. My gun was raised and I was holding damn still. I'm sure they were nearby. They always are."

"So being so close, you must have heard the shot and the whistles," said Jimmy.

"Yes, son. We heard both."

"And what did you do then?" Guthrie interjected again, to dampen Jimmy's enthusiasm.

"My guys *secured* me, as they like to say. And Ron tore off in his truck, back in the direction of the club, which is where it sounded like the whistle was coming from.

"What does *securing* you entail?" Guthrie continued.

"It means we move, fast."

"You mean, you run away?" Jimmy asked. When Jimmy lost patience he fell into baiting, like the school-yard bully he once was. Whitaker glared at him, not remotely amused.

"In manner of speaking, son, yes. We run away."

"Where did you go?" Guthrie asked preemptively, to head off the jab Jimmy was bound to have ready.

"I can't tell you that," Whitaker replied. "We have a procedure, which we followed."

"All right, who was the next person to see you?" Guthrie continued.

"As I say, we followed a security procedure, which meant staying away from the club. One of my guys returned to collect my things so we could go back to Washington."

"Detective Guthrie," Jimmy interrupted, "can we go back to the time of the shooting?" Jimmy's startling impertinence caught him off guard, and Jimmy mistook his silence for consent.

"So at the time of the shooting," Jimmy began, "you knew where Ron was, but you can't say for sure where your security goons were, is that right?" He was taunting Whitaker now, which caused Whitaker to relax and resign himself to giving the local boy his day.

"Yes, that's right, son, but you can be sure they were there."

"I'm sure that's right, Mr. Whitaker, and I'm not suggesting anything else, sir, I'm just thinking about the possibilities. And based on what you just said, it is possible isn't it, not likely, mind you," and now Jimmy was parodying, just for fun, Whitaker's manner of speaking, "but it is possible that one of them..." Surely Jimmy wasn't serious; surely he was tweaking Whitaker's nose because it was irresistible. But he was going too far, and Guthrie resolved to end it before his indecorous protégé accused a secret service bodyguard of murder.

"Jimmy!" Guthrie barked. "That's enough."

"I didn't come here prepared with alibis for my security detail, son. They're special agents, trained to keep me alive, not trained assassins. You're going to have a hard time with cooperation if your first instinct is to suspect those of us willing to talk to you."

"Mr. Whitaker, I apologize," said Guthrie. "My colleague is young and enthusiastic, as we all were once. In any event, I apologize," he said again as he turned to Jimmy.

"Let's give Mr. Whitaker's security detail the benefit of the doubt, shall we Jimmy?"

"The benefit of the doubt about what?" Jimmy asked. "All I wanted to know was whether it was possible one of his bodyguards saw the gunman, and didn't even know it because the gunman was a familiar face, like a guide." It was a possibility Guthrie hadn't considered and he felt chastened, but only slightly. Jimmy was wily enough to have a fall back if he failed to get a rise out of Whitaker. He stared at Jimmy doubtfully before turning back to Whitaker.

"At least we can say Ron was with you until after the shot was fired, so he can come off our list," he pronounced, running a thick black line through *Ron LeBeau* on the easel. "I feel like we're making progress." He was thinking hard about what he knew Jimmy suspected, which was that Whitaker couldn't be trusted and that his testimony, whatever it was, would always be a psalm shy of gospel.

The word of the Deputy Director gave Ron and his own body guards a rock solid alibi, but he was hardly beyond suspicion himself, which made their collective proximity to the murder all the more intriguing. Whitaker's security detail was parked right outside. Guthrie had seen them when he arrived at the stationhouse and he was half tempted to call them in for a few spontaneous questions.

But Whitaker had come voluntarily, in the spirit of cooperation, and now was the wrong time to question his storyline. Better to lose the scent, or leave that impression and let procedure bring it back around when it was harder to deny. The conversation stalled. By now Whitaker had learned more than he'd contributed, which was a barely serviceable alibi for Ron LeBeau, and Guthrie felt robbed. He'd placed his last dollar on the wrong horse, and Whitaker seemed to know it by the look of his superior gaze.

"I understand why Rick LeBeau," Whitaker finally said, "but why Dr. Achermann? You must be casting a pretty wide net."

"We're grasping at straws, Mr. Whitaker," Guthrie said, "as you can tell. Achermann took liberties, or so they say. She had the money and the motive to have it done professionally, as it appears it was. It's something we have to consider." Whitaker folded his newspaper, wedged it beneath his arm, and headed for the door.

"I'm sorry I haven't been much help," he said with a smile, "but let me know if there's something I can do." He pulled two business cards from his wallet and slid them down the table, a beltway parlor trick, guessed Guthrie, that he'd performed a hundred times before. The embossed gold seal of the United States and the colorful mark of the Central Intelligence Agency winked in the overhead light.

"You know, Mr. Whitaker, now that you mention it, there may be one more thing," said Guthrie.

"Why sure, anything."

"Who is Adam Woodcock?" Whitaker's eyes narrowed, the same way they narrowed at Jimmy.

"I don't think I know an Adam Woodcock," he finally replied. "Should I know him?"

"I suppose not. I just thought you might. A guy with an English accent, according to my source, who claims to work for Homeland Security," said Guthrie.

"A lot of people work for Homeland Security, Detective Guthrie. If he's telling the truth, I can find him if that would help."

"Word has it he's on the trail of a thief who stole some kind of biological warfare agent," Guthrie said, rising from his chair and reaching for a newsprint clipping pinned to the wall near the polaroids.

"Here's a story, from the *Washington Post*, on the day before the shooting. I presume you're aware of it."

"Yes, of course, Detective Guthrie, but not of an Adam Woodcock. Is there anything else I can do for you?"

"Well, it turns out, Mr. Whitaker, that this fellow, Adam Woodcock, from Homeland Security, recently paid Dr. Achermann a visit." Pay dirt, finally. Try as he might, Whitaker feigned disinterest poorly.

"And you're never going to believe this," Guthrie continued, feeling the advantage, "but this Woodcock character visited her in Atlanta at the Center for Disease Control." He paused, looking for a response, but Whitaker had turned to stone, absent of expression, devoid of emotion, a statue in fishing clothes and an ascot. The silence gave voice to the death rattle of a light bulb, which buzzed like static before a storm.

When Whitaker failed to respond, Guthrie forged ahead. "And according to Dr. Achermann, who was censured mid-sentence by a CDC staff member named…" and he snapped his fingers at Jimmy, who was waiting for redemption.

"Katrine Burkhardt," Jimmy said on cue.

"Yes," he continued, "according to Dr. Achermann, one of these biological agents turned up somewhere in South Africa, of all places." Again, he rested, but Whitaker was unbowed.

"Anyway, this fellow Woodcock shows up at the CDC within twenty-four hours of Dr. Achermann arriving with this biological agent, and then he starts asking a bunch of questions about Mr. Achermann." Guthrie concluded.

Whitaker finally smiled. "You obviously have more questions," he said, pulling a chair from the table and pushing it to the wall. He seated himself, stretched his shoulders, and propped a heel on the opposing knee. "Now what's the question?" he said, as if he were ready to talk all day.

"That's quite a coincidence, isn't it?" Guthrie said.

"What's a coincidence?"

"That this story breaks about someone stealing a biological agent, Mr. Achermann meets his maker the very next day, and his wife turns up with the same biological agent, hotly pursued by an agent from Homeland Security." Whitaker weighed the evidence.

"Yes," he finally said, "I suppose that is a coincidence."

Guthrie had heard all the evasions, obfuscations, and smart-ass answers from lesser subjects than Whitaker and he wanted more respect from a fellow law enforcement officer. He could be menacing himself when the situation warranted, and he hardened his eyes and ground his teeth in a show of dwindling patience.

"Homeland Security is one of my departments," he squeezed out of Whitaker. "I can try to find Woodcock for you if that would help." Guthrie grappled the table with his brutal hands and pulled himself to his feet, the weight of his torso coming to rest on the knuckles of his clenched fists.

"Mr. Whitaker," he began, "I understand there may be things you can't tell me…." he stipulated, hoping with sinking confidence that Whitaker would dispense with the charade.

"My job is to investigate this incident and to determine to the best of my ability what happened. I think I'm going to find out, whether you help me or not, and Jimmy and I, well, we're a little worried about what we might find. Are you sure there isn't anything you want to tell us? Are there things we're going to find out that…" and he paused for effect, "things… areas… matters the confidentiality of which you might like us to respect?" He was laboring to extend the professional courtesy he was being so thoroughly denied, even though he didn't expect Whitaker to reverse himself, especially in front of Jimmy.

"Detective Guthrie," Whitaker replied, "I don't know anything about this incident, why it happened, or even who Achermann was."

"I see. Then let's keep going, shall we? You ever heard of something called 'In-Q-Tel'?"

"Yes, I believe I have." Progress, an opening, perhaps a face-saving way to clarify misunderstandings and find their way back to center.

"It's an investment company sponsored by the CIA. They invest in technologies of interest to the security community. Things like communications, robotics, sensors, that sort of thing, I think," Whitaker offered.

"What about biological warfare? They ever invest in that?"

"I don't know."

"Well, it turns out, Mr. Whitaker, that Achermann's investment company and In-Q-Tel had interests in a company called Ribonetics, about ten years ago, and this company developed a biological agent, perhaps the very one Dr. Achermann retrieved from South Africa." Whitaker flashed a smile.

"And you think this incident, that silly newspaper article, and whatever Dr. Achermann has told you are all connected?"

"I told you we were grasping at straws, Mr. Whitaker."

"Until now I didn't believe you, Detective Guthrie. Don't you think you're making this more complicated than it is? Isn't it more likely a poacher made a mistake, realized what he'd done, and fled? Somebody gets shot around here every year. It happens all the time. I don't need to tell you that." Guthrie didn't appreciate the jab. It was classic city-slicker contempt: *you of all people should know.* He could feel Jimmy fuming in the corner, piqued by the mockery of his legwork.

"That's certainly possible, maybe even likely,… but let's assume for a minute it's premeditated murder; who would murder this guy, and on club grounds, and what would be the motive?" He posed the questions deferentially, but Whitaker passed on the bait.

"As you say, Detective Guthrie, probably a lot of people – his wife, his girlfriends, business associates? You don't achieve his level of success without making enemies."

"But a lot of people do without getting murdered," Guthrie noted. "Mr. Achermann was a new member at Donner's Forge, wasn't he?" he continued

"I believe that's right."

"I understand you wrote a letter supporting him for membership."

"I did. It was a favor to a friend. I didn't really know Achermann," Whitaker replied.

Only then did Guthrie appreciate Whitaker's comfort and facility with deception. He lied in his sleep, whether he needed to or not. He could tilt you at shadows, turn you in circles, like a setter with scent on the wind. If Whitaker didn't want to play there was nothing to gain.

"One last question, Mr. Whitaker, and then we'll leave you alone. Can you say whether Achermann was under surveillance?" Whitaker smiled, an inscrutable expressionless smile, his thin featureless lips knitted and taut like a scar holding his jaw to his face.

"Do you have reason to suspect he was, or should have been?" he said, answering Guthrie's question with a question. He was probing for what Guthrie thought he knew.

"No." Guthrie replied. "He traveled a lot, and in influential circles. Those are the kinds of folks the CIA likes to know, aren't they?" Two could play the question game, which Whitaker seemed to concede by ignoring the second and answering the first.

"No, I can't say whether Achermann was under surveillance." The diplomat-speak, *I can neither confirm nor deny,* was all the evasion Guthrie could stomach.

"Very well then, Mr. Whitaker, we appreciate your time. Enjoy the fishing, and thanks for your card." He worried about Jimmy who jumped to his feet, driving his chair hard into the cinder block wall behind him. He looked angry and frustrated and followed Whitaker into the hall before leaving him to find his way out. When Whitaker was gone he wheeled around.

"He's lying, boss."

"No kidding, Jimmy, you'll make a great detective someday."

"I hate people who lie to me," Jimmy seethed.

"You're gonna hate this job if you don't get over it, Jimmy."

"Shouldn't he be on our side? I mean, aren't we all trying to get the bad guys?"

"Who *are* the bad guys?" Guthrie posed philosophically.

"Isn't it obvious? Can't you see? The murderer and his accomplices, of course."

"Forget it, Jimmy, he thinks we're townies, hacks. It's contempt, that's all. Get used to that, too."

There's a moment, Guthrie thought, in every case when suspicions wake the instinct for self-preservation. It was like thunderstorms rising into the big sky over Wichita, when straight-line winds collide with an updraft and presto, a vortex as destructive and indiscriminate as anything in nature, climbing like Jack's beanstalk into the sky. It altered the landscape, leaving no one and nothing secure, and everybody paid; and so it was when suspicion and self-preservation collided. Everything got harder when the vortex took hold, when the scramble for cover began, and this is why he was hesitating.

These crossroads brought him back to the hellish inferno on the Colorado hillside. He attributed a great many sins to hesitation, which could always be laziness in disguise. The charter operator, the FAA, the pilots, the air traffic controllers – all were guilty of laziness, and the pilot of impulsiveness, like the impulsiveness he was trying to tame in Jimmy. The minutes passed as he evaluated his timing, weighing his options, Jimmy by his side.

"Jimmy?"

"Yes, boss?"

"Get a hold of that Burkhardt woman. See if you can get a picture of this Adam Woodcock off the CDC surveillance cameras, and go find him." Jimmy grinned.

"Yes, boss. I'm on it."

Chapter 17

Sam Dunkelsbuhler nodded off inside the main conference room at DeBeers headquarters in London. He was supposed to be paying attention to Freddie Gervers, Global Director Brokerage Operations, and Guy Lilienfeld, Global Director Marketing and Sales. Like him, they were direct descendants of the cartel's founding families who first contracted with Cecil Rhodes to buy South African diamonds. They were forty-five minutes into presenting Sam with the new plan for entering the U.S. market.

The company was already more embedded in the American market than a Georgia chigger, through U.S. sight-holders, and indirectly funded advertising campaigns. But the settlement of the U.S. price fixing case was a chance to relaunch the DeBeers brand, to build caché around diamonds sourced from the most revered South African mines, because there was nothing like wearing a stone spilled from the same vein as the Star of Africa, the world's largest cut diamond, on display at the Tower of London in the royal scepter.

These mines gainfully employed thousands of locals, liberated of late from the brutal repression of Apartheid. Lilienfeld wanted to build brand loyalty around mines that yielded some of the world's legendary stones, and by supporting the miners who dug for them. Sam agreed. Mines with pedigree were no less absurd than branded bottled water, and could be a powerful new weapon in the company's arsenal for demand management – a creative new way to *regulate* access to the U.S., the world's largest retail diamond market.

Sam was amused by Lilienfeld's obsession with the Chinese. They were "dealing like rice traders," he said, for raw materials to fuel the voracious Chinese industrial machine, not to mention a hungry new middle class thirsting for status symbols.

"I have reliable reports," said Lilienfeld, "of Chinese inquiries throughout the diamond and gold producing districts. They're bound to try, and they'll be formidable if we give them a toe hold." Sam was less troubled, because Lilienfeld was a hand-wringer, as sales executives are, and because no competitor in a hundred years had assembled all the elements required to build a vertically integrated production, cutting, and retail network to match the might of DeBeers.

There were always vulnerabilities somewhere along the value chain, and the company had a knack, like Paris for Achilles' heel, for exploiting them. Nobody should be overlooked, especially not the Chinese, but Lilienfeld's countermeasure looked promising, especially with the settlement behind them. He had already green-lighted Lilienfeld's plan, a preemptive strike in the form of a branded American retail network that would lock up the U.S. market before the Chinese could get started. It was a winner-takes-all bet, stacked by carte blanche access care of the settlement with the U.S. government.

"The Chinese can be mitigated," Lilienfeld was saying, "by painting them as the ruthless, government subsidized profiteers they are, and by highlighting their unscrupulous exploitation of the locals." It was a clever if hypocritical notion, but soporific, and Sam's attention wandered.

He looked around the room at the richly painted portraits. There was Cecil Rhodes, and his own great-great-grandfather Samuel J. Dunkelsbuhler, Ernest Oppenheimer, the older brother, and their younger brother, Otto. And Alfred Beit, a governor who suffered a heart attack when he heard the news that a turn of the century brick layer named Thomas M. Cullinan discovered a pipe so saturated with diamonds it would dwarf the company's best Kimberly mines.

Cullinan was deftly neutralized by Oppenheimer the moment Britain subdued the Boers. The Transvaal government owned a majority of the Cullinan find, which Oppenheimer purchased and Britain happily sold to recover costs from the war. The company had a legacy of improbable turnabouts, from rescuing investors in the Namibian beach discovery to securing new supplies from the Forminière mines in the Belgian Congo. State by state, region by region, mine by mine, governments, investors, and suppliers had been co-opted from every continent and every nationality.

Lilienfeld's plan was modest by comparison, but another chapter in a history of conquest to which the Chinese would be just as deftly relegated. He was proud they had honored their forbearers by preserving the resilience of the cartel. Their ingenuity and determination was every bit the match of their predecessors, as was their readiness to protect their legacy.

The soft resonating trill of a modern ring tone interrupted Lilienfeld, the velvety tone amplified through eight concealed speakers and modulated by the obsidian oak paneling, overstuffed leather chairs, and dense wool carpeting. Sam reached for the media control board and pressed a button.

"I thought we asked not to be disturbed."

"I apologize for interrupting you Mr. Dunkelsbuhler, but Ms. Stockton from the *Washington Post* is on the line." His assistant's mellifluous South African accent never got old. He reached for the control panel and lifted the handset which canceled the surround-sound, leaving Gervers and Lilienfeld in silence.

"Good day, Coco," Sam said solicitously, flashing his colleagues a disingenuous smile.

"Yes, yes, that is quite a development isn't it? Well, of course I couldn't tell you until it was resolved, don't be silly." He rolled his eyes, parodying for his audience the drama coming through the handset.

"Yes, of course. I have an early dinner engagement so I mustn't linger." She was being abrupt, uncharacteristically aggravated, and he wondered how much his colleagues could hear.

"I shall need final say, as is our custom," he confirmed. "Right-o, see you there," he finished and hung up. "Carry on," he said, and his colleagues obliged, completing the story of their grand plan for American conquest.

*****

Woodcock stewed in the *Washington Post* London Bureau conference room, feeling as addled as his interrogation victims. He was bleary-eyed and tense, poring through Coco Stockton's files. The files were a shambles - unintelligible interview notes interspersed with court records and newspaper and magazine articles. The connections he knew were there eluded his foggy, jetlagged mind. His laptop was open to one side, glowing in boring sympathy with the fading afternoon outside. It chortled now and again like a digital songbird with the receipt of unsolicited emails until one missive revived him. It was Hank Caldwell, leader of the rapid reaction team dispatched to Johannesburg to track Dr. Achermann's movements back to the Nama.

Adam: We found the park guide who brought Dr. Achermann out of Richtersveld Park, one Norris Sanderling. He was positive for DRX - in wretched shape - no time left and delusional so confidence in the following is low. He said he worked for DeBeers – that his job for the parks was a cover to observe the Nama. In the past month he delivered clothing and food supplies. He was suspicious – it was the only relief of its kind, ever - and they began getting sick. He feared a connection. Confirm the symptoms and progression of DRX. He died this morning...

The email trailed off into a sequence of lists cataloging names and places and plans, and qualified optimism for containing the disease. Caldwell's story was familiar, resonating with some other event. It was déjà vu of something he knew, an historical event on the tip of his tongue, if only he had more sleep. And then he remembered, an optional esoteric assigned reading at Sandhurst on settling the American west. Hadn't the U.S. Army seeded trading blankets with European smallpox to eradicate the more bothersome tribes? The results had been devastating, the tribes possessing no natural immunities. There was no denying the parallels. It bore a uniquely American signature.

He was contemplating the ironic methods by which the United States had spread freedom when Coco barged into the room.

"We've got our meeting, Mr. Woodcock. This afternoon. 5 p.m. at a small pub around the corner from DeBeers' office. I told Sam I would meet him there." He was still in the Sandhurst stacks as her words took a moment to register.

"Jolly good, Coco," he said, as the academy's Greek revival portico, which bore an uncanny resemblance to the White House, come to think of it, faded. Was his subliminal mind, the cultivation of which Whitaker so eagerly encouraged, seeing the outlines of an Anglo-American conspiracy? What could they want together, and from a situation like this?

He noticed her again, for no particular reason, the texture of her tousled hair. It was sturdy and supple like wind-blown wheat, bending with the curves of her cheeks. There was no likeness among the British of her gender to the peachy glow of her skin, or to the way it turned to blush around her ears, or to the fullness of her fleshy lips.

"You don't mind if I call you Coco, do you?" he heard himself say. "I would definitely prefer that you call me Adam," he said, spilling his words unrehearsed, raw and unrefined like an American.

"Okay, Adam. We have our meeting."

"As I say, well done, Coco." He liked the sound of saying her name. Charlotte was nice, too. What a shame the Americans contracted absolutely everything.

"I regret you can't come with me. I shall need you to point him out, but then I shall need to conduct the meeting alone."

"He won't talk to you. He doesn't know you. He won't trust you."

"Well, you have me there. He will not trust me, Coco, but he *will* talk to me."

"It's not fair."

"Yes Coco, you're quite right, but he may tell me more in your absence. I will be able to confront him with things that he will not want to discuss with a…" and he cut himself off.

"A woman?" said Coco. He saw the blush around her ears flare smoothly and suddenly across her cheeks.

"No, actually. To a newspaper reporter."

Ninety minutes later she was sitting by his side in a taxi on the way to Charterhouse Street. He felt better, more awake now that it was mid-day on the U.S. East Coast, and his circadian rhythm was sailing on a following breeze. They were on the bench seat like teenagers on a carnival ride and he was trying to stay calm as undulating streams of pedestrians seeped from the urban landscape to begin their great migrations home. They were clogging pedestrian crossings and slowing rush hour traffic that was already unbearably heavy.

"Don't worry," she said. "It's always like this. We won't be late." Her voice was comforting and feminine in a way that was new to him, and he caught himself sneaking childish glances at her which she didn't seem to mind.

At Charterhouse Street they exited the cab and walked northeast past a trendy night club that was hours from opening, and past an expensive looking restaurant with crisp white-jacketed waiters posted in the entryway. She slowed at the next street corner and faded into a doorway. When she pulled him into the shadows and started peering over his shoulders he felt himself thoroughly beguiled.

Her eyes were on the patron-packed tables outside an old-fashioned pub. The crowd was huddled close in the shade of beer-labeled umbrellas that floated like lily pads above the sidewalk. The smoking and drinking and chatting was well underway, the animated stories and exaggerated yarns making theater of office monotony. Alone in the crowd and comfortably ensconced sat a man with the tranquility of a tycoon. His back was turned so his face was impossible to see, but the work-a-day world was amusing him. His grey hair was swept back straight over his head, ending in a breezy curl that lapped like ripples on an ornamental lake at the back of his collar.

"There he is," she whispered, looking in the direction of the pub.

"Jolly good, Coco. I'll give you a ring tonight," he promised and bolted from the entry way. A step from the curb he wheeled around.

"Go stay with a friend tonight, Coco. Don't go home until we talk again, do you understand?" He saw her nod and then he was off across the street.

Chapter 18

"At first it made no sense," said Mort Depworm, pulling a large envelope from the parted jaws of a dilapidated medical bag that looked as anxious to disgorge its contents as a gavage-fatted duck. The Tomato seemed to be looking for a stethoscope. The faint smell of formaldehyde vied with the scent of wintergreen muscle cream, but it was impossible to say whether the bag or Depworm was the source.

"There was massive internal bleeding from the bottom of the esophagus, throughout his stomach, and into his upper intestine. It's possible but unlikely so much internal bleeding would have been caused by falling," Depworm was saying, "but of course he didn't fall, did he?" Depworm posed rhetorically. He was trying to sound intriguing again and it drove Guthrie nuts.

"He was sitting when he was shot."

Guthrie tolerated Depworm poorly, even in abbreviated form, which this meeting was proving not to be. He tried to look bored behind his grey steel desk as Depworm labored to concoct a mystery. It was the same old routine. Build the suspense until the audience couldn't stand it and solve the case with a flourish of scientific mumbo-jumbo to rival weeknight television. He already knew the answer was in the black-and-white photographs Depworm was clutching to his chest.

Depworm's unkempt white hair exploded in jaunty matted bolts, like loosely spun cotton candy. His thin drawn lips had a peculiar mauve tint that hinted at the use of lipstick, especially in contrast to his sallow complexion. He wore a faded green sweater vest, unraveling at more than one button hole, beneath a threadbare herring bone jacket. The Tomato was tracking, but with even less inspiration than usual.

"I'm not following you yet," said Guthrie.

"Normally, internal bleeding would be localized, the result of blunt force trauma, like a fall, or a blow. Only the shock wave from a very large explosion would cause the kind of generalized internal bleeding he suffered, and that would not be limited to the digestive tract," said Depworm growing animated.

"In any event, there was no explosion, was there?" he noted ironically. "So we would expect to trace the bleeding to a central locus, an area of severe trauma where the bleeding would be worse. This was not like that," he said, pausing for effect. "The bleeding was very consistent throughout his upper digestive tract, like something had sheared out his insides," he concluded, his eyes wide as saucers. Guthrie removed his glasses, which he did when enough was enough.

"What are you telling me, Mort? Do you have any theories, any conclusions? Shall we get to the punchline?" Depworm looked chastened and shed the affectations.

"It was like something he ate for breakfast dissolved his insides, but dissolved isn't the right idea. Under the microscope the damage looked more like tiny concentrated lacerations, like something got to his bloodstream by cutting its way through the walls of his digestive tract."

"So you think he was poisoned before he was shot? Is that what you're saying Mort?" Guthrie asked. The Tomato was annoying him, too, his eyes following the exchange like a tennis spectator, except he was perceptibly behind, like a dying metronome.

"Oh no, Guthrie, it's much better than that. When the toxicology tests came back negative, I took a swab from several locations throughout the area of internal bleeding, and this is what I found." Depworm deposited the photographs on Guthrie's desk like a royal flush. The Tomato slid forwards on his generous haunches and craned his neck to register curiosity. He studied the photographs briefly before relapsing into his previous angle of repose. Guthrie replaced his glasses, leaned over his folded forearms, and examined the photographs like a dinner menu. They looked like bad modern art, more and less concentrated blotches of small angular dots on a white field.

"So?"

"You know what those are?" said Depworm, full of suspense.

"Why don't you tell me."

"At first I didn't believe it, so I did a little a research. Sure enough, this was a tried and true method of the ancients. A fifteenth-century Turkish Sultan and a sixteenth-century Pope were murdered this way. Even Catherine De Medici dispatched several of her victims using this technique." The Tomato slid forward again, falling for the intrigue, to Guthrie's chagrin.

"Those are diamonds," Depworm said breathlessly. "It's diamond dust. The victim ingested diamond dust that morning. It was cutting his insides to ribbons. He would have been dead within a few hours anyway. His fate was sealed before he was shot," Depworm finished victoriously, his paintbrush eye brows raised in triumph and his hand latched thoughtfully to his chin.

"Wow," the Tomato blurted with a schoolboy's admiration. Guthrie gazed at the photographs. They were about to complicate his life far beyond the geometric simplicity of the shapes.

"Thank you, Mort," he finally said. "Impressive sleuthing. That's got to be a first for the Poughkeepsie coroner's office."

"You're darn right it is!" Depworm exclaimed. Guthrie drew a deep breath and leaned way back in his articulated chair. There was blessed relief from Depworm and the Tomato in the vacant space high in the eaves.

The case was on a reasonable path until Depworm dropped in. He had narrowed his suspicions to a business or personal relationship somewhere in the tangle of institutions represented by the two Achermanns and Whitaker. Depworm's discovery did not contradict his theory, but a second unrelated cause of death? It was unprecedented.

"Let's start at the beginning," he eventually said, and the Tomato and Depworm closed, like children at story hour.

"This is conclusive evidence that Achermann's murder, by at least one method, was premeditated. He was, as they say, 'dead man walking,' is that right?" Depworm contorted his face.

"There was no saving him, even if he'd been rushed to the hospital in this condition," Guthrie clarified, looking for Depworm to concur.

"Well, I didn't say that exactly, but I believe that's right." The air felt warm and oppressive like a standing room only subway car, and Depworm was nodding peculiarly, like holes might be opening in his theory.

"Yes?" Guthrie pressed him. "No? Maybe?"

"Yes." Depworm finally said, but with unconvincing resolve.

"So this plot, to poison Achermann, needs an insider, doesn't it? Someone to administer the poison, to spike his food, isn't that right?" The Tomato and Depworm appeared to be with him now, hanging like acolytes of Poirot on his words.

"OK, so we have an insider," he concluded.

"Now let's think about the shooting, assuming it was no accident. Doesn't that require an insider, too?" This caught them off guard, and Depworm contorted his face again.

"Most likely Rick LeBeau, possibly one of the other guides. We just don't know yet, right?" He surmised from their expressions he was moving too fast, so he circled back and retraced his steps.

"If the shooting was premeditated the gunman had to know where Rick was going to take Achermann, right?" Depworm looked satisfied, and the Tomato nodded along, his head weighing on his torso like a tree bending in the wind.

"You're certain about this, Mort? That he was doomed before he was shot?" he repeated, to reaffirm their progress.

"All I said, Guthrie, is that there's diamond dust in the victim's digestive tract. Of that I'm sure. I can tell you when it got there, and what the clinical effects were. Can I say with one hundred percent certainty it was fatal? No, I can't tell you that, but I can't imagine how he would have survived it either." Guthrie needed better than that. Since when was solving murders a one hundred percent certain line of work.

Here he was again, hanging on an expert opinion, and his expert was losing his nerve. They were known for this crap, all bluster and certitude until it was time to accuse, which always brought out the ninny. He needed conjecture, measured but deliberate, to go beyond the evidence because that's where the answers lay. Hedging was defensive, paralysis of the imagination.

Was there any being more cursed than a man like Depworm, perpetually in fear of his own work, forever diminishing himself before its consequences? This was the job, for God's sake. A lifetime of preparation only to cower in the moment for which he was made, for which he defined himself. How sad. It was the difference between men who hungered for taming the chaos, for railing against the storm, and men who had the training but not the courage to shape life. At some primitive level they distrusted themselves, and there were many more like Depworm with certificates of higher learning over their desks than there were riding tractors in Wichita or Dutchess County. It was a peculiar side effect of education, he thought. Mort could deliver the evidence but wanted no part of its meaning, which meant he'd exhausted his usefulness.

"Thanks, Mort. This is important. Anything else you want to share with us?" Guthrie asked.

"No," Depworm replied, looking visibly deflated. "I don't have anything else. The victim bled out from his throat. That's what finally killed him, but he was bleeding out, dying from the inside already."

"Okay then," Guthrie concluded. "We'll let you know if we need anything else." He was glad Depworm understood he was dismissed, and the coroner left, vapors of wintergreen and formaldehyde lingering in the air.

The Tomato was still swaying, his mind skipping like a record on the thought that put him in motion. He looked distracted and troubled, even more than his huge soft eyes and dreary olive complexion usually suggested.

"Hey Tomato, what are you thinking over there?" Guthrie asked, sensing the need to lift the Tomato's spirits.

"Let me guess, Tomato. You're afraid Kelley Sutton is involved," he said. He was well aware of the community ties that climbed like vines right into his own department. Personal entanglements were the nature of Poughkeepsie's public institutions, part of the grainy texture of small town life.

"No, boss," replied the Tomato, the spell of his gaze broken. He raised his cheerless eyes.

"I ain't afraid, boss. An' I ain't wonderin' *if.* I'm wonderin' *how much*," he said, his swaying subsiding.

"Did she tell you she's pregnant, Tomato?"

"Yeah, boss. How did you know?"

"I'm a detective, Tomato, remember?"

"It's bad, boss. She says she was raped, by this guy Achermann at the club New Year's Eve pahty. She says she was sleepin' in her car outside the club when he was shot, but she ain't got no witness."

"So you think she's our gunman?"

"Piece `a cake, boss. She's a great shot. Been deer huntin' all her life. She has motive, opportunity, ability, and no alibi. She was there that morning and any one of the guides coulda tipped her to where Rick was goin'. She's our gunman, alright. And that's not all, boss. She works in the kitchen, too, and did that morning. She's in this deep, boss, one way or the other."

He could see the toll of ratting out a friend weigh on the Tomato, and he had the impression there was more to come.

"What else?"

"It probably wasn't one a de odder guides dat tipped 'er. More 'n likely it were Rick himself. You see, dey been goin' together on and off since we was kids," the Tomato said, "and Rick knew that Achermann raped her. They're both definitely in on this one, boss."

Her inconstancy in love with LeBeau or anybody else was no surprise to Guthrie, and nor was her tangle with Achermann. Based on his observations at the Mad Hatter, and her tone of voice with Dirk LeBeau on the morning he walked in behind Dirk, she was a troublemaker. She enjoyed her effect on men, and used it to advantage. The prospect of her inciting the crime of passion wasn't just plausible, it was likely. He never saw her being the gunman, but suddenly *femme fatale* suited her. The Tomato's suffering was hard to watch, the tug between guilt and duty gnawing at his simple, honest mind.

"Don't beat yourself up, Tomato. It's all circumstantial, at least for right now," he said, "and what makes you so sure she's involved?"

"Who else, boss? It all adds up. Jus' like you always says, don't ovah complicate t'ings."

"I suppose she denied knowing anything," he probed.

"Ah cawse, boss. She must be de world's greatest liar," the Tomato moped, a lifetime of confidences shattered.

"But you don't *know* that she's lying," Guthrie countered. "Maybe you're too close to it." He regretted assigning Tomato the task, even though the job was well done and his suspicions solidly grounded.

"Although I will spot you motive, Tomato," he added. "If she's telling the truth she has motive, and that's not a bad place to begin seeing as she makes a good suspect for both plots."

"She's not lying about that, boss, I'm sure, and *I*'d 'a killed the bastard if I knew."

"Okay, Tomato, stop feeling sorry for yourself and let's start being smart about this. Let's assume you're right. She's guilty. Open and shut, as you say. What the coroner just told us means more than one person wanted Achermann dead, and that means there are at least two insiders. Let's say your friend Kelley is one. Who is the other?" The Tomato's unimproved expression meant he wasn't following. "Someone went to a lot of trouble to poison Achermann, wouldn't you say?" he said, trying to coax the Tomato from his lethargy. Inspiring the Tomato could be like driving a heifer from the barn.

"Where do you pick up diamond dust around Poughkeepsie anyway?" he asked, searching for levity.

"I dunno," the Tomato replied with the shadow of a smile.

"If you knew he would be dead in hours," he continued, "why would you go to the trouble of shooting him, too?" He could see the Tomato coming around.

What he could not bring himself to say was that he thought the Tomato was right. Sutton and LeBeau were involved, the both of them, but separately, each one defending her honor the best way they knew how; and both would likely face charges, one for premeditated murder and the other for conspiracy to commit. They would both end up in the big house, and probably for a good long time, passing letters between the bars, like a dystopian Romeo and Juliet, denied even the catharsis of death.

"There are cheaper, more common poisons than diamond dust, wouldn't you say? So let's start there. That's a signature of some kind. Let's find out whose."

His enthusiasm for widening the investigation gave the Tomato welcome relief, and he looked optimistic, like a battered but unbowed prize fighter.

"Look Tomato," he said, "Kelley Sutton didn't come up with diamond dust on her own, even if she did feed it to Achermann. And if she shot him we're going to need a lot more evidence to prove it." The Tomato looked puzzled, relieved for his boss's forbearance, but mystified all the same. Guthrie's logic was simple. The case had a long way to run, and plots and suspects were multiplying like dump rats.

"The tough part, my friend, is that you're going to have to talk to her again. She's played the sympathy card, now find out if she had revenge on her mind. She doesn't strike me as the defenseless type."

He knew the Tomato was at a disadvantage without sharing his suspicion of Whitaker, and he felt sure the CIA was involved. Whitaker's affiliation with the club and with the LeBeaus in particular was long, and Ron's law enforcement ambitions and Rick's military credentials made them natural allies, kindred spirits, especially if the cause were national security. He felt himself fumbling at the frayed edges of a tightly woven plot, and Whitaker's shadowy hand reaching like Fagen with federal powers into the private lives of the LeBeaus, exploiting the urge for revenge. But it was no use explaining that to the Tomato. It would only complicate his next assignment. What he needed from the Tomato was information from Kelley Sutton, and this the Tomato could handle.

There was still the puzzling matter of the Achermanns and their connection to the pilfered DRX. It was a bizarre and unlikely coincidence that was impossible to ignore. Did they start in cahoots and part ways, or was she spooked by his murder? Was she still planning to blame him to save herself, or was it just a change of heart; or perhaps her plan from the start was to serve him up like a fatted calf, just desserts for his indiscretions. Another shoe was bound to drop.

A straightforward crime of passion was acquiring appeal, especially if the Achermanns were in the agency's sights. Whitaker wouldn't bat an eye at using disposables like Sutton and LeBeau to do his dirty work. If that explained one plot, how to explain the other? Surely the agency had more confidence in its work than to require belt and suspenders, which brought him back reluctantly to the possibility of an accident, right where Whitaker wanted him to go.

It turned in his mind so convulsively that he lost track of the storylines, his theories and the evidence decoupling into nonsensical cubist art. What he needed was more information, better information, for which he was relying on his hapless henchmen, Jimmy and the Tomato. There was no way to know what Sutton and Woodcock might say, if Woodcock could even be found. And then he realized that Sutton and LeBeau were perfect marks for the oldest and most cunning of ploys for wresting confessions.

Chapter 19

Woodcock reached the rusty iron railing ringing the bustling sidewalk café tables, and noticed something familiar about the man Coco told him was Sam Dunkelsbuhler. He hesitated on the chance of a flash recollection, but the memory was too distant. As he approached from behind Dunkelsbuhler turned. Their eyes met, and Dunkelsbuhler smiled spontaneously, a broad, bright, welcoming, smile with so much goodwill it caught him off guard.

"Woodcock, old boy!" Sam exclaimed. He recoiled spontaneously with surprise, barely recognizing the face and certainly unable to place it. His reaction set Sam to backpedaling.

"Sam Dunkelsbuhler," he pronounced. "Eton, old boy. You were in Godolphin House. I was in the Timbralls. I was in Fourth Form when you were famously denied your goal in the E versus Chamber match." Woodcock's goal would have been the first point scored in Eton's legendary Wall Game since 1909, but the umpire did not see his throw graze the tree it was required to strike and would not allow what he had not witnessed, even over the opposing side's decency to concede the point.

The match to which Sam referred was the seminal confrontation between the two top teams in the arcane Wall Game, played nowhere in the world but Eton. They played against a wall built in 1717, almost two hundred years after the school was founded by Henry VI. The Wall Game was grueling and monotonous and almost always scoreless, a testament to stubborn British fealty to tradition. Even the school's catalog conceded *"few sports offer less to the spectator."*

"No reason you would remember me, Woodcock, but you were famous. Come sit for a minute if you can?" Sam proposed. His expectations of the encounter had been low, especially with the usual handicap of his CIA calling card. That Sam knew him in another context, from a simpler, more innocent time, before life took its inevitable toll, made the opportunity immediately more promising.

"Bloody good memory, Dunkelsbuhler," he effused. "I do apologize for not recognizing you."

"Why would you? I'm sure I don't remember any Fourth Formers from my last year." Sam virtually beamed with pleasure at being in the company of so revered a Senior Boy, even so many years later; and Woodcock felt unexpectedly at ease, basking in the intimacy of privilege only school boys of pedigree share.

"Meeting someone, are you?" Sam inquired, trying to keep him from feeling obligated.

"Not really, no," he said stalling. "Not that at all, really." He wracked his brain for an innocuous segue into why he had come.

"No, I'm afraid not, actually, Dunkelsbuhler," he began, deciding the truth might be best. "The reason I'm here is to see you." Sam's enthusiasm faded like a summer evening, and he began to look puzzled. He felt the reunion becoming a forgettable prologue and Sam's spontaneous elation sputter.

"You say you've come here to see me?" Sam finally said. "Come now, you wouldn't have known me if I hadn't recognized you."

"Yes, I suppose that's right," he agreed, waiting for Sam to make the connection to Coco Stockton.

"Well look, Woodcock, that's jolly good of you. I'm sure it's a matter of tremendous intrigue, and it would be bloody good fun to reminisce about the old days," Sam prattled, "but we may need to find another time. Someone will be joining me, very shortly," Sam said looking at his watch. "Not the sort to have around a chap's conversation. Would that be all right?" He sounded genuine and interested but the camaraderie was gone.

"Yes, of course, fine," Woodcock replied, trying to put Sam at ease "but you see, Dunkelsbuhler, I'm afraid I *am* your meeting. I had Ms. Stockton ring you because I needed to speak to you on a matter of some urgency. Please forgive my impertinence." Sam's soft Tuscan tan turned ruddy and hard like New England granite.

"That's a bit over the top, isn't it, mate?" said Sam, trading congeniality for street parlance.

"I didn't have time to call directly and risk being put off by someone in your office. I apologize," Woodcock replied. "I wouldn't have done it otherwise, do you see?"

"No need for apologies, old boy," replied Sam. "Anything for a fellow Wall banger and all that, though it's bloody discouraging you relied on an American journalist to find me."

"Yes, quite," he replied, reaffirming their peerage.

Despite the rocky introduction Sam appeared to be at ease, and he let the conversation run, falling into the cadence and phrases and rarified inflections that restore the tribal bonds of nobility. He was speaking more freely than he generally allowed, and to an all but perfect stranger. But Sam was emboldened by his confidences. He was on loan to the CIA from British intelligence, assigned to the Department of Homeland Security, of all the indignities, and he described his ascendance from interpreter to field agent. Fear in the United States had turned to panic, he said, which had spooked the intelligence community. It was engaged in monitoring the citizenry with the same troubling enthusiasm as the soviet era Stasi, he didn't mind saying. Sam listened carefully, waiting for the point.

"What brings me here, old chap," he finally said, "is one Harry Achermann. Do you know him?" he asked. At first he saw confusion, and then calculation, darting like a comet through Sam's eyes.

"Of course I know him," said Sam. "You should know I know him." At first he thought Sam meant by association with Coco, but something in his body language intimated more. He looked confounded, or perhaps imploring – like a hopeless child's tutor. He was yearning for Woodcock to make the connection.

"Why should I know that?" Woodcock finally said.

"Because…because your chaps…" and he watched Sam cut himself off as he realized how oblivious Woodcock was. He had lost the initiative and Sam knew it, and he felt the old order inexorably topple. They both shifted uncomfortably, Sam acclimating to the upper hand. Sam was the path to enlightenment now, and *rescue me* was the only way out. It would take his best performance before Sam let his tongue slip again.

"Tell me, if you would," Woodcock said, hat-in-hand, "how you came to know Achermann." The expressionless mask of Sam's face looked like a warning to trespassers, and he grew stiff and inhibited as he scanned the nearby tables for eavesdroppers. He completed his sweep and leaned across the table, acquiring a hushed, conspiratorial tone.

"Harry appeared in London some years ago, a bit of an uninvited guest as it were…" He said Achermann made himself a nuisance, ham-handedly courting company executives.

"He was keen on natural resources, diamonds in particular, and he wanted an African presence for his Global Strategy something or other," Sam snorted. "He was utterly, well *you* know, *American*. No inkling of the diamonds market, how it works, who's involved," he said. "I mean, it's not the bloody New York Stock exchange, is it Woodcock?" said Sam, wink-as-good-as-a-nudge.

"No, quite," he acknowledged, playing the new-boy, and rather well, too, he flattered himself. Sam carried on about Harry's presumptions and the embarrassment of his entreaties, which he invariably undertook at the most public social engagements.

"We treated him civilly, as one does, you see, but we paid him no attention, you can be sure."

He cringed and laughed and nodded like an ingénue while Sam worked a tired old theme – Americans in London, and their anglophile affectations.

"Look Woodcock," said Sam, tiring of his own charade, "what's your interest in Achermann anyway, if you don't mind me asking?"

"Of course, old chap, happy to oblige," he said.

"Achermann was someone of interest to the U.S. authorities. Not a very savory fellow, to be honest. Poked his nose in places he shouldn't, perhaps helping himself to things that weren't his. Did you happen to know his wife?"

"Did you say his wife, old boy? I should say not. Didn't even know he was married. He gave no impression of it, of that you can be sure."

"Yes, quite," Woodcock answered, moving slowly, taking Sam's measure. Sam might have the goods on Achermann, but if he was unaware of his wife, and more to the point, her possession of DRX, he might be less informed than he supposed.

"I've been trailing Achermann for months now," Woodcock began. "Seems he might have gotten his hands on a rather nasty weapons grade biological agent."

"Whatever for?"

"Well you might ask. To offer it for sale?" he said, lifting his eye brows suggestively. He studied Sam's face for the untamed flicker in the eyebrows, the impulsive purse of the lips profilers attach to concealment. But Sam looked away, then down at the pavement where his attention was drawn to the pulsating embers of a cigarette. And then he closed his eyes and rubbed his face as if he were waking to face the day. That sequence of gestures was precisely what Woodcock came for – a textbook display from the phase of his training called *profiling for beginners* – which included a video tape of President Clinton giving testimony under oath about the Monica Lewinski affair during which he perpetually rubbed his nose and covered his mouth, like a chronic sufferer of hay fever.

"A classic example of dissembling," said the narrator. "Acts of physical concealment are the surest tell of deception." It meant he was close.

"He never mentioned something for sale?"

"Don't be silly, Woodcock. We wouldn't involve ourselves with the likes of him," said Sam, "too much of a risk."

"So you had no dealings with him?" he persisted.

"None whatsoever, old chap. Wish I could be more help, I really do, but we avoided him like the plague." Like the plague. Really, thought Woodcock. If that weren't a subconscious cue they didn't exist.

"Is that *really* what this surprise encounter is all about, Woodcock? Harry Achermann?" Sam stole another glance at his watch. "I shall be late for a dinner engagement, old chap. We really must get together again when we both have more time. I hope you don't mind," he finished.

"Hang on, Dunkelsbuhler," he interrupted. "The plague is just what Achermann might have been offering."

"Offering?" Sam replied. "You didn't hear me. DeBeers has no interest in the Achermanns of this world, whatever he was offering."

"Not even if it eradicated an insignificant tribe that was just awarded mineral rights, including diamonds, worth billions of pounds?"

"You're bloody daft, Woodcock, that's what you are."

"Am I?" he persisted. "An engineered strain of the Ebola virus called DRX just turned up in Namaqueland, in Northwest South Africa. Are you familiar with that region?"

"I've heard of it, of course," Sam replied. He looked at the pavement again. The embers had burned themselves out.

"Our lads interviewed a park ranger, dead now, I'm afraid," he said, gauging the effect on Sam. "Said he worked for DeBeers. Believed there could have been something virulent in supplies he delivered to the Nama, the local tribe from that region that was, not coincidentally, just awarded mineral rights worth billions of pounds." Sam ignored him. "That part of South Africa is a diamond rich region, is it not?"

"Look Woodcock, I don't know what you're on about. Sounds bloody sinister to me – stolen viruses and tribal mineral rights. But you're up the wrong tree if you think we had anything to do with Achermann. You should really ask Achermann himself about all this."

"Yes, well, we were getting around to doing just that when he was murdered. Bloody nuisance, really." Sam hesitated.

"Yes, I should say so. Bad luck." Sam finally said. The flicker for which Woodcock had been waiting darted like a zephyr on still water across Sam's eyebrows.

"Poor bloody Achermann, and Mrs. Achermann, too, I suppose," said Sam.

Once they got started good liars strung lies like party ribbons, and Woodcock was in his element. If he could keep Sam lying, Sam would make a mistake. Lies were hard to keep straight under sustained questioning, and liars never quit, the success of the first few being its own reward on the path to the delusion of invincibility. Something about the arrogance of a lie, the delusion of the liar, kept them repeating the offense under the misimpression they could outwit everyone. If he could force Sam to say something inconsistent, catch Sam in his own tangled web, Sam might relent.

"Look Dunkelsbuhler, I don't give a toss about Harry Achermann, how he met his ill-timed fate, or the bloody Nama for that matter. My job is to recover every last trace of DRX Ebola. My lads are running around South Africa and London studying surveillance tapes and tracking down every last soul at risk of exposure. If you chaps have any DRX left, you better bloody well turn it over, or the company will feel the full weight of the U.S. government in a way it hasn't before," he said. "This is no bloody joke. Please think about it over your dinner engagement and give me a ring if you decide to cooperate. Here's my card." He leaned across the table tendering his business card the way starlets hold cigarettes.

Sam was staring down again, discouraged to have lost sight of the cold embers. He seemed to be weighing consequences, perhaps even capitulation, so Woodcock waited. When Sam looked up it was with Himalayan conceit, no effort wasted on disguise.

"Woodcock," Sam began, "are you aware of our... relationship, between us, our company, and the U.S. government?"

"No. I'm quite sure I'm not. Do enlighten me."

"Africa is a complicated place, as you might imagine, and we've been friends, quite good friends, actually, for a long time," Sam extemporized.

"Except the last ten years," Woodcock added.

"Oh that. A tiff. A spat, and we've made up, you see. But you know all that."

"Yes, but what was the trade? The settlement was window dressing, a slap on the wrist. What was the quid pro quo?"

"You poor sod, Woodcock. You really are short-sighted. Think man."

"....Achermann? But why?"

"Now, now. No jumping to conclusions, as people always do. It was the diamond curse."

"Whatever *are* you on about?"

"You've never heard the legend?" said Sam.

"No. I'm quite sure I haven't."

"Legend has it that diamonds don't take to misuse. You mentioned some other fellow. Had a bit of bad luck."

"Sanderling? The dead park ranger? Yes, I suppose that qualifies as bad luck."

"Yes. He was probably up to no good either. Struck down by the curse."

"Come off it Dunkelsbuhler. That's pure tosh."

"Is it? Think back on the misfortune of men with questionable intentions in the diamond trade. They come to no good. It's the curse. At least that's what we believe. One of our guiding principles, actually. We take our stewardship seriously."

"Nonsense."

"Do you believe in God, Woodcock?"

"No."

"No, I don't suppose someone in your trade would."

"What's God got to do with anything?"

"Do you remember your Keats?"

"I don't know. Try me."

"Beauty truth, truth beauty and all that sort of thing."

"Vaguely."

"Well that's diamonds, isn't it."

"Is it?"

"Yes, the perfect expression of beauty, God's beauty, here on earth. Won't abide anything but the truth."

"You're bloody mad, Dunkelsbuhler."

"Am I? How do you explain our survival, the prosperity of our venture all these many years? We're good stewards, and we encourage good stewardship. Insist on it, actually. They've looked after us and we look after them."

"Diamonds?"

"Of course."

"If diamonds are the work of God, then how do you explain the infamous blood diamond trade?"

"I should think it explains itself, doesn't it? Diamonds are a touchstone. They bring out the truth, reveal the heart. Love in loving hands, death for the damned. It's that simple."

"And you decide."

"No, we bear witness, as believers do. What do *you* believe, Woodcock?" For a moment he wasn't sure.

"Superstitions aside, old boy," Woodcock began, "are you saying you knocked off Achermann to ingratiate yourself to the U.S. justice department? So they would give you a pass to the U.S. market? Couldn't the CIA have handled the job themselves?"

"Well, you have me there. I suppose they could have, or maybe they did. I wish it were all that simple. But it isn't, quite. Look, mate, nothing I'm about to tell you is going to do you a bit of good, but you may as well know seeing as your superiors don't seem to keep you informed. We had a bit of a rogue on our hands. Yes, you're quite right, this fellow Achermann *was* selling your DRX and we weren't the least bit interested, I can tell you. But he didn't stop there, did he. Yes, of course we know about the diamonds in Namaqueland – have known for decades, actually, and the Nama were never the worse for their ignorance. But greed is a dangerous thing and once someone put them up to suing for their rights we all knew we were in for it. Achermann came to us with this plan to eradicate them using the DRX so the mineral rights, if they won them, would go to a tribal trustee from whom they could be purchased for quite a reasonable sum. He wanted to be paid for the arrangement as well as a share in the subsequent mining yields. It was madness. Shrewd, mind you, but stark raving mad. We sent him packing. But he was undeterred."

"Oh?"

"Yes. You see he got wind of the Chinese - convinced them to buy the Nama mineral claims even before they were awarded, and brokered the transaction for the Nama on condition they appoint him trustee to manage their windfall – several billion dollars U.S. I'm told. Not that your lads knew any of this until we told them." So Whitaker knew. He knew all along.

"In any event, I told you he was mad. Never thought he'd use it, the DRX I mean, but based on everything you're saying, apparently he has. Wouldn't be at all surprised if he was sticking to his plan - ridding himself of the Nama and making off with their trust."

"You mentioned a rogue. You mean Achermann?"

"No, not Achermann. We have this fellow. Sort of a peace keeper on the frontiers of our little venture."

"You mean your cartel," he felt compelled to note.

"Too much time with Coco, I see. Call it what you will. This fellow keeps our friends mindful of their obligations. You do *see*, don't you?"

"He sounds lovely. I don't suppose he's the sort who mightn't take nicely to a nosy newspaper reporter?"

"Ah, yes. Coco. No, he's no fan of Ms. Stockton's. Well, perhaps that's not fair. No fan of her dismal dealings with Achermann, but that's none of my affair."

"Dealings?" said Woodcock.

"Associations may be more accurate."

"Good with a camera, was he?" asked Woodcock.

"Don't know. He has quite a repertoire. Is that what she sent you here to investigate?"

"She didn't send me. I need to know more about Achermann and his professional associates, if you follow my meaning."

"Yes. Not sure I can help you there, old boy, beyond the information we've already supplied. In any event, we had been concerned about the Chinese for some time, and when Achermann's dealings came to light I fear this fellow, our peace maker, took matters into his own hands."

"And murdered Achermann."

"I don't know to be perfectly honest. We're not the micromanaging sort. But he was bloody angry."

"You're not too cynical, are you Dunkelsbuhler?"

"Oh don't be so earnest, Woodcock. Too much time with the Yanks. Perhaps it's time to come home. In any event, the agency was reasonably chuffed to know about the DRX and quite inclined to forgive us our little pricing misunderstanding on that basis alone. But when misfortune caught up with Achermann, as we suspected it might, they gave us full marks. Don't know that we earned it, but someone deserves credit. Bloody sinister chap if you ask me."

Why hadn't Whitaker told him? What possible risk did he present by knowing? Maybe Dunkelsbuhler was right. It was time to come home. He reminded himself of his assignment - containing the DRX. The CIA's network of "friends," as Sam had so charitably described himself, was none of his business and nor was the archive of backroom deals and quid pro quos the agency juggled to keep the wheels turning. The world was full of dark characters like Achermann who supplied their own reasons for an abbreviated life. He wasn't the least bit squeamish about eliminating them. Nor did he concern himself with due process of law, since it was barely operative in the handful of countries practicing it. His job was to mitigate the damage.

"So you knew he was dead?" he inquired.

"Or would be soon. It's not my place to know when or how these things happen. I only know they do." *Rescue me* had worked, but not sufficiently to recover his school-days seniority.

Chapter 20

Jimmy gripped the armrests as the enormous plane settled into slow flight and lumbered through final approach to Heathrow Airport, London. He was exhausted and disoriented from the overnight journey. He had ventured from New England barely more than half a dozen times, not because he was unadventurous, but because he knew what he liked, and he liked what he knew. This was his first journey beyond U.S. borders and he was not especially excited about it. Air travel didn't suit him, he knew that now, and but for his high-profile quarry, it was strictly routine: question, document, file and report.

Dawn was breaking over the dense ledge of clouds beneath the wing. The plane rose and fell like a horse on a carousel. The clouds looked so firm that he subtly braced for impact as they descended into the pall, but the plane continued its inexorable descent, slipping beneath the silvery mist and giving him vertigo as the window turned black like paper turning to ash. He peered apprehensively into the gloom, searching for the wingtip that moments before had been springing like the hands of a tap dancer with the twitching plane. For the longest time he hurtled through space, a planet spiraling out of orbit, until the wing tip reappeared and he relaxed his grip at the sight of the dreary countryside rising beneath him. The briefest watercolor images flashed like test screens through passing apertures in the low level clouds, and shadowy images of hedgerows and farmhouses smeared in the rain across his window. So the misty grey landscapes of Sherlock Holmes were just like in the movies, he thought. England was really like that, and he steeled himself for the sinister streets of Jack the Ripper and Jekyll and Hyde. The plane touched down with such a thunderous clatter that he was sure it would disintegrate, and he crossed himself twice.

But it held together until it reached the gate, where he waited forever to disembark, and then followed the crowd through corridors and switchbacks until he found himself amidst the throng waiting to clear customs in Terminal Four. The crowd looked like wildebeest fording a river in *National Geographic* with a gauntlet of emigration officers culling weaklings from the herd. He felt horrible, bewildered by jet lag and rocked by alternating spells of hunger and nausea. He thought he had seen everything in New York City, but the exotic occupants of the super-sized room opened his eyes. It was a whole new race, shorter on average he reckoned than Americans, since he was five foot eight on his toes and could see clear across the room. A few soared like baobabs on the Serengeti and spoke in belligerent, guttural tongues. These must be the ones whose ancestors crossbred with Neanderthals, according to an article he read about DNA to familiarize himself with the properties of DecimRiboX. And there were robes and scarves and sandals a plenty, with a potpourri of odors from cologne-masked body odor to aftershave and spice. It was Times Square at rush hour, times ten.

An hour into the line without a customs officer in sight, the novelty of the floor show had worn off and be began to think about finding Woodcock. It was sure he was nowhere nearby. He would stand out like an albino in a juke joint, and that's when he noticed the line of travelers on the far wall slipping through customs like turnstile jumpers beneath the *European Union passports this way* sign. That's bald-faced discrimination, thought Jimmy, and right at the crossroads of modern civilization. Since when did being American make you like riff-raff outside a New York city night club, kept waiting by design to keep the in-crowd feeling *in*. The ACLU would have a field day with this, he thought, and that's when Europe began growing on him.

He was eventually called forward by a Sikh emigration officer with a towering blue turban and a thick unkempt beard with such expansionist designs that his eyes, nose and mouth looked at risk.

"How long will you be staying in the United Kingdom?" the officer asked in a crisp British accent that took Jimmy by surprise. He couldn't help but expect the officer's head to bobble like a snake charmer.

"I'm not sure," he replied, earning himself a malignant stare, to which he responded with a self-amused grin.

"I see you're a U.S. police officer," the Sikh observed, "what exactly brings you here?"

"I thought you'd never ask," said Jimmy. "I'm looking for someone in connection with a murder back in the States." The officer's eyes opened so wide that Jimmy thought he'd been goosed by someone beneath his podium.

"Of course you are," he replied with a smile. "We have arrangements for that sort of thing, as you should know, my good fellow," the officer said, and his grip on Jimmy's passport tightened unpromisingly. Long before he was a cop, Jimmy made peace with the truth, using it to charm his way out of all manner of predicaments. He had a hunch that being explicit would serve his particular purpose, and he was relieved to be quickly rewarded.

The officer reached high above his towering turban and waved over a stern-looking Caucasian. The broad-shouldered supervisor had tightly cropped hair and the complexion of the British Isles - ruddy red cheeks and Dover sole skin. He wore a blue ribbed sweater with brass buttoned epaulettes and a stiff white collar that gave him the look of a priest. A radio microphone hung on one shoulder with a black spiral chord that corkscrewed like a sash to his waist. He swept in on the Sikh like a fish on a bait, with a serious expression for which Jimmy was prepared with more antics.

"Says he's a U.S. police officer on business," the Sikh reported, to which Jimmy flashed his most winning smile. The supervisor leaned into his shoulder mic and muttered something unintelligible and stern. He took Jimmy's passport and landing card and said, "Come with me please, Officer Doolan." They aren't much fun, Jimmy thought to himself, giving up on his charm.

The supervisor marched him to a steel door with a coded lock that was bordered by one-way mirrored glass panes. It opened on to a long hallway with aging linoleum tiles that curled like dog-eared pages. At even intervals down the hall were metal framed doors from behind which rose the stressful low hum of questioning, like murmurs around a casket.

He was led to an empty office and told to sit down while his escort guarded the door. A large unkempt man in a similar blue uniform materialized like a bouncer at a scuffle, dismissing Jimmy's escort with a nod. Enter the interrogator, thought Jimmy, who steeled himself for the routine. The new man looked tired and bored, and his belly parted the ribs of his sweater unflatteringly. His thick black hair twisted and waved in slow, greasy curls and dandruff spotted his epaulettes. There was nowhere to escape his rancid body odor, and the folds of his abdomen settled like ties on a roast when he pulled on his waistband. He dumped himself into a chair behind the plastic veneer desk, and the seat howled in unholy protest as he set to work on Jimmy's passport and landing card. A computer screen on the desk flashed to life as he scanned Jimmy's passport, and Jimmy was waiting with a smile when he finally looked up.

"Look, mate," said the interrogator in an accent Jimmy couldn't place, "what are you doing here?" His breath was a stew of semi-digested vapors, including cigarettes and coffee.

"I'm looking for someone," said Jimmy, taken aback by the interrogator's candor. Maybe he'd gotten lucky and this was the end of the shift.

"Who?"

"Someone called Adam Woodcock. At least that's the name he's using. This is what he looks like," said Jimmy offering the interrogator his cell phone. The interrogator ignored him and studied his screen like a replay official. He finally looked satisfied and leaned back in his chair, which yelped again beneath him.

"First time out of the country then, is it?"

"Yes, actually. First time anywhere, really," said Jimmy.

"Good idea of where to find him then, do you?"

"No, not really. I thought you might be willing to help me out," said Jimmy, beaming. The interrogator grunted. He must have seen the youthful innocence gambit before.

"He's not a suspect or anything, I just need to talk to him," said Jimmy, trying to recover.

"Have you tried ringing him up?" said the interrogator with a sneer. A monosyllabic chuckle gurgled from his gut and he rippled like a walrus.

"I wouldn't know where to reach him. Probably wouldn't talk to me over the phone anyway," he said, pausing for effect and doing his best to look discouraged.

"But," Jimmy finally said, producing a blank landing card, "you know where he's staying, don't you?" and he pointed to the address line of the card. He reached into his collapsed overnight bag and produced his New York State Lieutenant Detective badge. "Check me out, boss. Take as long as you want. The sooner I find

Woodcock, the sooner I can leave." The officer looked disdainfully at the badge.

"Bollocks, mate. Don't mean a bloody thing here. You're in the wrong bloody country, aren't you," he said, and snorted and rippled again.

"What's this bloke's name again, Lieutenant-Sir-James-bloody-Doolan?" he said, inspecting Jimmy's badge.

"Woodcock, Adam Woodcock," said Jimmy. "He probably came through here the day before yesterday, or maybe yesterday." He felt himself mix days the way tourists mix phrases. The interrogator leaned forward into his computer screen and pecked at his keyboard with his index fingers.

"'Ere he is, mate," he said. Something he saw piqued his curiosity because he made a quizzical sound like a flummoxed cartoon character. "Hmm… British passport, U.S. government employee. That's a bit unusual, isn't it?" he observed. Apparently a British national working as U.S. government agent presented something of a common threat, for he welcomed the opportunity to demonstrate his powers of surveillance.

"E's staying where they all do, 'round the corner from your embassy on Grosvenor Square," he said. He scrounged a tired notepad from the desk drawer and scratched out an address, stamped Jimmy's passport and folded the address inside it.

"Good luck, mate," he said, "and don't stay too bloody long."

"Thanks, man," said Jimmy, "I won't." He shouldered his bag and extended his hand as a plume of new breath enveloped him - the price of the assist, he told himself - and he smiled with gratitude through the interrogator's limp handshake. So far the plan was working.

He was studying door numbers and estimating the location of the hotel to which the interrogator had directed him when he saw Woodcock emerge from a taxi and enter a doorway. It was columned and grand like the others on the street, and he double-timed it to the steps which he bounded like a delivery boy in twos. There was a beveled brass plaque imbedded in the door with letters worn smooth like ancient hieroglyphs from polishing. He pushed through the door into a small reception area that felt more like an opulent home than a hotel lobby, and the door swung closed behind him sealing out the street noise outside. Somewhere in the distance an elevator door that had seen better times ground shut, and there behind reception stood the most astonishing woman. She was well-groomed and Indian, posed like a runway model, with moist white teeth and dark red lips, and she seemed to regard him with skepticism.

"May I help you?" she asked.

"Ah, yeah," Jimmy stuttered, adrift on the lilting delivery of her British accent. She had glistening green eyes and green silk lapels that shimmered in iridescent harmony, and a translucent silk blouse that flattered her counters in a way that revived his senses. Her springy bob brushed against her neck, the smoothness of which left him speechless.

"I'm looking for one of your guests, Adam Woodcock," he blurted, the coarseness and volume of his voice embarrassing him.

"Mr. Woodcock?" she smiled, and she pointed around the corner to the elevator. "You just missed him, I'm afraid. You can ring him on the house phone, over there in the corner. He's in room sixteen." He stood there feeling foolish, spellbound by her manner until she said, "is there anything else?" and tucked a springy course of her shiny black hair self-consciously behind one ear.

The sitting room to which she directed him was small and sumptuously appointed. Dried flowers and peacock feathers potted in matching oriental vases rose from the corners in thick symmetrical fronds, and tapestries hung from the walls. A rich Turkish rug covered all but the perimeter of the parquet flooring and a heavy glass table with gold painted legs divided the room into intimate seating. He was feeling like Lawrence of Arabia when the elevator halted on the landing beyond the sitting room.

"Detective Doolan, is it?" said an Englishman as the door ground open. He exited the elevator and closed the separation in four strides. The beguiling receptionist turned at the word *detective*. "Yeah, that's right, but Jimmy's fine," said Jimmy, hoping to make himself sound more approachable. "You must be Woodcock, am I right?"

"The very one. Whatever brings you all the way to London, from Poughkeepsie, is it, you say?" Jimmy had only heard about proper British snobs, but he was already getting the picture.

"I came to see you," he said.

"That's a bloody long way, isn't it? It must be important."

"It is, like I said on the phone."

"I'll tell you what, my good man, I'm in a terrible rush. Suppose you ride in a taxi with me and tell me what this is all about."

They were in the street beneath a darkening sky when a cab heeded Woodcock's call and pulled to the curb, and the first heavy drops of a cold spring rain began to fall.

"Royal Marsden Hospital, please," said Woodcock to the driver through his window.

"Right, Gov," Jimmy heard the driver say as he piled in the rear behind Woodcock.

Jimmy wasted no time and led with the facts. Achermann was a sitting duck, shot dead, or almost so, the flesh of his throat flayed like a songbird on a windshield. The Poughkeepsie police thought it was a setup, meant to look like a hunting accident, but they weren't buying it.

"That's all very interesting Detective Doolan, but what on earth does any of this have to do with me?"

"Oh please, Mr. British-secret-agent-man, don't embarrass yourself," said Jimmy reaching for his phone, and he summoned the same security camera photograph by which he had been served so well in customs only a few hours before.

"Because that's a picture of you visiting Achermann's wife at the CDC in Atlanta a couple of days ago where she's been quarantined for exposure to DRX Ebola, which you and your employer believe Achermann stole."

"My employer, Detective Doolan? And who would that be?"

"You tell me. Homeland Security is what you told Dr. Achermann. Now tell me something, Woodcock, how well do you know Jack Whitaker?" Jimmy got his answer in the blankness on Woodcock's face.

"Thought so," he concluded. "That's funny. He said he didn't know you either. I think you're both lying. Here's why."

"Doesn't everybody?" interrupted Woodcock.

"Doesn't everybody what?" answered Jimmy.

"Know Whitaker. He *is* deputy director of the CIA."

"Yeah, no shit, Woody. That's not what I meant. Did you know he was there when Achermann was murdered? Did you know he and his goons were less than a mile away, armed, and that the goons have no alibis but each other at the time of the murder?" He wanted to be careful, to guard against sounding hysterical, but pretensions of office made him mad.

"Please forgive me, my good man, but are you suggesting the deputy director of the CIA and his security detail were somehow involved in a murder?"

"I'm not suggesting anything. I'm reporting the facts. You would know better than I. But if eliminating Achermann had to done, as a matter of national security, in an accessible place and an unsuspicious way, wouldn't this fit the bill? In plain sight, and all that?" Woodcock looked at him cock-eyed like a clown, afraid and amused all at once.

"Anyway," said Jimmy, "we questioned him, and he said he had never heard of you either."

"Did you say you questioned him? The deputy director of the CIA, Jack Whitaker? You questioned him?"

"Of course. He was there when it happened, nearby, like I said. We're questioning everybody who was at the club that morning. So you admit you know him."

"I told you I knew him. You weren't listening, Detective Doolan. I'm in direct contact with him on this DRX problem, as a matter of fact," he sniffed, "the top secret nature of which you would oblige me by keeping. You *can* keep a secret, can't you? Until the public is out of danger?"

"Then why did he deny knowing you?"

"I can't say, except there's no reason for him to think you needed to know. There's more at play here than meets the eye, my American friend. One wants to be careful in such situations," he cautioned in a way that could have been a threat.

"Where are we going anyway?" Jimmy demanded.

Chapter 21

"He's here," Guthrie barked.

"I see him, boss," said the Tomato. They were both expecting him, but not fifteen minutes early. The Tomato probably needed the time, thought Guthrie, to steel himself like an army chaplain with bad news. They could both see him waiting at the intake desk, peering into the station house like he was casing the joint. Nothing about his appearance today betrayed his years in the army. His hair looked longer than normal and unkempt, and the patchy unevenness of his two-day stubble gave him a mangy, unsanitary look like a bum. Only his sinewy bare forearms, which lay across the desk, gave any hint of his athleticism, and he looked about the stationhouse, calm as the clergy, waiting for someone to notice him.

Guthrie watched the Tomato amble reluctantly to the front where he greeted his old friend like a stranger. They weren't the first of friends to be parted by the hundred year old wood. It was grey and faded and worn at the center like the steps of an ancient cathedral, except the devotions it witnessed were dismal and dark, like car theft and drug dealing and prostitution. The shades of Poughkeepsie left it scarred like old skin, a chronicle to rival all one hundred of its growth rings.

"Hey Frankie, what's this about?" Guthrie heard Rick ask. He sounded uncertain and familiar, like a family member but estranged.

"We gotta ask a few more questions about 'de Achermann 'ting," said the Tomato. "Why don' you take a seat out here," the Tomato instructed his friend, and pointed to the chairs in the waiting area. "You're a few minutes early. I'll be right back," said the Tomato as he turned in retreat toward Guthrie. Over the Tomato's perpetual slouch he watched Rick study the seating until deciding on a chair that gave him a view across the intake desk into the stationhouse. Rick faced himself in from beside the front door and began tracking the movements of stationhouse staff, his eyes following the Tomato until he stood by Guthrie'e side.

"He's watching us, Tomato," Guthrie said to his protégé.

"Yeah, not surprised, boss. He sees everything."

"You think he's got us figured?"

"If he don't now he will soon, boss."

"Fair enough, Tomato. Let's see where it goes."

"I wish we didn't have to do it this way, boss. Sometimes I don't like your procedures."

"I know you don't, Tomato. I don't much like it myself. Come in here with me," he said, herding the Tomato into the conference room where the evidence decorated the walls, and where the Tomato planned to question Rick.

"You still game for this?"

"Sure," said the Tomato. Guthrie left him there for the cubicle outside the door. It was ideally situated to eavesdrop on the questioning and observe the proceedings at the intake desk. The time passed slowly until the stroke of 8 a.m. when an imposing black female police officer assumed her position at the intake desk. From inside the cubicle he couldn't see Rick, but he could see duty officer Chantelle Washington, and she was staring at Rick disparagingly. She looked that way at everybody called for questioning to the stationhouse because her Rasta-themed dime-store reading glasses saw no reason to hope for any of them.

"Can I help you?" she finally asked Rick.

"Waiting for Frankie," Guthrie heard Rick say. Officer Washington lowered her chin. She had the practiced disdain of an inner-city school teacher which she was presently leveling on Rick.

"I mean Detective D'Amato," Rick corrected himself.

"I see," she said, as if she had already heard enough. And then daylight filled the waiting area as the front door swung wide and in stepped Kelley Sutton, moving tentatively. She did not see Rick behind the door as she crossed the threshold, but there was no way for him to miss her, and she stepped forward into the glare of Officer Washington's Rastafarian readers looking scared and disorganized.

"I'm here to see Frankie," Guthrie heard her whisper.

"Do you mean Detective D'Amato?" Officer Washington bellowed. "Why, he is popular today, isn't he?" she blared like a town crier. Count on Chantelle to find the bright side, even in moments like this, Guthrie thought.

"And what might your name be, friend of Frankie?" she bellowed again.

"Kelley Sutton," she said even less audibly.

"You're going to have to speak up, Miss Sutton," said Washington, "if you want to be heard. You can have a seat right there," she said, pointing to the seats around the room, "in line behind that young man, who is here to see Detective D'Amato, too." He saw Kelley turn and see Rick for the first time, and she froze like a cast from Pompeii.

"Hi Kel," he heard Rick say. She clutched her shoulder bag like a security blanket and disappeared from view, taking the closest seat to the intake desk, Guthrie presumed. Officer Washington swiveled on her captain's chair and leveled her readers on Guthrie. Her patience for his procedures was never unlimited and she was ready to start the show.

"Hi Ricky," he heard Kelley say. "What are you doing here?" Washington swiveled back like a vigilant librarian determined to keep things under control.

"Frankie asked me to come," said Rick.

"Oh yeah? Me too," she replied sounding relieved, and a very long silence followed. Let it simmer, thought Guthrie, let the emotions rise, and then we'll go to work.

"She's here," he told the Tomato through the open conference room door. "You almost ready?"

"Ready as I'll ever be, boss," droned the Tomato. "You want me to go get him?"

"Not yet, Tomato. Let 'em get reacquainted, and then we'll see what they know." He let the time pass until Officer Washington swiveled again and he felt himself in the cross-fire of her readers and the Tomato's soulful stare.

"OK, Tomato, one at a time."

"I got it, boss, one at a time," and he lifted himself reluctantly. He ambled past Guthrie, down the passageway, past the darkened offices, and through the door into the waiting area.

"Frankie," he heard them say in unison like they had said it together before.

"Hey Ricky, hey Kel'," said the Tomato before they bombarded him with questions that cancelled each other out before reaching Guthrie's ears.

"We'll talk it all through," he heard the Tomato assure them, before he told Kelley to wait.

"Come on, Ricky," he said, holding open the waiting room door.

Rick followed the Tomato into the passageway back to the conference room, studying the stationhouse as he went. When his eyes found Guthrie in the cubicle outside the conference room, they crackled disquietingly in his cool, composed face. He acknowledged Guthrie with a dip of his chin and followed the Tomato into the conference room, leaving the door ajar.

"Wow, Frankie," said Rick. "You guys been hard at work," he observed as he took in the evidence on the walls.

"Yeah Rick. This is what we do. You wanna a coffee or somethin'?"

"Nah. I'm fine. Is Guthrie out there joining us, or are we doing this alone?"

Officer Washington swiveled again and glared at Guthrie from her captain's chair, and this time he gave her the nod.

"Miss Kelley," she announced so the stationhouse heard, "come with me please," she instructed and dismounted her chair.

"Why's she here, Frankie?" Rick asked. "She's got nothin' to do with this."

"What makes you so sure?" said the Tomato in a way that made Guthrie proud.

"Detective Guthrie?" Kelley said as she and Officer Washington approached the conference room. "Why are we here? Did you ask Frankie to bring us here?"

"I did," said Guthrie, standing to greet her just outside the conference room door where Rick would be sure to see her.

"Why?"

"Because, Miss Sutton, and I'm sorry to say it, but we know something happened... something unfortunate, upsetting... between you and Mr. Achermann." She glanced into the conference room where she found the Tomato, and gave him a Judas worthy look.

"Don't blame him, Miss Sutton, he's doing his job. He thinks you're both innocent, that's why you're here, because he's sure you can clear yourselves as suspects, given the chance - a chance you're getting courtesy of Detective D'Amato." She seemed to go cold, as if the Tomato's confidence were misplaced.

"It's a chance I'd take, Miss Sutton, if I were you. If what you told Detective D'Amato is true, it's a compelling motive, the only one we have so far, so please cooperate with Officer Washington, here, and tell her everything you know." She stood in stunned silence, and glanced back at the conference room where Rick was already sprawled like last year's scarecrow across a chair, except his crackling blue eyes. With so many years of shared intimacy between them Guthrie imagined they cued each other in invisible ways, and he watched especially closely to see what they might divulge to each other.

But she turned back to Guthrie looking lost and scared.

"But you don't believe him, do you Detective Guthrie? Because you already think one of us done it." Officer Washington was standing close by.

"Officer Washington," said Guthrie.

"Come with me, please, Miss Sutton," she said heading for the darkened office next to the conference room, and flipping the light switch on the wall as she passed through the door.

"Your friend Detective D'Amato will spend some time with Mr. LeBeau while Officer Washington spends some time with you. I'll be right out here if either of you needs anything. There's nothing to worry about, Miss Sutton, if Detective D'Amato is right." Officer Washington closed the door behind them after Kelley entered the room, and Guthrie closed the door on the Tomato and Rick, and returned to his station in the cubicle.

The quality of construction by the lowest bidder on the stationhouse contract ensured he would hear the majority of both conversations. The glass panels beside each door leaked sound like the walls of a cheap motel, while the cinderblock wall dividing the rooms had an altogether different effect. The wall filtered words but not sound, meaning but not sentiment, the way frosted glass obscures form but not light. It was bound to unnerve them and that was his plan.

"So, Ricky, we got a lot to talk about, don't we?" the Tomato began.

"Frankie, I don't know what you mean. I didn't have nothin' to do with all this," he said, waving his hand at the evidence on the walls around the room.

"I know it don't look good, being with him and all, but I already told you everything I know. Honest. I been over it so many times in my own mind that I'm getting things mixed up myself," Rick confessed.

"Ricky, there's gotta be more than your remembering," D'Amato replied. "Or than you're tellin'." That-a-boy, thought Guthrie, you have to be tough. But the silence that followed gave him cause for concern. They were still in discovery. They were trying to learn, and if Rick stopped trusting them now they would miss an opportunity. He sat in his cubicle waiting for the conversation to resume, and the longer he waited the more he despaired. It was probably the first time in their lives either Rick or the Tomato had doubted one another.

"Don't give me that look, Ricky," he heard the Tomato say.

"What look is that, Frankie?"

"That *I been to war and killed tougher guys than you,* look. You know what I mean."

"Miss Sutton," Officer Washington was saying, "I need you to tell me why you had nothin' to do with this, and I need you to speak up, 'cause nobody but you comin' to your rescue, understand?" Neither subject uttered a word, as if they'd taken a vow of silence.

"I'm not scared of you, Ricky," he heard the Tomato say, "so you can stop lookin' at me that way. You weren't ruined or broken by goin' off to war. No, that's not what scares me. I'll tell you what scares me, Ricky, is that it just made you tougher. That you've changed, one way or another, and it's nothin' for you to kill this guy and let Kel' hang for it, 'cause you think they both deserve it. Tell me I'm wrong Ricky. Please tell me I'm wrong."

"And Guthrie said you thought I was innocent," said Rick.

"I do. Least I want to think so, Ricky, but you ain't helpin' me any."

"What do you want to know?" Kelley was saying to Officer Washington. "What do you want me to tell you that I haven't told Frankie?" she whined, "and that he hasn't told the whole world."

"Ricky, why aren't you talkin'? What do you got to hide?"

"Frankie," said Rick, "I got nothing. I told you everything. Everything. There ain't nothing more to tell. You're looking for something that isn't there." He sounded frustrated, maybe annoyed, but not guilty. It was the sound of a clear conscience, thought Guthrie, at least for now.

"What about her?" the Tomato continued.

"What about her, Frankie?"

"Come on, Ricky. You know what I mean. She can't account for where she was at the time of the murder. It don't help she can shoot the nuts off a squirrel, and if what she says happened..."

"It happened."

"Well all right then."

"What does it matter?"

"It matters, Ricky. If she did it, she's going away for life."

"So what?"

"What a sweetheart you are. Man, have you changed."

"I just figure they deserve each other, know what I mean."

"I know you don't mean it, Ricky. I know you don't."

"Don't be so sure."

"Well you ain't off the hook either, my friend, and it don't exactly look good. There's nothin' I can do unless one of you starts talkin'." The Tomato was on it, drawing him out, finding his anger and probing for flashpoints.

"If you don' wanna talk to me, Ricky, Guthrie is gonna take a run at you, and he ain't gonna be so nice about it," D'Amato warned.

"Aren't I entitled to a lawyer or a phone call or something, Frankie?" Rick asked lackadaisically.

"You ain't entitled to shit, Ricky," said the Tomato, raising his voice. "This is still informal. You pull that shit and you'll be named a suspect. Then you can have a lawyer and a phone call and all the attention you want. Is that where you wanna go, Ricky?" The Tomato's outburst hushed the conversation next door, and Guthrie hung on who would speak next.

"Well I ain't gonna tell you Kel shot him, if that's what you're askin', 'cause I don't know if she did." His voice rose optimistically as if the possibility excited him.

"Fact is, it never occurred to me, but it's a damn good idea. I hope she did. Som' bitch deserved it."

"Please don' do that," Guthrie heard the Tomato say, and that's when he remembered the whole family carried, and they never checked for his weapon coming into the stationhouse. "Put it down, Ricky," said the Tomato, sounding more perturbed; and Guthrie was on his feet, headed for the conference room door when he heard the touch tones of a cell phone key pad and froze.

The sound of a speed dial warbled through the air and Guthrie bent his ear to the door.

"Hey, Pops?" said Rick. Even through the door he could hear Dirk LeBeau's baritone resonating like a kazoo with loose parts in Rick's phone.

"They've got me and Kelley down at the police station asking us questions we can't answer. I don't know what to tell them." Dirk reacted badly, the tone of his unintelligible words carrying through the phone.

"He's with you?" said Rick, "yeah, sure, put him on." Whoever the next speaker was he was magnitudes more measured, almost impossible to hear.

"Un-hunh," said Rick, taking direction, "sure. I understand. Thanks, man. Yeah, I'll see you soon." And then he heard Rick flip the phone shut.

"Prisoners' dilemma!" Rick shouted. "Is that what we're playing at, Guthrie? Prisoners' dilemma? Don't say nothin', Kelley. Don't say another word," he bellowed, silencing the stationhouse. Guthrie felt naked, eavesdropping by the door.

"You shouldn't a done that, Ricky," droned the Tomato. "This was your chance to make it easy. It's gonna get hard now. I'm sorry." Guthrie heard him rise and pace toward the door, and resisted the instinct to bolt for his cubicle. He was standing there grimacing when the Tomato opened the door.

"I'm sorry," he said before the Tomato could speak. "You gave him a chance."

"Big Dirk's on his way over, boss."

"I know," Guthrie said, turning to Rick. "You're free to go if you've nothing else to say. We can't hold you," he said, "until we bring charges." Rick's eyes crackled. His body stayed loose.

Guthrie was standing on the steps of the stationhouse when Dirk and Ron LeBeau tore into the parking lot. His knobbled fists were perched on his hips, clenched like medieval maces, and his generous arms spilled from his shoulders like flying buttresses. His jaw was set like a stone mantel and he stared disparagingly at the old pick-up truck as it ground to a halt in the shadow of the stationhouse. The brooding engine idled in cycles like a foreboding Greek chorus chanted in rounds.

"Why'd you come all this way, Dirk?" Guthrie bellowed over the din. "You can't do any good here." He could see Ron LeBeau on the far side of the cab. "You neither, Ron. You should know better than to interfere with this. You two go on home." Dirk cut the engine and shifted in the driver's seat. He tipped his camouflage ball cap over the crown of his head and draped his left arm like a side of beef on the outside of his door. He was looking through the windshield, gathering himself to speak.

"Those two kids had nothin' to do with it," Dirk finally said, finding Guthrie with a withering stare.

"They been havin' a real bad time. And this Achermann character, he put 'em in a real bad place. But they didn' have nothin' to do with it, see." Guthrie descended the last step of the stationhouse and approached Dirk's window. He gripped the driver's side windowsill with his powerful arms, as though he might toss the whole thing like a piece of luggage.

"And what makes you so sure, Dirk?"

"Because I been…holdin' somethin'… scared half to death…" began Dirk, before his baritone broke. He looked away, then down at his lap where a crumpled paper bag was nested between his legs.

Guthrie stood by, waiting on the finished thought, when the sun cleared the stationhouse behind him. A pinprick point of iridescent light sparkled from the fiber optic barrel site of a high powered rifle pointing straight at his head. It was resting in the gun rack on the rear panel of the cab, and mounted over the breach was a telescopic lens. The finely-ground super-magnified convex aperture glared at him menacingly, bending the morning light in a perfectly distorted reflection of himself. Suspended from the gun was a fraying shoulder strap.

"Is there something you want to tell me?" Guthrie asked. Something in the strap caught him by surprise. Dirk lifted the crumpled paper bag from between his legs. It rocked in his open palm, weighted at its center.

"I don't know what you're gonna find when you take a closer look," Dirk said, "but I don't like it, and I'm prayin' to God my boy didn't have nothin' to do with it."

Ron looked baffled, blinking like an owl from the passengers' seat.

"You want to tell me what it is, Dirk," said Guthrie, loosening his grip and ignoring the bag like hot merchandise.

"And why you would give it to me if you're afraid it could implicate your boy?" he said softening his voice to respect Dirk's distress. Then he glanced back at the strap. There were patches of bark ground into the fraying pile padding.

"Look, Guthrie, my boy's no angel. And maybe he was involved with somethin' and maybe he weren't. I don't know. But if he had any part in *this*," said Dirk, looking pointedly at the bag, "thank the Lord Achermann died another way." Guthrie was distracted by the muzzle of the gun, and by the bark on the strap beneath it, and he worked to keep his eyes on the bag in Dirk's palm.

"It's a shell, Guthrie, been handling them all my life. But never one like this. You hear what I'm sayin'?" said Dirk, annoyed that Guthrie appeared to be preoccupied.

"I hear you, Dirk, there's something suspicious about the shell."

"It ought to be looked at by somebody who knows ordinance."

"And why is that, Dirk? What's so special about it?" Guthrie asked, studying the bark on the strap.

"It came from Achermann's gun," replied Dirk. "The shell he never fired. The gun was on the ground next to Achermann when I got to him and my boy, and I ejected the shell and put it in my pocket soon as I picked up the gun. Wasn't until I put up my coat and dumped out my pockets that I noticed this shell were different, a dud maybe, so I put it aside and thought nothin' more of it 'til you and your boys started askin' questions. I should'a brung it to you sooner," Dirk said. He looked troubled and tired, unbefitting his usual countenance. Guthrie lifted the soft paper bag by the neck like a cub.

"Okay. We'll take a look, Dirk," he offered, searching Dirk's eyes. "Anything else you want to tell me?" Dirk wasn't the sort for unburdening moods, and it was plain there was more on his mind.

"No, not yet. You tell me what you find in dat shell, and maybe I'll have more to say. I'm jus' guessin' right now."

Chapter 22

Events of the past forty-eight hours swirled through Woodcock's mind, like the brooding river rushing at his feet. Across the Thames the lights of south London beamed and flickered in Easter egg pastels as the hum of the city behind him softened. Now and then the sound of a lone motor car broke the peace, zooming along the embankment roadway, before the growl of the straining exhaust faded in the night. Huddled beneath his arm, taking refuge from the chill, was the girl he met yesterday morning. They were sitting in the shadows of a heavy balustrade on an ancient stone stairway that descended from the embankment overhead to the water at their feet. It was one of many landings on the manmade river bank that channeled salty water inland and brackish water seaward when the river reversed course twice a day. The two of them must look like migratory birds, he thought, clumped in the lee of a gale. He distrusted to his core the protective instincts she ignited in him when he scooped her from a Chelsea side street, arriving like the cavalry with her bureau chief in tow to rescue her in the nick of time; and he had attended her pursuer's bedside before he died in the hospital that afternoon, accompanied by a brazen American detective who came to find him from Poughkeepsie, New York, of all places.

The American had appeared like an embarrassing relative at his hotel bearing a disconcerting theory and credible evidence to explain the untimely death of Harry Achermann. What detective Jimmy Doolan lacked in refinement he compensated for with candor. He had introduced himself over the house phone without the faintest nod to courtesy.

"Adam Woodcock?" he had said, "I'm detective Doolan with the Poughkeepsie Police. I'm investigating the murder of Harry Achermann, and I think it was a hit you know something about." He was boorish, indelicate, but his resourcefulness and persistence were their own reward.

"Nobody would be surprised to find his wife behind it - so many mistresses," Doolan had assured him in the hotel lobby as he flashed a badge that looked like a gold-plated almond cluster. The Americans loved their showy symbols of power, and they rode together in a cab across town while the American pressed his case.

"Could also have been a business deal gone bad. You know, he pissed somebody off, lost or stole some money, so they clipped him. But then, we found his wife at the Center for Disease Control in Atlanta where she showed up last week with this DRX biological agent. And guess what? It had been lifted from a government lab. But you already knew that, didn't you, because you work for Homeland Security, which, according to the papers the day before Achermann got clipped, is looking for the missing DRX; and that explains why you got to her before we did. Do you know Jack Whitaker?" he had finished anticlimactically, plainly pleased with his thoroughness.

There was no diverting him. He had an ironclad timeline of the seventy-two hours from the publication of the news stories, to the murder the next day, to the appearance of Mrs. Doctor Achermann the following evening in Atlanta, and Woodcock's arrival there the following morning. "Here's the clincher, the keystone," he said, "you know, the stone at the center of a span that all the other stones lean on," he expounded, using a worn-sounding metaphor he had plainly used before.

"Achermann and one of his company subsidiaries were mixed up with a CIA investment company called In-Q-Tel, and guess what?" the stout young detective had posed triumphantly, "they ended up owning a company called Ribonetics, the company that developed DRX. I think Achermann stole DRX from the CIA, his own partner in Ribonetics, and he got clipped for it. And that's why I think you know more than you're tellin'," Doolan had concluded breathlessly. "It's okay, Adam," he said, just like a Yank to be so familiar. "Everybody lies to us. We're cops. We expect it. But you have to admit, if you're not lying, finding you in Atlanta at the CDC is a helluva coincidence. What I can't figure is how Mrs. Doctor Achermann comes up with the DRX and brings it straight to the CDC."

It was on Woodcock's orders that the dying man's brain had been basted like a Thanksgiving turkey in sodium pentothal. The truth had spilled in dollops, like swigs from a bottle, and the unnerving detail had conquered what remained of his skepticism. The longer the dying man spoke the more evident it became he was Dunkelsbuhler's man, his *peacekeeper*, whose brain they were wringing for every last confession. They managed to pry loose his craven crusade – to eliminate Achermann before "they beat me to the punch," and to "make that harlot journalist pay." Woodcock had been satisfied with that. It made sense of the murder as well as the car chase, and meant Coco was probably out of danger; and it was consistent enough with Dunkelsbuhler's story to mean DRX was probably not in the hands of terrorists. But the American had persisted in relentless pursuit of the *they* to which the dying man referred – the *they* he feared would *beat him to the punch*.

"Who?" Doolan had demanded, "tell me who?" he said as the man in the bed began to fade.

"The Americans..." the man murmured.

"Whitaker!" exclaimed Doolan. "Whitaker?" he attempted to confirm. He had shaken the bed like a pan of reluctant popcorn to bring the weakening man around, but the subject had spoken his last.

"I knew it! I told you so!" his brash young companion concluded. There was no way to prove it, or even reason to suspect it, for who could read the dope-addled mind of a dying fanatic. And yet his testimony could hardly have better corroborated Dunkelsbuhler's narrative. Even a common corporate thug had been better informed than Whitaker had kept him and it rankled.

Whitaker had been his inspiration in a dark time – his irrepressible persona, his engaging, relaxed charm, and the steam boiler work ethic that drove him. He had a solitary faith, a spiritual self-sufficiency with mysterious headwaters that spun him like a weathervane to face the storm. He had been easy to admire, someone new to believe in, and that had been good enough - until now.

He had called Whitaker after leaving the hospital, and probed without revealing his sources. But Whitaker had disavowed everything. It was true, he had said, just as Doolan alleged, that he was nearby when Achermann was shot.

"But if we wanted him dead, as we would have eventually, can't you think of better ways and less conspicuous places to do it?" And "Yes," he also conceded, it was "probably true, but entirely coincidental" that the CIA and Achermann had invested together.

Whatever he'd been told by whomever he spoke to at DeBeers was apocryphal. There was no such affiliation, to that company or any other, and the idea of "exchanging commercial rewards for eliminating traitors is preposterous. You sound tired and upset," Whitaker had said condescendingly, and suggested it was "time to come in."

Whitaker's argot for rest and recuperation would have been music to his ears under any other circumstances. But it sounded vaguely unreliable in the context of Whitaker's defensiveness, and did little to corral his suspicions. When he mentioned the girl because he feared for her safety, Whitaker reacted surprisingly.

"Nonsense!" he barked. "Forget the girl for Chris'sake. What do you expect from a porn star reporter who's mixed up with a guy like Achermann. You've gotten too close to this thing. I'm telling you, come in."

His indictment of her felt callous, a conspicuous overreaction as if something else were eating him. She wasn't so far beyond the pale, he told himself, for an assertive millennial woman. She had embraced her independence, and built a career, and indulged her conquests as openly as a man; or were these ill-fitting rationalizations that had failed before to make sense of his fated first love, or worse yet, the dim logic of desire he felt sordidly swirling like the river carp feeding at his feet.

"But sir," he had persisted, "if these are secrets that need to be kept I can keep them. I need to know what I'm dealing with." Whitaker remained steadfast in his denial, unequivocal in renouncing the moral hazard of associations with "soulless commercial enterprises," and explicit in repudiating such "idle speculation." *The lady doth protest too much, methinks,* he had concluded reluctantly after the call, and the blind faith with which he had followed his mentor weakened. He prayed he was wrong but there was no ignoring past lessons. Trust was scarce, and scarcest sometimes among the most intimate of confidants.

Someone was lying, Whitaker or Dunkelsbuhler. Suppose they both were, he thought, as he remembered Dunkelsbuhler covering his face. The dying man was not conscious enough for his last words, *the Americans...* to be false. There was truth in it, he was sure. *Idle speculation,* Whitaker had said, like the idle speculation of Katrine Burkhardt at the CDC, whose suspicions ran to an experiment by the U.S. government in the remote desert sands of Namaqualand, and the windfall Sam Dunkelsbuhler had accused Achermann of scheming to take for himself, except Achermann was dead now. And so was the park ranger, an employee of the enterprise, who feared the disease had ridden on relief supplies to which the Nama had never been treated before. It was no secret anymore that the U.S. government and the CIA in particular had experimented unethically before, with radiation and disease, and chemicals and toxic substances on prisoners, minorities, the sick and mentally disabled. Why would it hesitate with the Nama?

And then it dawned on him. What if Achermann was never the enemy, only the facilitator, a soldier in a conspiracy that would have never come to light but for his do-gooder wife's impromptu visit to her medical school chum at the CDC, and Whitaker and Dunkelsbuhler were racing to cover each other's tracks?

"Puts *you* in a spot, don't it?" said Doolan, who read his mind on the sidewalk outside departures at Heathrow airport only hours before. And he thought he had been discrete with his fears.

"Yes, quite," he had said, because there was nothing else to say.

"Maybe you've taken this thing as far as you can. You know, without... without getting yourself in a pickle. Maybe we should take it from here," Doolan had volunteered, sounding genuinely concerned. "We're not on the inside, so what do we know. Suppose we just stumble through the evidence, ask the inappropriate question, like the simple country cops we are?"

"Yes, maybe."

Woodcock felt stupid to have exposed himself so naively to Whitaker. If the girl had posed a threat to DeBeers without even knowing of its CIA ties, or of the exposure they both shared to Achermann, then imagine the danger in knowing what he now knew, and saying so to Whitaker, of all people. The dead man, a hatchet man, had sung like a canary, and he had been stupid enough to carry the tune right back to his boss, the composer.

"Suppose you disappear for a while," Doolan had suggested, "can you do that?" Woodcock had dismissed the suggestion out of hand. He was certain he could play along with Whitaker and return unobtrusively to the business of supervising the mop up of DRX, assuming Whitaker let sleeping dogs lie. But would he?

The report of footfalls on the embankment pavement above them gave warning of the approaching intruder. He drew Coco close, concealing her in the shadow of the balustrade. Was it possible he was already being hunted? The steps moved on quickly, fading in the night, and he chastised himself for losing his composure. Fatigue was making him paranoid, he told himself. Nobody silenced their own people anymore. The punishment was costlier than the crime, and lousy for morale, and he wasn't missing yet, for God's sake. Missing. To go missing, as Doolan had suggested, like an overdue ship in the night, and perhaps forever lost at sea. Could it be done without spending life on the run?

He had driven Doolan back to Heathrow airport mainly because he needed the company. By the time they parted ways and Doolan melted in the crowd they had a common interpretation of events that left them with decidedly different burdens. Doolan's excitement was palpable. He was off to bring down the deputy director of the CIA, while Woodcock was nothing but vulnerable. He would be looking over his shoulder for a lifetime, however long that might be, for dutifully reporting his suspicions. His discovery in the wrong hands would be devastating, to the intelligence community, to the administration, and to Whitaker, a man who operated unchecked, it seemed, without regard for laws or borders. It was the sort of intelligence the bloody Americans would convene a Congressional committee to explore twenty years from now, if it meant clearing their righteous Puritan consciences, and Whitaker's survival hinged on it.

He was in rotten psychological shape to be piling into intimate relations, but he had called Coco anyway on the way back from Heathrow and arranged to pick her up at the office. There was nothing to lose by feeding the hunger with which he held her now, and it settled his mind while he weighed his options: to report for duty come what may, or listen to Doolan and go missing. The latter was naïve, he knew. There would be no clean breaks or turning over new leaves. They would find him, eventually, and punish him if the secret remained safe, or kill him if it didn't.

It was pointless at such times to wish for the clarity and peacefulness of dawn breaking over the heath behind his childhood home, but it came to him in his mind's eye, a time and place uncomplicated by oaths of duty to commander-in-chief, or king and country, or whoever it was he had sworn to serve.

It made him snort, a contemptible, involuntarily sort of snort, at the wretchedness of his lamentable circumstances. What could be further away than childhood?

"What was that for?" Coco inquired. Her low muffled voice drifted up from where her head was pressed against his chest, resonating like a tuning fork with his insides.

"Nothing, really," he replied.

"You were thinking something."

"No, nothing."

"Nothing will come of nothing," she quoted.

"Yes, quite," he conceded. "I was thinking, 'What a tangled web we weave…'"

"When we practice to deceive?" she answered on cue.

"You know your Shakespeare," he said like a talent scout.

"It's Sir Walter Scott, actually," she corrected him, "often misattributed."

Who was this troublemaking, careless American of letters? She had drawn him from across the water into unenviable circumstances, and she was bound to do herself in. His heroics had merely postponed her fate; yet here he was with her, by choice, as though somewhere, fairly recently, annihilation grew on him.

"I was just thinking," he said, "wondering really, about what I do now."

"You go public with it, you report the story," she murmured, her voice agitating his organs again, and bringing his insides to life.

"Don't be daft, Coco. It can't be proven, and it's a jolly good way to get us both killed."

"You wouldn't be the first to risk your life for the truth," she persisted.

"Bloody hell," he whispered quietly. Could there be a worse companion for a British intelligence officer than a female American journalist?

"It's not as silly as you make it sound, Adam," she continued.

"I'm afraid my sort banished the crusading part of our natures to foreign shores centuries ago, where they found fertile ground, it appears." There was a comforting presumption in baiting her, as though they had long been friends.

"Well, shame on you," she whispered, "you can abdicate your responsibility if you want. I hope you don't think I'm going to."

"And what if I ask you not to?"

"Because it puts you in danger?" she replied as she rooted in his chest. She seemed to weigh his companionship, as if it might be worth trading for a good story.

"I wouldn't be a very good journalist, would I," she observed, "if I didn't write all the things people asked me not to write," she said with inevitability, as though the truth and a good story always out.

"That's a nice way to thank me for saving your life," he replied.

"Nobody murders journalists in the free world anymore, Adam. Maybe it still works in Russia or China, but it's a lousy way to bury a story," she whispered.

It must be simple and exciting, he reflected, to find sanctimonious outrage in the commonest conceits, and to spill them over city dailies and ruin people's lives in the interlude between the newsstand and the dustbin. He realized then that the people she wrote about were dispensable - fictional characters in a meaningless novel. What he needed to show her was how keeping his secrets meant lasting security, a life not lived on the run.

"Think, Coco," he said. "If you write the story it will be denied, and there's no proof of anything. I doubt very much the Agency or the company will experience a sudden bout of altruism and come forward. And then you've played the only cards we have." He paused as the water grew still. "And if I change my story, you have no story," he finally said. "There will be nobody to corroborate it. Sam certainly won't."

He had in mind something better, a strategy for disappearing without running, for living in plain sight by preserving the threat to reveal every last detail of the DRX debacle, from its existence to its use in manipulating world diamond markets, to its role in a murder at en exclusive hunting retreat; and to name names in the process. The deal he had in mind was keeping his silence so long as Coco and he remained safe. She could help him document Doolan's research which they would supplement with the deathbed confessions of Norris Sanderling, the dead park ranger, and Coco's pursuer, regrettably pulverized in Hyde Park. They would load the information into email blasts programmed to release automatically unless he remained alive to override the programming. The blasts would target all the major news organizations and media outlets, and arrive with covering messages to investigate his whereabouts since only his disappearance would explain its receipt. For the first time all night the water at his feet stood still, poised to change course for the return trip to the sea.

Chapter 23

"Pick up, Jimmy," Guthrie whispered as Jimmy's phone rang a third time and launched him into voicemail.

"It's your lucky day!" announced the recording, "This is detective Jimmy Doolan of the Poughkeepsie police. I'm out chasing bad guys, so leave a message." He waited for the beep.

"Jimmy. It's Guthrie. I need you to pinch-hit for me this morning. Dr. Achermann got out of quarantine a few days ago and she's on her way up here for a briefing and to claim Achermann's things. I said I'd drive her out to Donner's Forge, but Dirk left a message late last night that he had to see me right away, couldn't wait. Something he needed me to see. I need you to meet Dr. Achermann at the stationhouse between eight and nine this morning, and give her a ride to Donner's Forge. It's six o'clock and I'm heading out there now. Call me to confirm you got this. See you out there," he said and hung up.

He pulled up to the farmhouse through a dense dawn mist and spotted Dirk waiting for him in the window overlooking the valley. Dirk seemed to wake from a trance as Guthrie cut the engine and the headlights flickered out. He was silhouetted in the open farmhouse door by the time Guthrie finished rooting for his boots in the trunk.

"Good mornin'," Dirk hailed from the stoop.

"'Morning," he replied. "This fog is something. Never seen it like this."

"Aw, dis ain't so bad. Kind'a normal this time of year," Dirk assured him. He approached Dirk where he stood in the door and looked up into his eyes.

"I hope this is good, Dirk."

"I believe you'll think so."

"I've got something for you, too, but it might not be so good," said Guthrie.

"How's dat?" asked Dirk.

"That shell you gave me. You were right. The lab said it was packed with C-4 explosive and a detonator. If Achermann had pulled the trigger it would have blown his head off, and maybe killed your boy, too," he said. Dirk exhaled, the warm air from his lungs precipitating on the cold country air.

"Damn fool," Dirk said to himself, looking across the parking area to the distant hillside rising from the mist. It looked further away than usual, immutable and remote, like a vision in a dream, a place where things happened beyond the imagination.

"You know where he got it?" asked Guthrie. "It wasn't homemade, Dirk. It was a professional job." Dirk was catatonic, staring into nothingness.

"De guides carry de shells," Dirk finally replied. "Dey carry special turkey loads… Rick gave Achermann de shell," Dirk conceded.

"I didn't mean 'where did *Achermann* get the shell,'" Guthrie interjected. "I already knew it came from Rick. I was asking if you had a hunch where *Rick* got the shell. I doubt he cobbled it together in his basement."

"I shouldn'a ever gave it to you."

"You're wrong, Dirk. You gave it to me for a reason."

"Oh yeah? And what was dat?"

"Because you know who gave it to him. And you'll be damned if your boy is going down alone."

"Maybe. We need to get movin'," Dirk said, stepping off the threshold.

"Where we going?"

"Back to the hill. Let's ride the Gator." It was parked beside the farmhouse and Dirk closed on it quickly, his hands plunged deep in his camouflage jacket, his oversized boots grinding pebbles to dust.

"Almost forgot," Dirk said, stopping midstride. "Need my gun."

"Why?" Guthrie asked.

"'Cause I need it to show you what you need to see."

"Your gun?"

"You'll see. It'll ruin the fun if I tell you now." Guthrie felt for his thirty-eight tucked in a holster beneath his armpit. Good. It was there. Dirk reached his truck and wrenched free the driver's side door, its hinges howling fiendishly. He lifted the gun from its rack, checked the breach, and shouldered the firearm by its strap. The rifle looked small against his back, and comfortable, like the yoke on a seasoned draught horse.

"Let's go," he said, slamming the door of his truck. He looked like an aging warrior, thought Guthrie, the muzzle of his rifle riding by his ear, his camouflage hunting cap askew his gigantic head. They converged on the Gator and Dirk slid the rifle into a hard plastic case secured to the flatbed before they craned their heads to clear the roll bars and landed in unison in the vehicle's front seats.

"I think I know where he got dat shell, but you won't believe me if I tell you," Dirk said.

"Don't kid yourself, Dirk. Try me."

Dirk cranked the ignition, and the Gator rattled to life belching plumes of blue smoke into the crisp dawn air. He threw the bucking two-stroke engine into gear, accelerated across the parking lot and over the edge into the sea of mist between the mountain and the farmhouse. Soon they were shouting to make themselves heard.

"So where do *you* think it came from?" Dirk boomed, peering ahead through the bars of the roll cage.

"We'll get to that in a minute," Guthrie said. "First tell me about Kelley Sutton."

"What do you want to know?" Dirk bellowed through the gloom.

"We know about her long-running relationship with Rick," said Guthrie.

"Star-crossed lovers. That's what I always told 'em. They never could get things figured out." The Gator lurched in fitful strides shaking them like rag dolls.

"And then something bad happened, didn't it, Dirk."

"Don't know what you mean."

"With Achermann, I mean. Between Kelley and Achermann. Last New Year's Eve." Dirk kept driving, urging the Gator ferociously ahead. Guthrie seized the roll bar and Dirk braced himself with the steering wheel as the Gator accelerated menacingly.

"Hey, take it easy," Guthrie ordered. The ride leveled out with the flattening terrain, but they were flying like a projectile through apogee, sailing on their own momentum.

"Yeah, somethin' real bad happened," Dirk acknowledged.

"Gives them both motive. You understand that, right? They both have motive," Guthrie hollered. They drove on, the clatter of the engine reverberating through the mist.

"And she's a damn good shot, I'm told," he added, "and has no alibi for the time of the shooting," he said, looking for a reaction from Dirk.

"Nah, she didn't do it," Dirk finally rumbled through the clatter.

"Why, because she's not up to killing? Not even after what she claims Achermann did to her?"

Dirk slowed the Gator to a fitful crawl as they approached the wooded hillside rising from the mist.

"I didn't say that. I suppose anyone is up to killin' if you give 'em a reason," said Dirk, as he cut the engine and his voice boomed like a signal cannon on the still morning air.

"So you *do* think she could have killed him?" Dirk turned in his seat, pivoting like a frigate bringing all guns to bear.

"No," he said so low that something loose beneath his seat resonated with his voice. "She didn't do it," he said.

"You mean you don't think she shot him." Dirk did not respond. "How do you know?"

"You'll see when we get there." Dirk dismounted the Gator, marched to its rear, and unsheathed his gun like a cutlass.

"What do you need that for?"

"Part of what I got to show you."

"If you're sure she didn't shoot him, do you think she could have poisoned him?" he pressed. Dirk studied him defiantly. For the first time Guthrie felt exposed, to a brutal man in his element.

"Poison him? What's poison got to do with anything?" Dirk asked.

"Yeah. I probably forgot to mention," he said, "Achermann had been poisoned. Most likely at breakfast. Certainly after midnight. He was bleeding internally before he was shot. Would have been dead within hours anyway. There was no saving him. Kelley was in the kitchen that morning. She had motive and opportunity to poison him, too." Dirk smiled and doffed his cap, and scratched at the bristles on his scalp.

"I'd say someone wanted that som' bitch dead. Exploding shells? Poison? Both beat to the punch by a plain ol' fashioned bullet."

"I s'pose that's about right," acknowledged Guthrie. "Maybe more than one person. That or someone with a gift for thoroughness. What do *you* think?"

"Well, if Kelley did poison him, and God bless 'er if she did, I'm glad it weren't the coup de grâce."

"Why is that?" Guthrie probed.

"So she ain't guilty of murder, of course. Jus' hope it didn' come too soon for him to suffer some."

"It's still attempted murder."

"Even if you find the murderer?" He wasn't sure what Dirk was asking.

"You offering me a deal, Dirk?"

"No. No deals, but if you catch your murderer why do you need the ones that should'a murdered him?"

"Because it's against the law." Dirk stared him down, underwhelmed, apparently, by the logic. "It's procedure," Guthrie added, to support his position; but it sounded defensive, he knew.

"You ready?" Dirk asked, slinging his gun. Guthrie nodded and abandoned the Gator. "Come on then, let's go," said Dirk, and turned into the woods. Guthrie followed him into the shadows and they began their ascent beneath the canopy.

He watched Dirk climb, his footing sure, twigs and branches snapping sacrificially under his weight and loam churning beneath his feet. Dirk moved fast, leaving Guthrie to stutter-step like a firewalker to keep pace. He was breathless and perspiring in less than a hundred vertical feet, while Dirk pressed on, alighting on a narrow plateau ahead. There he paused to watch Guthrie struggle, for his own amusement, presumably.

"Dirk," Guthrie gasped on reaching the plateau, "I can't tell you we'll get the trigger man, but that may be the least of our problems."

"How's dat?" said Dirk.

"There's a lot going on here, more than meets the eye, involving people and events that may never come to light. Maybe Rick knew about the shell and maybe he didn't. Maybe he was supposed to die with Achermann. You ever think of that?"

Something distracted Dirk. He put his index fingers to his lips to hush Guthrie's voice. He heard or saw something down in the woods off the trail, and he peered in that direction with maniacal intensity.

"You hear anything?" he rumbled soft and low.

"Like what?" Guthrie whispered. Dirk stood still, every fiber of his soul tuned to where he was looking down the trail.

"Anyone know we're here?" Guthrie asked.

"Not unless you told 'em. Did *you* hear something, or is my mind playing tricks?" Dirk rumbled so low he sounded like distant thunder.

"No. I didn't hear anything," Guthrie said, and waited. When Dirk seemed to be satisfied Guthrie resumed his train of thought.

"Anyway, the point is that Rick, and probably Kelley too, if they're involved, could be pawns. There's others that wanted Achermann dead."

"What others?" Dirk asked.

"Others for whom Achermann was making a lot of trouble. Others that we're never going to catch, whatever Rick or Kelley tell us."

"Why?" Dirk asked defiantly.

"They're too big. They're too powerful. And…we'll never get the evidence." This time Guthrie heard the footfalls down the trail and turned abruptly to where Dirk had just been staring.

"What're you lookin' at?" Dirk asked.

"I heard it this time. Someone's down there," he said.

"Now you're making me nervous," said Dirk. He stepped around Guthrie, shouldered his gun, and peered through the scope. He swung the high powered rifle slowly through forty-five degrees, scanning the forest to both sides of the trail, and down to where they had entered the wood.

"I can't see nothing,'" he whispered before lowering the gun. "Probably some critter, or deer maybe." He looked at Guthrie and lifted a flap over his breast pocket. The brass caps of three rifle rounds protruded from a soft elastic bandolier sewn into the inside of the pocket.

"If someone *is* out there they best not come too close without makin' themselves known," he said, and let the flap fall back over the rounds. He slung his gun back over his shoulder. "Let's keep movin'. You were sayin' something about too big and too powerful."

Dirk reverted to the incline, and Guthrie followed him in unsteady pursuit.

"What I was saying is that Rick and Kelley, if they were involved, could have been used by people, maybe several people, who all wanted Achermann dead. And if those same people were willing to kill someone as… as visible as Achermann…"

"Den dey won't stop there to protect themselves…" said Dirk, finishing the thought.

"I'm not saying I think Rick or Kelley are in danger, and I'm not anxious to put them in danger. At least not yet. Fact is, even if they did talk there's probably no credible evidence. And their story wouldn't be believable. It wouldn't hold up," he said. And then he had an epiphany. "That's why they were picked."

Dirk's stride quickened. His boots chewing up the hillside and kicking out mashed detritus as a seething anger found purchase on the mountain. He advanced on the incline in furious silence, lengthening his lead with each stride. He was fifty yards ahead of Guthrie by the time he reached the gentle slope where Achermann and Rick had positioned themselves. Only then did he turn to see Guthrie struggling to keep up.

He unslung his rifle, and backed into a giant oak a few feet from the perimeter of the crime scene tape. It hung in languid arcs from an orbit of saplings encircling the tree where Achermann was sitting when the bullet tore out three quarters of his neck. Dirk's titanic mass came to rest against a pillar of bark, the convexity of the trunk fitting neatly between his bulging shoulders. He looked like an Elgin marble holding up the tree, and might be there as long, thought Guthrie, as he tried to catch up. When he finally arrived, gasping and disheveled, Dirk stepped forward from the giant oak. He looked somber and tormented, his rifle hanging limply from one hand.

"I can't tell you where Kelley would'a gotten no poison, but I'm pretty sure I know who gave Rick dat shell," he said.

"It doesn't matter, Dirk, you said yourself that's not how Achermann was killed, and it won't do Rick any good to help us hunt down his handlers. Besides, we think we already know who they are, and it doesn't go anyplace good. Certainly not anyplace that leaves Rick better off." Dirk stood there dumbfounded. "That doesn't mean we're letting them go. It just means we're saving them for later, in case we come up empty-handed looking for the gunman. But I won't be too surprised if finding the gunman leads us back to the same nice folks who gave Rick the shell, which will spare Rick more trouble than he's already in."

258

"Supposin' it don't," Dirk grunted, "or you don't find the gunman?" Guthrie pushed his index fingers beneath his glasses and ran the tips along his eyelids to wipe away the sweat.

"I don't know, Dirk," he finally said. "Let's worry about that when we get there. What we really need is evidence that leads to the gunman. Tracks, a boot print, something he dropped. Anything that would tell us more than we've got right now, which is nothing. Is what you wanted to show me something like that?"

"Sort'a," said Dirk. "You mind if I go inside the tape?" he asked, gesturing at the crime scene.

"I suppose," Guthrie replied, hoping Dirk had done nothing foolish like plant evidence on a processed crime scene. Dirk leaned his gun against the great oak and approached a low point in the tape where it swung like a listless gallows inches off the ground. He cleared the tape, removed his hat, and picked a sturdy crooked branch from the forest floor.

"Stop," Guthrie said, and looked at his watch. 7:30. Still too early for Jimmy, who should be calling soon if he got the message.

"I hear a car, coming up the drive. Are you expecting somebody?"

"That'll be Kelley, or Whitaker." He listened. "It's Kelley. Whitaker's cars run a good bit smoother," he said, smiling. "Whitaker's on the fishing schedule today. Should be along shortly."

"With his goons, no doubt."

"Always," Dirk assured him. Terrific, thought Guthrie. Alone in the woods surrounded by suspects, and every one of them a marksman, and he still didn't know what Dirk had in store.

"Okay to move?" Dirk asked.

He took his hat and braced it low against the tree with the branch.

"Dat's about where his head were, I figure." The brim protruded with hip-hop attitude down the old logging road.

"That ought to do it," Dirk said. "Let's see what dat looks like from up 'dere."

The ghostly call of a distant owl carried through the desolate woods; and across the mountainside turkeys retaliated, shock gobbles rolling in waves down the valley.

"Too bad we ain't out here to bag us a turkey," said Dirk, pausing as if to consider the possibility. "If we took our time, and set up just right, we could probably get 'em all," he speculated. "But that would be against the law, and you only need one to put on the dinner table, see?"

"I hear you, Dirk, I got it. Now show me what you want me to see."

"Follow me," Dirk said, and they moved shoulder to shoulder up the rise. "Now where's that X," he said as they arrived on the ridge. Guthrie remembered and led him to the base of the tree.

"Here," Guthrie said, squatting by the base and pawing at the leaves in search of clues.

"What you lookin' for?" Dirk asked.

"Not sure," he said, rising to his feet. The view down the valley was breathtaking, the farmhouse in the foreground and the foothills to the east, and a field in between caught his eye.

"That's where Whitaker was that morning," he said, pointing, "wasn't it?"

"Yeah, and Ron, too."

"And Whitaker's security team," he felt compelled to note. He studied the topography between the field and the ridge, realizing for the first time that the road through the woods on the back side of the mountain led directly to the field in which Whitaker had been hunting. The terrain between them was more easily covered on foot than he first imagined.

"...the same team that can conveniently vouch for each other's whereabouts without saying where they actually were," he added. He turned ninety degrees to his right and focused on the farmhouse.

"And Kelley was down there. A lot closer," he said. "She could have made it up and back in no time at all. One of Whitaker's guys would have taken longer. But they could have done it, with no pressure to get back."

"...'less Whitaker and his boys didn't think the shell was gonna go off," Dirk finally muttered.

"What's that?"

"I'm just sayin,' they had no reason to shoot Achermann. They was the ones who gave Rick that shell," Dirk said, his eyes wide and dark, loaded with accusation.

"Yeah, I figured that," Guthrie replied. "What about Kelley?" he continued.

"What about 'er?" said Dirk. "Thought you said she poisoned him."

"I never said that, Dirk. I said he was poisoned, and she was in the right place to do it." Down in the valley, a furlong from the farmhouse, a sleek black sedan turned into the Donner's Forge drive way.

"Whitaker," said Dirk. The phone in Guthrie's pocket vibrated.

"Jimmy?" he said, answering the call. "Good... thadda boy... no delay, you understand... what's that...she told the Tomato that? Well I'll be... That answers that, then. Get yourself here soon, understand?" and he disconnected the call.

"Answer's what," Dirk said.

"Who poisoned Achermann. Jimmy Doolan found a guy, died very soon after Jimmy hunted him down. The poison was special, rare, and this guy Jimmy found could have easily supplied it."

"So?"

"So this guy lived in London, England, which is where he died last week, and Kelley Sutton ID'd him yesterday; said he came around a few months back." Dirk grunted dismissively, and swelled with new resolve.

"Let me show you what's on my mind, Guthrie," Dirk said turning his back on the valley and moving towards the tree.

"Now you look down there at my hat, you see it?" He didn't, at least not right away. The camouflage was hard to pick out in the shadows, against the forest, but eventually the peak and brim came into focus.

"Here, use my scope, it's easier," said Dirk. He dipped his shoulder and swung the rifle off his back, opened the chamber and checked it was empty, and then presented it with both hands like a Broadsword. Guthrie took the gun and dropped to his knees, surveying the target downrange. Then he tipped himself forward into a crisp bed of leaves until he was prone, his elbow lodged in the soft loam, the rifle barrel cradled in his hand. He squeezed his head against the stock and peered through the telescopic lens.

"I guess this ain't *your* first rodeo," Dirk said.

"Nope," said Guthrie, pulling himself off the ground. "That thicket, about half way down. It blocks the base of the tree. If he shot from here he...or *she*, would have to have been standing. What's your point?"

"That is my point. I don't think he shot from here. I think we're lookin' in the wrong place." Guthrie had been thrown red herrings before and this smelled like one.

"He couldn't have shot from his feet?"

"You tell me. Take a look for yourself," said Dirk. Guthrie moved up close to the tree, wrapped his left arm through the rifle strap, cinching it tight around his forearm, and shouldered the gun. He leaned against the tree to steady his arm and peered again through the scope.

"Yeah. Perfect," he said.

"Perfect, hunh? Go ahead. Try to make that shot standin'. Here," Dirk said, reaching beneath the flap over his breast pocket and producing a shiny brass thirty-aught-six caliber round from the elastic bandolier.

"You look like you know what you're doin.' See if you can hit my hat," Dirk dared.

Guthrie took the round, opened the bolt, dropped it adroitly into the breach, and drove the bolt home. He studied the target again, stretched his neck, hugged the stock, and bore down on the rifle, addressing the scope with his eye. Dirk was right. The gun was heavy and increasingly difficult to steady. The crosshairs gyrated wildly on the magnified image of the tree, the hat easily frustrating his attempts to target it. He tightened his grip, but the tighter he squeezed the more violently the magnified image gyrated. And then he remembered a small but important detail, and relaxed his grip and dampened his breathing until he felt the slow steady pulse of his heartbeat. He centered the crosshairs on Dirk's hunting cap downrange, waiting for the pause between heart beats to fire, and squeezed the trigger. A plume of black earth lifted off the forest floor ten yards short of the target as the report echoed through the stillness. The wood fell silent in the percussive vacuum.

"Short," Dirk pronounced, "by a bit." Guthrie stepped away from the tree and ejected the hot casing.

"The gunman was a better shot," Guthrie conceded.

"Maybe," said Dirk. "And maybe you ain't used to shootin' downhill. The round falls faster shootin' downhill, so you have to aim higher," Dirk said. "Mind if I giv'er a try?" he asked. Guthrie handed him the gun.

A look came over Dirk that left Guthrie cold: violence and peace all rolled into one, like an executioner with his axe at the wheel. He looked Guthrie straight in the eye before his hands went to work. He unclipped the shoulder strap at both ends from the "D" rings by which it was fastened to the gun, and leaned the rifle against the tree. The strap he lassoed around the trunk, clipping the ends together and twisting them tight until the strap was cinched against the tree at shoulder height. Moving with taunting deliberateness he picked up the gun, inserted the muzzle through a small loop where he had joined the bitter ends and flipped the gun quickly by its stock through two turns, tightening the strap like a tourniquet around the trunk. He rammed a shiny brass round indelicately into the breach and locked the bolt home, and then he glared for just an instant before stepping into the gun. As he filled the scope with one eye the fatty folds of flesh on the back of his neck tightened like an accordion, raising the bristles like the hackles on a wild boar. Without delay he fired.

Downrange a fibrous white halo exploded like confetti in the air, the pulverized synthetic fill hanging in the atmosphere, glinting like radiation before drifting softly to earth where Achermann had fallen before it. Dirk ejected the hot casing, loosened the barrel from the strap, and released the strap from the tree. As he removed the strap from the trunk Guthrie realized Dirk had placed it on the very same scar they had found in the bark just a few days before, and the scar had grown.

"Wrong place, hunh?" Guthrie said, in awe of Dirk's deviousness. He was thumbing his nose, reenacting the crime in a way that left legitimate explanations for the scar on the tree and the bark in his rifle strap. Clever, damn clever, thought Guthrie, to cover his tracks be retracing them in plain view.

"I guess that makes me a suspect, don' it," said Dirk. Guthrie searched him for meaning. There was nothing to fear in his demeanor, nothing criminal or untamed. He stood there placidly, dawn breathing color into his camouflage as he flawlessly melded with his surroundings.

"I guess it does," Guthrie concurred as he lost sight of Dirk's outline. His pale whiskered head appeared to float amidst the trees, his primal vigor defeated, a weary, vacant blamelessness in his eyes.

He seemed on the verge of confessing, and Guthrie hoped he wouldn't.

"Of course we would have to be able to prove it, wouldn't we," he heard himself say, "and how would we do that... especially with so many other plots afoot."

"I don' know. Not my problem," Dirk replied indifferently. "I's jus' sayin' there's plenty a folks 'round here dat could'a made dat shot."

The blindness was immediate, a searing burning heat in Guthrie's eyes, and he covered his face and fell to his knees.

"Roll! Roll!" he heard Dirk yell.

"What the hell is it?" Guthrie shouted, throwing himself down the rise. He could feel Dirk near him, rolling along side, until he felt Dirk's arm arrest his advance.

"Stay put, Guthrie. Don't move. Let me take a look around."

"What the hell was that?" he said, opening his watering eyes and adjusting to the light.

"A laser sight, pointed right at your head. Stay down," Dirk said before he took to his feet, and Guthrie heard him dash back up the ridge.

Chapter 24

He was probably gone for less than five minutes but it felt like an eternity, and his vision was back by the time Dirk landed in the leaves beside him.

"I didn't see nothin'. Someone's tryin' to scare us. They'd a shot if they meant to. Come on, let's get off this hill," he said as Guthrie felt himself lifted by the armpit and planted on his feet. He surprised himself with his sureness of foot as they moved quickly downhill. They were in the lurching Gator and cresting the rise into the parking lot when Guthrie saw Jimmy Doolan's car, tearing like a drag racer up the drive. It very nearly left the ground encountering the lip of the parking lot and came to an abrasive halt in the gravel apron in front of the farmhouse. Jimmy leaped from the car and met the Gator as it pulled in.

"Everything okay, boss?" Jimmy yelled before Dirk cut the engine and it sputtered like a lawnmower and died.

"Yes," said Guthrie. "Did you bring Dr. Achermann?"

"Yes, sir. She's in the car. Should I get her?"

"No need," Guthrie heard a woman say. She was coming across the parking lot like a squall, dressed for the country in high leather boots, shooting slacks, a herring bone blazer and a colorful silk scarf drawn loosely around her neck. She was standing beside Jimmy before Guthrie could get to his feet.

"Dr. Achermann," she said, firmly extending her hand.

"Dr. Achermann, this is Detective Guthrie," Jimmy said.

"Yes, we've spoken on the phone, haven't we Detective Guthrie. Nice to meet you." She was even more striking in person, though the photographs belied her presence.

"I'm sorry, Dr. Achermann, for your loss," said Guthrie.

"Thank you," she said. "Shall we get on with it? I can't be here all day. And you are?" she said, reaching across Guthrie to extend Dirk her hand.

"Dirk LeBeau, Club Manager, ma'am," said Dirk, surprised by her vigorous handshake.

"Very well, then. Would one of you kind gentlemen show me to my late husband's things?" she asked, standing close enough to Guthrie that he knew she missed Jimmy smirk.

Guthrie held the door for her and she stepped into the front hall and followed the light into the dining room on the right.

"Pardon me," Guthrie heard her say.

"Other way, Dr. Achermann. Lockers are to the left," Dirk rumbled from where he was entering the front hall behind Guthrie, who had already turned behind her.

"Why Detective Guthrie," said Whitaker, rising to his feet at the sight of the lady. "So very good to see you again. To what do we owe this fortuitous encounter?"

"Mr. Whitaker," Guthrie acknowledged. "Kelley," he added, acknowledging Kelley Sutton, who was pouring Whitaker coffee when Astrid stumbled on them in dining room.

"Hello, Detective Guthrie," Kelley whispered, taken aback to see him. Whitaker was showing undisguised interest in an introduction to the lady standing before him.

"Dr. Achermann, this is Mr. Whitaker," Guthrie said obligingly.

"Jack," Whitaker corrected him. She took his extended hand and shook it savagely. If he realized she was the widow of the man murdered on the club grounds two weeks before, he didn't show it. Kelley cowered and turned for the kitchen.

"Kelley," Guthrie said, "this is Dr. Achermann."

"Hello," said Astrid, softening as if addressing a patient.

"Hello, Mrs. Achermann," said Kelley, shifting uncomfortably. Astrid studied her.

"Did you know my husband?" Astrid asked.

"My condolences," Whitaker interceded. "We were here with him that day. We're so very sorry for your loss."

"Jack, is it?" she said.

"Yes."

"Jack... Jack Whitaker. Of course. I know you," Astrid continued, "I read your name in the paper. CIA. One of your field agents visited me in quarantine – a sort of fussy British fellow. Accused me of collaborating with my late husband to steal a doomsday virus you wonderful people developed, and that you lost, or maybe you're testing on a tribe called the Nama in South Africa."

"Now, now, Dr. Achermann, let's not get carried away," Whitaker replied.

"I'm a relief doctor, Jack, and I wouldn't be a very good one if I got carried away, would I."

"I beg your pardon, Dr. Achermann," said Whitaker.

"I was treating the Nama, as you probably know, so they put me in quarantine for long enough to be sure I wasn't sick," she said, approaching the table across from Whitaker, and subtly leaning in on him. "One of the fringe benefits of my work is that I've developed the constitution of a horse, the immune system of reptile. Disease rarely afflicts me, but that doesn't mean I don't carry a few," she said, exhaling coolly at him.

Guthrie was gathering himself from being targeted in the woods, and speculating on who was trying to intimidate him, when Astrid's rebuke of Whitaker raised his spirits. She had turned the tables in a sentence or two and he was anxious for Whitaker's response.

"If you'll show me to his things, Detective Guthrie, I'll take them and go," she said turning for the door.

"It's not that easy," Guthrie said spontaneously, trying to preserve the tension.

"And why is that?" said Whitaker.

"Because there's been a murder," Guthrie said, glancing at Dirk, "and it's an active investigation, and someone just aimed a gun at me up near the crime scene," he said.

"Does it surprise you he was murdered?" Astrid asked, "after everything Jack's field agent alleges he was doing?"

"Mr. Whitaker has not shared that information with me, Dr. Achermann, and yes, every murder surprises me," Guthrie said.

"Truth is," Jimmy interrupted, "your husband's murder is no surprise to anybody here, is it?" he said, grinning at Whitaker and Kelley.

"Easy, Jimmy," said Guthrie.

"Oh?" said Astrid, her curiosity piqued.

"Please excuse the eagerness of our local constabulary, Dr. Achermann," said Whitaker. Guthrie felt his anger rise, anger he hadn't felt since testifying before the National Transportation Safety

Board, anger he was helpless to contain, and he could see Jimmy's body twitching, too.

"Be careful, Mr. Whitaker," Guthrie heard himself say.

"I beg your pardon?" said Whitaker, puffing his chest like a rooster.

"You heard him, sir," said Jimmy, acquiring his signature wanna-fight look.

"Perhaps you'd like to say exactly what you mean," Whitaker said.

"Dirk," said Guthrie, "Do you have a 12-gauge shell handy?" Dirk rifled his pockets and handed Guthrie a bright red cartridge. Guthrie approached the table until he stood beside Astrid facing Whitaker and stood the shell on its end in the middle of the table.

"Mr. Whitaker, sir. Imagine that were packed with C-4 explosive instead of shot. What do you think would happen to the hunter when he pulled the trigger?" Whitaker's lips tightened and his eyes narrowed.

"Yes, I thought that would get your attention."

"You're on a witch hunt, a goose chase. They're out of their depth," said Whitaker, turning to Astrid. "This is all nonsense, and highly unprofessional, Detective Guthrie. Please remember yourself."

"Maybe it's nonsense, and maybe it isn't. We'll see. Come on, Jimmy, Dr. Achermann, let's show Dr. Achermann to her husband's things. These are questions for another time."

"Are they?" Whitaker asked.

"Yes," Guthrie replied. "We'll let the courts decide, according to the law."

"Who's law? What law?" asked Whitaker.

"Amen," Astrid murmured, and for the first time he heard the Bible Belt in her voice.

"Thank you for driving me back," she said twenty minutes later as Guthrie eased his sedan west toward Poughkeepsie through the flashing light crossroads at the heart of Highrock. "Your colleague, Mr. Doolan, supplied a bracing ride out, I can tell you," she said, taking in the shimmering foothills and brilliant blue sky overhead.

"He's not entirely to blame. I told him to get out here fast," Guthrie said, recalling his orders from the hillside earlier that morning. "Jimmy's very good. You were never in danger."

"What was the rush?" she asked. *Where to begin* he was inclined to reply. How much did she know, or want to know, had she the luxury of forgetting everything he could tell her.

"That was very generous of you back there. Those were beautiful guns," he said, changing the subject.

"I have no use for them, and now they'll be used by men who appreciate them." She had taken him by surprise by gifting all of her deceased husband's belongings to the club staff, including three beautiful shotguns, one to each of the LeBeaus, for flying to her husband's side in a doomed effort to save him. If she only knew what he suspected. He was glad to leave the club behind and to have Jimmy tailgating him in his rearview mirror. Maybe, for once, they could take their time about interviewing Dr. Achermann. People around Achermann had been so hard to pin down.

"You're stonewalling me, Detective Guthrie," she finally said after a few minutes of silence. "I confess I don't like it."

"Please call me Wayne, and I'm not sure what you mean. I'll tell you anything I can."

"Then you must call me Astrid, and what you *can't* tell me sounds much more interesting. For instance, Whitaker, what do you make of him? Sly, or there's no such thing. And what was that stunt with the cartridge all about? And that girl, Kelley? Whatever Jimmy Doolan said made her want to die."

"You don't miss much, Dr. Achermann," he conceded.

"Astrid," she corrected him. "And the LeBeaus," she continued. "The dad was so aloof, so quiet, without so much as a condolence, and Rick materializing like a ghost behind me, before I knew he was there."

"Yeah, he does that," said Guthrie, thinking back to the woods.

"Well? Am I missing something, or was there a whole lot more going on in that room than met the eye?"

"I just don't know yet, I really can't say," he said.

"That's nonsense, Wayne. You just don't want to say. I have a right to know, don't you think? ...unless you suspect me...so that's it. That's why you wanted to see me, and why Jimmy Doolan is back there, meeting us back at the police station." She was a quick study, he had to admit.

"My alibi is pretty solid, don't you think?" she said and smiled. The truth was she was still in the suspects column back on the easel at the stationhouse, even though Dirk's impressive marksmanship that morning had weakened the assassin-for-hire theory considerably.

"So here's the deal, Wayne. I don't talk without a lawyer unless you tell me where you are on this, with the investigation, I mean."

"Right now?" he asked, aware of the moment slipping away.

"Right now," she said.

"We suspect everyone in that room today, Dr. Acher..., Astrid. And we have good reasons, and in some cases evidence."

"You mean they were all in on it? All of them, together?"

"Not exactly, no, but they all have motives, some of which a couple of them share." She continued to peer out her window, no more moved than if she were watching the evening news. You would never know, he thought, she had lost a husband of many years, or that she knew she had faced the suspects in his murder only minutes before.

"You don't seem surprised," said Guthrie.

"I suppose I shouldn't be," she said distantly. "Of course he had enemies. How could he not? But that's not how I pictured them, men like that."

"Don't forget Kelley, she's got motive, too."

"Oh God, please don't tell me why. And Whitaker, why on earth him?"

"Seems your late husband did some business with the CIA, and crossed them... in a fairly unpatriotic way." Now they were into it he felt powerless to hold back. She knew more about the origins of DRX than he, which explained Whitaker easily enough, and he told her about the cartridge and how the sniper beat it by seconds to finishing its job. He knew less about her husband's dealings overseas and expected to know much more soon, but there was evidence he may have double-crossed someone in the diamond industry and he had been poisoned with diamond dust only a few hours before he was shot. Had the bullet missed and the cartridge failed, the diamonds would have killed him in the end. He had come between Rick and Kelley in an unfortunate way that they agreed to avoid discussing, but suffice it to say that Rick and Kelley both had motive and probably delivered the cartridge and the poison.

"Together? They did both?" she whispered as they crossed into the Poughkeepsie city limits.

"Oh, we don't know, Astrid. We think probably not. We think maybe they each took matters into their own hands, encouraged by Whitaker and whomever your late husband crossed overseas. There's evidence for both, and that each was acting alone…as if…"

"As if what?" she said more urgently.

"As if killing him could put them back together, if you believe in crimes of passion, which I'm afraid I do."

"So what about the bullet?" she asked. "Whose idea was that?"

"I'm still working on that one. Just before you drove up this morning, I thought I might be close to getting a confession."

"From Dirk LeBeau?" she asked.

"And why would you think that?" he replied, surprised again by her intuition.

"It doesn't take a genius, Wayne, that's who you were sitting with when I walked up to you."

"Yes, maybe, but I can't be sure. He had just shown me how easy it was to do, almost like he was saying he did it himself, and he has no alibi for that morning. But I can't for the life of me figure a motive, though that doesn't mean there isn't one. And the timing, the timing, so flawlessly preemptive," he said, catching himself thinking out load.

The stationhouse came into view, with Jimmy still full in his rearview mirror, when he noticed Astrid smiling. She was still looking out her side window, but he could tell from her cheek, which was raised and plump and flush in a swell of emotion. The topic had been so dour, and he had probably gone too far, so he was very pleased to see her that way, and rather than inquire or distract her from the moment, he left her to savor what pleasure she was feeling. He pulled the car to a stop in a space reserved for police vehicles and cut the ignition reluctantly fearing it would break her spell.

"You know," she said turning to him and wiping clean her smile, "it's obvious, isn't it? He did it to protect his son, and the life he might have with Kelley, because he knew they were up to something, and it was important for him to move first, in case someone had to pay for the crime."

And that's when it came to him, unsought and unwanted, the flawlessly improper end to a flawlessly improper life. Astrid was probably right. Dirk murdered her husband to protect the freedom of his son, who aided and abetted by Whitaker, planned on executing

Achermann himself - and Kelley had been ahead of them all. Their fitful devotion to each other, ransacked by Achermann, made them willing volunteers, lustily moved by revenge to the cynical bidding of mysterious forces whose motives they never understood; and the warning in the woods had been clear: *leave well enough alone.* He sat there a moment, reckoning with his powers, when he was gripped like an atheist by an unwelcome revelation: the forbearance that was his right to leave just crimes unsolved.

Words from the Author

I was born to a by-the-book lawyer. He loved the underdog and detested bullies. Fairness, to his mind, was no abstraction, and the rules were the rules. Between my father, English primary school and three years at an austere New England boarding school my path was narrow and straight, with grave consequences for straying.

And then came a chance encounter, a person of pure, unadulterated evil, to whom the narrow and straight was contemptible if it were understandable to him at all. I never met him in person, but watched him destroy lives and businesses. He brought out the worst in everybody. Fairness, to his way of thinking, was the language of patsies, and he reveled in destruction for his own gain. Machiavelli? A prude by this fellow's standards. Knowing him, however briefly, opened my eyes to evil, and gave good new meaning. He taught me why people murder, and why murder, now and then, needs no justification.

Made in the USA
Middletown, DE
28 October 2015